BROKEN DOVE

L A Kent

Published by WillowOrchard Publishing

www.lakent.co.uk

Broken Dove

First published in Great Britain in 2016 by WillowOrchard Publishing

Copyright © 2016 Louise Harrington and Andy Sinden

Photographs and Drawings © 2016 Louise Harrington and Andy Sinden

Louise Harrington and Andy Sinden writing as L. A. Kent assert their moral right to be identified as the Authors of this work.

Published by WillowOrchard Publishing.

978-0-9575109-3-7

For information about the Treloar series, the characters and the authors, and beautiful photographs of Cornwall where the series is set:

www.lakent.co.uk.

For Mo

The Treloar homeland. Near St Ives, Cornwall

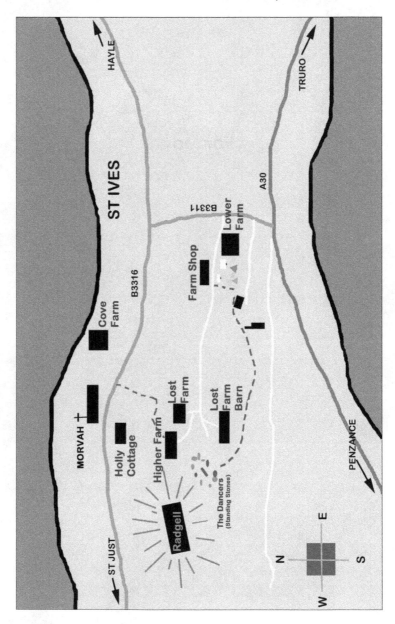

The Island Park - St Ives ** NEW **

New this year, The Island Park offers great facilities and accommodation for the family looking for an upmarket self-catering holiday in individual seaside chalet style cabins. A splendid water complex with three swimming pools, climbing wall, trampolining, fully equipped gym, tennis and basketball. Two bars and a bistro plus a well-stocked shop with an excellent deli counter. Just 2 miles from St Ives with its abundance of shops and restaurants and its safe, sandy beaches.

A great new addition to our guide.

www.summeringincornwall.co.uk

One

'It started as an ordinary day. It was busy, yeah, and hellish noisy; everybody was amped, but what do you expect?' Harry Stokes told the dude from BBC Spotlight.

It was May 1st, half term and a gloriously sunny early summer's day, busiest of the year so far at The Island Park 'holiday haven' near St Ives in Cornwall, where Harry was in his second week as a lifeguard. And it had been a normal afternoon until that one piercing scream cut through the cacophony of yelling and laughter, whooping and squealing which echoed around the heaving swimming pool complex, and then those words:

'There's blood in the water!'

Harry reacted. He blew lengthily on his whistle and slid down from his ladder seat, shouting at the top of his voice, 'OUT OF THE WATER! NOW!' as if that were necessary as the water churned with thrashing bodies dragging themselves to the steps at the shallow end, the more athletic hauling themselves out at the sides. In no time the pool was deserted. Nobody was drowned, nobody was injured. Harry sighed with relief; he had done his job.

Everyone relaxed: a hoax, a prank. Among the detritus floating in the abandoned pool they found a deflated rubber ring oozing red. As Harry said, it wasn't very big, but hell you don't need a lot of blood in water, just some prat having a joke with red dye or pigs' blood.

But then they discovered that two little girls had gone missing; and then they discovered that the blood was human.

The owners of The Island Park were devastated. They'd done everything right, everything. They'd passed all the inspections; they had lifeguards trained with the RNLI at the Leisure Centre in St Ives; they had 'swim-minders' and they were getting CCTV coverage of the entire pool complex, it would be in place for the season, and nobody had expected this weather in May, nobody had expected all these people, nobody!

Two

♪♪♪ Summer is a-coming in
Loudly sing cuckoo
Groweth seed and bloweth mead
and springs the wood anew
Sing cuckoo! ♪♪♪

Detective Sergeant Samantha Scott of Devon & Cornwall Police sang along with the car radio as she navigated the narrow lanes on a glorious afternoon. She smiled as she remembered the song from school. It was 1st of May, an early summer's day full of promise, she was in love, and all was right with the world.

She had left her home in Truro, Cornwall and travelled west down the A30 turning off towards Lelant then bearing left up Mill Hill, passing through dappled woodland to join the B3311 which runs between St Ives on the north coast and Penzance on the south. Here she turned left towards Cripplesease and Nancledra. As she crested a hill she indicated right and turned onto a narrow lane with passing places where a newly erected sign on the grass verge read 'Lower Farm Holiday Cottages and Camping', and beside it an older brick and slate sign read 'Lost Farm Farm Shop'. After 50 yards a whitewashed farmhouse with roses around the trellised entrance appeared on her left with an old sign on its wall – Lower Farm. Outside the gate, draped along the hedge, was a hand-painted banner reading 'For cottages and camping pitches apply at Farm Shop - 50 yards on your right', and indeed shortly she passed a purpose built rustic building with a gravelled car park where a small refrigerated truck sporting Roskilly's dairy's distinctive playful livery was reversing. She was looking forward to the evening.

After another couple of minutes she passed a rough track leading uphill to her right with a worn sign indicating Lost Farm and Higher Farm but she continued on. She opened the front windows of the car to a dusty airflow with the slight scent of cow manure and a stronger vegetal smell. An urban girl born and bred, she quickly closed them again, laughing. Finally she came to a gap in the hedgerow where a brightly coloured garland of paper flowers was strung across the opening: Lost Farm Barn, home to her boss, the object of her secret affections, Detective Inspector Félipe Treloar, and today the venue for the annual May Day Treloar family party.

Samantha Scott was on a fast track with Devon & Cornwall Police having joined from Bristol University where she had attained a 2:1 in History. This had earned her the nickname 'Samba' –Sam B. A. - with some of her colleagues which she took in good spirit. Sam worked on major crimes in a small team led by Treloar which included D S Colin Matthews and a new member, D C Luke Callaway. She was expecting to see them at the party that evening.

Sam turned in under the garland and drove onto a field where a large number of cars were already parked. She pulled up alongside a beautiful old golden Mercedes and climbed out of her Brilliant Red VW Beetle. The boot of the Mercedes was open and a portly balding man with a bushy grey beard was rooting about inside muttering to himself.

'Hi Doc,' Sam called out pulling two bottles of wine from the rear seat. Sam was a good looking tall woman with a shapely athletic build from regular visits to the gym, thick dark blonde hair and bright turquoise eyes.

'Good afternoon my dear,' replied Dr. Anthony Tremayne, police doctor and Treloar family friend, 'somewhere in here Molly has secreted a bumper box of my cheese and pea pasties, but I can't for the life of me… ah, yes here they are.'

He lifted out a cardboard box and closed the boot. Just then a buxom middle aged woman with thick chestnut hair and a broad gap-toothed smile, dressed in bright floral shorts and a white man's linen shirt, emerged from the side of a dilapidated stable block.

'Jesus Christ Tremayne what are you doing?' asked Molly Rackham, Tremayne's wife good-naturedly. 'Hello Sam, lovely to see you again. What is my idiot husband up to?'

'God Almighty woman, why did you hide these pasties under all that rubbish?' he huffed. 'Well, I have them now so we can all go join the fun!'

'Come along then, follow me,' Molly said, 'Oh and watch your step Sam. Phil's done wonders but the going's still rather uneven underfoot.

The wonders Molly was referring to were a major refurbishment and conversion of a group of old farm buildings. The son of a

3

Cornish farming father and a Spanish mother, Félipe Treloar had grown up in west Cornwall on the family farm near Zennor. Four years previously, he had acquired the Lost Farm Barn site from old family friend Edmund Maddox, owner of the Lost Farm estate which consisted of three separate farms: Lost Farm, Lower Farm and Higher Farm. The sale had not however been without the fierce opposition of Edmund's elder son, Dylan, who managed Lower Farm with his wife, Hope. Dylan was intent upon the redevelopment of the Lost Farm holdings as tourist accommodation and a major entertainment complex.

However, younger son, Rees, and daughter, Megan, had sided with their father in selling Lost Farm Barn and the surrounding buildings along with twelve acres of woodland, moorland and sloping pasture to Treloar. Further to Dylan's disgust, this had been at a below market price. Since the sale Treloar has spent all of his spare time and leave on the conversion, doing the majority of the work himself. As Sam and the Tremaynes rounded the corner of the stable block they surveyed the fruits of his labours.

'Wow!' exclaimed Sam, 'he's done so much since I was last here.'

They had emerged into a cobbled courtyard flanked by the stable block and two long sheds, one open on one side. Making up the square was the main building: Lost Farm Barn. This was in fact two barns connected by a pitch-roofed glass atrium. Today the yard was lined with huge coloured flags, depicting fish, flowers and wildlife, on extensible poles, and a mismatch of wooden and plastic picnic tables with bright umbrellas was ranged across the cobbles. There was the noise of laughter and soft music, clusters of people were eating and drinking and gangs of children chased about, shrieking.

'I see Ochre's been having a field day,' Dr. Tremayne said.

'Who?' asked Sam.

'No slacking, follow me with the goodies,' Molly interjected. 'This way,' and she strode on through the crowds, heading for the barn.

As they progressed through the throng, Dr. Tremayne pointed out a couple deep in animated conversation. The two women were of a similar age but very different in appearance. One was statuesque with masses of blonde hair piled and somehow secured on top of her head. She was dressed in a multicolour kaftan with rope upon rope of beads around her neck. The other could not have made a sharper contrast, being small and slight with cropped steel grey hair and dressed in a plain black shift dress.

'The Amazon is Ochre Pengelly, local artist, writer and entrepreneur and the other, well that's Phil's eldest sister, Eva.'

'I'd never have guessed; she's nothing like Phil.'

'No she takes after their mother, Inés, the two are very alike. You'll see when you meet her,' said Molly steaming ahead.

'Look there's John and Priss over there with Colin,' she added waving at a tall thin man standing closely beside a beautiful black woman talking with a taller younger man who stood at a slight distance from them. John was Dr. John Forbes, local pathologist; Priss, his psychiatrist wife, Dr. Priscilla Forbes and Colin was Sam's colleague D S Colin Matthews.

'Well the gang's all here,' said Dr. Tremayne.

'Give me that box Tremayne and I'll take it through,' said Molly. 'You join John and the others. Come on Sam let's deliver our gifts and find our hosts.'

With that she grabbed the box from her husband and sailed on towards the barn with Sam in her wake suppressing a grin. Molly Rackham was indeed something to behold.

Three

Detective Sergeant Tom Grigg was depressed. He hated child abductions, hated them. It was clear, at least to him, that the girls had disappeared, they hadn't just wandered off, run away, got lost or trapped or shut in. No, some bastard had them.

The two girls were nine years old and had met for the first time that week at the holiday park. One was local, daughter of a friend of a manager at The Island Park, one a visitor from Ludlow. They had both been at the Splash Pool adjacent to the main swimming pool without any parental supervision. It always amazed Grigg how people on holiday behave in ways they would never dream of when at home; leaving their children alone or with strangers, getting drunk, wandering about at night, driving under the influence. He hated the summer season: too many people being stupid, too many cars, too much of everything. God he was turning into a curmudgeon. His wife Lizzie said he had forgotten that when their children were young he allowed them out to play for hours on end, especially in the summer and when they were away on holiday. He pointed out to her in return, that that was then and this was now, a point she conceded without really understanding its relevance; sometimes, it definitely wasn't worth the argument.

The local girl was Lily Warren, the girl from Ludlow, Tamsin Thomas and they were both going to turn up dead, Grigg knew it, the parents knew it, the press knew it.

'For fuck's sake Dan don't be stupid, I can't do THAT,' Dan screeched. 'It's fucking mental,' he went on, looking first at the table and then the wire and books on the floor.

'Of course you can, just imagine it, like he said, and try ……… it'll be a laugh. Christ, we'll all seem like idiots as well ……… stop whining and just give it a go,' Dan replied then looked across to the cool looking guy in the larger group with long black hair and raised her eyebrows; he winked back quickly and surreptitiously. Her shoulder length blonde hair was in a ponytail tied with a long red ribbon which matched the bright red A-line skirt she was wearing that stopped short of her knees, even though the emailed instructions for the session had strongly urged jeans or trousers for everyone.

Nor had she worn the loose fitting sweatshirt or jumper they had suggested, but the blue taffeta Donna Karen blouse with long sleeves that she knew didn't show off her figure too much, just enough, and only the top two buttons were undone. Christ she'd even worn a bra ………… and silver studs in her ears instead of the usual drops or big hoops. A slight waft of Gaultier Classique had followed her into the room.

The trainers that had been suggested weren't going to work with the skirt and she had gone with the pink Jimmy Choo block sandals - not too plain, but not over the top either, and comfortable for hours. She'd even toned down the make-up, only the simple matte gloss for her lips, no face make up to speak of, just the Sheer Horizon eye shadow; no Lash-bold or Brow-sculptor, not even in the small red patent shoulder bag she'd chosen.

Dan limped across the large reception room, scuffing the floor with the inside of his left foot at the end of each step as it drew level with his right foot before sitting down. UPSTAIRS AT THE CHAPEL was printed in light grey at the top of the back of his black tucked in T shirt, in a semi circle curving upwards towards his straggly black hair. RETRO NIGHTS IN ISLINGTON was printed underneath in yellow in a semi circle that curved down. He wore black soled black Adidas hi-tops and bright yellow socks under a pair of cuffed and faded mid-blue Levis. Anyone seriously interested might guess that they were custom distressed 1947 501s.

He had gone to stand near the corner of the room with the

7

other three who were playing this evening's session and as he looked at the square coffee table in the corner that was supposed to be the freezer, he shook his head. Dan turned round revealing the picture of Blondie's Debbie Harry kneeling, holding a bulbous microphone close to her mouth, that was on the front of his T shirt.

He ran his eyes over the cable that had been pulled out from the skirting board to run across the floor about five metres from the wall and the row of books lying flat on the floor that marked out the other shorter wall. The cable and the books, along with the real walls, were marking out the old family kitchen that Dan had paced out, at about eight metres by five, once he'd thought back, after being asked by Ivan to remember.

Ivan was standing with the others, fourteen of them; they'd had to turn away another seventeen which was why the camera was being used - to video the session for the whole group to look at and discuss the following week. Ivan wouldn't allow more than the eighteen, 'and that's pushing it', he had told the organisers. Plain plastic chairs, some a faded red and some a faded blue, had been moved into three rows following the round circle discussion and were now across the corner diagonally opposite the freezer in 'the kitchen'.

The video camera was on a tripod in the fourth corner, recording to DVD. Ivan had set it up so that it was recording everything that happened in the rest of the room, including all of the kitchen and most of the currently empty seats where the rest of the group would be. He had been pleased with the F2.8 wide angle lens and the Sony professional camcorder. It was getting everything he wanted and had nearly paid for itself already with the fees generated by this session and next week's discussion group.

'Right, brilliant,' Ivan said, 'now what about the table, how big and where, and the cooker, and where's the fridge and washing machine?'

After a couple of minutes the table was being played by beige coloured masking tape that someone had thought to bring along, with an actual chair on each side, the fridge by a large empty cardboard box and once Dan had remembered where the doors were - from the kitchen into the garden and out to the hall - he had marked their openings with more books, stacked four high so they wouldn't be confused with the wall. Someone rushed off and found a large yellow plastic linen basket for the washing machine which Ivan had congratulated them on.

It was the Friday night 'Friends of Omega' session, and this was the occasional 'special' run by a professional outsider rather than the usual regulation encounter group run by one of the staff, often by the long black haired guy who had winked at Dan. This was a psychodrama 'special' and the Friends had been looking forward to it for weeks.

Omega House is a residential therapeutic hostel for drug addicts and alcoholics; a large detached house, originally a pavilion of the Latchmere hospital, which evolved into the Richmond HM Remand Centre which was recently closed and the grounds sold off for private development. Convoluted changes of use and ownership had left the pavilion as a half-way house for selected inmates of the Remand Centre, before they were fed back into society, even though it was still owned by Surrey County Council. When the Remand Centre closed, the Council changed its use yet again, opened it as Omega House, and majority funds the operating costs.

Publicity material says it is run by professional staff, several of whom are past addicts having been through Omega-like programmes in other therapeutic communities. Some important finance is provided by Friends of Omega, a registered charity, which raises money and practical support from a range of local and regional businesses and individuals - some of whom attend the weekly Friends' encounter groups, for all sorts of reasons. Some go because they are basically nosey and just want to know what goes on in the house, some because they want to know how the therapy works because they have relatives or friends with drug or alcohol problems, and some go because they have their own personal issues.

According to the literature a minimum annual donation of £350 guarantees attendance at Friends' groups at least six times per year and any smaller amount is appreciated because it makes a real difference. A drop-in visit to the House can always be arranged for Friends to have a tour and meet with staff and residents.

Omega staff occasionally invite professionals - social workers, probation officers, therapists etc - wanting to know more about the techniques used in the house, and sometimes those thinking of making a serious financial contribution are invited by the House Director or, with her permission, the Council. Sometimes group members are invited by staff wanting to impress friends, but this shouldn't happen and most staff consider it irresponsible and an abuse of responsibility.

'We've only got three hours,' Ivan had said during the round circle discussion after everyone had spoken for two minutes, 'so we need something clear cut and interesting, and I think you've got the something we can work with Dan.'

Dan had not liked it, and glaring at Dan had hissed harshly, 'this is bollocks'. Ivan had selected the three for the support roles after Dan explained more about the kind of situations frequently found at home, and the video had captured it all as Ivan had planned.

'Right,' said Ivan after Dan had described his parents and the way they had behaved towards him.

He had also spoken about listening to the way they used to speak to Dan, overhearing their conversations and how the two of them were treated differently.

'When they died, life was loads easier, it was a relief,' Dan went on, 'they were bastards; I was always second best, not wanted, resented ………. I know they hadn't wanted me but didn't think an abortion was right after what happened, I used to hear them going on ………. I was always too much to think about, too much ………. especially getting between them and Dan. They didn't care what I thought, were always going on about how fucking great Dan was and how useless I was ………. I used to hear them. Why this, why that, why the fucking other?! Impossible questions, you know, like 'why were you born young man? Why don't you speak like your sister? Why don't you read more? What are you doing here now ………. shouldn't you be outside?' All polite like, why, why, why, all the time ………. either that or going on about Dan ………. Dan this, Dan that, Dan the bleeding other!'

'What about you Dan,' Ivan asked, 'how were they with you? Your turn to think back now ………. what sort of thing did they say if you came in late or didn't get your homework done, or got good marks at school, or didn't want bacon and eggs for breakfast, or wanted to go away with mates for the weekend? What about sex, did you talk about it ………. with either of them, what about boyfriends, TV programmes, videos you wanted, loud music ………? What about your adoption, did you ever talk about that? What about Dan, what sort of things did they say about Dan?'

After listening for around fifteen minutes, which included four interruptions by Dan with embellished but carefully thought through corrections, Ivan broke in, 'right, we've got enough to go on now, so here's what you're going to do.'

Chris and Sophie, who were both in their late thirties, were not related, and whom Ivan had picked out at the end of the round circle session to play the father and mother, had been taking notes as they'd been asked to.

'I want both of you to get into your roles right now. If you have any questions before we kick off please ask them in-role. To

11

repeat, it is really, really important that you stay in-role until I tell you that the role play part of the session has ended, before we get back into the full group to discuss it; do you both understand and agree?'

They both had. In the round circle introductions Chris had explained that he was in his thirties, was divorced with two early teens kids who lived with his ex and her new husband, and that he was a senior draughtsman for an environmentally conscious building cladding fabricator. Sophie told the group she was newly returned to work after getting her kids off to university and was training to be a probation officer. They moved closer together as they became father and mother to their adopted daughter Dan, and her three years' younger brother, Dan.

'Dan and Dan, I know this might seem hard but this is going to be set three years ago. Dan, you are thirteen years old and Dan you are sixteen; you are now in your roles. If you have any questions please ask them in-role, and please stay in-role until I say your role is over at the end of this part of the session.'

Dan had curtsied, put her hands together behind her back, smiled demurely at Ivan and said 'OK' before looking across to the cool guy with the long black hair; she tilted her head slightly, and puckered her lips almost imperceptibly in a mock kiss. He nodded, smiled, and wagged his finger at her before she looked back at Dan as he said 'right'.

'Now,' said Ivan, 'it's mid-morning on a normal quite warm sunny Saturday in early June. School is five or six weeks from breaking up, end of year exams and 'O' levels will be happening shortly. You're going on a family holiday in late July but you're not sure where yet. The holiday, near Bordeaux or Nice in France, on the Algarve in Portugal, or Tenerife in the Canaries - that's a Spanish island but not far from Morocco in the Atlantic - has been the main topic of conversation over the last couple of weeks between mother and father. It has to be booked by this coming Tuesday to take advantage of a deal being offered by the travel agent; Dan and Dan, you are aware of this. Discuss this, and anything else that develops from it, in the kitchen over the next forty five minutes to an hour.'

'I'd like you sit on the chairs in the kitchen, spend the next five minutes thinking about these issues and what else might come up, what you might say, and make notes to help you keep on track.

12

When I say 'go', father and mother stand and begin talking. Dan and Dan stand over there in the hall and go into the kitchen when you feel ready. Try not to leave it longer than 10 minutes, and don't forget that it's Dan we're trying to work with mainly here, and please ………… think about what you would normally have been doing on a Saturday morning, and planning for the afternoon. Now ……… we want this to be as realistic as possible so raise your voice if your role requires it ………… swear even, if you feel like it, and stand if you like, but NO physical violence, let's just see where this goes. If any of you would like a time-out for any reason, questions, uncertainties etc, just raise your hand and say TIME-OUT. If I think a time-out is needed, I'll interrupt and say so.'

'The rest of you,' Ivan said looking back at the larger group, 'please look, listen, and take notes. We'll discuss any points you want to raise afterwards. Please, no talking while they're in role. Thanks. Right ………… go, I'll tell you when the five minutes thinking time is up.'

Five minutes later Dan and Dan were standing outside the kitchen and mother and father were sitting at the table.

'So, shall we book the Algarve or not?' snapped father 'I want to ring them today and pay before we lose it, I like the idea of Portugal and the house is close to the beach and town, so there'll be loads for us to do and the clubs and cafés look good for Danni, so we'll all be happy, OK?'

'Yeah right, brilliant ………… and what am I supposed to do when you two are baking yourselves silly in the sun ………… stay in with the air-con blasting and read no doubt, or go see if Eddy Jordan still goes to the beach café up the coast with the sea breeze?...... Christ!'

'Oh come on it's not going ……..,' father was interrupted as Danni walked in.

'Bloody hell you two, I've told you I can't go anywhere, even if Portugal does sound cool, I can't be away for that long. If we have to go, why can't we go just for a week? I could live with that, as long as you'll let me go to that club we looked at and Joni comes with us, she reckons her mum and dad will be OK with it.'

Dan limped towards the kitchen and there was a sharp intake of breath from the group as he stumbled when his left foot scuffed against the slightly raised edge of a carpet tile. He hesitated and looked thoughtful, then reached down and picked up one of the *books that was marking the door frame - it was a hardback - weighed it, then turned round and limped back again with the book clenched tightly across the spine in his right hand.*

'Oh, bloody hell what's wrong with everyone? .... OK we'll take Joni, as long as her mum and dad pay and she brings her own spending money, but it's two weeks and you'll bloody well enj ....' Father was cut off by Dan shouting from the hall.

'Oy .... more sun!!? I don't want to go on bloody holiday, I told you,' Dan whined as he limped back and through the door, 'I'm going with Craig to Center Parc, haven't you spoken to his dad yet? .... you said you'd do it ages ago.'

'Oh, come on Danny .... why?' mother said, 'what do you want? You know you can't be without Danni. You don't really know Craig, why are you saying that?'

'Look,' father said, 'why do you want Center Parc when you can have a lot more fun with us?'

'Well he'd be able ......,' Danni was interrupted by mother.

'And you'll be outside not shut up with the TV all day, and the swimming will be outdoors. Why can't you be like normal kids and ....' mother was interrupted by father.

'Besides, you'll like it, and we'll be together as a family, that's what we all want isn't it?'

'Well, I think I'd like to try and ....,' Danny was cut off by father again.

'So what is it about Craig anyway, why, when he's not even your friend?'

'I'll get the orange juice,' mother said as she stood and walked over to the fridge, 'who wants crisps?'

'So why? Why Craig? .... Why not us? .... Why?' Father asked.

'Anyone?' asked mother. She looked at Danny as he limped over, then turned away from him and flinched, just before he slammed the book he was holding against the top of the fridge.

Danny turned, his face contorted, and blustered through gritted teeth.

'Well .... I wonder why that might be, why? Why do YOU think?' Danny had said before picking the book back up and limping back to the table; then standing, glaring at father.

Father looked concerned and glanced first at mother and then Danni before turning to look at Ivan and shrugging his shoulders in question, as if to say 'what now?'

Ivan, looking unconcerned, simply leaned forward in his seat, nodded, held out his right hand with forefinger extended and rotated it three or four times away from his body, and mouthed 'carry on'.

'Well, why? .... come on, why?' Danny blustered, 'come on, I really want to know .... why?'

'Christ, what's going on .... can't you just tell him,' said Danni, 'what's the big deal anyway?'

'Oh for goodness sake .... come on then, but tell us about Craig .... seriously, why, what's made you change your mind?' asked father, 'Why don't you want to come with us?'

'I haven't changed my mind, I never wanted to go away with you .... I told you, I said I wanted to go to Center Parc and that Craig said that was OK; ages ago when you first talked about it .... what's up with him?' Danny growled looking at Mother, 'You said you'd talk about .... ' he said before father butted in with a patient but raised voice.

'Oh come on Danny, why, what's the matter, why don't we ask Craig to come with us? Why haven't you asked him ....? Why don't you ring ....?' Father said before Danny cut him off angrily.

'For fuck's sake I don't want to go with you on holiday, I want to go .... bloody hell what's the matter with you for Christ's sake? You're bloody mental and you never listen to me or treat me like a real person it's all Dan, Dan, Dan and you, you, you, you bloody bastards,' Danny said, his rant getting louder, as spittle flew at father, 'I'm fucking sick of it, I'm going out and I'm NOT GOING TO FUCKING PORTUGAL OR FUCKING FRANCE OR ANYWHERE WITH YOU, YOU MENTAL FUCKING TOSSER' and Danny hurled the book overarm at Father's head and it hit his nose and left eyebrow before he could move and then Danny was taking long even heavy strides towards the door and then through it and Danni ran after him. Ivan and the rest of the group sat stunned, staring in wonder at the empty doorway with mouths open and there was silence until the front door of Omega House very loudly slammed shut.

15

Four

Sam and Molly crossed the courtyard to an open stable door which led directly into the barn's kitchen. Every work surface, table, cupboard and shelf in the large sunlit room was covered with plates of food. There were huge bowls of salads, quiches, tortillas, empanadas, plates of cold meats, patés, cold salmon, various breads, nuts, olives, pickles, trays of fruit and cheeses and three large flat cakes. Ranks of wine bottles were lined up beneath a large wooden table. Ahead of them glass doors were open onto a patio where Sam could see Félipe Treloar standing with two women, one small and wiry, dressed in a black calf-length cotton dress, her long silver-streaked black hair swept up into a loose bun at the back of her head, the other simply stunning; a tall lithe beauty, her long black hair falling in a single plait over her left shoulder.

'We come bearing gifts,' Molly called out.

The smaller woman broke away from her companions and hurried into the kitchen smiling, leaving Treloar with the other woman. Sam watched in dismay as he pulled her towards him, his hands on her shoulders and kissed her on the forehead.

'Molly! How wonderful for you to come,' the smaller woman said taking the box of food Molly held out to her.

'Inés, this is Phil's colleague, Samantha Scott, Sam meet Phil's mother, Inés de Santangel.'

Seeing no alternative Sam put the bottles of wine down on the floor at her feet and took the woman's hand, 'I'm so pleased to meet you Ms de Santangel.'

'Oh Sam, please this is such a mouthful, call me Inés.'

Sam smiled distractedly trying to keep one eye on the couple on the patio.

'Félipe, Lucia, come in to greet our new guests!' Treloar's mother called out.

Treloar and the beauty walked in to meet them. Sam was transfixed by the woman. She was about Sam's height but in her black stiletto heels stood almost as tall as Treloar. Her hair was lustrous and her eyes large, the deepest brown and expertly made up. She wore a knee length black linen pencil skirt and a sleeveless red silk shirt and Sam hated her on sight. Treloar took his arm from her shoulder and crossed to kiss Molly on the cheek.

'Molly, great to see you,' he turned and smiled at Sam.

'Molly Rackham, how wonderful to see you,' the beauty said in a deep sonorous voice that made Sam think of molten chocolate. She crossed to join Treloar and kissed Molly on both cheeks, then turned to face Sam, 'and who have we here?' she asked.

Treloar draped his arm back across her shoulder and smiled at Sam whose heart sank. She glanced down at her own attire of washed-out Weird Fish T shirt, cut-off faded Levi's and ancient tennis shoes. She felt horribly as if she were about to burst into tears.

'Sam Scott, meet Lucia Lo Verde,' he said beaming as the two women shook hands, 'Lucia, Sam works with me, she's my right hand woman so to speak.'

'Delighted to meet you Sam. I hope you keep Flip in order, he needs a firm hand I imagine,' she added with a deep chuckle.

As Sam stood speechless, rooted to the spot whilst the beauty turned and said something to Inés and the two of them walked over to one of the food-laden cupboards, Treloar spoke.

'Let me get you a drink ladies; what will you have? How about a glass of Asti? Lucia brought it. It's wonderful, nothing like the sweet stuff,' he walked away towards a huge American fridge.

Sam heard Molly chuckle at her side.

'Sam sweetheart, don't look so crestfallen. Lucia Lo Verde is an exceptionally beautiful and accomplished woman, she is a brilliant photographer and expert swordswoman, but she also happens to be one of Phil's three sisters.'

Sam felt her cheeks burn and a wave of warmth flood through her body: relief.

The public and press were responding rapidly to the alert. Radio appeals were going out, and Twitter and Facebook alerts. Posters with the girls' photographs were being printed, everybody was being asked to search everywhere: cars, caravans, tents, boats, sheds, garages, outbuildings, farm buildings, shops, beaches. There had even been a light plane trailing a banner along the coast, sponsored by a local building firm, calling for people to be on the lookout. Grigg had to admit that he was impressed with the speed and the extent of the response, but the stats were all too bleak. What was it, 80% of abducted children dead within the first 24 hours? Still, he could always be pleasantly surprised.

D S Grigg and a female constable, who was acting as family

liaison, were standing in the conservatory at the back of Rebecca and Guy Warren's Victorian terrace house in St Ives. Rebecca and Kate Thomas were sitting together on an over-stuffed cream sofa. Their husbands were out searching.

'People say it's like an endless screaming in your head, but it isn't,' said Rebecca Warren in a tear-strained voice. She was a small plump thirty something with dirty blonde tousled hair, barefoot and dressed in jeans and a baggy Fat Face T shirt. As she spoke she was unconsciously wringing the neck of an old teddy bear clutched in her hands. 'It's like an endless panic attack. I feel like I'll never breathe normally again. I feel like I'm drowning. The doctor came but I can't take anything, not now, not yet. I just can't stop thinking about what's happening to them. I just cannot bear that,' tears rolled down her face as she spoke. 'Guy and Sebastian are out looking for them but we all thought I should stay here, we should be here, in case Lily can find her way home.' She looked at Grigg with pleading eyes.

'I think that's a very good idea,' he said softly, dropping to one knee before her.

Kate Thomas had said nothing. A tall thin woman with long dark red hair, wearing a short denim dress and red flipflops, she sat staring fixedly at a basket of dried flowers in the corner, showing no emotion, her hands folded calmly in her lap.

As PC Fiona Sinclair walked Grigg through the hallway to the front porch she spoke quietly.

'There's something not quite right here Sir.'

'I know. The Warren woman is behaving exactly as I would expect, but the other woman ... well she's just too calm.'

'I know. She's been like that since I arrived. I'm wondering if she's taken something?'

'Possibly, but it's more than that. She's concerned, worried even, but she's not frightened, she's not frantic like Rebecca. She's anxious but she's not terrified. It's odd. Keep a close eye on her in particular.'

April, the previous year

He smiled as he remembered his first day in the room at the top, fourth of the fourth, four days after the bastards had died, not long after April Fool's Day. It had been brilliant; he knew he'd remember it forever. He would be left in peace with Dan to get on with his life; they just had to persuade the sucky fucking social workers that they would be OK on their own.

They would have loads of money to live on from the insurance, the house was paid for - by gran and pops, ages ago - so there would be no rent or whatever. The solicitor had told them the interest from the life insurances would more than cover the bills and food and the rest of it, and there might still be insurance from the farmer .... ha, talk about luck, straight through the hedge on the bend and into the slurry tanker, old, nearly empty, broke down they said, shouldn't have been there, still pressurised whatever that meant, full of gas, bang, fire, brilliant, better than he'd thought possible .... and all the pensions, and the investments they were still sorting through, so they would be able to do whatever they liked; he could leave school if he wanted, even though they'd told the sucky workers he'd stay on, fucking idiots.

Dan was an adult, OK only eighteen but nearly nineteen, but he was sixteen, Christ he could die for his country, he could get married, so they were sure she could 'look after him' - he didn't need it anyway, it should be just a formality the solicitor had said, maybe after some kind of formal interview. The bastards had wanted Dan to go to university and that had always been the plan. She was going for computer science, the fancy one with the human interaction, it was a natural after the mocks – A's in Maths and Computer Science and B in Chemistry; she had already found a flat in Manchester, well Didsbury, she had got it after going up for the interview and tour.

The University had been understanding and said she could defer the start for a couple of years, but the arsehole who owned the flat wouldn't give the deposit back. Christ, there was still months left to get someone else. She was pissed off about that, but what was a few weeks' rent anyway? She seemed more excited about staying in town, free, doing whatever she wanted.

He laughed to himself as he remembered holding up his Smartphone and the surprise and pride that he had felt as Dan walked out of the bathroom in a towel. She'd just had a shower, her blonde hair was brown and still dripping, and the towel had flapped at the top of her thighs as she walked.

He laughed again as he remembered switching on the TV on the wall, using the remote to change channel, then seeing the much bigger picture that was coming from the tiny scope lens in the corner of Dan's ceiling in the bedroom below, Christ it was like a pin head. The video's quality was amazing, full HD, and the sound wasn't too bad, and it ran first to his laptop which he'd set up as the video server, and was then relayed to wherever he wanted to see it.

All he'd had to do was drill a small hole and push the lens and mike end of the fibre optic cable through when Dan was out. A quick look downstairs, a rub over the edge of the hole with a piece of sandpaper and a smear of white paint and you couldn't see it unless you were looking for it. That had been the easy part.

The bloody software and receiver box manuals had been a nightmare and it had taken the whole of that Saturday to get it all connected, but he had switched it on and there she had been, getting ready to go out. Well worth it; much better than squeezing his eye up to the hole in the wall between their bedrooms before the bastards had died. Even though he had been excited and chuffed with himself, he'd known he would wait until she'd finished her hair, as usual, before going downstairs to wait until they went down the road to The Chapel.

She didn't usually finish her hair until her makeup was on, and he could remember watching the brilliant new movie with a real sense of achievement; he had realised a lower camera would give a better view when she was standing or sitting and realised he could probably get one tucked in just below the windowsill. He had made a plan as he had watched, involving bricks and cables, thought it through ……….. daydreamed ……… later, when he had tried it, it had worked.

'Come on you,' she had said at the bottom of the stairs, 'let's get there before the seats all go, it's Blondie night tonight, it'll be packed.' He remembered laughing as she turned and pulled the hooded black leather bomber jacket from the coat stand, to wear over the short red dress that he had known she had on before she came down. The bottom had flicked up as she turned and she flashed the lacy tops of the hold ups he'd also seen going on earlier. Her blonde hair was comb handle styled, straggly, and he'd been chuffed that he had well-sussed the red high heels.

Five

'Who's that? Christ, I seem to have spent the entire evening asking that question, perhaps I should have written it on a card and worn it around my neck,' Sam said with a smile. She was standing in the courtyard with Lucia and Treloar's neighbour from Lower Farm, Hope Maddox, a pretty girl with golden tresses and dimples. A tall man with long grey hair had rushed into the courtyard from the hill beyond, followed closely by a big shaggy mongrel dog. Both appeared agitated. They headed for the kitchen where the man made a sign to the dog which then sat obediently at the door.

'That's my father-in-law, Edmund. I expect he's been arguing with Dylan again,' Hope answered softly. 'Dylan wouldn't come this evening. Oh he made the excuse of baby sitting Bethan, but one of the girls from the village would have been happy to do that. No, he's just being bloody about Phil having this place and we're all sick to death of it. He's completely obsessed and it makes me mad. I told Edmund it just wasn't worth the effort, trying to persuade him to change his mind about the party, but he wanted to try. I'd better go find out what happened. I love Dylan but he's just so …. angry these days,' and with that she turned towards the kitchen.

'Poor Hope. I feel so sorry for her,' said Lucia.

'No way!' said Beatriz arriving with a fresh plate of food. Beatriz was the youngest of Treloar's sisters and the most like him physically, tall with long blonde hair and the same bright blue eyes. 'Hope's tough; she's a diver. She dived the cove loads after Papá went, you know, just looking for any sign. Found nada. No, Hope's strong. We used to say she grew up underwater. She put up with all that mermaid stuff, you know, what with us all being brought up near Zennor and the famous mermaid,' she put on a mock tour guide accent, 'who lured poor Matthew Trewhella to his doom and is now commemorated on a bench end in St Senara's Church. It's only that prick Dylan who's ruined her life, forcing her onto the land.'

'What my sister means Sam,' said Lucia, 'is that since Hope had Bethan, she has worked in Lost Farm's shop. But she has a creative outlet too, she does all the advertising and marketing materials for Dylan's empire. She has a really upmarket computer setup in the office at the farm shop. I've borrowed it a couple of times when I've been here. She's hardly tilling the soil, Bee.'

'Might as well be,' muttered Beatriz, 'it's no place for a sea creature like Hope.'

'Bee, enough! She's coming back. I thought you were handing out that food. Vaya! Go!'

At about ten o'clock the wind had picked up and heavy showers were blowing through. Most of the families with children had left and the remaining guests were mostly drifting indoors. Sam found herself in the main sitting room with Dr. Tremayne.

'I love the airy feel of the place don't you?' Sam asked Dr. Tremayne, but he was gazing into the middle distance, clearly paying no attention.

'You seem distracted Doc.'

'I was thinking about something very strange I heard from Charlie Hendra. You remember him, the Community Sergeant on that Porthaven case?'

'Yes, I remember. Good bloke.'

'He thinks, well he's adamant, that he saw Jago Treloar at the weekend.

'Jago Treloar? Phil's father who went missing years ago? I thought he was presumed drowned?'

'Indeed Sam, indeed.'

Sam took another sip of her wine. Having now become firm friends with Lucia she had been offered a bed for the night at Cove Farm, Treloar's family home, so she was free to enjoy a drink as she would not be driving.

'Where was this? I mean where does he think he saw him?'

'Ah well. It was in Plymouth, down Union Street, at the tail end of a rugby club night out. No doubt a few gallons of ale had been sunk by all, but nevertheless ... Charlie is convinced and Charlie knew Jago well; they were in the same choir for years.'

'Well Charlie Hendra doesn't strike me as a fanciful man, but surely it seems very unlikely after all this time?'

'Quite.'

'How long ago was it anyway, that he disappeared?'

'Must be .... six or seven years now.'

'Has Charlie said anything to Phil?'

'Lord no. He has told me and I have told you and I think for now it should stay at that, don't you?'

'Oh yes. Christ knows what Phil would do. Still, I could take a sneaky peek at the CCTV coverage, if I knew who I was looking for. What do you think?'

'I think that's an excellent idea. As for who you're looking for …' he pointed to a row of framed photographs lining the walls of a passageway which led through to the kitchen, 'I'm sure we'll find him there. Let's stroll over and take a look.'

They made their way through the crowd and studied the faces on the wall. There were pictures of family gatherings with younger versions of the Treloar family on picnics, on a beach, somewhere hot and mountainous, presumably in Spain, gathered around a huge Christmas tree, standing beside a huge horse. Tremayne pointed out a photograph of a younger beaming Félipe standing with his arms around the neck of an older seated man whom he resembled greatly.

'That's Jago Treloar,' he said.

'I can certainly see the likeness. That's a great photograph it really captures the mood: happiness. Several of these are very good indeed.'

'Yes; the handiwork of the lovely Lucia. She had a brilliant eye for composition even as a child.'

As they stood looking at the photograph, the kitchen door was thrown open and a curtain of heavy raindrops splattered across the tiled floor. A strikingly beautiful young woman, a dark silk dress clinging to her body, dashed in shaking her arms and brushing the hair from her face. To Sam she looked familiar yet out of place.

'What a totally awful place to find,' the woman shouted slamming the door behind her.

'My God, it's the Ghost of Summers Past,' Dr. Tremayne said softly to Sam. As he spoke she sensed a lull in the conversations around them spreading out like a shock wave as group after group fell silent. All eyes were on the late arrival.

'Whose past?' asked Sam.

'Well actually, Phil's past,' answered Molly who had joined them with a plate of food.

'But isn't that Lamorna Rain, the supermodel?' asked Sam.

'Oh yes indeed,' Tremayne answered, 'her real name is Amy Angove, and she is the former Mrs Félipe Treloar to boot.'

'All we need now is Banquo's ghost,' whispered Molly Rackham to her husband.

'Indeed,' he murmured in reply, 'or the long lost Jago.'

In the sudden quiet with just the background sound of soft music drifting in from the sitting room, the staccato sound of high heels approaching rang out as Lucia strode into view.

'What in the name of God is she doing here?'

'Light of my life, I really don't believe your brother invited her, he looks as stunned as the rest of us,' said Dr. Tremayne soothingly.

As they stood watching the newcomer Eva also joined them.

'Lucia, stop,' Eva placed her hand on her sister's arm. 'The Treloar May Day party is open to all. Always has been. You know that. Let her be. Her parents are still family friends, particularly to mother, and they're here somewhere, I've seen them. Leave it. It is not your concern. Let Flip decide how he wants to handle this. It is not up to you.'

'And Bee makes three,' muttered Tremayne as Beatriz rushed across.

'Well fuck me it's Girlie Goosegrass. Why is she here, surely Flip didn't invite her?'

'Enough, both of you. I shall speak with her,' Eva commanded.

Six

By half past one in the morning Ochre Pengelly had her audience in thrall but Amy Angove in particular seemed transfixed. Ochre was telling the story of past owners of Lost Farm Barn.

'Their name was Pitt-Townsend and they farmed the whole of the Lost Farm estate now owned by Edmund and his family, and well Phil of course, but then it was known as Last Farm estate. The name came to be changed in reaction to the dreadful events that ensued.'

Her audience gathered closer with bated breath as she lowered her voice for dramatic effect.

'Simon, the eldest son returned home from the First World War with severe shell shock, his two younger brothers already killed in action. At first all seemed well but after several months the grief-stricken mother was clearly declining into madness. Then, just before the summer solstice she hanged their only sister, her only daughter, in an act of total insanity. A farm worker found the body swinging in the cool morning air in the derelict engine house of the abandoned mine workings that are still to be found on Dylan's farm today.'

'No!' Amy cried.

Ochre ignored her and continued gravely. 'The father sold up and moved away with his remaining disturbed son. Then, when he himself, the father, died in the influenza pandemic of 1918/19, the last son returned to Cornwall to commit suicide in the same way, at the same spot as his tragic sister.'

'You mean she was hung, hung by her own mother?' Amy asked

'Hanged, Amy, hanged; pictures are hung, people are hanged,' said Ochre in a patronising tone.

'But that's so terribly, terribly sad. Tragic … just tragic. Dreadful. Awful. You couldn't make that up. You aren't making that up are you, Ochre? All of them, the entire family just … lost. All of them?'

'Indeed Amy, and since that time the farm has always been known as Lost Farm, and the doomed siblings are said to be seen late on summer evenings wandering the empty mine workings.'

'But does Pippit know this story?' Amy asked breathlessly, 'Does Pipit know?'

'Pippit?' asked Sam under her breath.

Lucia rolled her eyes. 'That's her name for Flip. He always loathed it.'

'Of course he does,' Ochre spat, 'everybody who knows this land knows the story. Frankly Amy I'm amazed that you don't.'

'But how can he live here, how can he have bought this horrid place?' she cried in genuine anguish, startling the others, even Ochre.

'Hush it's OK, it's OK, it's all a long time ago sweetheart. I've never seen any ghosts here,' said Hope Maddox, putting her arm around Amy's shoulder and leading her away, casting a frown at Ochre who shrugged her shoulders in reply.

'Well that woman doesn't get any smarter with age,' Ochre declared to her remaining audience.

'Really Ochre you are a beast, you know how gullible she is,' Lucia said.

'I believe their spirits still roam here Lucia, even after all these years.'

'Well I don't and neither does Flip.'

'He knows the story then?' Sam asked.

'Yes of course. I must agree with Ochre on that point. Everyone knows the story, I can't believe it's news to Amy. Maybe she just forgot.'

Just then Eva strode through from the kitchen, hands on hips.

'Really Lucia what have you been saying to Amy now, she's in floods of tears all over our brother?'

Sam bristled and Lucia threw her arms up in exasperation.

'Not guilty, not guilty, Sam is my witness and Ochre here is the culprit.'

'I should have guessed. At times you are unconscionable Ochre; you know how delicate she is.'

'Well she didn't have to stay and listen, she could have joined you and the others in the kitchen, couldn't she? I didn't pin her down.' Ochre said.

'No but it was a very absorbing story,' Sam said, 'and she was right about the tragedy of it.'

'Well anyway, I was coming to fetch you Lucia, and Sam. Mamá is ready to go home now so we're off. You are staying with us I gather Sam?'

'Well yes, thank you, if that's all right?' she answered

looking to Lucia.

'Yes of course it's fine isn't it Eva?'

'Indeed it will be a pleasure,' Eva replied flashing one of the characteristic, glorious, Treloar smiles.

Sam bit her lip as she found herself about to ask whether they shouldn't give Amy a lift, but stopped herself just in time realising she would come across as a jealous teenager. As if sensing her discomfort Lucia spoke up.

'Are we taking Amy?'

'No, she wants to talk to Flip and then she's going with Ochre, isn't that right?'

'Yes, yes. I'm happy to drop her back to her parents when she's ready. The least I can do.'

'Right then. Let's away. Have you seen Bee?' asked Lucia.

'Yes she's in the kitchen waiting,' Eva declared.

As they were speaking a piercing, terrified scream rang out from the courtyard. Sam and Lucia rushed from the sitting room out through the atrium into the night. Amy Angove was standing alone pointing into the gloom. She turned her huge eyes, wide and unblinking towards them.

'Look, look, look!'

They looked in the direction of her outstretched arm. There, in the middle of the courtyard shining in the light from the patio lamps, was an old-fashioned gas mask.

Early May – the previous year

He had tried hard not to trip off as the psychologist was talking, it had been bloody hard. The guy had been old, spoke softly and carefully, stared when he was listening and cocked his head to one side like a dog. He had tiny round black glasses, scruffy grey hair and a beard, and a moustache. Christ he had looked like that guy, the statue just down the road, Lenin, scruffy, or that other one, Freud, up at Hampstead, but older; in the right place alright, right next to the antique market, Camden. Ha.

Dan was waiting outside and he had promised that he would concentrate and not drift off like he sometimes did. He had tripped back to the night they had gone to the Blondie night at Upstairs at the Chapel, the first day with the new system, and the buzz he had been on from seeing it work, it had actually fucking worked! He remembered sitting with Dan on high stools at the bar and how much time the guys spent looking at Dan's legs; he couldn't blame them, and he started to smile as he remembered the two that had come up separately to ask Dan if they could put a twenty behind the bar for later, and the disappointment on their faces as she had reached over to hold his hand and told them she was already taken for the night, and how their eyes couldn't help following her hand as it pushed his own hand down, each time, onto her leg, above her knee.

She had rewarded the one that had asked if he could put a fifty behind the bar with a slow re-crossing of her legs while she looked as though she was thinking about it, and held his hand again before pushing it onto her leg, and told the guy, who she had known was a regular, that he should have known better because he could see that she was with Dan. Islington was great, no-one cared when they were together, Upstairs, at the cafés, the pizza places, the pubs, or wherever .... Upper Street locals were well-cool.

'Ahem,' the psych had coughed politely, 'what do you think then, why is that? '

He didn't have a fucking clue. 'Sorry, I was thinking about something you said before, what did you say? '

'Hmmmm, well Daniel I was wondering about the limp, and asking whether or not you'd ever had any treatment for it. I can't see anything about it in the file we received from your doctor, but it looks quite bad. Does it hurt, what's the matter with the leg, or is it

the foot?'

'My name's Danny. I don't know, it doesn't hurt but it pisses me off that I scrape my foot and can't walk properly. I don't understand it; sometimes it gets worse and it's hard to bend my leg, but it doesn't hurt. Afterwards it aches sometimes, above the ankle. Mum didn't bother with the doctor because it doesn't hurt. It's just there, that's how it is. Why, what's that got to do with it?'

The sucky workers had told them that the psychologist was an independent professional they often worked with and they should think of him as part of their team. That he would talk about the same sort of things they had, but because he wasn't a social worker his questions would be slightly different. He wasn't a psychiatrist, and there was nothing to worry about. 'Yeah right, better not be,' Dan had thought, and Dan had agreed. He had rooms just behind Camden Passage, they had been told, not too far from Gibson Square where they lived, and he worked there two days a week.

He heard the clattering of the rear roller door of a box van being pushed up, then a heavy thud as something dropped onto the van floor and a scraping sound as it had been pushed inside the van. He had thought it must have been the long dirty table they had walked past, it was only just over the road.

'Nothing really, I'm just interested to know what the problem is, how long have you had the limp?'

'Always had it, like I said, no problem.' There was a lighter sound, almost a tap, then a much softer scraping sound, and he had realised they must have started loading the ratty looking chairs. Concentrating on the psych had been a bitch. He wondered how much the table and chairs had cost and how far they were going - staying in Islington, maybe going to that place in Gibson Square that had just been done up, or miles? The van had been white with long slightly dented grey scrapes along the side, with brown rust spots; hadn't looked like it could go far at all.

'What about school, sports, that kind of thing? Do you play football or cricket? Tennis, anything, have you ever done sports at all .... swimming .... what about first school, was it bad then?'

He remembered thinking about it for two seconds before raising his voice, he was getting annoyed, and saying, 'That was ages ago, I don't know, Christ what ARE you talking about, that was years ago, I don't fucking know. He remembered remembering he should behave and get on with this guy and said, 'Oh Christ, sorry, if I knew I'd say ……… and no, I don't do sports, they don't make me because of the leg, it doesn't bother me, I go to the computer room instead'. He had remembered as he had said it, thinking that this guy was about what he'd been expecting after reading an on-line article in one of the sucky worker mags, a fucking tosser.

Psychological Support In The World Of Child Care had warned about the good and the not so good, the genuinely knowledgeable with relevant experience that brings useful perception, probing and communications skills to the party, and the talkative zealots, and how to tell the difference. There had even been a critical points' list for scoring out of ten. This guy was getting twos and threes. Christ, he couldn't even get the name right.

'What about Dan, how do you get on with her, how is she with you, how do feel about her being adopted, do you know why your parents adopted her?'

'She's great, just like most sisters I suppose, we get on fine……… yeah they told me, they couldn't have kids but wanted one, just one ……… went for adoption, Dan came, they were chuffed, then I came. Their little accident, they were pissed off - that never stopped. Dan's fine, we're good.'

'So, how did you get on with them ……… how did you feel about them being pissed off with you?'

'OK, what, nothing, yeah we were OK.'

'Look Daniel, you're not a child anymore, and you're old enough to understand that what I'm trying to do is get to know you a little bit, to be able to tell the social workers if you'll be OK living with your sister or not, so I'd appreciate a bit of help here, and being vague isn't doing it. I know you don't want to be here and that you don't want to talk to me but it's not helping!'

'It's Danny ………… why don't you write down your questions, I'll wait. I'll come back next time with the answers.'

He had thought that was pretty clever, and then he had been surprised, 'Perfect. We'll call it quits then. I'll see your sister now.'

Late May, the previous year

They knew before they went that the psych had sent his report to the Social Services. He remembered thinking when the sucky worker had started talking about the Omega House recommendation that his technical achievements and viewing pleasures had seriously improved since they'd seen the psych. It had only been three or four weeks but the motion sensors and two extra lenses, including the one in the sitting room, and extra hard drives had been well worth the effort. Dan with boys, Dan with girls, Dan on her own, brilliant.

'.......... June, what about it?' he had heard.

'Well,' said Dan, ' if you're saying you think we should go, we probably should, and I guess meeting the .... what did you say .... facilitator, first is probably a good idea as well. I guess next week is good, what do think Dan?'

He didn't have a clue, but if Dan thought it was a good idea he probably ought to agree. 'Yeah, OK, cool.'

'Right, I'll confirm with John that you'll be there to see him on Wednesday morning then, you can look through this first so you've got a better idea of what it's about before you go,' he remembered her saying as she handed Dan the leaflets and papers. 'They can be a bit picky about who they allow in, so I think you should read it. Impressing him won't do you any harm, and if this goes well, as the psychologist thinks it is likely to, we'll be able to sign off on your case, er .... situation, and be out of your hair. He thinks the session he's suggesting will help Dan begin to begin talking more about his feelings and this particular facilitator, John, will explain more about what to expect. It'll be a kind of interview .... but I'm sure you'll be able to impress him without too much trouble.'

The Sucky Worker had smiled then, and he had thought maybe she wasn't that bad after all, then he had started thinking about Joni and wondered what she would be wearing when she came to see Dan later. He would be Upstairs at The Chapel .... in the Blondie Endangered Species hoodie, the grey one, with the American dates .... but knew there would be loads to see when he got back, laid on courtesy of the motion sensors, he would be wondering about what they were doing, and .... would she turn her head slightly and wink and wave her shiny tongue at the camera again .... Christ he'd nearly died the first time, he had

31

wondered how long she had known; he didn't really care now, it didn't matter anyway.

'.......... about two weeks afterwards then. Hopefully the legal bods will agree and that will be that,' he had caught, drifting back after Dan had coughed then glared at him.

'Great,' Dan replied, 'We're looking forward to getting out of your hair too, getting all this finished with. Bye, see you then,' Dan had said.

'Yeah, bye, Cheers,' he had said, and remembered turning and getting out as quickly as possible, holding that week's Time Out over the biggest fucking hard on he he'd had since last night!

Seven

Sam opened her eyes and remembered where she was. She felt very anxious about how the party had ended. Eva had accused Ochre of putting the gas mask in the courtyard to enhance her ghost story. Ochre had denied this vehemently and when a heated debate had ensued she had stormed off leaving the hysterical Amy in the arms of Treloar. Eva and Inés had agreed that it would be best for her to stay at Lost Farm Barn and Beatriz had decided that she would also stay to help with Amy and with the clearing up, although from the glances exchanged between Beatriz and Lucia, Sam felt that she also had another agenda, namely keeping an eye on what Amy might get up to.

When Sam had arrived at Cove Farm at two thirty that morning it had been dark and she had been distracted by thoughts of leaving Treloar with a hysterical Amy Angove, so it was only since waking that she had been able to appraise her surroundings. The room she had slept in was on the first floor of the main farm house. Its walls were painted the palest luminous blue and the furniture was made of heavy dark wood with ornate carvings.

She climbed from beneath a white duvet under a hand embroidered coverlet and crossed the room to throw open the white wood-framed windows. Outside was one of those glorious top and tail days of early summer when the air is warm and still and the sky a hazy blue. She could see that the main house was washed dirty cream and set in a square flanked by stables, sheds and barns. In the yard were masses of terracotta pots and troughs filled with herbs and flowers.

From her lofty position she could make out poppies, ox-eye daisies, and something blue she thought might be lavender. To her left was a walled vegetable garden with rows of raised beds packed with greenery, small fruit trees and a large old wood-framed greenhouse built along a south-facing wall which was lined with espaliered fruit trees. She could see Inés Treloar working inside. She wrapped herself in a large beach towel that was lying on a wicker chair in the corner of the room and headed to the bathroom next door that she had been shown earlier that morning. After a brisk shower, Sam dressed and made her way along the landing and down the stairs through a door which opened onto the huge kitchen.

This is a splendid room thought Sam, looking around. To her

left stood a large scrub table set against the wall, with a long settle on the wall side and a variety of chairs grouped around it; some plain wood, some gloss in bright primary colours, some washed pastel emulsion. To her right, a double Belfast sink sat under the window which looked out onto the yard and a stable door stood open. Ahead of her was a large open hearth with a log grate and some evil-looking fire irons. Curled up in the grate, yawning and eyeing her with vague interest, was a big black cat. The room's walls were washed in dayroom yellow.

Along the wall containing the door she had walked through was an Aga flanked by an enormous pine dresser and mismatched cupboards. The dresser was crowded with Spanish plates in vivid colours, patterned with coloured circles, naïve flowers, bright lemons, and spots and jars of olives, preserved fruits and vegetables. A drying rack suspended from the ceiling held copper and enamelled pans and bunches of dried herbs. The table was strewn with more of the Spanish plates, some crumb-covered, a large loaf of crusty bread on a dark wooden board, a dish of butter, various pots of jams and a second board with several cheeses.

Standing barefoot at the table end, pouring from a pot of coffee into a large cup like the ones Sam had admired in Treloar's kitchen on her first visit to Lost Farm Barn, was Lucia. She looked disgustingly alive and beautiful for someone who had had four hours' sleep, dressed in blue jeans and a baggy primrose yellow sweater which could only have been cashmere. She flashed her dazzling smile and Sam felt dishevelled, depressed and horribly human.

'Buenos dias. Coffee and something to eat? All homemade I promise, but not by me I hasten to add.'

'Good morning,' Sam replied drawing up a chair, 'I'd love some coffee.'

'Here,' Lucia poured some and handed her a cup, 'you really should try this,' she picked up a cut glass bowl containing orange jam, 'spiced peach preserve. Mamá makes it with fruit and chillies from the glass house.'

Sensing the movement of food on the table, the black cat rose, stretching, from the grate and strolled across the flagstone floor towards them.

'Lo siento querido,' Lucia said softly, stretching down to stroke the now purring cat, 'there is nothing here for you Jools. Ah wait,' and with that she cut a small piece of brie and held it out to the cat who licked it suspiciously and took it gently from her.

'Jools. An unusual name for a cat,' Sam said, sipping the delicious coffee.

'Jools, as in Jools Holland. Beatriz is a very good piano player and she names all the animals. Most of the cats are named after piano players or composers, apart from Flip's Barça boys. We now have goats called Burnt Sienna, Indigo and Vermillion. Beatriz chose their names as an homage to Ochre Pengelly. To be fair, Ochre was marvellous with Bee after father went. It was a tremendous relief to the rest of us because Bee was inconsolable, desolate and seething, totally bereft. It was a huge strain on mother. We thought she might have a complete breakdown but Ochre took her under her wing. She had infinite patience and limitless time for her. You'd hardly believe it meeting her would you, she seems so self-focused, but it's true. We are all eternally grateful.'

'Ochre is also an unusual name,' Sam said.

'Chosen. Her given name is Loveday, Loveday Demelza Pengelly. But she hates it and she is an accomplished artist, so she chose an oil paint colour,' Lucia added pointing to the wall behind her. Above the settle hung a large beautiful watercolour of Cove Farm on a winter's day, with snow in the yard and a shire horse with steaming breath.

'The horse is Errolan. He was named after a Basque giant. That must be years ago now. It was the winter after my father went. It was a strange day; sudden freak snowstorm, well a fierce flurry to be truthful, but Ochre, as I'm sure you can imagine, was ever one for a little artistic licence. She took Bee to Tresco that autumn; rented a cottage right on the beach. At the time I thought it was rather crass, with what had happened with my father I mean, but I suppose back on the horse and all that, and it worked. When they came back Bee was so much better; less frantic, calmer, accepting that Papá had gone. All that summer she had been like an Elizabethan fire-ship; rudderless and out of control, burning fiercely, singeing and scorching everyone she came near. It was terrifying. No one could approach her, no one but Ochre. Ochre was spending a lot of time here to be with Bee and she painted that for Mamá for Christmas.'

'Do you mind talking about it?'

'Me? No. But be careful around Bee.'

'What do you think happened?' Sam asked gently. She had decided to keep Charlie Hendra's apparent sighting of Jago Treloar to herself, at least until she had done some investigation.

'I've no idea really but I just don't believe he drowned. He was too strong a swimmer and very fit.'

'I've heard there were bad riptides that day. Could they have played a part?'

'No. Rip currents occur on beaches not in sheltered coves. I suppose there could have been a freak current but his body would have washed ashore. No. He's still out there somewhere I'm sure of it and so is Mamá. A tragedy; a sudden death, a disappearance, you don't get over it, you get beyond it.' With that Lucia stood and walked over to the stove to refill the coffee pot.

Sam looked at the painting again and then glanced at the other walls. Either side of the hearth were two framed Jóan Miro posters. One was the official world cup poster from 1982 – COPA DEL MUNDO DE FUTBOL ESPAÑA 82, the other showed a black teasle-tailed creature facing right with the Barcelona football club badge incorporated in its body: FUTBOL CLUB BARCELONA 75 Anniversari (1899-1974).

'Phil told me that your mother is a great Barça fan,' Sam said munching on a piece of bread spread with the peach preserve, 'this really is wonderful.'

'Mamá is a magical cook and a Barça nut,' Lucia said returning to the table, 'she was at the Nou Camp in '82 for the semi-final between Poland Italy. Italy won 2-0 and went on to beat Germany at the Bernebau in Madrid. Oh Phil phoned by the way. He'll be over soon. He's taking Amy to her parents and bringing Bee back.'

'I was very surprised by Lamorna Rain; she seemed so ... blonde, ditzy, I don't mean to be rude but I can't picture Phil married to her.'

'Well he was very young and she was, is, very beautiful and so terribly vulnerable. Seems she still is. But fear not, his tastes have changed. He now goes for the sophisticated and intelligent,' Lucia added with a sly smile.

'I didn't know your brother had been married.'

'No reason why you should. It was years ago and it didn't last long.'

'You don't seem too sad about that, if you don't mind my

observation.'

'Christ no. I can't stand the cow, neither can Bee. Eva and Mamá suffer her. We just don't see her, haven't for years thank God.

'How did Phil meet her?'

'Oh she's local. Her real name is Amy Angove and her parents used to farm along the coast from here towards St Just. Old Cornish farming family like ours. She was in my class at school. They married when she was seventeen and Flip was... twenty three. It was before he joined the police. He was working in marine conservation.

'They were very young then.'

'They were, but my parents married very young so they were OK with it. Anyway she was so lovely to all of us, couldn't do enough to please his family and his friends, right up to the wedding. Then, when she had that ring on her finger and we were no longer of use to her, you know, approving the marriage, encouraging them ... well she dropped us all, cut us dead.'

'How extraordinary.'

'Yes. It was like a candle being extinguished. But God did she cling to him, suffocating, all-consuming, trying to block out all his family and friends. That's why Bee calls her Girlie Goosegrass, its that weed that looks like ivy and smothers everything, growing up through trees and shrubs, killing them.'

'So what happened?'

'Ah. She was 'discovered'. That summer she was working in a shop in Fore Street in St Ives and some model agency type who was 'over-summering' in the town walked in and saw her. That was it. She had dropped us and now she dropped Flip. Moved to London and the rest is history. He cherished her and she discarded him, dropped him for her new rich and famous friends. She's a user, a manipulator, a parasitic creature. If she's back here and seeking out Flip, she must want something very badly.'

'I wonder what?'

'Oh we'll find out be sure. And don't worry; Flip has no feelings for her now. Her being in London was one of the reasons he didn't join the Met when he had the chance. Oh don't get me wrong, staying to be near Mamá mattered, but she has got Eva and Bee at home. No he wanted to steer well clear of that bitch.'

'What about you? I understand you live in Barcelona now?'

'Yes, well Barcelona and Milan. My husband lives in Milan. The boys are with him at the moment.'

'You have sons?' Sam asked.

'I have two beautiful boys: Cesare and Angelo, 6 and 4.' Lucia replied with her beautiful smile.

'But you live apart from your husband? Forgive me, too used to asking questions,' Sam said with a laugh.

'It's fine. I met Luca Lo Verde at Biffi restaurant in the Galleria in Milan. I was in Milan on a photo-shoot for Armani. He lives there, he is a designer for Ferrari in Maranello but it's only 160 kilometres from Milan, and Milan is a beautiful city full of beautiful people and things, just like Luca and his cars. Luca is a very Italian man and he can be tiresome and demanding. We do well when we live in separate countries and meet from time to time. There is no animosity, no bitterness and we share our sons. We even have sex from time to time and it's as good as ever.'

Sam blushed and Lucia laughed.

'Querida you are so English! You should just grab Flip by the cajones and lead him to bed. God knows it would be good for him.'

'Christ is it so obvious?'

'That you care for him? Only to some; certainly not to him. But you are a beautiful, intelligent woman why are you not already taken?'

'It's complicated. I thought I'd found the right one, but I was very wrong about him. I finished with him but he still put me in the hospital.'

'Ah yes, I remember Mamá telling me about that, but querida, Flip would never hurt you, he has never raised a finger to any of us and I can tell you I could be a monster when I was younger. I will find out how he feels about you.'

'Oh no, no! Please don't let him know how I feel.'

'Nonsense. If you two need a push, I, Lucia di Santangel, shall provide it.'

At that moment they heard a scurrying on gravel and two ginger cats hurtled through the open kitchen door.

'Hola Mamá! Great. Looks like critters for lunch,' said Lucia as Inés walked through the open door smiling, carrying a large wicker trug filled with courgettes, spring onions and mint.

'Critters?' asked Sam. 'I thought you were vegetarians?'

'We are. Well mostly. That was Bee as a toddler: courgette fritters – critters. It's stuck ever since. Flip adores them … I'll have to give you the recipe,' she added with a sly smile.

Early September, the previous year

The sitting room had been quiet, well .... apart from the amazing audio from the surround sound, that went with the video he had been watching, incredible, one of the best. He had seen it loads of times and still wasn't sure if they had known too, or if Dan did all the manoeuvring knowing what turned him on. But he remembered he had still wandered, drifting first out of the sitting room's ground floor window to the Park.

The sky had been really blue, the trees really green, the bloody kids shouting as they kicked the ball about and he could hear screeching from the playground. He remembered thinking they'd all be back in school in a week, and when Dan's breathing and squeals broke through the drifting he remembered knowing he had been right about what to do instead of school; fuck the sucky workers. He knew the basics, just had to get better, needed more practice, different kit, new camera, no problem .... then he had drifted back to Amsterdam.

'Bloody hell, that's awesome,' Dan had said, 'fucking great, and we'll be back on Sunday so I can still see Jodi. She's been texting me ten times a day since she's been away. Bored out of her mind for two weeks just 'cos her parents wanted their last bloody family holiday ever. You're a genius, let's get ready and go. One bag, fifteen minutes .... GO.'

So, they had rushed around and packed a bag each, made sure they had passports just in case - they hadn't known where they would end up - and he had remembered to take his two favourite cameras. The Powershot with the amazing 80x zoom and the 600D were packed, with chargers and plenty of spare batteries and memory cards just in case. They both did good HD video and you never knew what you'd be shooting, and this WAS Dan he was going with.

They had called a cab and were at the London City airport forty minutes after deciding they would catch the first plane out, wherever it was going provided they could fly back on the Sunday, and have as much fun as possible.

He smiled as he remembered throwing two twenty pound notes through the cab window before running at a racing hobble through the entrance to the small terminal, then rushing over to look at the departures board behind the information desk on the left and seeing that flights to Paris, Glasgow and Dublin were flashing closed but the 13.50 to Amsterdam was still open with take off twenty five minutes away. There were no queues at the information desk and Dan, arriving first, had already established that there were seats and even though it wasn't normal to buy tickets at the airport they could do it this time and they could get on the flight as you could check in with hand-baggage only up to 15 minutes before take-off but that it would be expensive as only Club Europe was available and it would be around £850 each to come back on Sunday with British Airways as well.

Christ what a rush! They had paid, checked in, gone up to departures, straight through to the gate and onto the plane, and it was in the air just over an hour after they had decided! Only one minute of that time had been spent standing still - when Dan was persuading the middle aged businessman in seat 3A to move to her allocated seat, 10B, so that they could sit together.

It had been really steep going up he remembered, and when they turned towards the coast almost straight away he remembered looking out of the window and seeing the Thames and then it was the sea. He remembered being surprised that even though it was sunny, the sea was grey. It had seemed that only five minutes after they had been given their drinks they were being asked for the empties and the descent had begun. Christ, incredible, not even enough time to look through the hotels in the flight magazine. Then they were at Schiphol, straight off the plane, miles to get out! Christ, no bloody auto-walk, what a bastard!

They were in a cab asking for a good hotel, not a big one, when they realised they needed Euros; but the driver had said not to worry, Christ the Cloggy had perfect English, they could pay with a credit card, and not too long afterwards, even after going slowly until they could get round a tram which was well-weird, they were at the Dylan Hotel! Christ, named after a fucking Welsh poet. They only had a couple of big rooms left and they ended up in a "loft style suite" looking out over a canal, ha, that wasn't hard, there were loads of them. 'Not far from everywhere in town,' they had been told when they were checking in.

They weren't wrong. Back downstairs in the bar for a drink and a look at the map, he had noticed a classy blonde with a bright yellow shopping bag over her shoulder with OBEY THE BODY on it in blue. White dress, short, tight, exactly like Dan's. It was amazing, she had just taken it out of the bag and unrolled it, then put it on; no creases. Fitted like a glove, no straps or lines, anywhere, brilliant, why would there be? The blonde had bright pink mid heel shoes and she was picking up a key; Dan left him to carry on noticing and went over to the guy on the desk by the door for advice. He saw him look at her scarlet shoes and first nod his head, then shake it before picking up the phone and two minutes later a taxi had pulled up.

He remembered it hadn't taken long for the quick stop at the bank machine to get some Euros on a card, then the taxi stopped outside The Grasshopper Coffee Shop not long after Dan had told him the Concierge had agreed that the Red Light District, except he'd called it the RLD, would be fun and that on the way they should call in at The Grasshopper to see what it was all about. 'Too far to walk in high heels,' he had said, 'even though it's not far, so make sure you tip the driver well.' So they had, Christ, thirty Euros for ten minutes including the bank stop! Even the fucking tram hadn't held them up, just overtook it, nothing coming the other way. Still, what was money? Ha!

According to the map The Grasshopper was even closer to the RLD than the hotel but he'd had a feeling that they would need another taxi. Even without the heels. Ha! Hassle free dope, Starbucks it wasn't; he remembered thinking as they had walked in that he'd get a beer with the smoke.

Fuck, what a bummer, they'd ordered the spliffs before being told there was no booze! Quick smoke, a fucking latte, a drinking herb-house restaurant recommendation in the RLD and they were out of there. At least the bargirl had called a cab. They were going to eat drink and smoke then slow-cruise and maybe sample. They hadn't been sure and would just see what happened.

OK, the first part had been fun alright, he smiled as he remembered the atmosphere, the slight haze over the tables, low lights, dark but happy, the blues in the background, he'd had a white beer while they waited then another, and Dan had had her fucking hair cut! Over in the corner was a big poster, "CUT THROAT BARBER ON THE ROAD," with a picture of two guys with black hair and beards and a big cut throat razor underneath. She saw the poster and just got up and walked over to the corner table underneath the poster, spoke to the guy, who ran his hands through her hair and pointed her at one of the seats at the table. The waitress went over with the white wine Dan had asked for before seeing the poster, just as the guy finished cutting nearly all the hair off one side of Dan's fucking head! It was rolling down the red cape the guy had wrapped round Dan's shoulders when she sat down.

Five minutes later and he had done the same to the back and the other fucking side and was back to the first side with a cut throat fucking razor! The guys hands were moving too quickly to see what he was doing, apart from every few minutes when the guy stood back to look for himself. The waitress walked over with another glass of wine for Dan and she smiled and gave Dan a thumbs up, and he could see Dan's ears as she reached for the glass. Christ!

When Dan came back, three quarters of an hour after she went over to the guy, she had short hair all over apart from sideburns halfway down her ears and spikes on fucking top! She told him it was called a spiky razor cut, that it was really cool on guys and would be soon on girls, that the guy was from New Zealand and his name was Carl, and that it had cost twenty euros. Fuck!

They had shared a thin crust pizza and drunk white wine. The waitress had stroked Dan's hair and smiled at her when she brought the wine over, then they had carried on drinking; this time with spliffs, three types of weed, one bitter, two sweet, couldn't remember what they were called, they had taken the bargirl's recommendations and Dan had persuaded her to roll them too, brilliant.

Then the fight, Christ! Well nearly. He had taken photos of girls in three windows with open blinds, some had been drawn and the little red lights over the doors were not on, the girls were busy, and they were still enjoying the third who was wearing a black corset, open topped, well it was after nine o'clock, with black hold ups and black high heels; she was holding a cock ring in one hand and pushing the business end of a red riding crop through it with the other and smiling at Dan when he was roughly shoved in the chest and the Powershot was snatched from his hands.

He stumbled backwards, shocked, and heard the arsehole shouting. Couldn't understand it, why hadn't the bastard run away, he was shouting and fiddling with the back of the camera. Dan started shouting at the arsehole who had stopped and was fiddling with the back of the camera and then he held it away from Dan who was trying to grab it back. Everything had happened so quickly and the next thing he remembered was the arsehole's shriek and then he was groaning loudly as Dan's left heel jammed hard onto his foot and the bastard fell over.

Dan had grabbed the camera back and the fucking idiot was speaking, hissing the words he couldn't believe through his clenched teeth; tears were in his eyes. 'I'm only doing my job,' he stammered, 'stop, bloody hell you fucking ……… leave me alone, I'll call the police. You're not supposed to take pictures, everyone knows, bloody hell you ………' He remembered looking at Dan and them both staring at him open-mouthed as he went from mugger to fucking jobsworth as they watched. Still mildly stoned they had started giggling and couldn't stop. Still giggling, Dan had held out her hand and he had reached up and held it and he had been so small she had pulled him up with no effort. Christ! What next? The girl in the window was knocking on the window with one hand and wagging the forefinger of her other hand at them and then started curling it in invitation.

With the blind down she had explained the no photos rule and told them the wardens and police upheld the rule, which was actually a law, quite seriously, but that it was unusual to see such a small warden behaving like that. They normally walked up to people and asked them politely to stop using cameras, and normally people did, some even deleting the pictures and videos they had taken.

He had been a bit knackered after all that and they booked an hour with her for the Saturday, paying a 100 euro deposit which 'allowed for any combination of eventualities from the menu,' she had explained in perfect English. Then he had said, 'Yes,' to the invitation to video her bending over the desk doing interesting things with the crop then, 'No,' to having interesting things done with the cock ring. Dan had smiled, taken the crop from the girl, held the business end up close to the camera and slowly turned it; then smiled again as she handed it over saying, 'tomorrow ……… we'll see you at ten.'

Eight

At Lost Farm Barn that morning the mood was very different from the relaxed one at Cove Farm. Beatriz and Treloar had risen early to clear the debris of the party, pack and stow away the leftovers and run three cycles of the dishwasher. With the last of the glasses drying on the draining board, they were sitting on the rear patio in the warm late morning sunshine enjoying a well-earned coffee. Amy was still asleep in the far spare bedroom, cocooned from the noise and activity in the kitchen.

'So tell me again, what exactly is she doing here?' asked Beatriz dipping a churro in her steaming cup.

Treloar reluctantly drew his gaze away from the pair of raptors circling high above the wooded valley which ran from the rear of his property down to a distant sparkling sea.

'Christ Bee I've told you twice. She's been having some problems, some sort of harassment in London and she wanted to get away.'

'Mmm, fair enough. But why has she come here?' she asked pointing to the building behind her. 'I know her parents live along the coast, but what brings her here to your place?'

'Well I suppose she knew her parents would be here.'

'Then why didn't she leave with them last night?'

'I suppose because they left early and she wanted to stay on. Ochre was supposed to be taking her back remember?'

'Yeah, and that's another thing. Why was Eva giving Ochre all that grief over that stupid gas mask? If she said it was nothing to do with her, then it was nothing to do with her, and Eva knows that.'

'I know Bee, but you've got to admit, it was the sort of thing Ochre might come up with to embellish her story, and it was late and Mamá wanted to go home and tempers were running a little frayed. They'll both forgive and forget; you know them.'

'Mmm,' Beatriz said munching, 'we'll put it down to just another example of Girlie Goosegrass causing havoc wherever she sets her dainty feet. She probably brought the gas mask herself.'

'Come on Bee,' Treloar said refilling his cup from the cafétière and offering it to Bee, 'you don't believe that. Perhaps it was one of the kids who were here?' but he didn't really believe that and the incident troubled him.

45

'Anyway what's all this about harassment?' she asked.

'I don't know, she hasn't given me any details yet.'

'Well let me know what it's all about when she does,' she declared, pushing back her chair and standing to stretch her arms above her head. 'Right I'm going for a quick run up by The Dancers and then, if Sleeping Beauty has stirred, we can head off. You can drop her at her parents first then take me home.'

'At your command querida,' Treloar said, smiling as his youngest sister tied her laces.

As he watched Beatriz run along the patio and head off uphill towards the ring of ancient stones, The Dancers, which stood to the north west of the barn, he heard the patter of feet on the kitchen flagstones and turned to see Amy emerge into the daylight, rubbing her eyes and pushing her long pale blonde hair back from her face to tie it in a loose knot behind her head.

'All alone?' she asked with a yawn.

'Yes,' he replied, 'Bee's just gone for a run. I'll fetch you a cup.'

He stood and moved to pass her but she grabbed his right hand.

'Thank you Pippit darling, thank you for letting me stay.'

He pulled his hand from her grasp and walked into the gloom of the kitchen without a word.

Treloar and Amy sat on the patio in companionable silence. The atmosphere was calm if not entirely relaxed.

'I remember these donut things,' she cried in delight grabbing a churro from the plate, 'your mother used to make them. Are these hers? Remind me, what are they called?'

'Churros, and yes my mother did make them.'

Amy tilted her head back and raised her face to the sun.

'I can see why you bought this place Pippit, it's very you: so far from the crowd. I'd absolutely hate it here, it's too, too quiet.'

'Yes that's one of the best things about it: the quiet. That and the space.'

'And such wonderful views. Look, right down the valley to Mount's Bay.'

'Yes. Now Amy, are you going to tell me about this harassment?'

Amy pouted and looked up at him from under her lashes in a gesture reminiscent of the late Diana.

46

'Oh Pippit. It's such a beautiful morning, must we spoil it?'

'Suit yourself. It's not my concern after all. If you're really worried you should report it to the Met.'

'Well I don't want to look like a paranoid celebrity,' she said stirring a third spoonful of sugar into her coffee. It was the cause of much chagrin amongst her peers that Amy's metabolism allowed her to consume anything she wanted with no effect on her weight or appearance. 'Perhaps I should bounce it off you, just to get an expert opinion I mean?'

'As you wish,' Treloar stated tonelessly.

'OK fine. Do you have any Champagne?' she asked.

'No Amy'.

At Cove Farm Lucia was taking Sam on a tour of the farm gardens. In the walled garden they strolled between the raised beds where Lucia pointed out baby squashes, courgettes, netted rows of salad leaves and bamboo tripods sporting French, broad, borlotti and other beans Sam had never heard of, and the names of which Lucia only knew in Spanish. They laughed as Lucia tried to describe the dishes they would be used in, but Sam, a devotee of fish and chips, bangers and mash, and steak and kidney puddings was none the wiser. Inevitably, their conversation turned to the previous evening.

'It seems a shame that the idyllic nature of Lost Farm Barn as Phil's home should be tainted by the unpleasantness with Hope's husband,' Sam said.

'Dylan? Yes it is sad. He wasn't always like this: bitter and angry, when we were growing up he was great fun, always laughing. I don't know what happened. I moved away, well Flip and I both did. It can't be to do with Hope; she's so lovely, so loved by everyone, truly. I have never heard a bad word said about her by anyone. I remember their wedding. It was such a happy day. Dylan was so proud; it was as if he had won a great prize.'

'Perhaps it's the child?'

'Bethan, no, surely not … why would you say that?'

'Some men, they resent their children especially when they are babies. They're not all adoring of their offspring like Luca. The baby takes the attention the man used to receive. The man is jealous. I've seen it a lot in domestic violence situations.'

'Well it's possible I suppose. I mean I don't doubt you're right about it happening, I mean it's possible in Dylan's case.

47

Looking back, there was something at the wedding, something disturbing, unwholesome about his … gloating.'

A sudden shower brought a drenching of sparkling raindrops and a scattering of tiny white blackthorn blossoms, then, as swiftly as it had arrived it cleared leaving a translucent pale blue sky. Lucia laughed nervously and rubbed her arms, 'it's the bucca, the spirits,' she said.

'Do you think Dylan could be a danger to them: his wife and child?' Sam asked, a question which would return to her in later days.

'Danger? No. No I don't believe that, I think he's just going through a bad patch. He'll come round about the barn as well. He can't hold a grudge for ever surely? And then of course there's his brother and sister, Rees and Megan. They were both in favour of selling the barn to Flip. They think Dylan has more than enough on his plate with all the renovations and the new build at Lower Farm, not to mention the Farm Shop.'

Lucia stopped at the end of a row of exotic vegetables and pointed at the large old wooden glass house built against the far wall. 'Those espaliered trees are the peach trees for the preserve we had at breakfast. It's always been Eva's absolute favourite food, even when she was a small child.'

Sam realised with surprise that she had not seen Eva that morning, nor had she thought to ask her whereabouts. Of all the Treloar children Eva was certainly the least distinct, almost a shadow by comparison with the others.

'Where is Eva?' she now asked.

'Friday is fish day,' Lucia replied,' we are mostly good Catholics and Eva will have gone to St Ives to exchange eggs and vegetables for something fresh from the boats. I expect she'll be doing deliveries too. Cove Farm sells produce: eggs, cheese, vegetables, fruit, herbs, whatever is in season to the restaurants and hotels. Mamá has quite a reputation for excellence and quality. Fridays Eva does St Ives. She'll be back after lunch. She always gets an offer from one of our customers and she enjoys the change from the farm and the female company.'

They wandered back towards the end of the walled garden. As they emerged through the faded red painted door in the wall into the yard Sam could not keep the butterflies from her heart or the smile from her face: Treloar's ancient Land Rover was parked by the far stable.

Still early September, the previous year

They had slept late, Christ! What a night. Brilliant, drinks in the bar before going up with beer and wine, sitting out on the balcony people watching, God, more like boat watching! Fucking loads of them. He had gone back in to lie on the bed and watched the video again, and again, and thought about tomorrow night, before Dan came in to join him. What a night!

They were still drinking orange juice and figuring out what to have from the weird buffet, Christ it was all cheese, salami, and cakes, when the blonde from yesterday walked quickly to the apple juice, poured a glass and stood and sipped at it. She wore a bright yellow dress with a short flared skirt, bright yellow plimsolls without socks, and laid her bag which was small, red, and had BODY in white on the side they could see, on the table next to the juice and looked as if she was daydreaming. Her lipstick matched the bag.

They sat and watched, wondering what she was thinking. Dan had been tapping her own plimsoll, bright red, against the table leg as she watched the blonde. It matched her bright red dress with the short flared skirt; she had thought it went well with the small yellow handbag - with MIND in white on his side; he knew BEAUTIFUL was on the other side, and thought Ha! as he had wondered about the other side of the blonde's BODY.

Weird or what! Same in reverse! Or something. Even the fucking hair was the same! Incredible; Short hair, longer sideburns. OK, not spiky on top, but still fucking spooky!

'Right,' Dan had said, 'screw the Canal trip, if she's not as much fun as she looks I'm a fucking llama. Let's see where she does it .... and how,' she said as she got up and walked off following the blonde.

Out of the hotel, sunny but fucking windy, a flag pole by the canal bloody rattling, they turned right, past the row of bikes in a rack along the other side of the road, a long one .... hundreds of them, canal just behind. Walking on the footpath on the same side of the road as the hotel, Dan was around thirty metres behind the blonde as she crossed the road, straight over a crossroads, not many people about and the roads were narrow. Dan was close, around five metres in front when she started crossing the road and her dress had blown up, like Marylyn Monroe's, but she didn't bother pushing it down .... great arse, and he remembered smiling .... someone whistled, he was still smiling as he looked right for traffic just before stepping into the road then was scared shitless and jumped back as something hard hit his stomach and he tripped backwards over the kerbstone.

The bastard had shouted something as he sped off .... he'd heard the noise but not the words because he had been on his fucking arse sitting on the kerb in fucking shock. Then three more bikes came at him down the slope from the bridge over the canal, handlebars over his head, peddles just in front of his eyes and wheels just missing his feet, riders laughing, two men and a woman. Bastards. He could still hear their fucking cloggy cackles as they slowed down and turned right, down the road that ran behind the Hotel. The wind carried the sounds of something heavy being thrown into the back of a small white van not far from where they turned.

He smiled as he remembered Dan looking back from the other side of the road and laughing when she saw he was OK, then turned and carried on. What a fucking game, the racing hobble was cool, he could keep it up for ages, but being taken out by a bike, fuck that! He got up, looked left, waited for a car he hadn't heard, looked right and heard the white van start up, then crossed and upped the hobble until he was close to Dan.

Same as the last street. Long row of bikes in a rack by the side of the canal on the other side of the road, then cars parked then another rack with bikes, shorter, no hotel though, just houses, some with steps up to the doors, some two storey some three storey, one with scaffolding, a pile of sand instead of cars opposite, and pallets with bricks, and Dan walking past it, the blonde turning right up ahead at a crossroads away from a three arched bridge on the left over the canal, a café with outside tables was on the corner. Dan looked back before hurrying to the corner and her dress blew up again as the wind whipped it as she stood at the corner waiting, looking at a poster in the window.

Another fucking canal! The blonde was walking into the wind, the smaller canal on the right, bikes chained to a railing by the side, she walked on the pavement next to shops and more cafés on the left. The wind was whipping at the back of her dress and it was flapping like the flags on poles next to the canal that sometimes sounded a bit like whips and their ropes were clanking against the poles. They followed the blonde side by side, the path was wider now, stepping into the road when they had to walk round the café chairs, and hurried when she took the next left, then saw when they got to the corner that the road she was on was wider, with pavements and houses on both sides, mix of two and three storey again, no scaffolding, no bricks or sand, no canal.

The pavement was wider and they walked together then after around a hundred metres the blonde walked up to a T junction and stopped, her dress blew up and she quickly pushed it down and held it, shame, and Dan looked at him and smiled and raised her eyebrows and the blonde crossed the road and went into an alley on the other side of the road. A white baseball cap rolled across the front of the alley from the road on the right and disappeared up the road on the left and a tall black kid appeared from the right and ran after it.

It was narrow, maybe two metres, brick walls each side, a no cycling sign at the entrance. He smiled at Dan and waited for her to set off, took the Powershot out of his pocket and switched it on then followed, stopping around ten metres from the junction and lining up the camera just before she got to it and her dress blew up and she didn't hold it down; just stood waiting for it to fall on its own and for the shots to be taken before crossing to the alley before the blonde disappeared.

They were halfway down the alley and over Dan's shoulder the blonde was a silhouette at the end, black against the bright open space of wherever she had stopped to look at. Looking over Dan's shoulder, he saw her set off, holding down the dress and she seemed to just disappear, just walked straight into a fucking mob at the end of the alley. Christ! People everywhere. Dan looked back and laughed, said, 'Wow, come on!'

People going past the alley one way, then the other, fucking loads of them. They came out of the alley and braked, no wonder the blonde had; after the quietness of the backstreets and the dark of the alley it was weird, noisy and light. A shock. Crowds. People walking both ways on the pavement, bumping, shoving, men, women, kids, old, young, holding hats onto their heads, couples, women hanging on to kids hands, push-chairs being shoved through, tall, small, fat, thin, carrying shopping bags, carrying hats, carrying handbags, stopping jackets flapping, holding onto

51

hats, bags blew along the ground and into ankles, from right to left and the blonde's head had threaded its way through and stood at the edge of the flagstones looking at a big old building like a massive church across the road with big signs either side of a big arch; MAGNA PLAZA, white capital letters from top to bottom on a blue background.

She was starting across the road, hurrying and Dan said, 'Fuck me, quick or we'll lose her, she's going in there. Come on,' and started through the mob, fucking two-way river, mad. Tall bastards too, fucking Cloggies, the blonde's head kept disappearing behind them, still moving towards the big arch. Dan looked round, still laughing, and bumped into a red headed guy who looked down at her and apologised and she looked back again and was giggling and waving him on. Christ! Fucking mental or what? They were both giggling and dodging round people who were coming at them from both sides and Dan made it through first and stood looking at the blonde who had made it across the road, onto the pavement the other side and was almost at the arch.

The people were all on this side, a fucking trickle on the other side and a fucking flood on this. Christ! Dan looked round, she wasn't far in front now, maybe a couple of metres and there were only four people to dodge round to reach her; the last one was stuck, standing still, a woman, wondering which way to move to miss a white guy with dreadlocks jogging on the spot, wondering which way he had to move to miss the woman who had long black hair, wore a black leather jacket, and long dangly earrings. Dan laughed and said, 'Brilliant, let's go,' and looked right as she stepped off the kerb, disappeared and THUD!! and the flashing windows of a light-blue and white tram were there instead.

The black haired woman screamed and screamed, the guy with the dreadlocks stopped moving and stared at the ground near the woman, some of the other people that were close stopped moving and were pushed over as the ones that hadn't stopped ran into them, then more people started screaming and it was fucking havoc.

The tram screeched and shuddered and stopped with the back carriage five metres past Dan. She was on her back lying still, on the kerb lengthways, half on the pavement and half in the gutter. Blood was pouring from the back of her head. Dead.

Nine

You cannot miss the Gurnard's Head Hotel, it can probably be seen from space: it is the colour of peeled ripe mango: glorious orange. Whilst Sam and Lucia were touring the gardens of Cove Farm, just down the road Dr. and Molly Tremayne were enjoying an early lunch. They had spent the night there, along with their friends and colleagues John and Priscilla Forbes, having left the party at around midnight.

'Here we are, some of the happy few, as the Bard had it.'

'Yes dear we all know, Henry V. It's what my husband calls the people in permanent residence in Cornwall seaside villages rather than the second home owners and holidaymakers. Rather juvenile I think but I have learnt to humour him, though I do get cross when he rails against Germans in motor-homes.'

'Well for Christ's sake why must they take to country lanes which they cannot negotiate? They cause havoc and road rage, and delays for those of us going about our business.'

'Enough now Tremayne,' she said with a smile, punching him gently on the arm.

'Well if Lucia and Beatriz had had their way I think Ms Rain would be in need of your husband's services, Molly,' said Priscilla.

'More likely your estimable husband, Priss dear,' Tremayne replied, referring to her husband's profession of pathologist.

'What's the history there then?'

'Ah well … it's a long story, but let's just say that when Phil's marriage came to an early and very sudden end, his younger sisters were not at all happy at Amy's treatment of their brother.'

'That family have certainly seen their share of unhappiness,' said John Forbes, returning from the bar with a tray of drinks.

'True words, true words,' said Dr. Tremayne. 'When Jago Treloar disappeared,' he continued, 'Inés started sleeping in Zawn Cottage overlooking the cove where he was last headed. She did not want to sleep in the farmhouse without him and wanted some time to herself. She had no trouble being at the farm during the day but not at night. And it has been thus ever since. I don't know whether she expects him to rise from the waves like Aphrodite one day but perhaps she does. It would be the most extraordinary reappearance since Bobby Ewing stepped out of the shower.'

'Bobby Ewing?' asked Priscilla.

'Before your time my dear - American TV series, *Dallas*.'

'Oh yes, I remember,' Molly exclaimed. 'Bobby Ewing was played by actor Patrick Duffy. He was a main character and very popular with the audience but he decided to leave to pursue other opportunities. So, the scriptwriters killed him off, having him run over by a car or some such thing. Anyway, things evidently didn't work out and Duffy wanted to return and the season without him had not been as successful, so in the next season there he is stepping out of the shower, and the entire previous season, throughout which he was dead, must have been more than twenty episodes, the whole thing is explained away as his wife Pam's dream! Extraordinary! You don't see on-screen deaths of major character in US dramas much now - just in case! But really Tremayne, you shouldn't, really you shouldn't,' she said shaking her head, smiling at her husband.

'And what was wrong with Sam? She seemed fine until Lamorna Rain, aka Amy, appeared and then she was totally different; quiet and preoccupied,' said John Forbes.

Molly and Priscilla rolled their eyes in unison.

'Really, men,' said Priscilla

'A classic case of UST,' Molly declared.

'UST?' Tremayne asked.

'Unresolved Sexual Tension. Much loved by American TV writers; think *Castle*, think *Moonlighting*'.

'*Moonlighting*?'

'Yes Tremayne, you loved that series, you must remember it; Bruce Willis and Cybill Shepherd.'

'Ah yes, Cybill Shepherd. Very sexy lady, Cybill Shepherd.'

'Anyway, that's what's going on with Sam and Phil. Take my word for it. Priss has noticed. You men are so useless in these matters.'

'Really Molly, you shouldn't be discussing my colleagues, even with my colleagues.'

'Oh stop it Mr Pompous. They're my friends.'

'Well with Amy's unexpected reappearance in his life I expect Phil has enough on his plate woman-wise,' said Priscilla.

'Oh yes. That is bizarre. What with how Sam feels about Phil and how Lucia and Beatriz feel about Amy, I really don't think it bodes well for any of them.' said Molly, 'I cannot imagine what she was thinking of just turning up like that. It all ended so bloodily when she left him.'

'Well, not literally thank God, but I know what you mean' Dr. Tremayne said, 'I recall you telling me about it at the time, endlessly as I remember,' he added with a grin. 'I'm concerned for Phil, I didn't know him when Amy left but I remember you saying how devastated he was.'

'Yes. I'd just started teaching Beatriz piano,' Molly explained. 'It was a very difficult time I recall; a tense, strained atmosphere at Cove Farm. The girls were secretly pleased to be rid of her but Phil was broken and Inés and Jago were at a loss as to what to do for him. Then one day he just seemed back to normal as if he had accepted the situation and moved on. I know Inés was greatly relieved. I think it was around that time he decided to join the police.'

'Ah, so we have Amy to blame then,' said Dr. Tremayne.

Molly punched him on the arm.

'Really Tremayne, you have no sense of … fellow feeling'.

'Gossip, you mean.'

John and Priscilla Forbes smiled as they watched their friends perform their usual double act. They often spoke of how it was like watching a fencing match or a tennis game.

'Enough,' Molly declared. 'Now order me the lemon posset please, I'm off to take a photograph of this wondrously coloured building, and if you don't behave I'll paint your den the same colour!'

Ten

After a lazy lunch at Cove Farm punctuated by the delightful squabbling of the siblings, Sam and Treloar had bade their farewells and given Sam's thanks then headed back over the hills to Lost Farm Barn. Sam was going to collect her car and head home with memories of two splendid days in early summer. She felt an instant rapport with Lucia, and Inés and Phil's other sisters had welcomed her warmly and put her at her ease. All in all she felt mellow and content.

As they walked through the stable door into the spotless kitchen Sam turned to Treloar with a grin.

'Wow, you guys did a tremendous job in here,' she said.

'Don't look at me, this is Bee's handiwork. I just do as I'm told, she has the master plan. I think it comes from her job: she's an apprentice chef in St Ives.'

'Really, where?' Sam asked with the genuine interest of someone who loves to eat out.

'She's been working at *Seafood on Stilts* ... well, it seems like forever. She started doing weekends and holidays when she was at school and now she's making a career of it.'

'Well good for her. *Seafood on Stilts*,' Sam said, an impressed tone to her voice, 'they've got a brilliant reputation.'

'Yes it is very good. And they're a customer of Cove Farm too, so it's all very neat. Plus Bee's seeing the son, Jory Nancarrow. He's a good kid from what I've seen.'

God he sounds like her father not her brother Sam thought, but bit her tongue before putting voice to her thought.

'Yes he's a surfer and a saxophonist. They play in a band together, Bee's a great jazz pianist and double bassist. Mamá is very happy with the relationship but she's not so keen on the younger brother, Cadan.'

'Why?'

'Cadan's troubled. I don't know the details but he's been thrown out of a couple of schools. He's a surfer too and I think he truants a lot. Anyway, enough of the Treloar family, would you like coffee?'

'Please,' Sam said taking a seat on a high stool at the worktop.

But as Treloar ran the tap at the sink, the phone rang in

another room.

'I'll just see who that is, but I'll call them back later,' he said turning off the tap and strolling from the kitchen along the passageway to the sitting room.

DI Treloar's boss was Detective Superintendent Suzanne Winters, known as 'Frosty' to her staff. They had never been great allies: she resented his hallowed status with the Chief Constable as the handsome Cornish media darling. But he had been forced to reappraise the woman after she had proved totally onside when Sam had been attacked a while ago. Their relationship now, whilst scarcely warm, was at least civilized and underpinned by a grudging respect on both sides. She was even supporting his upcoming promotion. She it was on the phone.

'Hello, Treloar,' he said lifting the handset.

'Suzanne Winters here. I know you're on leave but I need you to come in. I could really use you, not least because of your local knowledge.'

'What's happened?' Treloar asked, totally focussed.

'You clearly haven't heard. Two girls, aged nine, were taken yesterday afternoon from that new Island Park complex. No sign since.'

'What do we know?'

'Not much. They were taken from a swimming pool, there was blood found but we think it was just a distraction; it proved to be human, but nobody was injured and it didn't match the blood group of either girl. We've done the usual thus far: people at the pool, thorough searches including with the helicopter and the lifeboat, media appeals, parental checks, CCTV review, offenders' register, you know the drill. There's a briefing at 18:00 at the Island Park, We've commandeered a chalet; there's ample space, good access and parking which as you know is a boon in St Ives. Can you be there?'

'Of course. I'll contact the team. Who's the lead at the moment?' Treloar asked.

'Tom Grigg. I've spoken to him and he's more than happy to have you on board.'

'Good bloke. Bit glum but bags of experience and common sense.'

'OK I'll see you there, and thanks,' and with that she was

57

gone.

'No worries,' Treloar said to the dead line.

He walked quickly back into the kitchen where Sam had made the coffee and was putting out cups.

'No time I'm afraid,' he said, 'well maybe we've time for one cup.'

'What is it?' Sam asked, frowning at his serious expression.

'That was Winters. We've been called in. I'll get on to Col and Luke.'

'What is it?' she repeated.

'Child abduction: two nine year old girls. Twenty four hours in.'

Sam felt her heart fall. It had been such a wonderful day, a day she knew she would always remember, a day full of light and warmth, of promise and hope. But now it was a day ruined; a day gone dark. A day she would never forget. She, like DS Tom Grigg, hated child abductions, but for very different, very personal reasons.

'Hola!' Eva called as she scurried through the open kitchen door and dropped a heavy striped wicker basket on the floor.

'Where have you been, I was starting to worry?' asked her mother.

'It's mayhem out there! The whole town is under siege, swimming with police. I was stopped four or five times and asked to check the back of the van. I nearly abandoned the deliveries,' she flopped into a chair at the kitchen table and pulled the espadrilles from her feet.

'What's going on?' and 'Did you get the fish?' asked Lucia and Beatriz simultaneously, the latter's mind never far from the main event: food.

'What?' asked Eva distractedly, rubbing her foot, 'Oh yes, some little girls have gone missing from a swimming pool, and yes I got some beautiful lemon sole and gurnards, large ones.'

Still early September, the previous year

Christ what a hassle. He'd been bloody gobsmacked, speechless, stunned, shocked, out of it ..... police, nurses, doctors, hospital, lawyers, vicars, more police, embassy people, funeral directors, hotel people, he had been a passenger, in slow motion .... for ages, not really .... just a couple of days. Woken up on the third day by a knock on the door, he had seen from the bedside clock that it was nine thirty and guessed that it was breakfast arriving and remembered thinking he should have cancelled it. He remembered seeing the empty bottles and crisp packets on the table and realising that it was time to stop being a passenger, make a plan, start doing something.

He had started planning as soon as the room service girl had gone and he had surprised himself by picking at a sausage then rapidly demolishing the carefully laid out full English he had forgotten ordering the night before. Good job, he was starving. Christ, they'd even got the fried bread right, amazing, and tinned tomatoes, brilliant.

There was no way he was going to stay there for a month, waiting for the bloody police or whoever it was to let him take Dan or her ashes back, that was the first thing. Then, did he want to take Dan back to England anyway? What about a funeral, who else would go, Joni he supposed, who else, what if he decided not to go back, what if Dan had decided she didn't want to go back, what would she want to do now anyway?

He remembered looking through Dan's things: the passport, credit cards, seeing the driving licence and staring at it until he wasn't seeing it anymore, then coming round and seeing her picture again; Christ she had looked great even on the licence photocard, even with no make-up and her hair tied back, how was that possible? He remembered seeing the paper part of the licence she wouldn't use again, Christ she'd not even used it this time, only brought it in case they decided to hire a car.

Then everything had stopped when he saw the address - Didsbury, Manchester, Dan's escape route from the bastards.

They had promised her a car if she passed her test, hadn't said anything about not getting her what she wanted, so when it came to it she had accepted the Fiesta with a smile and decided at that moment to apply for her full licence using the Manchester address .... even though she'd talked them into getting the top of the range. She persuaded them that with the motorways being so busy she needed to feel safe and a small car needed to be quick to be safe. Yeah right, nought to sixty in under seven seconds and one hundred and thirty mph top speed! She'd got the Audi soft-top that she had really wanted after they died, ha!

She had told Dan about the plan when he had asked her why she was looking at copies of electricity and water bills with the Didsbury address and handwritten notes at the top, and turning the tenancy agreement over and over in her hand. The notes had been written by the landlord-to-be, confirming that she was now living there and paying her portion of the bills. 'Well why not, try it, see what happens, it'll be a laugh. What have you got to lose?' Dan had said and he had looked nervously round the room to check. No-one there. But he had nodded and said 'Yeah right, why not?'

Once he had decided, he had realised there wasn't actually very much to do, just call the funeral director, tell her he'd be back in four weeks for the cremation and to pick up the ashes, which he wanted in the bright yellow jar she had told him she was sure that Dan would like, and pay for the crematorium reservation using a credit card. Then pack, check-out, taxi to Schiphol, taxi home, think about the rest of the plan on the way.

Packing had been bad. Going round picking up Dan's things even though there weren't that many, it was slow, but it didn't last long and then he was slouching, in a big moody, along the never fucking ending corridors at Schiphol, right to the gate at the end. He had picked up a bottle of Orange Gin on the way through and started drinking it while he waited. Christ, the Cloggies had invented it. Who knew THAT?

There weren't many others waiting to be called to board, but if he had noticed he would have seen quite a few of them looking down their noses at the scruffy red-eyed guy who slouched in his seat and looked like he'd slept in his hoodie and ripped jeans for a week and probably stank, who was probably high or pissed or both, sitting on his own with TWO bloody carry-on bags, staring .... at the wall. They were all hoping they wouldn't be sitting anywhere near him.

He remembered the gin, Christ, it was brilliant stuff, stuff to *get foodies and drinksperts well excited he had thought stupidly, and remembered wondering why he was thinking like that. It was well strong, dry and sweet and syrupy at the same time, hot from the chillies and tasted of orange, brilliant.*

He remembered the blurred haze from the staring, just looking, looking at the wall, and the picture that slowly appeared. It was a framed poster on the wall that he had been looking through; a sexy girl in a yellow dress with a red Gucci bag slung carelessly over her shoulder, looking back and pouting her red lips at him. Her blonde hair was tied back in a pony tail and it was swished to the left. 'Cool, do it,' Dan had said from behind him.

An elderly couple looking at him wondered why he had suddenly smiled and turned to look behind him, raised his eyebrows and said 'Yeah, right, brilliant,' before turning round and taking a swig from his bottle then staring at the wall again. They had looked at each other, raised their eyebrows, then looked down at their boarding cards, hoping for plenty of spare seats just in case.

Eleven

DC Luke Callaway was the new boy on the major crime team but he was proving to be a useful addition with his combination of excellent IT skills and the brawn which comes from years of competitive rugby. DS Colin Matthews' nose had initially been put out of joint by somebody usurping his established role of team techie, but Treloar had pointed out that Callaway's involvement would free him to concentrate on the forensics aspects which were his true passion and Matthews had fallen for this reassurance.

The team had assembled at a large chalet at The Island Park which the owners had been only too happy to put at their disposal. Detective Supt. Winters had been grateful for the space and more significantly the access and parking, both of which were notoriously difficult in St Ives during the holiday season. Although it was only half term, the exceptional weather meant the town was crowded with visitors and day trippers.

Detective Superintendent Winters had addressed the assembled team, stressed the obvious as was her wont, and handed over to Treloar before leaving to prepare for a press conference. When she left, the team in the room consisted of DI Treloar, DS's Sam Scott, Colin Matthews and Tom Grigg, DC Luke Callaway, and PC Fiona Sinclair who had been temporarily substituted as Family Liaison to give her impressions of the families. Everyone else and his dog, literally, were out searching. Treloar rose to speak.

'OK everyone let's get to it. First I want to ask Tom Grigg to fill us in on the story so far as he was called in at the start. Tom?' with that he took his seat beside Sam.

Tom Grigg stood and moved to the front of the circle of assorted garden and kitchen chairs.

'Right,' he said consulting his notepad. 'We were first called in to an incident at the main swimming pool of the complex at 15:34 yesterday. A member of the public had called 999 when blood was seen in the pool and all hell broke loose. As you can imagine the pool emptied fast and anyone in the vicinity came running to see what the commotion was all about. Our uniform boys arrived at 15:46, just after the community first responder and the paramedic, and it was quickly established that the blood was coming from a deflating rubber ring floating in the pool. At this point the vigilant member of the public was beginning to feel a bit of a plonker, when one of the guests came forward to say that his daughter, who had been at the pool, was nowhere to be found. After a quick canvass they also established that a second girl who had been playing with the missing child was also AWOL. At this point they called me.'

'Didn't anyone see them go; wasn't anyone watching them; where were their parents?' asked Sam, with an unusual degree of vehemence, Treloar thought.

'Right, let's get to that,' said Grigg nodding. 'The family staying here are Sebastian and Kate Thomas and daughter Tamsin, aged nine. He was working in the chalet and the mother was in town. Apparently they felt it fine to leave Tamsin at the pool with the supervision provided onsite.'

'Fucking idiots,' Sam muttered.

Treloar looked at her in surprise.

'The other girl is local, Lily Warren, also aged nine. She was at the pool as a guest of one of the site managers who is a neighbour. She has often been here in the run up to the opening and has never come to any harm.'

'Typical,' Sam muttered.

What is going on with her? Treloar asked himself. 'Did anyone see anything?' he asked Grigg.

'Nada. You can imagine the noise and pandemonium. And before you ask, nobody saw anything before the blood appeared in the pool, nobody saw how the rubber ring got into the pool, and nobody remembers seeing the two girls in particular, but the place was heaving with kids, a lot of them around that age, nearly all of them strangers to each other. Welcome to my world in the season.'

'Great,' Treloar said glumly, 'and no CCTV I understand.'

'Coming soon,' Grigg confirmed. 'I have asked everybody on site to hand in their cameras and phones and we have people going through them for anything that might have caught the girls. Nothing yet. And as Frosty said, all the searches, appeals, canvassing, all that's underway. Tamsin had a new iPhone but she didn't have it with her at the pool and Lily doesn't have a phone so we've no hope of tracing them that way.'

'Good,' Treloar said, nodding. 'Thanks Tom. Right, let's look at the families. Luke, I understand you have that for us. Let's make this fast but thorough.' Tom Grigg took his seat.

Callaway had been gathering information from government

sources and social media and had collated everything into a PowerPoint presentation which he projected onto a blank white wall in the chalet's sitting room. At this point Colin Matthews sat up straighter and paid particular attention to the upstart, pulling out a small tablet from his pocket and extracting the stylus ready to make notes. Treloar looked to exchange a smile with Sam but she was clearly miles away, staring into the distance with a slight frown on her face. Callaway cleared his throat and picked up his pointer.

'Thank you Sir.'

'Phil,' Treloar said.

'Sorry Sir, err Phil.'

'OK. I've started with the visitors: The Thomas family,' Callaway said as he clicked and photographs of the Thomas family appeared with brief biographical bullet points listed beneath each picture. Colin Matthews grunted, hopefully in approval Treloar thought.

'Father is Sebastian Llewelyn Thomas, known as Seb, aged thirty nine. Founder and Chief Exec of his own company, **Sebware**, based near Ludlow in Shropshire, which makes, "colourful ceramics for the catering industry", restaurants, hotels and the like. Business is thriving, no financial worries, business or personal, no criminal record, no civil judgements; married Kate Thomas twelve years ago,' Callaway looked around for any questions, but no one spoke.

'Mother is Katherine Elizabeth Thomas, known as Kate, aged thirty seven. Design engineer, met Sebastian when she joined the company where she still works part-time. No financial issues obviously, but one criminal conviction two years ago for drink driving: one year ban.'

'Interesting,' said PC Fiona Sinclair quietly.

'What makes you say that?' asked Treloar.

'Well Sir, it's just I noticed this morning when she was at the Warrens, Becky was drinking camomile tea but Kate was on the white wine at ten o'clock. I put it down to stress but maybe it's more than that.'

'Good observation Fiona. Sam, make a note of that, it might be significant,' he said turning to his sergeant but she was still staring into space. 'Sam, are you with us here?'

'Yes, of course,' she snapped, 'mother drinks; noted'.

'Please continue Luke,' he said calmly, but he was becoming

increasingly concerned by Sam's weird behaviour. She was normally the consummate professional, the least emotionally involved colleague he had worked with, but here she was scarcely paying attention and reacting to this abduction, when she reacted at all, with what seemed like anger.

'Daughter is Tamsin Abigail Thomas aged nine. Attends private school, does ballet, swim club and ponies. Family live in a listed Georgian townhouse in Ludlow. They holiday in Cornwall every year and chose this place for the water complex.'

'So your basic coalition government success story: prosperous, prospering hard-working family,' said Tom Grigg and a soft chuckle spread around the room.

'Yeah, but what lies beyond that?' Sam asked.

'Well,' said Callaway with a slight grin, 'I have been poking around in social media and I would say from some of her selfies, that Kate definitely likes a drink, and from some of her posts, that she's not a happy woman. Seems to me that she spends a lot of time on her own talking to cyberspace.'

'And you can tell all that from Facebook?' Sam asked with a snarl.

'Well,' he answered, 'basically, yes I can derive that from her Facebook and Twitter accounts.'

'Fine,' said Treloar firmly not wanting a petty argument to break out, 'let's move on children. What about the Warrens?'

Callaway clicked his pointer to bring up the Warren family. 'They live here in St Ives and have for years, currently in one of those Victorian terraces. Father is Guy Gregory Warren aged forty five. Ceramic artist and potter, reasonably successful, no financial issues, no criminal record. All round nice guy, excuse the pun, from word on the street; popular with the art scene and neighbours, friends and associates. Fairly active in eco stuff; Surfers against Sewage, Greenpeace, various protests but certainly nothing violent.'

'And the mother?' Sam asked.

'Rebecca Rachel Warren, known as Becky, aged forty five. Married Guy last year but they've been together for years. Runs her own business, *Lily Delicious*, making desserts and puddings. Supplies local pubs and hotels, some shops, and the business is growing rapidly. No financial worries, nor criminal record. Also much liked. Daughter is Lily Louisa Warren aged nine. Attends local state primary, seems to be very artistic like father, otherwise average. No health issues, mental or physical, for either child, no history or suggestion of physical or sexual abuse in either family. That's what I've come up with so far Sir, sorry, Phil.'

'Thanks Luke,' said Treloar standing again. 'So to summarize: nice respectable families, no criminal associations, no financial or personal skeletons with the exception of Mrs Thomas' apparent fondness for a drink, successful growing businesses, lovely homes, lovely children.'

'Just the luck of the draw then,' said Tom Grigg, 'he came; he saw; he wanted. Pure fate, could have been any of the young girls at that pool.'

'….Maybe,' said Treloar.

'Phil?' asked Grigg.

'Not sure Tom. Something's off. How could he get two girls away like that, even with all the hullabaloo? Kids these days are pretty street smart and it's not as if he could have driven up and bundled them into a car; they must have walked away with him.'

'Or her,' Sam commented.

'Or her,' Treloar conceded. 'Then there's what you told me earlier about Kate Thomas, her strange attitude.'

'Well she's certainly not behaving as I would have expected, she seems a bit anxious but that's all, she's hardly climbing the walls like Becky Warren as young Fi will confirm. She noticed and she's even greener than young Luke here.'

'Careful Tom,' said Colin Matthews with a grin, 'that's almost two charges of discrimination and harassment against colleagues. Good job Frosty's gone.'

Everyone ignored him and the grin fell from his face. Poor Col, Sam thought, he's trying too hard because Luke's been centre stage.

'Why would she be like that, almost unconcerned?' Treloar asked 'Any thoughts people?'

'Well maybe she doesn't give a fuck about her daughter,' Sam stated harshly.

'Or maybe,' Colin said slowly, 'maybe she knows she'll be OK. Maybe she knows something we don't, like there's been a ransom and they've paid up already.'

'Interesting idea Col,' Treloar said.

Well played Phil, thought Sam, as Colin Matthews visibly

puffed at the praise.

'But we mustn't just assume we're dealing with a predatory paedophile here, and close our minds to the other possibilities. This could be a kidnapping for some type of ransom; it could be an abduction; it could be that they've wandered off and for whatever reason they're trapped or injured somewhere,' Treloar continued.

'Or dead,' Sam said bluntly.

'Yes Sam, that is also a possibility,' he added looking at her sharply.

'But if it's a kidnap for ransom, why take both?' Luke asked.

'Well, if they were together you couldn't just take one,' Tom Grigg answered, 'the other one would make a fuss, attract attention and raise the alarm.'

'Yeah,' said Luke nodding his head, 'I can see that.'

'Right: actions', said Treloar clapping his hands, 'Tom, you, Sam and I will go see the parents. They're all at the Warrens?'

'Yes Sir,' said PC Fiona Sinclair.

'And we'll take Fi back with us to relieve the temporary Family Liaison, I want one set of eyes and ears on them as much as possible and Fi's clearly doing a good job.'

The young PC blushed violently.

'Colin, you and Luke double check around here, ask the questions again, we may have missed something, or more likely someone; people on holiday come and go, they don't sign in and out. I'll double check with Frosty that she's got the families' phones covered in case there's any calls. Tom, you take Fi then you can go on from there; check the reports on the usual suspects, I'll take Sam.' He looked at Sam with a stony face, 'Sergeant, with me.'

Twelve

Whilst Treloar was running the briefing at The Island Park, a few miles away his youngest sister, Beatriz, was busy in the kitchen at *Seafood on Stilts*. *Seafood on Stilts,* true to its name, was mainly a fish and shellfish restaurant with a minimal meat offering. It was located on two floors of a building overlooking the harbour, with a bar at the rear of the ground floor and open seating out front, above which, effectively on stilts, was further seating. The restaurant and its sister establishment The Cuttlefish Café, were owned and operated by chef Jowan Nancarrow and his wife Joanna, known as Jazz, who also worked part-time as a local GP.

Jazz had been in charge of style and décor, and whilst accepting that it was hardly original, had opted for the 'washed driftwood in pale yellows and blues' theme prevalent in Cornish seaside restaurants: 'if it ain't bust don't fix it'. The exception to this was the bar area which was fitted out in dark panelled wood and brass, with large glass vases filled with bold flowers such as iris or gladioli. The upper tables were formal with cloths and napkins in white linen, those below less so: white-washed wood and cotton napkins in primary colours.

On the upper floor an artfully casual scattering of tall potted palms and folding screens broke up the seating and offered a degree of intimacy, and the walls throughout housed paintings by local artists, including a huge primitive acrylic of a mermaid by Ochre Pengelly.

Although brought up as a vegetarian, Beatriz Treloar would now eat most foods, as would her sister Lucia, and that evening she was on fish preparation at which she had become highly proficient. The kitchen was redolent with the smells of baking bread, coriander and garlic oil, roasting peppers and simmering fish stock. She could easily have been at home at Cove Farm. Just before seven the door from the rear alley burst open and Jowan Nancarrow made his way through to the kitchen struggling into his chef's whites.

'Sorry gang, sorry!' he shouted across the clatterings and bangings of the busy kitchen. 'Everything under control Bee?'

'Yes, we're on schedule. You OK?' she asked raising her eyes from a pile of haddock fillets.

'Yeah, yeah. Just my precious son Cadan causing problems

again. I've left Jazz to it. She can handle him better than me anyway, you know that.'

'What's happened now?' Beatriz asked, her attention back on the fish.

'Oh the usual: trespass, graffiti, vandalism; some South West Water pumping house – Save our Surf, Clean Seas before Profits, etc. etc.,' Jowan replied wearily.

'They're good causes Chef.'

'I know, I know, it's just such a hassle, and one day soon it'll be more than a caution. Anyway,' he clapped his hands,' enough of my spawn. How're we looking tonight?'

'Not bad at all. We're about 60% booked and there's a hell of a footfall out there with this weather.'

'And all the people looking for those little girls. One of them is Becky Warren's daughter, Lily. You know, Becky who does the puds?'

'Jeez, I never made the connection. Bad stuff. I expect Flip'll be called in.'

'Oh yes, sorry, how was the party? Shame we had to miss it with work.'

'Pretty good, except Amy Angove turned up.'

'What the ex?'

'Yeah.'

'What the hell was she thinking?' Jowan mumbled through a spoonful of crab sauce he was tasting.

'Don't know… but I'm going to find out.'

A voice rang out above the hubbub: 'One fish soup, one whitebait, one squid, one Greek!' And with that conversation died down and service was underway.

Treloar threaded his way through the traffic cluttering the narrow winding streets of St Ives. Sam was sitting silently next to him gazing out of the window. Whenever she visited St Ives in the season she parked at Lelant Saltings and took the train. It was a short but splendid ride right along the coastline and avoided the hellish traffic; everyone and their dog seemed to flock to St Ives, except on rainy days when they all went shopping in Truro.

'What the hell is the matter with you Sam?'

'Nothing,' she muttered without looking in his direction.

At that moment his phone rang. It was Tom Grigg who was

just arriving at the Warrens' house.

'Phil, I've just heard that a girl has just phoned in who says she knows something about the girls and it seems kosher. Do you want to take it?'

'Yes Tom. You go ahead with the families. We'll take this girl, see what she has to say, and then come join you there.'

'What girl?' Sam asked.

Still early September, the previous year

Back home he had finished the gin and gone to sleep downstairs on the sofa. No TV, no music, he had woken up still bloody pissed off, but thinking. The house was quiet, Christ, fucking terrible, Saturday, it would be busy in town, he remembered thinking he could start today. Try the credit card, take the car out, no that could wait, Christ, a bit fucking different from first thing last Saturday morning.

He hadn't changed for days or showered and knew that would need to stop now, no more slobbing around, what a mess in the mirror, Christ, had to re-cool, get going. Still a month to wait for the ashes, still not sure what to do with them, or who to invite, or tell about Dan. Anyone? Just needed to get going. Decide later.

Showered and got ready, through the lane to Sainsbury's Local in Upper Street for pizzas .... Pizza Express Sloppy Guiseppes and Pollo Pollos - as many as he could carry, and milk .... and chocolate Special K for breakfast. Christ, talk about domesticated .... he hadn't seen that coming, and what about the bloody cleaning, fuck that, he'd think about it later.

Looked up the road and saw The Chapel, Christ, another world and years ago since they'd been there, wondered what was happening tonight, not for long, needed to concentrate, get on. 'Right, good, about time, you're better than that,' Dan had told him as he stood looking up the road before walking into the lane. She had looked great, red heels, spikey, red blouse, pleated short yellow skirt, short hair, spikey on top. He remembered not being surprised. 'True yeah,' he remembered he had said and laughed out loud.

He had decided on Oxford Street. He could have a quick look in Adidas to see if they had any new trainers in, and Selfridges was only just over the road. He knew they sold Gucci because he had been there with Dan. Unless he lucked into one, he figured the best way to find one was to go to where they bought the stuff. Wearing the hooded grey Levi leather trucker jacket, faded blue 501s and the black hi-tops, he had put the PowerShot in one of the top pockets, a load of cash in the other, and set out for the Angel tube station.

Not that far and he knew where all the tricky paving stones were, Christ he'd been finding them and either stumbling over or laughing at them for long enough. Laugh, what? He'd been just outside the station when his foot dragged into the raised edge of a newly re-laid slab and nearly went arse over tit when he looked across the road at a blonde who had caught his eye. Bastards, they'd dug up the pavement while he was away and the fuckers hadn't put the slabs back properly.

Hadn't had to wait long, good job, loads on the platform on a Saturday, train wasn't too bad though. Had a good look down the carriage just in case, hadn't wanted to miss one. Only two stops to Euston, pick up the Victoria Line, then only two stops to Oxford Circus, up on the south side and a gentle stroll towards Marble Arch, keeping an eye out.

Bound to happen wasn't it? Christ, everyone got off at Euston and went in the same direction!! Southbound Victoria. The crowd grew as it got nearer the platform and when he shuffled onto the platform he saw it was at least six deep, fuck; he carefully shoved through until he was close to the front, wanted to be sure of getting on, didn't want to be right at the edge of the platform .... you never know!

Didn't have to wait too long for the train, then everyone somehow squeezed in, Christ, maybe he should have waited until Monday - no, less chance of success, fewer people about, not just on the tube. Because he had been near the doors he ended up being shoved on, then pushed, shuffling halfway down the carriage, standing room only. At around the same time the people that had been near the platform edge at the other door to the carriage also arrived; pushed together, tight, then squashed, tighter. Christ, no-one would need the hanger straps, they couldn't fall anywhere!

Stopped at Warren Street, waste of time, only a couple of people on the platform, heard the doors open, couldn't see them, couldn't tell if anyone got on. Christ he was getting hot, maybe he should have worn a thinner top, it would be hot outside too; no, the Levi was the best hoodie he had, shit. Still, next stop now.

He didn't use the tube much and had always found it a bit weird going from the underground up to street level, especially on hot sunny days. Bright real light gradually replaced the crappy yellow light as he climbed the steps up to the street and left the crowd behind - loads not sure which exit to use on their way out and some not sure which platforms to go to or where they were and looking for maps or helpful underground staff and some not sure where or how to get a ticket and others just walking round the wanderers, quickly, knowing exactly where they were going.

He had gone straight over to the Benetton shop window for a breather; it was showing off a few brightly coloured wellingtons, on display in front of a few brightly coloured ladies raincoats with brightly coloured polka dot umbrellas next to them, and more hanging upside down over the display from the ceiling. Walking slowly in the direction of Marble Arch he saw in the next window naked gold and silver adult mannequins, alternately, with bright yellow cards covering their mannitalia. Each card had a single word in black – GREAT... INDIAN ... SUMMER ... THE ... JOKE'S ... ON ... US ... A space of three or so metres separated the last one from two others, a female and a male, she wearing a bright orange bikini and he wearing turquoise shorts. He was holding a card in the air saying BUT NOT US and she held a polka dot umbrella over her head shielding it from a bright yellow spotlight, with a yellow card in her other hand saying A FEW LEFT, 25% OFF!!

A noisy bus woke him up and when he turned around he looked at the car-free Oxford Street and saw a queue of buses and black taxi cabs; they were waiting for an idiot in a black Range Rover that was trying to turn in from Regent Street to get out of the way while three Boris bikers followed a guy on a Harley threading its way through the mess.

He had looked around, no, Selfridges was still the best bet, and he set off. Christ, so many people, so many shops, how many foreign exchanges and McDonalds could one side of one street need? And all the phone shops, Christ! Loads of buses and taxis going each way, the occasional car with the driver looking either lost because they were, or furtive because they weren't and were hoping to get away with taking a short cut, a mix of Boris and ordinary bikers, and the odd courier biker in lycra. As he walked along, looking for the blonde hair Gucci combo there were a few motorbikes too. No more Harleys though.

Pull & Bear was big into footwear, cool stuff they said. Bollocks it was, he was looking at the flashy display in the first window, all plimsolls, 'no good to me,' he had said, 'the zippy ones look OK but cheap, and why don't they do trainers anyway?' He was looking round for Dan, didn't see her then heard a lot of clapping from over the road; there was a big crowd looking at something. He couldn't see what, just a black and white triangle jogging about on the other side of the crowd, just above it, maybe in the middle of it, and no-one looking in the John Lewis windows right next to it. 'Fuck, what's that all about?' he said, then Dan was there and she said 'come on, move it, Adidas is only just up the road, concentrate for fuck's sake!'

As he walked past HMV the clapping started again, he could just hear it in the distance, this time with cheering, and a picture of Debbie Harry caught his eye. She was on a poster, and underneath it in the window was a mix of Blondie CDs and vouchers, and Albert Hall tickets. He had smiled, knowing that he already had all of their albums, and two front row tickets for the gig in February, said, 'gold-dust, see yah there man,' and laughed and carried on.

A few minutes later, not far from Adidas, a flash of bright orange in a window caught his attention and he did a double-take at the pyramid of Orange Gin bottles in the window he was about to walk past. The bottles glinted and the bright orange Vs on the white labels really stood out. A tall out of scale white windmill with diamond shaped orange sails stood next to the pyramid. He'd stopped and fucking gawped, completely fucking gawped, he looked round, Dan would be embarrassed. 'Fuck, what's this?' he had said to himself as he looked open-mouthed at the three small tables, one of them with two women sitting drinking tea, on the pavement at the side of the door. He had still been gawping when he saw the circular BULLDOG LONDON logo on one of the windows with a cartoon bulldog, its tongue hanging out, a studded collar around its neck inside the circular words: COFFEE SHOP was in big red letters underneath. A sign hanging on the inside of the door said 'Cheapest ho(s)tel in London!! 15 rooms, 4 free.'

'Christ, what's that about?' He had gone close to the window and looked in, shielding his eyes to stop the reflection, and could see red and yellow tulips at the side of the windmill and tulip petals around the base of the gin pyramid. 'Wow, fuck, another time,' he had said, then looked up and across the road at Selfridges, then back at the window and smiled.

At Adidas there was nothing new, that he wanted anyway, 'Bollocks, anyway who cares?' he said as he left, 'only here for Gucci,' and he scrambled quickly across the road diagonally towards Selfridges between buses going up towards Marble Arch, catching his foot on a raised section of asphalt then stopping in the middle of the street, 'bastard, that was close!' he spat. Then he had noticed a courier bike heading towards him, down the middle of the street before spotting an almost gap between two black cabs heading towards Oxford Circus and stumble-ran through to the pavement. His trailing foot caught the kerb, 'fucking high one, bastard,' he said, then, 'Shit,' looking back at the seriously busy street, 'lights next time,' he thought to himself and looked around for Dan, not seeing her.

He was looking at the store layout plan in the window at the side of Selfridges main entrance to check he was right about where Gucci was when her reflection walked by, out of the shop. He saw she had blonde hair held back with a bright yellow band, and wore a long tight fitting yellow T shirt with small red dots. She had a shoulder bag with a long strap, and when he turned to look properly it was only red fucking leather with the Gucci fucking monogram stencilled all over it! How fucking amazing is that?! She turned left, walking in the direction of Oxford Circus and he started after her.

Back the way he had come, but on the other side of the road. Didn't want to get too close - find out where she lived, that was the plan. 'Great arse,' he thought, 'even if the skirt is a bit long, shouldn't be too much of a problem following that! Brilliant, easy.' She walked quickly along the crowded pavement, easily stepping round people of all shapes and sizes and colours and ages, some going slowly, some standing still, some going quickly, it seemed in almost every direction. He remembered feeling really excited, with a tension in the pit of his stomach. He didn't know that if Dan had been watching she would have seen no sign of a dragging foot.

'Fuck, great,' he said as he crossed the side street at the end of Selfridges, following about six metres behind. She occasionally slowed to look in shop windows, but didn't stop until she got to the last of three small narrow shops. He stopped and watched her looking in the window for a minute before going in. 'Shit, now what?' he thought, before walking slowly to the window himself, to see if he could see what she was doing. He couldn't, it was a full height display space full of knickers and bras on what looked like artistically sculptured body parts. 'Shit,' he muttered, then walked towards the door. He saw her in the shop talking to an assistant who nodded her head and pointed towards some stairs halfway

down the shop and the girl walked over to the stairs and up to the next floor.

He couldn't see any obvious way out through the back of the shop, turned around and noticed a stone bench seat at the edge of the pavement, no back, no-one on it, and walked over and sat down where he could see anyone leaving. Breathing a sigh of relief, he looked up and saw the shop was called Intimissimi, and that it looked as if it was on two floors but could have been more. After a few minutes he felt like a bit of a prat, just sitting there, looking in through the door of a women's underwear shop, a bit obvious as well, 'Christ, should have bought a magazine to read ...... or newspaper .... no, no good .... an A - Z map to look ...... looking lost ...... next time maybe.'

'Christ! What the fuck IS that?' he said after hearing the sound of clapping again, and cheering, in the distance. He moved down the bench, turned to sit on the end, facing down the street towards the noise. Couldn't see much, people in the way, but he could look sideways every few seconds to see if his girl had reappeared. 'Shit, too fucking obvious,' he said to himself after what seemed like ages, and he got up and went to look in the Aldo window next to the knicker shop. He could face the plimsolls and shoes and trainers and pretend he was looking while he was actually looking for her to come out, 'pretty clever hey?' he was thinking as she walked back into the street. 'Christ, let's go,' he muttered, and began following again, noticing that she was carrying a large white rectangular bag.

As he walked he reached into his pocket and took out the PowerShot, switched it on and quickly checked that it was set to automatic, then moved to the edge of the pavement while still walking, stepping smoothly around people all the time, then, still walking, held the camera above his head, pointed it, as near as he could tell, at his girl and took six photos. Christ, nightmare, couldn't stop to see what they were like. Carried on walking, across a sidestreet, she stopped to look into the big window of a big shop. A big sign said TRAIN 25% OFF, 2 NIGHTS IN PARIS 50% OFF. Christ, it was Disney, she was thinking of going to Paris, brilliant, not been there before. Took three more pictures while she stood looking before setting off again. 'Should be good,' he said to himself, there had been no-one between them when he took the photos; even though the camera had been at thigh height he was pretty sure it was pointing in the right direction.

She had carried on, just walking around people, occasionally stepping into the street to pass slow walkers and pavement blockers or to move out of the way of oncomers, looking behind to check traffic, before stepping out but not looking at him at all. Great. They were getting nearer to the crowd and noise next to John Lewis, just past a big kiosk with a blue and white striped awning; selling build it yourself sandwiches and rolls by the ton.

She paused to see what the crowd was looking at, he stopped too and looked, all he could see was the blur of what looked like halos being juggled, by someone wearing a tall black and white hat that kept disappearing and reappearing. The halos were going miles into the air, five of them, no six. Every few seconds there was the rattle of a snare drum and then the thump of a bass drum and at the same time the hat disappeared and reappeared. Then, he looked back and his girl had disappeared.

'Shit! Fuck!!' He ran into the road and around the crowd, got to the main John Lewis door but she had gone. 'Bastard!' he shouted and a few people looked at him just standing there, still trying to spot her on the pavement, and failing. He walked over to one of the windows, out of way of the bastard crowd, and looked at the photos to see what they were like. Not great; one of the shots from the hip shots had worked, showed her looking in the window, holding the Intimissimi bag; the head in the crowd shots, the ones he really wanted, were useless; then he had an idea and walked back to look at the juggler, who had stopped.

The crowd was breaking up but lots of people were walking up and throwing money, notes as well as coins, into the now upside down snare drum. The juggler, dressed in a black and white clown outfit and still wearing the hat, was lazily shaking out another hat from one of the halos then flicking his wrist to shake it back in to the halo shape while saying thanks to the money throwers. He could see that the hats were like tall cones, with brims, from the front the left half was white and the right half black. The left half of the jugglers jacket was black, the right half white - the opposite from the hat, and the trousers were opposite from the jacket, like the hat, and his left shoe was black and the right one white. They were long, with big swollen toe sections. Fucking amazing!!

The juggler looked at the drum player and nodded every few seconds. She had short spiky red hair and was dressed as a ringmaster, wearing a white top hat, a tight fitting sleeveless red tail-jacket with black lapels and nothing obvious underneath - he could see a flat stomach below the jacket's buttons, skin-tight white trousers with narrow black stripes down the side from waist to ankle, and black high heeled boots that stopped just below her knees. A black whip was tucked into a black cummerbund round her waist and she was twirling the end of the whip's thong in her right hand. She had one foot up on the base drum, the heel tapping softly in rhythm with the twirling thong and was smiling at the dispersing crowd and talking; to the juggler or the crowd he couldn't tell.

He had waited until the crowd had gone; the ringmaster walked over to the kiosk and he walked over to the juggler, told him the juggling was amazing, and asked about the halo hats. Turned out they were collapsible Pierrot hats, named after a French clown, and they were specially made at a custom hat shop in New York. The juggler handed him one, it was so much heavier than he was expecting that he almost dropped it. 'Christ, amazing!' he said. Shaken out into a hat, it felt solid, just like a real hat.

Tall, about half a metre high. He flicked his wrist and the hat folded in on itself and became a disc again, with a solid steel rim. 'Christ, fucking perfect,' he thought, flicked it out again, tried it on and it had even fitted perfectly, took it off again.

He told the juggler he'd put a hefty donation in the drum in return for the hat he was holding and after not too much negotiation he counted three hundred pounds in twenty pound notes from the bundle in his top pocket and handed it to the juggler who laughed out loud and said 'Wow man, enjoy!' Turned out that three hundred pounds would keep the juggling drama student in beer for a couple of months and he had a couple of spares anyway.

Turning to leave, he saw the HMV shop up the road on the other side and remembered The London Bulldog next door, smiled to himself, walked up to a pedestrian crossing, waited for the light to turn green and crossed Oxford Street with the crowd then walked to The Bulldog. Only one of the outside tables was free now and he took it. When the waitress came he asked her for a neat Orange Gin, a double. It arrived with a round paper mat to stand it on, a menu, and a gift list.

Thirteen

'Right. Start from the very beginning. When did you first come into contact with this "dude"?'

Treloar and Sam were at St Ives police station talking to a couple who had come forward having seen the posters with the photographs of the two girls. They had come back into town that evening having spent the previous night camping above Zennor and most of the day walking the South West coastal path. Rick was a lanky dreadlocked blonde in his early twenties; Moonsong a small hennaed redhead of nineteen. They intended to spend the summer in Devon and Cornwall supplementing their generous parental allowances with a little busking, face-painting and hair-beading.

'Well,' said Rick, 'we were working the pavement opposite The Tate, doing a bit of trade, and we noticed him in the café over a couple of days.'

'Why? Why did you notice him in particular?' Treloar asked.

'He was there a lot, and always on his own, and he looked so sad,' Moonsong said, 'and ... well he gave us twenty pounds each day, just dropped it in the guitar case.'

'Yeah, that's very noticeable,' Rick added with a grin, 'and then he asked if we wanted to join him for lunch.'

'When? Which day was that?' Treloar pressed.

Moonsong bit her lower lip and counted on her fingers. 'That would've been the third day we were here, Tuesday.'

'Was he local?' Sam asked, reassuring Treloar that she hadn't fallen asleep.

'Don't know; he didn't say,' Rick answered as Moonsong shrugged her shoulders.

'Well ...' Sam went on speaking laboriously, 'did he sound local, or Spanish or Scottish or American, or like Prince Charles? Did he have an accent?'

'No, not really. Sounded like you and Moonsong: bit posh,' said Rick.

'So, describe him. What did he look like?' Treloar intervened, glancing at Sam with a 'cool it' look.

'He was nice looking,' said Moonsong smiling, 'he looked a bit like Captain Jack, you know the guy in *Torchwood*; tall, dark haired ... great teeth. You know what, I bet he was American.'

'I thought Rick said he had no accent,' Sam snarled.

'He didn't. But I bet he grew up there. It was the way he ate lunch; he cut up his food with a knife and fork, then put the knife down and ate just with the fork. They do that, Americans, I've seen it in films and on TV. And then what he ate was weird too,' Moonsong continued.

'How?' asked Treloar.

'Well, at lunch Rick and I had burgers and chips with beer, but he had nothing but chocolate: hot chocolate with marshmallows floating on the top, and two sorts of chocolate cake: well odd.'

'Yeah,' Rick nodded, he was a well weird dude.'

'Still,' Moonsong looked at him, 'he was really nice and really upset about the little girl.'

'Yeah, and he paid,' Rick added, grinning.

'Right. So let's get this straight. Tell us about the little girl,' Treloar said.

'Well she's his daughter isn't she, and that wife of his and her new bloke won't let him see her,' said Rick indignantly.

'It's true. He was so upset, crying even, and he had these beautiful photos of them together; they looked really, really happy. He needed our help. He gave us one so we'd be able to … pick her out,' Moonsong faltered.

'Where is it?' Sam snapped, glaring at her.

'We gave it back when we met up later,' Moonsong mumbled.

'Describe the photograph Moonsong,' Treloar said softly, 'Where was it taken, inside or outside? Who else was in it? Close your eyes and picture that photo. Tell us what you see.'

Moonsong dutifully closed her eyes and furrowed her brow in concentration.

'It was summer. Looked like a garden; looked like England. They were laughing, heads touching. Looked like a selfie. That's the one he gave us. I didn't look closely at the others, but there were loads.

'Loads of photos you didn't look at,' Sam snapped again. 'What about you?' she turned to glare at Rick, who meekly shook his head and looked down.

Treloar gave Sam another sharp look. Her outrage at these people's behaviour was threatening to scupper the interview and Moonsong at least, was providing useful information. Something was going on with Sam and he was determined to find out what later.

'So,' he said calmly, 'he gave you a photo of his daughter and asked for your help. What did he ask you to do?'

Sam rolled her eyes and sighed. Rick was staying silent, head down, eyes fixed on his hands in his lap, but Moonsong was in the moment.

'He handed me the photo, stroking her face as he passed it across the table. He told us that she was staying at that Island Park place. He said she was bound to be at one of the swimming pools because she loved the water so. He asked us - well me actually – to let her know he was here, show her the photo, and ask if she wanted to come with us to see him. Well, when we got there it was manic; people shouting and clambering out of the pool, but we spotted her and showed her the photo. She was made up; absolutely delighted. She clapped her hands, grabbed her friend's hand and said something like: "It's Willy, it's Willy. Come on let's go see him. Do come Lily it'll be the best fun ever, you'll see."'

'She called him Willy, not daddy. Are you sure?' Treloar asked.

'Oh yes. But some people do don't they?'

'And what about when you met him, how did he introduce himself?'

'He didn't say his name come to think of it, did he Rick?'

Rick shook his head.

'You didn't even get his name?' Sam spat, 'And talking of names, what is your name, your real name. I'm not calling you Moonsong.'

'It's Matilda, but I hate it. Everyone calls me Moonsong.'

'That's fine, we respect that and we will call you Moonsong,' Treloar looked pointedly at Sam. 'Now, what about the rubber ring?' he asked, 'When did he give you that?'

'What rubber ring?' she frowned at him.

'Right. So he didn't give you a rubber ring to put in the pool?'

'No of course not. Why would he have done that? We showed her the photo and then we left, the four of us.'

'And then what?' Treloar asked as Sam sat, arms crossed, staring at the ceiling.

'We all got in the car and drove back to the car park near the café opposite The Tate. And I'll tell you what,' Moonsong continued glaring at Sam, 'when we got there and she saw him waiting by the wall, she leapt out of the car and ran to him laughing, calling the other one to follow. She was happy. I'm telling you she knew him and she loved him.'

'She's right man,' Rick spoke for the first time in a while, 'she was well happy to see him. He was no stranger, no paedo.'

'Did you see him when you were at The Island Park?' Treloar asked.

'Of course not,' Moonsong said indignantly. 'He couldn't go in case the mother saw him.'

'And what about the mother or the other girls' parents, did you see any adult with the girls?' Sam asked.

'No. Just the girls on their own. No one came after us,' Rick said.

'Didn't you think you were doing something wrong, something bad, just taking two nine year old girls?' Sam asked, her voice quaking with anger.

'No. And I still don't. She loves him, any fool can see that, and that bitch mother wouldn't let her see him. That's what's wrong lady!' Rick shouted.

Treloar grabbed Sam's arm as she started to rise and dragged her back down into her seat.

'Sergeant!'

He turned to Moonsong, 'did you see where they went from the car park?'

She was staring at Sam wide-eyed. 'No,' she said shakily, 'no we couldn't stop. You know what it's like; there were no spaces, and people honking horns, and shunting about: nightmare. When the girls got out we just drove off, and when I looked back they were gone.'

'So tell me, why have you come forward now?' Treloar asked gently.

'Well when we got back we saw all the posters,' Rick said, 'and we wanted to let everyone know they're all right, they're with the girl Tamsin's dad.'

'So all this was from the goodness of your hearts?' Sam said staring at the floor.

'Of course,' Rick mumbled.

'Tell them Rick,' Moonsong whispered.

'What?' he looked at her.

'Just tell them.'

'Well,' he mumbled, 'he did slip me £500.'

'For your information, your new pal "Willy" is not Tamsin's father. Tamsin's father is with her mother, sitting with Lily's parents at their house, waiting for news, out of their minds with fear and worry, you IDIOTS!' and with that Sam stormed from the room.

'Fucking idiots,' Sam spat as she paced the corridor.

'Never mind them,' Treloar said. 'if you can't control yourself in interviews Sergeant, I want you off this enquiry.'

'I'm fine,' she muttered.

'No you are not. I've never seen you behave with such little discipline. If you can't see past the anxiety that child abduction causes for all of us, then you are of no use to me. You are acting like a wounded animal, lashing out, blind to anything but pain. Get a grip or get off the case. Think about it and let me know.'

And with that he strode off and out of the station door.

Mid September, the previous year

Back home that afternoon it hadn't taken long to rig the camera, he already had all the kit and knew it inside out. He was chuffed, only forty five minutes from start to finish, then less than two to realise it was never going to work. 'Christ, what a fucking idiot,' he said to the pizzas stacked on the cold hob, then, 'Fuck, I'd better get them in the freezer.'

It had all fitted together perfectly, brilliant set up, pictures could be taken at will through the tiny lens mounted in the top of the hat, then transmitted down the fibre cable inside it, and the focus on the phone's camera app was preset so that everything between six and twelve metres was sharp. Holding the phone in his hand to see what would be in the picture, he could twist the hat on his head to alter the direction of the shot easily enough, then press the shutter button to take it. Perfect. But when he took off the hat and flicked his wrist to close it back to a disk the fibre cable got caught inside and so mashed up it was fucking ridiculous.

Bummer, the height was perfect. He wanted to take the pictures of the girl at a distance, giving her a chance to see the hat before he took it off and collapsed it, before vanishing into the crowd. Then, he was going to post or deliver the photos to her house.

'Fucking stupid,' he said to himself as he lifted the pizzas into the freezer. Staring at an old toasting fork hanging on the wall that had belonged to his gran he said suddenly, 'Christ, brilliant, fucking idiot, selfie stick!!'

It wasn't four o'clock yet, the shops on Upper Street would still be open. The 3 or Orange mobile shops were bound to have them, so he racing-hobbled out of the house and sure enough twenty minutes later he swapped just three scruffy five pound notes for an orange-handled selfie stick. Brilliant.

In the kitchen again he set up the stick with a spare phone he had used in his video set-up upstairs, linked it by Bluetooth via an app he made ages ago to his phone and saw the image from the end of the selfie stick on it perfectly. Took test pictures using the shutter button on his phone, played them back, brilliant, fucking perfect!!

Knackered, he whacked a Sloppy Guiseppe pizza into the oven, got a bottle of Sol from the fridge and finished it before the pizza came out. Put it on a board and carved it into well-sloppy slices, took it with another bottle of Sol into the living room where he switched the TV on. First thing in the morning he couldn't remember what he had watched before crashing out on the sofa.

On Sunday morning he woke up early, well early for him, at around seven o'clock, excited, even butterflies, keen to get moving, but it was too early. Needed to grab some thinking time, so he finished off the pizza with a black coffee while he did. Halfway through, he had fished the folded Bulldog gift list from his pocket, looked through it to make sure he was right about a couple of things, and smiled to himself and nodded.

The weather was still good and after a shower and checking on-line when The Bulldog opened, he had dressed in yesterday's 501s and had put on a black Parallel Lines T shirt, before thinking he should be more anonymous and switching it to a plain white T shirt, and a plain light grey hoodie. He'd been too hot yesterday and didn't want a repeat. Plain white socks and the black hi-tops went on last.

On the way downstairs he remembered he'd been looking at crappy boring American real-crime stuff on the TV last night, laughed out loud, and went to the kitchen to get a pair of the thin rubber insulating gloves he used when he was doing electronics from his toolbox and put them in the right hoodie pocket. The selfie stick and phones were in a light brown leather shoulder bag, switched on, connected, ready to go, like him.

Nearly. He took some twenty pound notes from his wallet, folded them and put them in a back jeans' pocket, and looked at Dan's Visa card and driving licence before deciding he wasn't ready for them yet, didn't need them yet anyway, and leaving them there. Then he had turned back and taken the credit card - just in case.

Taking the same journey as yesterday, leaving the house just after nine o'clock, he was looking at the Benetton mannequins, still with umbrellas and wellington boots in the window, just after 10.00 o'clock. He had been walking more slowly and there were longer waits for trains than on the Saturday, but by 10.30 he was sitting outside The Bulldog in the sun and ordering a white beer and a bag of peanuts. Going slowly with the beer, with good reason - he didn't want to be caught short while on the follow - he said, 'No thanks,' to the waitress when she asked if he wanted a second, but he did ask for a packet of tulip petals and a small windmill.

Selfridges didn't open until 11.30 on Sundays so he had sat in the sun and thought and fantasized, and thought and fantasized some more, while keeping his eye out for another one, just in case. When the waitress came back and asked if he was sure he didn't want another beer he realised he had tripped off and he needed to go so he said, 'No thanks,' gave her a twenty pound note saying, 'Thanks, great, keep the change,' put the petals and windmill in the shoulder bag and wandered a few metres towards Oxford Circus before crossing the road at the lights outside John Lewis, then walking back on himself towards Selfridges. Not quite as many people about as yesterday but the weather had bought out enough and the crowds had thickened even while he had waited over the road.

At Selfridges he had stopped outside again just in case one came out, no luck this time, so after a minute he went in and took the escalator up to the second floor, walked past Gucci Men, which had an offer on shoes, saw behind the shoes some hi-top trainers that he might come back to look at, but went straight past towards women's hand bags. Great plan, he was looking for a present, easy; but really ...... find, follow, freak ...... whatever .... and he'd had plenty of ideas about that!

A sexy high pitched giggle followed by a female but deep and husky laugh caught his attention and between rails of T shirts blouses and dresses on the other side of the GG red carpet between the departments he saw two of them. Shoulder length blonde hair, sexy attractive, young, one in a bright yellow sleeveless top and the other in a matching but red top, both with Gucci shoulder bags. They both had their backs to him and one held up a long red skirt with a bright blue bird with a curved orange beak and long black shimmering tail on what looked like the front. The other one had pulled at the side of the long red skirt and held open the thigh high gap. He wondered what they were laughing about.

The second girl pulled an orange skirt off the rail, held it up next to the first one, the same bird was on the front but with a black beak, and they giggled and laughed again, nodded to each other and walked off towards the cash desk, giggling.

He carried on browsing the handbags, but watched as they

went to the desk then giggled again while talking to the Gucci girl at the till. The one in the yellow top, who he could now see wore a short red skirt and red plimsolls with yellow soles, took the long orange skirt from her mate, took a big gold card with a number 2 on it from the till girl, put her bag on the counter while talking to the till girl because it was slipping off her shoulder, then they both walked in the direction that the till girl had pointed; to the changing rooms he thought - ha, he was fucking bright like that.

Seemed like ages, he kept waiting for them to reappear, but nothing except shrieks and laughter from the changing rooms. Then, 'Fuck me noooooo, you won't,' from the changing room, then, 'You fucking wait and see,' and more laughter, louder now. The till girl looked round, not many customers in yet, when she saw him browsing the bags she shrugged her shoulders and smiled then set off for the changing rooms.

'Fucking hell, go, go, go!' said Dan, who was suddenly at the till, waving him over, and he walked quickly to the shoulder bag on the counter, putting on the gloves from his pocket as he went, opened it and soon saw a driving licence and memorised the name and address and put it back, then quickly emptied the packet of tulip petals into an unzipped side pocket before closing the bag, taking off his gloves, putting them back in his pocket and walking quickly back to carry on browsing the bags.

Fourteen

'Right,' said Treloar, 'let's look at Moonsong and Rick's story. I agree that they've been stupid but I think they're genuine. Just because the girls are missing doesn't mean they're being held in dripping drains or filthy cellars, tethered by the neck. I think this is positive news. Tamsin obviously knows this "Willy" and was clearly delighted to see him. If she is happy that will keep Lily reassured, at least for a while. He could have left Lily on her own in that busy car park, but he didn't. That's something; he's showing some responsibility.'

'It's definitely time to talk to the parents again, especially the Thomases. There is clearly something they're not telling us. Tom Grigg and Fi Sinclair were right about that.'

'What sort of name is "Moonsong" anyway? Obviously Mummy and Daddy weren't bestowed with much good sense,' Sam said. 'You're setting a lot of store by that pair.'

'I know, but I believe them. We'll keep them at the station for now but I don't think they're any more involved than they've said. And if you think about it with a cool head, neither do you. And she did tell us her real name is Matilda, so I don't really think you can blame her parents.'

Sam turned to look at him. They were in his Land Rover driving up out of St Ives town centre towards the Warren house. 'OK fine. I agree. I think they're on the level. But what about the business with the rubber ring, that can't be a coincidence?'

'No, I think that was him. They wouldn't have dreamt that up. Obviously now we know from DNA that the blood wasn't that of either girl, but look at what happened: a major distraction whilst our pair took the girl. And think of the fear. Missing girls and blood where they were last seen. That's frightening, and who would be most frightened?'

'The parents.'

'Indeed. And as he didn't expect Lily, it's Tamsin's parents he's looking to scare. There's a relationship there, a connection, has to be. For a while nobody connected the blood with the rubber ring. All they had was blood in the pool and two missing girls at the same time. Again, surely not coincidence? Panic all round'.

'But why involve Rick and Moonsong at all if he was going to be there himself?'

'Well would you trust that pair to pull it off? No I think he went along as a fallback in case they bottled out or fucked up, and the ring was there to help, to cause a distraction if he needed to act alone. Then of course he saw the bonus of the confusion and panic it would cause in such a crowded pool. If the pool had been quiet, he would have risked somebody seeing the girls going off and the blood would have grabbed everybody's attention. As it was it did take the immediate focus and delayed attention switching to the missing girls.'

'Our pair says Tamsin was delighted to see "Willy" but they didn't say she was surprised or shocked. Perhaps she was in on it; perhaps she threw the rubber ring in the pool, part of the lark?'

Treloar glanced at her, 'Tell me, where would a nine year old girl on holiday in a strange place get a rubber ring filled with human blood?'

'Yes well, when you put it like that I suppose. But she might have known what was going to happen which was why it was so easy to take them?' How would "Willy" have known she would be at that water complex at that holiday park at that time and without her parents, if she hadn't been in on it? It would explain a lot.'

'Except, why **he** involved Rick and Moonsong, and why **she** involved Lily?'

'True enough.'

As they drew up outside the Warren's Victorian terrace house, Treloar switched off the engine and pulled out his mobile phone.

'Let's go ask some questions of Mr and Mrs Thomas, but first I'll check in with Col and Luke, see if they have anything new. You go ahead, I shouldn't be long.' And with that Sam climbed out, grabbed her bag from the back seat and walked up the drive towards a warm glow shining through the coloured leaded lights of the Warren's front door.

As it transpired, Colin Matthews had discovered something which would prove of tremendous significance when put together with other threads, but at the time it seemed insignificant to him and so he did not mention it to anyone else.

Hal was pissed. Goddamnit. It was not supposed to go like this. It was just supposed to be a neat way to fuck with Sebastian. The man was such a total asshole and Hal enjoyed messing with him. But those idiot dopeheads had brought along the other girl and that was serious bad news. She'd have to go. Shit.

Fifteen

'You do forget when you sleep, if you sleep. But then I wake up and for a moment I'm totally lost: I can't remember who I am, where I am. But then the reality lashes back like a severed cable and it literally knocks me down; I fall down. Guy can't assimilate it at all; he's in a mess, I've never seen him like this.'

Whilst Treloar and Sam were talking to Moonsong and Rick, Fiona Sinclair was sitting in the conservatory of the Warren house talking with Becky Warren.

'My mother watched Detective Superintendent Winters on the television news at lunchtime; she said she was very good, very … efficient.'

'Yes. She has a good reputation,' Fi said struggling for words to help this woman.

'Did you see that French television programme? I think it was called *Les Revenants*, The Returned Ones, something like that; it was about dead people coming back into their own lives, just back … alive. Do you think such things are possible?'

'Becky, we have absolutely no reason whatsoever to believe that Lily is dead.'

'Guy doesn't believe it. He says the dead are in another country and the borders are closed. Perhaps he read it somewhere?'

As Becky Warren sat on her sofa methodically wringing the neck of the battered teddy bear, Fi pondered the change in the woman from when she had first met her the previous day. When she had arrived on the doorstep that evening with Tom Grigg, the door had been opened by a pretty smiling woman, glowing with life and health. Now she was looking at a sunken spectre with hollow eyes, lank hair and a deathly pallor. Had it not been physically impossible, Fi would have sworn the woman had lost six inches in height and two stone in weight. When the door opened and Tom Grigg walked through with yet another tray of tea, Fi sighed with relief.

Placing the tray on the low table Tom took a seat opposite the sofa and smiled softly at Becky. He's good at this Fi thought; he's a good, kind man. He fears the worst, believes the worst, but you would never know it in this house.

'Does Lily keep any kind of diary or journal? I know she's

young, but I remember that mine did that sort of thing in the summer holiday, school project, that sort of thing.

'No, nothing like that. Nothing … official. She does keep a sort of picture book, scrap book thing where she draws things she comes across. Would you like to see it?

'Yes please,' Tom replied.

Becky Warren tucked the teddy bear under her left arm, pulled herself to her feet like an old lady and walked slowly from the room.

'Does it matter Sir, what she drew?' Fi asked.

'What she's drawing Fi, remember to use the present tense. It's very important for the families. If they think we've given up hope, what's left for them?'

Becky Warren slowly climbed the stairs to the first floor landing. She opened the door to the back bedroom which overlooked the garden. Looking in she saw that her mother was asleep on the bed, snoring gently. The sleep of the drugged or the exhausted, Becky thought, wondering if she would ever sleep soundly again, naturally again. Downstairs she heard a knock at the door and then voices as the policewoman let in a second female.

Closing the door softly she carried on up a further flight of stairs to the top floor where Lily had her room immediately above the one in which her grandmother slept. The door was closed. The police had been in there but Becky had not, not since Lily had been gone. Luckily she would not have to go in there now. Lily's drawing book was in the front room, the one above hers and Guy's, the one that served as Guy's studio.

She opened the door and walked in. This was a lovely airy room with a large bay window opening to the east, letting in the light from across the bay where she could just make out the lighthouse on Godrevy Island. Those windows need washing she found herself thinking, absurdly. She wanted to stay and study the paintings and drawings pinned to the walls, to inhale the smells of paints and clay, to touch the little figures of animals and angels that Lily had made last Christmas which were now lined up on the wonky shelving that Guy was meaning to fix, next weekend, soon, over the summer.

Somehow something more interesting, more fun always intervened and so the shelves remained wonky. Becky smiled. But the policeman wanted that book, so she walked across to the old pine table in the window and pulled it from beneath a pile of Guy's sketches. With one last glance out across the bay, she turned and left the room, closing the door firmly behind her. As she reached the bottom of the second flight of stairs and stood in the hallway with the front porch to her right, ahead of her, the sitting room door had come open. Guy must fix that before the autumn she thought it lets in such a draft if it's not closed properly.

As she stood at the foot of the stairs thinking idly about the autumn and whether Lily would be home by then, she could hear urgent angry lowered voices coming from her sitting room. Their tone was furtive and squabbling and Becky wondered who could be acting like that in her house at a time like this. Quietly, she walked forward and rested her head against the partially open door.

'Look you foolish woman. Remember when this happened before, two years ago? We were told not to go to the police and we didn't and we got her back safe and sound. Hold onto that. We can't tell anyone this time either, if it's him.'

'If it's him?' Becky recognised the slurring drawl of Kate Thomas. 'And what about Lily, what about her, what will he do to Lily?'

'Nothing. He didn't hurt Tamsin last time so why should he hurt either of them now? I'll pay him and it will be over. Lily's just happenstance: wrong place, wrong time; collateral.'

'Well let's just hope she's not collateral damage!'

Becky flung the heavy door open as if it were made of plywood sending it slamming into the wall of the sitting room sending a large pottery giraffe crashing to the wooden floor, shattering into pieces which scattered across the room hitting tables, chairs and landing in the open fireplace like hailstones.

'What do you know?' she snarled, 'what do you know? WHAT DO YOU KNOW?'

The clamour brought Fi, Sam and Tom running in from the conservatory.

'What is going on in here?' Tom Grigg asked in his severest tone.

'They know something. This has happened before. I heard them, I heard them. Somebody took Tamsin two years ago and they paid to get her back and they said nothing, nothing. They know something, they do, just ask them, ask them, ASK THEM!' and with that she rushed across the room still clutching Lily's drawing book and set about beating Sebastian Thomas across the head with it. At this, Kate Thomas burst into hysterical laughter.

'Right. Fi help me take Becky through to the conservatory, Sam you stay with these two.' With that he crossed the room and firmly took Becky's arms and folded them behind her back, taking the drawing book from her grasp and handing it to Fiona. Sebastian Thomas regained his composure and slapped his wife across the face as Tom Grigg marched the distraught woman from the room in sobs, Fiona closing the door behind them.

A stunned silence filled their wake. Kate Thomas sat slumped on the floor, her head in her hands. Her husband stood by the mantelpiece visibly shaking. Sam advanced to the centre of the bay window and surveyed them both with a withering glare.

'What the fuck is going on here? Tell me now and tell me everything or I swear I'll make sure you both pay for this with more than money.'

Whilst emotions ran riot in the Warren house Treloar sat calmly in his Land Rover talking to Colin Matthews and Luke Calloway. He had already spoken to Detective Superintendent Winters about the interview with Moonsong and Rick and she had agreed that they should be held whilst their story was checked. She also agreed that it sounded plausible. Colin and Luke were now tasked with canvassing The Island Park for any sightings of "Willy" using the description of Captain Jack, proffered by Moonsong. They were then to ask in the café opposite The Tate.

Having closed his phone, Treloar got out and locked his vehicle and started up the path to the Warren house. As he approached the front door he became aware of raised voices. The door was opened by Fiona Sinclair in a flustered, breathless state. The raised voices were coming from behind the closed door to his right.

'What in the name of God is going on here?'

'It's the Thomases Sir. They know something, and Mrs Warren lost it completely and attacked Mr Thomas and Sarge and I had to take her out to the conservatory before she had a fit.'

'Calm down Fiona. Why the hell did Tom leave them in there on their own?'

'They're not on their own Sir … Phil,' she continued,

breathing deeply, 'Sergeant Scott's in there with them.'

'What ...?' he asked grasping the door knob and pushing it open.

Standing in the doorway Treloar took in the scene in the sitting room. A large amount of shattered pottery was strewn across the floor; Sebastian and Kate Thomas were standing stricken faced side by side at the fireplace; but most alarming of all Detective Sergeant Sam Scott stood with her back to him, haranguing the couple at the top of her voice.

'And how do you know what happened to her? Are you qualified to establish that? Did you take her to a counsellor? Did you take her to a doctor? Are you qualified to establish whether she was raped or sodomised? Who knows what harm you've done to her on top of whatever harm he did, who knows what he's doing to her, doing to Lily right now?' and with that she crossed the room and struck Sebastian Thomas hard on the side of his face.

'SERGEANT!' Treloar barked, 'A moment please?' He stood back holding the door for the red-faced Sam who walked out past an astonished Fiona Sinclair. 'Fiona, please join Tom in the conservatory.'

As Fiona retreated to the conservatory Treloar closed the sitting room door and turned to face Sam.

'Why are you behaving like this? It's never personal; you know that.'

'It's not personal,' Sam replied sulkily, 'it doesn't have to be your dog he's kicking to know a man's a total shit.'

'I have no idea what is happening with you but I do not have the time to deal with it now. Go and sit in the Land Rover until a squad car comes to fetch you. It will take you home and you will stay there until you hear from me. You are off this enquiry as of now and if the Thomases make a complaint you may well be off the force.'

'But I ...'

'Just go,' he said gently handing her the keys, 'don't make this any worse for anyone.'

And with that, she took the keys from him, as tears streamed down her face, and let herself out of the front door closing it softly behind her. Treloar rubbed his hands across his face, suddenly overcome by an intense fatigue. God what a day, he thought as he

94

turned back to the sitting room.

Sebastian and Kate Thomas had regained their composure and were sitting at opposite ends of the crimson covered sofa facing the fireplace. Some attempt had been made to shovel the pottery shards into a pile next to the empty log basket in the hearth.

Sebastian spoke. 'I assume you are someone in authority? I cannot say that I have had dealings with this police force before, but never in my …'

'For fuck's sake Seb shut up you pompous prick.' Kate Thomas said slowly but clearly. 'I'm sure that your colleague does not normally speak to the public in that fashion, but what she actually said was entirely reasonable, if a little harsh in the delivery.'

'Yes, my apologies to you both, Mr and Mrs Thomas; emotions do run high in these circumstances. I am Detective Inspector Félipe Treloar. I am leading this enquiry and I would like to understand what has happened here this evening. But first, if you will bear with me I would like to check on Mrs Warren.'

'Please do Inspector, please do.' Kate Thomas said waving a hand towards the door.

In the conservatory Treloar found Tom Grigg standing by the open door to the garden sipping a coffee. Treloar looked longingly at the pot on the table and recognizing the need in his colleague, Tom bent to pour him a cup then handed it to him proffering the sugar bowl. Treloar shook his head, taking the cup with a grateful nod. Sitting on the sofa next to Fiona was a small woman with a tear-streaked face, clutching an old teddy bear.

'Phil, this is Becky Warren, Becky this is Inspector Treloar,' Grigg said quietly.

Treloar downed his coffee, put the cup back on the tray and knelt on one knee before the woman, taking one of her hands in both of his.

'Hello Mrs Warren', he said, 'I'm sorry this has happened to you, but we're doing everything we can to get the girls back.'

Becky nodded mutely and continued to wring the teddy bear.

'Will you excuse me for one moment whilst I catch up with Tom?'

Becky looked up at him and nodded again. Treloar held out

an arm to the garden door and followed Tom Grigg out into the evening.

'Christ Phil what the hell has got into Sam? I don't know her well, mainly by reputation but she doesn't normally lose it does she?'

'Never. Beats me. She's outside in my Land Rover. I need to get a squad car to take her home. If there's a complaint she's fucked. What the hell happened here?'

'Well all was calm when we got here from the briefing. The Thomases were in the sitting room talking quietly and Becky was out here with her mother. Then the mother excused herself and went upstairs to lie down and Fi and I were talking to Becky. I asked if Lily kept a journal and Becky said she had a sketch book and went to fetch it. You never know there could be something in it and at least it was keeping her occupied.'

'Good thought, Tom.'

'Anyway the next thing, Sam arrives and we're out here with Sam telling us about your interview with the couple - that sounds encouraging by the way, I'd like to tell Becky – then we hear Becky screaming in the sitting room. We get her out of there back down here and leave Sam with the Thomases. Well then you arrive and Sam goes mental. From what I can get out of Becky, she came downstairs and heard them talking about how Tamsin had been taken before for money a couple of years ago, and they paid up and told no one. What did they tell Sam?'

'No idea. I just needed to get her out of there.'

'What have they said about Sam?'

'Well he started spouting off and she shut him straight down, more or less said that Sam was justified in what she said, just a bit … forceful.'

'Could be OK then?'

'Yeah, if Sam hadn't hit him.'

'What?'

'Yeah, smacked him one in the face. Extraordinary.'

'Listen Phil, I know it's your call, but if you get the uniform boys to take her home, it's going to get out one way or another. If the Thomases say nothing, and it sounds like they've probably good cause to keep their heads down, it might just slide you know?'

'OK but what am I going to do with her? She can't sit in my car all night.'

'Well, you're here now, why don't I take her home? I can be up to Truro and back in no time and no one the wiser. Or if you're worried about her, I could take her back to mine. Lizzie won't mind.'

'Tell you what, let me make a call and I can sort this quickly and quietly.' With that he took out his phone and pressed a speed dial number. After a few rings Tom heard a distant "Si?" and Treloar spoke.

'Lucia, querida, I need a favour …'

Still mid September, the previous year

The shouting and laughing and giggling had stopped when the till girl went over and sounded like a school teacher at them, apart from a couple of giggles when she was halfway back to the till. She turned and looked back but it was quiet after that. Not long afterwards they both came out of the changing rooms, went back to the till and the girl in the yellow top bought both skirts. Christ! Made of money, incredible.

He had gone over to the rail the skirts had been on to see them close up, see what they felt like, what they cost, £1,550 each. Fuck! He browsed the scarves while she paid and the skirts were folded and bagged up, checked that his hood was still pulled as far forward as it would go, then followed them over to the escalator where they stopped to talk before splitting up, laughing and waving. Red-top shouted, 'See you at eight!' down the escalator before looking round, spotting the lifts then walking towards them.

He was already walking to the escalator, around ten metres back, when he had had to stop while red-top shouted, but was on it and on his way down well before yellow-top was anywhere near the bottom. At the bottom she had just turned and stepped onto the down escalator to the Ground Floor and, his luck was in, she had gone straight to the main door and out onto Oxford Street then turned right, up towards Marble Arch. Brilliant.

Got a bit closer, plenty of people about, slow past Marks & Spencer, loads of people looking in the windows, fuck knows why, he almost stopped, trying to concentrate on getting the selfie-stick out, it was catching on something in his bag, looked back up, thought he had lost her and stepped round a beggar with his hat out and on to the road, trotted looking to his right and saw her, slowly edging through the M & S window watchers and could see a big SALE sign and curtains being pulled back either side of it, Christ!

He was to the side and slightly in front of yellow-top, who couldn't move now, when he stepped back onto the pavement, finally dragged out and extended the selfie-stick, held it up and saw her face in the crowd on the mobile's screen in his hand, looking seriously pissed off, and clicked three quick shots before collapsing the stick. He held on to the phone and the stick, just in case, rather than putting them back in the bag.

She got going again and he slotted in behind, around four

people back, then suddenly she turned right, up a side street. Shit, not many people, he held back and let her get well ahead before following, not too far back, but there was nowhere really for her to go, unless she was going to the Thistle hotel. There was a sign to it, pointing left, above a parking sign pointing the same way. He put the selfie-stick and phone back in his shoulder bag.

Suddenly she had turned left, going quickly and was out of view so he sped up to the corner, looked round it carefully and saw her walk past the back entrance to the hotel towards a big blue sign saying Bryanstone Road Car Park, and past a builder's skip, in front of a blocked off door, with a chute above it held to the wall with scaffolding. A taxi was parked up on its own three car lengths from the skip. Christ! Didn't look like any multi-storey car park he had ever seen. Windows, loads, more like an office block, and a fucking big gym sign and entrance the other side of the car park barrier, maybe she was going there. Suddenly she stopped, opened a door just before the barrier and was gone. Fuck, now what?

He ran up to the door, pushed it open and quickly stepped through it and it slammed loudly behind him. Couldn't see her on the ground floor, saw the stairs on his right and heard someone going up them, couldn't think of anything else but running up them himself so he did. Got to a landing with a door out to the first floor, hadn't heard a door open or close and could still hear someone going up, so he ran up the next flight to the second floor, still no door slam, still someone going up. Stopped to catch his breath, wasn't used to running, especially up fucking stairs.

Then he thought .... 'Idiot, not a problem, you've got her address anyway.' He heard the footsteps above speeding up, was enjoying himself more than he had in fucking ages, and ran up the next flight, then the next and was halfway up the next when he heard a door squeak open then slam shut and he ran up, could see there were no more stairs so he waited a few seconds, went through the door which had 'ROOF' painted on it and it slammed loudly behind him. She had stopped, her free hand was in her shoulder bag and she was looking back, straight at him, fifteen metres away; she looked scared, he smiled, and waved.

She looked around, looking for her car he thought, took her hand from her bag and held up what he thought were keys and a second later he saw the indicators of a red BMW Z4 flash twice with a beep. She turned towards the noise but hadn't seen the flash, stood still and pressed the key again as he started walking towards her. She saw the indicators flashing, they were way over on the other side of the roof, about 50 metres away, then looked back at him, still smiling, and walking towards her.

Suddenly she ran into a gap between a big silver Lexus and an orange Range Rover, towards a door that had 'NO ENTRY' painted diagonally across it in big black letters, pulled it open and ran through, holding tightly onto the Gucci shopper, and the door slammed loudly. He ran after her, opening and running through the door then stopping quickly and the door slam was mega fucking loud as it closed just behind him. He couldn't walk much further without walking into her.

The stairs to the right were blocked off with piles of bricks and there was a blue tarpaulin in front of the wall that she was standing in front of. She turned around quickly, holding up the Gucci shopper and looking seriously scared, really seriously, Christ! Fucking brilliant! He smiled as he took two steps towards her, nodded at her, then stopped; she seemed relieved and nodded back and tried to smile. Didn't work, but he enjoyed seeing the effort. Mascara was running down her cheeks and he saw dark sweat marks on the yellow top under her arms.

He took his gloves from his pocket and put them on, then took the shopper from her and put it on the floor beside his right foot, then took two more steps towards her with his hands open and out towards her neck. Just touched it with his fingertips, and laughed as she backed up to the tarpaulin, which moved backwards with her; then she had gasped, thrown her hands forward clutching at nothing, and disappeared. Fuck! He looked through the hole where the tarpaulin had been and down at the pavement. Christ!

Sixteen

As they drove up to Cove Farm, it seemed impossible to Sam that the last few hours had passed and things had changed so utterly, totally and probably irrevocably. She felt worse than she ever had. It seemed she had ruined her life, both personal and professional, in less than an hour. Could that be possible? How would she ever explain to her parents, to her friends, to the team and most of all, worst of all, to herself? If she had blown it all, she would never forgive herself, never.

Earlier she had been sitting in abject misery in Treloar's Land Rover outside the Warrens' when he had emerged from the house. As he walked down the path she had noticed a white Citroën Berlingo van draw up alongside her. Treloar had opened his driver's door and leaned across the seat towards her.

'Sam, I've asked Lucia to take you back to Cove Farm for the night.'

'But ...'

'No debate. I don't have time for this now. Go with Lucia and stay there tomorrow until you hear from me. I'll tell the others you're unwell. When I have time I'll come up to the farm. You can explain yourself then.'

'Thank you,' she mumbled.

'Don't thank me. It was Tom's idea to keep this between ourselves. Lucia is here. Go.'

With that he had walked around to speak to Lucia and Sam had clambered shakily out. Misery, misery, all is misery she had thought as she climbed into the van's passenger seat. On the journey up to Cove Farm, Lucia had asked no questions and merely expressed the view that in her extensive experience of disastrous situations, absolutely nothing is ever as bad as you think at the time. Sam had nodded bleakly.

When they arrived at the farm Sam had asked if she could just go to the room. There she had found that someone had laid out some faded sweat pants and a baggy jumper which obviously didn't belong to Lucia, fresh towels and a huge towelling dressing gown. The bed had been changed and there were fresh wild flowers in an earthenware pot on the deep windowsill. Sam had sat on the bed and burst into tears.

As Sam wallowed in misery, Lucia was sitting at the kitchen table gazing intently at the screen of her laptop. Spread across the table were piles of photographs. Something from the party was troubling her. Over the course of her brother's barn conversion, whenever she was in Cornwall, Lucia had taken photographs, some of which were now framed and hanging on the walls of Lost Farm Barn. Ever the perfectionist, at the party she had noticed what appeared to be a blemish or smudge on several of the photographs; perhaps it was a smear on the paper, in which case she intended to reprint and replace the prints. She was sure that it was not a scratch on the camera lens as she would have noticed it with other subjects. As she scrolled through the images in her folders two things struck her: all the photographs were stills captured from video, and more bizarrely, the flaw only appeared in shots featuring Beatriz.

'Hello,' said a voice to her right, startling her and setting her heart racing.

'Jesus Christ Sam you made me jump!'

'Sorry,' Sam said glumly.

'Oh come, come and sit down and have some coffee. I told you, it's never as bad as you think. When I think of how I have felt after dreadful scenes and hurtful fights with Luca, and yet here we are, still friends. All things pass.'

'Thank you for the loan of the clean clothes,' Sam said.

'Oh that's OK, they're some of Bee's, she won't mind.'

'Is it just us here?' Sam asked looking around the kitchen.

'Mamá and Eva have gone to Mass in St Ives. They'll be back at lunchtime. Bee is still asleep. She worked last night and then she was playing at the R & B bar 'til the small hours. Really, I do not know where that girl gets her stamina. Lucia pulled a pile of photographs towards her across the kitchen table. 'Here, you're the detective, come and help me with this.'

'What are you doing?' Sam asked, intrigued despite her depressed state.

'Come look. Here, sit next to me,' she added shuffling along on the settle so that Sam could sit beside her. 'I noticed the other night that some of the photographs at Flip's place had a fault so I'm checking them out.'

'You took all those photographs at the barn?'

'Well no, obviously not the ones when we were small or the ones I'm in of course, but a lot of them, and I did a series of the

102

conversion and that's where I spotted the problem.'

'OK. I'm no expert on photography though.'

'That's fine, it's more that I need a second opinion and to prove that I'm not seeing or imagining things.'

'Right. I'm all yours,' Sam nodded, glad of the distraction.

Lucia picked up her mug and took a sip.

'Qué asco! That is awful. Let me make some more. Do you want anything to eat?'

'No thanks.'

Lucia shuffled out from the table and crossed over to empty and refill an ancient Bialetti coffee maker which she set on the Aga. She opened and closed several cupboard doors before pulling out a battered biscuit tin from which she took tiny round biscuits which she put on a bright red plate she took down from a shelf. She took the biscuits with two cups across to the table.

'These are Mamá's nut biscuits. They're like panellets, a traditional Catalan treat for All Saints' Day, but Mamá bakes them all year. These ones don't have pinenuts. Try one. They're very light, and perfect to dip in coffee. Would you like some milk or sugar?'

'No, black will be fine thanks.'

Lucia brought the coffee across and stood the pot on a battered green enamelled trivet. She shuffled back along the settle.

'Look at this.'

Lucia dragged a pile of photographs across the table and spread them out.

'OK, what am I looking for?' Sam asked.

'These are a series of photographs taken over several months during the construction work at Flip's barn. They are actually all captured from video. Tell me if you notice anything.'

Sam picked up each print in turn to study it closely. They showed various groupings of people in differing locations around the barn site. The first set was clearly from an early stage of the conversion when the two barns were still distinct, separate buildings.

It was obviously Christmas because Beatriz, Eva and their mother were laughing and decorating a fir tree in a terracotta pot with silver tinsel and glass baubles. They were in the courtyard outside the kitchen door dressed in trousers and coats. Treloar was standing to one side, hands on hips, grinning.

103

In the next shot the decoration of the tree was complete, and Beatriz was reaching to place a silver star on its top. The others stood to the side watching and they had been joined by a second man, his face half-obscured by a scarf as he watched Beatriz. He was shorter than Treloar with ragged brown hair and he was dressed in jeans and a thick navy blue fisherman's sweater. He was holding a white envelope and a bottle of what looked like wine, wrapped in red paper.

'Who's that?' Sam asked pointing at the figure.

'That's Dylan Maddox,' Lucia replied.

Looking more closely at Beatriz Sam noticed that as she had stretched to reach the top of the tree her coat collar had slid down on one side to reveal a chunky bead necklace, not unlike something Sam could picture Ochre Pengelly wearing: a gift from her perhaps? In the next print Beatriz, Eva and Inés stood by the tree facing the camera with broad smiles but Treloar and Dylan Maddox were not in shot. All looked much like the previous print, clearly taken just moments earlier, except that the beads had gone from Beatriz's neck.

The next sequence was obviously from months later: it was summer and the glass atrium between the two barns was in place. A larger group of people was assembled on the half-finished patio at the rear of the barn. Sam recognised Treloar, Inés and Beatriz. Next to Treloar stood a young man of similar height with striking copper coloured hair and a broad grin. He was leaning on a garden fork. Both men were stripped to the waist, Beatriz was in shorts and a T shirt and Inés wore a simple black dress.

'And this guy?' Sam asked pointing at the young man.

Lucia glanced across from her laptop screen. 'That's Bee's best friend, Jory Nancarrow. I don't know if it's friends with benefits, but I hope so; he's a really lovely guy and very sexy.'

Sam laughed and moved on to the next print: the same scene but with the addition of Dylan and Hope Maddox who was holding a tiny baby as they stood by the open kitchen door. Inés was absent, and Beatriz and Jory were now sitting on a travel rug spread on the patio. Everyone was smiling at the camera with the exception of the baby, obviously, and Dylan who was staring at the couple on the rug. Sam focused on Beatriz. There, around her neck, were the beads again. She started to speak to Lucia only to find that her mouth was full of delicious biscuit. She looked down to see that the plate was almost empty. Noticing this Lucia laughed.

'Don't worry querida. Not even God himself could eat only one of my mother's biscuits!'

Sam finished the last of the biscuits, pushed the plate aside and turned to Lucia. She spoke slowly.

'Well, there is something odd here. In two of these prints, clearly taken at different gatherings, Beatriz appears to be wearing a chunky bead necklace one minute and then not the next.'

Lucia's eyes flashed in triumph.

'Exactly, exactly and what's more Bee never wears necklaces, beads, chains, pendants, nothing other than a ring that belonged to my grandmother. She hates the feel of jewellery and says it gets in her way when she's playing her double bass. Anything else, any other observations?'

'Well, the only common factor I can make out is that in both the prints where she seems to be wearing the beads, Dylan Maddox is present.'

Lucia was silent for a while. 'So it's not just me then,' she finally said, her hand pressed to her heart, 'I'm looking for the originals. Perhaps we can see something on them?' Her fingers flew across the keypad, then she started to click rapidly through galleries of prints.

'I don't have the original video here, I'd need to get it sent over from Barcelona, but I do have the print copies I emailed to Eva. Right … here we go.'

She pulled up two images side by side on the screen and zoomed in on Beatriz. Suddenly she let out a gasp and pushed herself violently back from the table, banging her head on the painting of Errolan behind her on the wall. Her face had drained of colour.

'Jesus, what is it?' Sam cried as Lucia turned the screen toward her. There it was beneath Beatriz's smiling face, circling her neck: a greyish brown band. But it was not a bead necklace; it was a rope noose.

By 22:00 Sam and Lucia had checked all the images on the laptop. Whenever Beatriz and Dylan Maddox were both in the shot there was the rope noose. No Dylan – no noose.

Still mid September, the previous year

Christ! Rush or what?! But he was calm. Amazing! He had stepped carefully around the bag on the floor, taken off his gloves and put them in his pocket, walked to the other side of the roof and down another staircase, not too quickly, with his hood still up, down to the ground floor, out at the side of the gym entrance, then to Marble Arch tube station, got on the first eastbound Central Line train and off again at Oxford Circus then back to the Angel.

Fucking incredible; three trains, six stops, and under an hour after he had nearly had his hands on her long fucking neck he was back in Islington, hood down, walking easily through the warm Sunday afternoon crowds in Upper Street going to and leaving the pubs and restaurants and Camden Passage, stepping easily over the feet of a lazy busker sitting on the uneven flag stones and leaning against the wall of a Barclays bank, and was nearly home, not even two o'clock. Brilliant!!

Even using cash to buy tickets instead of his touch fucking in and touch fucking out travel card, how cool was THAT!

He had whacked a pizza in the oven and tripped off ...... shame about the time, too short, miles too bloody short, not in the plan, better than last time, but should have been better, shouldn't have been seen, not then, shit, fuck, need to get better. Had her address, knew what else he wanted .... bastard. He'd found, he'd followed, he'd freaked .... freaked her right out, scared her, well scared her, not much more, really .... he was only going to stroke her neck, both hands, up and down, freak her, and she was good, really good, so he wished he'd followed better, for longer, again, and again, and done .... more, not sure what, seen her scared again, and again. Still, no-one had seen him, with her, at least he was pretty sure, anyway he had kept his hood up until he was back in Islington, so the cameras wouldn't have caught him. Could he have used his own camera? No time, or opportunity, definitely, no, luck of the draw; he had dealt with it pretty well. Still buzzy, and calm.

He had taken the pizza to the sofa, switched on Sky News, just left it on and waited. Nothing. Switched over to BBC News, for ages, nothing. Drifted off to sleep and was woken up close to seven o'clock by the BBC London News music. The lead story was his! Fuck!! Young woman's body found in mysterious circumstances, near a car park close to the Marble Arch end of Oxford Street, Police investigating and appealing for witnesses, death referred to the coroner, contact numbers for the Metropolitan Police, Christ! That was him! DID anyone see him? Did any cameras pick him up? Christ, there were thousands of them, Fuck! Turned off the TV and played it all back in his mind, fast forward, from the girly giggle in Selfridges to getting back on the tube train at Marble Arch, cool, he was cool, and went upstairs to bed.

By the time he was watching the BBC London News just before seven o'clock on Monday morning she was the pretty Melissa Stanley-Beale, just nineteen years of age, who had still died in mysterious circumstances which the police were still investigating, and witnesses were still being asked to come forward. There was a photograph now and a description of the distinctive clothes that she had been wearing - a bright yellow sleeveless shirt, red skirt and red plimsolls with unusual yellow soles. She had been carrying a large red Gucci shoulder bag. Wow! Shit! That was him!! Brilliant, no knocks on the door in the night, hadn't really expected them, but still, fantastic!

On the Monday afternoon he had walked down to the Angel tube station to pick up copies of the London Evening Standard and the Metro, there had been nothing in the national papers he'd picked up from the newsagent on Upper Street, and when he got back he eventually found the basic 'Body found and witness appeal' story in the Metro, then after what seemed like fucking ages he found a slightly longer story in The Standard; it included how she had been shopping on Sunday and what she had brought, how she had been missed at a party on Sunday night, and how there had been construction work going on in the car park.

He had never been that interested in the news, so it had been a real surprise when he counted, on Friday night just before going out to The Chapel, twelve newspapers in the pile on the kitchen counter; and those were just the ones he had kept because he was in them ..... and not! Ha!!

They were going to get some other poor sod for it!! Brilliant, you couldn't fucking make it up! He had practically skipped all the way to The Chapel; Jodi was probably going to be there and he had wondered what she would be wearing - it was a Blondie night and he wondered if she would be wearing her fishnet stockings, and what else, and what the fuck he would say about Dan?

107

Hadn't been hard, in the end he had said Dan had gone up to Manchester early, to get furniture and stuff for the flat, get settled before Uni started full-on, that Dan sent Jodi her love and had said she would see her at Christmas or maybe earlier if Jodi wanted to go north for a weekend. Dan had been standing behind Jodi at the time, looking at him over Jodi's shoulder and shaking her head. Jodi was pissed off, especially because Dan hadn't been replying to texts or phone calls since Amsterdam, and she hadn't even said goodbye; Jodi seemed to like the idea of going up to Manchester for a weekend though and brightened up. Dan was still standing behind Jodi, just to one side, looking really great in a tight short yellow dress and red high heels, but still shaking her head and he heard her say, 'No way!'

He had told Jodi it was all because Dan had her head in textbook and reading lists all the time and not to worry and Jodi had seemed fine with that. They had danced and Jodi had told him how great he was moving, and when he got back home he went straight to bed and slept without dreams for ten hours straight.

Seventeen

The previous evening when Phil walked back up the path to the Warren house after Lucia had collected Sam he was feeling dead on his feet. He had no idea what was wrong with Sam. They had been in highly charged situations before, he had seen her lose her temper before, but never had he seen her totally lose control, let alone physically assault someone. He was at a loss. First she had been aggressive and negative at the briefing. Then she had lost it with Moonsong and Rick. And now she had hit one of the parents. He would get to the bottom of it but for now he needed to find out what Kate and Sebastian Thomas were hiding.

When he knocked at the door Tom Grigg let him in. He was frowning.

'What's up Tom?'

'I've been thinking and something's not stacking up.'

'How do you mean?'

'Sam told me that the couple, the pair you interviewed, came forward because they recognised Tamsin from a photograph on a poster in the street.'

'That's right.'

'And that was a recent photograph, taken here, this week.'

'Yes.'

'And they also recognised her from the photo our man gave them in the café, the one with him in it?'

'Yes.'

'Well then, that photo must also be recent. Becky heard them say Tamsin was taken two years ago. The photo he gave your pair can't be two years old. Trust me they change a lot at this age, especially girls. He's been with her recently.'

'Christ Tom you're right. And she was happy with him in the photograph and she was pleased to see him yesterday. He's no stranger to her. What the fuck is going on and what aren't the Thomases telling us?'

'Shall we go find out?'

'Yes let's do that. Is Fi with Becky Warren?'

'Yes and her mother's with them too. She's phoned Guy Warren and he's coming home.'

'Right. Mr and Mrs Thomas. You ready?'

In the sitting room the Thomases had not moved from their places at opposite ends of the sofa, but there was now an opened bottle of red wine and a glass infront of Kate on a low coffee table.

'It never ceases to amaze me how cavalier people are with other people's time. If you waste my money, I can make more, replace it; if you waste my time, that time is gone, I can never get it back. I cannot replace the hours I have spent in this house this afternoon: time is the only non-recoverable resource. If you were in business you would understand that.'

Treloar and Tom stared at Sebastian Thomas in amazement.

'Yes he really is something else isn't he?' said Kate. 'Our daughter is missing, another child is missing, and all he can think about are his bloody business resources.'

'You don't complain when you're spending the money, do you?' he spat at his wife.

'Stop. Both of you,' Treloar said holding his hand up palm outwards as if directing traffic. 'This afternoon, matters have come to our attention which require explanation. I am now convinced that you have not been entirely honest with us. You know more about this abduction than you are saying, and I want to know what that is, and I want to know it now.'

'This is all your fault,' Kate hissed at her husband, 'if you'd kept your mouth shut when they were taken she'd probably be back by now. You're an idiot.'

'Oh yes, and how was I supposed to keep quiet? It was the manager who noticed that Lily was missing. He asked around and people told him she'd been with Tammy. Tammy was also nowhere to be found. It would have looked bloody strange if I'd ignored that, done nothing. I had to raise the alarm. It was the only thing to do.'

Kate Thomas merely glared at him. Treloar continued.

'Firstly, a young couple have come forward who were involved in taking the girls from the Island Park. They were approached by a man who claimed to be Tamsin's father ...'

'That's ridiculous,' Sebastian interrupted, 'I'm her father.'

'I'll finish, then you may speak,' Treloar fixed him with an icy look. 'This man had a photograph of himself with Tamsin in which they were clearly not strangers; he claimed that Tamsin's mother and her partner were refusing him access to his daughter.'

'What utter crap,' Sebastian shouted.

'Please Mr Thomas, let Inspector Treloar finish, then you will have an opportunity to explain your behaviour,' Tom said.

Treloar resumed. 'They state that they approached Tamsin at the pool and explained that they had been sent to fetch her. They showed her the photograph and she was clearly happy and excited at the prospect of seeing this man who she called Willy.'

At this point Treloar was surprised to see Kate Thomas roll her eyes and tut. Tom noticed too and Sebastian shot her a sharp look.

'When they told her they would take her to him, Tamsin grabbed Lily by the arm and insisted that she accompany them. They then drove to a prearranged meeting place where they left the girls with the man. It was clear to them that Tamsin was delighted to see him and rushed happily to greet him.'

'They must be mistaken,' Sebastian said without conviction, 'how could she have known him?'

'Indeed,' said Treloar. 'Now we come to the incident this evening with Mrs Warren. She claims, and we have no reason to disbelieve her, that she overheard you talking about the abduction and that you stated that this had happened before, two years ago, that you had told no one, that you had paid a ransom and that Tamsin had been returned unharmed.'

'She must have misheard,' Sebastian mumbled.

'No, from her extreme reaction, I don't think that's the case,' Tom said.

'Look Inspector, I have no intention of sitting here whilst you accuse …'

'Shut up! Shut up! Please Seb, please, just tell them.' Kate Thomas looked at her husband, her eyes brimming with tears.

Sebastian Thomas sighed deeply and rubbed his face with his hands. 'Very well,' he said softly.

'It was two years ago. Tamsin was taken from a pony trekking centre in the Lake District. Kate had taken her up at the autumn half term. I wasn't there: there was a big contract bid on and we were up against a deadline.'

'What happened exactly?' Treloar looked at Kate who had recovered her composure.

'We were staying in a beautiful country house hotel. Tamsin was in her element: the only child there and showing off shamefully. We had adjoining rooms overlooking Windermere. The

111

views were quite stunning and the food was to die for. Anyway, they offered pony trekking at a nearby centre through the hotel. Well Tamsin is an avid rider, positive star at our local pony club, so I let her go. Personally I cannot abide the beasts, so I stayed at the hotel.'

It was about four o'clock when one of the staff approached me in the bar and told me that the centre had telephoned to say that my husband had collected her. Well obviously I thought that was most unlikely given his precious deal in the offing so I called him. He said he had been trying to get hold of me on my mobile to tell me that some man had phoned to say he had Tamsin and he wanted money.'

She paused for a moment and poured herself a glass of wine. Sebastian picked up the story.

'Yes I received a call through the switchboard at work. He said he had Tamsin and he wanted 100,000 euros in cash or we wouldn't see her again.'

'Did you ask for proof?' Tom asked.

'He put her on the phone. She was totally unconcerned. I asked her where Mummy was and she told me what had happened, about the pony trekking I mean, and how Kate had stayed at the hotel. In the bar no doubt.' He glared at his wife. 'Tammy said they were having a lot of fun on a house boat on the lake and she had just had 'the bestest ever' chocolate cake. He came back on and told me not to go to the police and to get the money ready for the next day in Cumbria.'

'So what did you do?' Treloar asked.

'Well I got the money of course. I arranged for one of my people to drive it up to Kate at the hotel and I told my wife to keep her mouth shut.'

'You didn't go up?' Tom asked unable to keep the outrage out of his voice.

'No it wasn't necessary. Kate was quite capable of handling the money. She's had enough practice. The next thing I knew was Kate phoned me to say that Tammy was back and they were coming home.'

'So what happened Mrs Thomas?'

'Somebody called me just after breakfast to say that a note was waiting for me at reception and would I like it sent up or was I coming down. I had them send it up with coffee and some of their very fine spice biscuits. Anyway it was typed or printed or whatever and it told me to take the money in one of the hotel's carrier bags and leave it in the summer house at the end of the front lawn overlooking the lake at 11:30 that morning.'

'Did it mention Tamsin?' Tom asked.

'Tamsin? No,' she seemed surprised at the question, 'no, just to leave the money and return to the hotel and to make no attempt to watch the summer house. Oh, and to leave the note in the bag with the money. So that is what I did.'

'And then?' Tom said.

'Well I went back up to the hotel and sat in the bar. About fifteen minutes later in strolled Tamsin just full of her great adventure. So I order some lunch for us both and listened to her endless gabbling on the subject of the wonderful Willy and their trip on the boat and the marvellous chocolate cake. It was obviously the highlight of the trip for her, even better than the pony trekking.'

'Did you ask if she was molested in any way?' Tom asked.

'No I didn't need to. She was clearly unharmed and she would have mentioned anything like that. Tamsin is not a shy or secretive child. It was Willy this and Willy that, quite sickening actually. So after lunch I called Sebastian to tell him everything was resolved. We travelled home the next day as scheduled.'

'And you never mentioned this to anyone?' Treloar asked.

'No.' Sebastian replied. 'She was back, what was there to say and to whom? We forbade her to mention this Willy again and put it behind us. What would the police have done if we'd come forward? It was dealt with and we wanted it forgotten.'

'Did it not occur to you that having extorted the money from you so easily he would do it again? Did you not think that Tamsin might be suffering some trauma and be in need of professional help?'

'Tammy was absolutely fine,' Sebastian snapped, 'and hindsight is a wonderfully exact science Inspector. Obviously we were naïve.'

'And have you received any contact this time?'

'Not yet.'

'So it may not be him,' Tom said. But Treloar knew they both thought it would be too much of a coincidence for it be someone else called Willy with a predilection for chocolate.

Just then there was a screaming from the back of the house.

113

Treloar and Tom Grigg leapt up and ran from the room almost colliding with Fi Sinclair who was hurrying along the corridor from the conservatory, mobile phone in hand.

'That was the Superintendent. She was trying to get hold of one of you. It's Lily. She's free; she's on her way home.'

'And Tamsin?' Tom asked though he anticipated her reply.

'No. Just Lily,' she said quietly.

'What is it, what is it? Is it Tammy?' Sebastian had followed them into the hallway followed by his wife.

'No I'm sorry. Lily has been found but there is no news of Tamsin.' Treloar said gently.

Sebastian Thomas groaned and put his head in his hands in despair. Treloar looked at Kate. To his astonishment he watched as a momentary expression crossed her face before she too covered her eyes with her hands. It was subtle, fleeting, but it was unmistakeable and it was there: triumph.

Mid to late September, the previous year

So far so good, another week and a half had gone by, more stories in the papers, even made the nationals, still no knocks on the door, and here he fucking was, back in fucking Amsterdam, well, near enough, without all the tourist bollocks at least. Bastards!

He'd turned the sofa round in the room and was sitting on it and looking out the window, thinking, tripping off .... find, follow, freak .... how the plan to use Dan's credit cards and licence and passport and car, to be where he wasn't, had come together, fucking brilliant! All that time when they were kids practising to sign the same signature, just fun then - Daniel with a curly up stroke to the l, a flourish one of the teachers had called it, and Daniele with a short last stroke of the e. Made them look the same.

Dan getting her original surname back and using the Manchester address for the licence and passport - fucking brilliant, even the pictures, she was on a red-head thing at the time, and her hair was tied back, photo-booth pictures, washed out, looked black and white whichever way you held them! And all because of the fucking suffocating bastards. Never saw this coming though, Fuck!

TV news on all the time at home, going through the papers, every day, ALL of them ..... fuck! Anorak now? No fucking chance, got to stay on top, in touch. It was a fucking pain fetching them all, and a complete nightmare to find them, the stories were never in the same bloody place, even in the same paper. Reading them though, about it, about her, what they thought had happened and who had done what and why, fucking brilliant!!

He'd started cutting them out, even dating them! Nineteen now. Time was a bummer - hour and a half in the morning to get the nationals; two hours, including the time to get to the shop and back, two and a half if he looked at the online stuff, it was quicker, he could auto-search, not the same as actually finding though, and half an hour in the afternoons, over an hour with the time to get down to the Angel station and back to pick the locals up. Worth it!? Too right, fucking awesome!!

The funeral director had rung him out of nowhere, told him the police had said he could bring the cremation forward; he'd already dealt with all the paperwork. So, did he want to? They'd already talked on the phone a few times about the arrangements, and he had finally chosen the custom urn and matching wrist flake cylinder pendant on leather cord option, in yellow with red highlights, Christ!

'Are you SURE you're not turning into an anorak?' asked Dan, smiling; she stood, leaning back against the wall by the window, arms folded, wore a black leather bomber jacket with yellow piping up the sleeves. The collar and cuffs and zip were yellow and matched her short flared yellow skirt. Her shoes were red, Jimmy Choo patent stilettos. She gave him a twirl and he saw that she was wearing hold-ups, sheer, and he looked past her, back out the window at the water outside the hotel. Didn't know if it was a lake or the sea, at least it wasn't a fucking canal!

He was in Volendam, north and east of Amsterdam, about 10 miles, he'd found it on TripAdvisor. It was a lake, he had been looking at Markermeer, he read about it in the room infopack. Used to be the Zuiderzee, then they were going to drain it, then they were going to build houses, then they were going to build a nuclear power plant, then .... yabba yabba yabba .... Christ! Who cares?!

He had booked the hotel before deciding how to get there, and when he thought about it he decided to go for it and try out the 'being where he wasn't,' plan; see if he could get away with using Dan's stuff. He checked the Satnav in the Fiesta to see if it had Dutch maps loaded and it did, uploaded the Samuel (where the fuck do you think YOU'RE going motherfucker? Turn the fuck around NOW) L Jackson voice to it from a CD he'd burned off the web, found out online that he could get a ferry from Harwich, which he had never heard of, but which wasn't too far away, to the Hook of Holland which he had never heard of either and turned out to be near Rotterdam which turned out to be not that far from Amsterdam, and that getting out of Hook of Holland, round the Rotterdam ring road, up the motorways, round the top of Amsterdam on the ring road and then to the hotel should be pretty easy, even on the wrong side of the road.

So, here he was, ten hours after leaving home, knackered. Still, the plan was working; he had tied back his hair but no-one really looked that closely at the passport anyway, and using one of the credit cards to pay for petrol on the motorway and check in at the hotel had been a breeze, no signature, just the magic code then a card swipe!

He ordered a steak sandwich from room service, booked a taxi to the crematorium for the morning, and drank beer from the mini bar while he listened to the Crematorium playlist for the morning in his earphones; all Blondie; **The Tide is High, Rapture Riders** *(OK, Blondie AND the Doors, fucking amazing!), and* **One Way or Another**.

He ate the sandwich staring out over the dark lake and listened to the playlist again and tripped off in the chair thinking about his favourite stories:

BODY FOUND NEAR OXFORD STREET CAR PARK

Standard 15 Sept Monday

Police are appealing for witnesses after a young woman's body was found in circumstances police are describing as unusual. Melissa Stanley-Beale, who was nineteen years of age, appears to have fallen to her death on Sunday afternoon from the roof level of the Bryanstone Road car park just off Oxford Street near Marble Arch.

Melissa was found by two passers-by who called an ambulance but she was found to be dead at the scene. CCTV cameras show several people entering and leaving the car park in the early afternoon of Sunday at around the same time as Melissa, and the Metropolitan Police are asking anyone who may have seen her in or on the way to the car park to get in touch by phone or text using the contact details underneath the photo of Melissa at the end of this column.

The death has been referred to the coroner at Westminster Coroner's Court, and it is thought that a post mortem will be carried out in the coming days. Meanwhile Melissa's parents and brother are said to be devastated and....................

MELISSA HEALTH & SAFETY CONCERNS

Standard 16 Sept Tuesday

The London Evening Standard understands that the Health and Safety Executive have been asked by Police to investigate possible Health and Safety regulation breaches at the car park from which Melissa Stanley-Beale (aged 19) fell to her death last Sunday 14 September. Police have confirmed that the death is now being considered as suspicious.

Maintenance work was being carried out at the car park although the London Evening Standard understands that no building work was actually scheduled to take place on the site at the time of the death.

Melissa's parent's made an appeal this morning, asking for anyone who saw Melissa in or near the car park on Sunday to contact the police. 'We are shocked and absolutely devastated by Melissa's death,' they said, 'We just can't understand how she could have fallen. Where she fell from is so far away from the stairs she would have used to get up to the roof level and it was not on the direct route to her car either. We are praying that the police find out exactly what happened just as soon as possible.'

A recent picture of Melissa is shown below. On the fateful Sunday she was distinctively dressed, wearing a bright yellow sleeveless top, a red skirt, and red plimsolls with yellow soles. She was also carrying a large red shoulder bag and a large yellow Selfridges carrier bag.

CCTV cameras in the car park show several people in and around the building early on Sunday afternoon and police are asking anyone who may have seen Melissa to contact them as soon as possible using the contact details underneath Melissa's photo.

MELISSA TRAGEDY, BROTHER AND FRIENDS' ANGUISH

Metro 18 Sept Thursday

Harry Stanley-Beale, the older brother of Melissa, who died after apparently tragically falling from the Bryanstone Car Park near Oxford Street last Sunday was joined by Melissa's best friend, Trudy Parker, yesterday outside the car park itself where they asked members of the public for their help.

Harry and Trudy stood solemnly in front of the many bouquets of flowers, notes and other tributes, pictured below, that friends, relatives and members of the public have left on the pavement where Melissa was found early last Sunday afternoon. They told The Metro (London) that they had been surprised by the number of tributes that had been left and wanted to come and see them for themselves after seeing them on the TV.

'Melissa was a darling,' said Trudy, 'we all loved her, she was the life and soul of the party and we just don't understand what happened. She had loads of friends and we are all missing her terribly. The last thing I said to her was see you tonight.....I mean you don't expect something like this do you? she was so happy and really looking forward to the party.' Trudy was clearly upset and tearful as she said, 'If anyone...... anyone at all saw what happened, or saw Melissa on the way to the car park, please....please get in touch with the police and let them know.'

When The Metro (London) asked Harry what his thoughts were he said, 'Of course the family is absolutely devastated. We loved Melissa very much and miss her very badly. It is made worse because we don't know how Melissa came to fall, so if anyone remembers seeing her at all, on the way to the car park or actually in it, please DO get in touch with the police. The support the family is getting from friends as well as the public is tremendous and does help, but we would just like to know what happened.'

The owners and management of the car park have not been available for comment about the tragedy.

MELISSA TRADEGY, WHAT REALLY HAPPENED?

Daily Mirror 23 Sept Tuesday

We can reveal sadly, that no one really knows yet, but it is looking more and more like a tragic accident, compounded by Health and Safety irregularities with the construction work being carried out at the car park from which Melissa Stanley-Beale fell to her death over a week ago.

Our own investigative reporter, Joanna Jones, posed as a shopper walking on her way from Selfridges to the car park that we are all now so familiar with, and easily stepped round police barriers to see for herself the place from which it is believed Melissa fell.

The roof of the car park and staircase used by Melissa to reach it from the pavement are still supposedly sealed off and are being investigated by police and the Health and Safety Executive to discover precisely what happened.

Joanna carried out her investigation in the early afternoon of last Sunday, one week after Melissa's death, after discovering from people close to the official investigation that not all of the CCTV cameras in the car park were operational at the time of the death, including two that normally record 24/7 full colour video of the roof area from which Melissa fell.

It is believed that builders carrying out repair works at the car park switched off the electrical circuit supplying the cameras in order to safely carry out their own work and provided neither temporary power to the cameras for the duration of their work, nor switched the power back on when they left the site for the weekend on Friday afternoon.

Joanna was able to see for herself the tarpaulin covered hole in the wall through which Melissa is believed to have fallen,

122

which had been left as the result of removing a full height window, which was in the process of being replaced, with a one and a half metre high wall and a smaller window.

Two pieces of tarpaulin were being used, each fastened at the wall, floor and ceiling but with no fastening between them, and just a slight overlap hiding the view to the outside. Joanna herself was able to easily put her head through the overlap and see the pavement below to which Melissa sadly fell.

Joanna also saw the spot close to the window where Melissa's shopping bag was found, and the parking space where her car had been, and commented, 'It is not obvious what could have drawn Melissa towards the window, as it is around twenty metres off the path she would have been expected to take from the

staircase she used to get up to the roof of the car park to her car.'

'It is also unclear why she would have placed her shopping bag carefully on the floor, two metres away from where she fell, yet still have been holding her shoulder bag when she was found on the pavement. This is a real mystery that may have already been solved if the CCTV cameras had been operational. Ironically, there are several CCTV cameras between Selfridges and the car park which were in full working order, but according to sources close to the investigation none of them shed any light on this tragic mystery.'

Police are still appealing for witnesses and anyone with information is asked to contact them on the numbers below the picture of Melissa.

MELISSA MANSLAUGHTER CHARGE

Early this morning Stan Briscova, owner of SB Brothers Builders, which is carrying out construction work at the car park from which nineteen year old Melissa Stanley-Beale fell to her death almost two weeks ago, was arrested and charged with corporate manslaughter. He remains in custody, and it has been revealed that the case will probably be scheduled to be heard at The Old Bailey in December, possibly sooner.

It is unusual for manslaughter cases to be heard so soon after charges are bought, but The Evening Standard understands that this case will be heard relatively quickly because a great deal of evidence is already in the hands of the prosecutor, the Health and Safety Executive (HSE). A key witness is understood to be helping them with enquiries, a previous employee of SB Brothers Builders who knows the Company well. It is understood that the HSE has had an unusually high level of ready access to Company documentation including Health and Safety risk assessments, and other ongoing site management documentation used by SB Brothers.

The Evening Standard also understands that the Company has been the subject of previous Health and Safety investigations but is prevented from writing about them in these columns prior to this manslaughter case for legal reasons.

It is notoriously difficult to successfully bring corporate manslaughter charges as there must be very clear lines of responsibility and the individual or individuals responsible for health and safety breaches that lead to the death must be very clearly and unambiguously identified. The Standard understands that in this case the paper trail is indeed clear and unambiguous.

Melissa's brother, Harry Stanley-Beale, told The Standard, 'the family is relieved that the person responsible for Melissa's death has been apprehended and we hope he has the book thrown at him and faces the full force of the law. What a bloody shame they didn't stop him hurting people when they looked at him before though. If they had, our Melissa would still be alive today.'

Eighteen

'What happened?' Treloar was speaking to his immediate boss Detective Superintendent Suzanne Winters.

'Lily was dropped off in the street opposite the police station in Penzance. She was told to go in and to give them her name and address and to ask to be taken home. That's exactly what she did. And of course they recognised her from her photograph. They put her in a car and she's on her way over to you. They've been told not to ask her anything, just to answer any questions she has. When she gets there, get her to change her clothes and get her stuff to the forensic guys. You know what we need.'

'Of course.'

'And obviously we'll need to know if he hurt or molested her in any way and what has happened to Tamsin Thomas?'

'Of course.'

'But we need to be gentle and let her tell the story at her own pace. Am I teaching you to suck eggs Inspector?' she asked with a soft laugh.

'Not at all. I'll play it by ear and keep you informed. I've had the Thomases taken back to the Island Park. I'm not at all satisfied with their behaviour and I'm sure that Mrs Thomas is still not telling us everything she knows, but obviously this latest development has upset them and they don't want or need to be here when Lily gets home.'

'Quite right Phil. Oh by the way what is wrong with Sergeant Scott? I understand she has gone off sick. Not very convenient with this abduction business. Is there any news on her?

'I think it's just one of those nasty 24 hour stomach bugs. Came on earlier this evening.'

'OK. Well let me know how things go with Lily Warren. I'm calling another briefing for tomorrow morning at the Island Park. It's a useful location and handy for you if you want to see the Thomases again.'

'Right. I'll call you later.'

With that they ended the conversation and Treloar thought again that he must make time to speak to Sam before the briefing and how, not for the first time, he was surprised at how well informed Winters was. Someone was telling tales.

He had made the call to Winters from the garden of the

Warren house. It was cool and peaceful and the temptation to lie down on the soft lawn was strong. Inside the house the atmosphere was highly charged: a mixture of overwhelming relief that Lily was safe and on her way home, fear at what she would have to say, and residual worry over the fate of Tamsin. Guy Warren had turned up just after the news of Lily's release and the departure of the Thomases.

Treloar had been impressed by the calmness that he brought with him into the house. Becky had gone from near hysteria to quiet acceptance in a matter of minutes. Her mother had handed over responsibility for her to Guy and retired to bed exhausted. Tom Grigg and Fi Sinclair were still there preparing them for what would need to be asked when Lily arrived. Everybody was acutely conscious of the fact that Tamsin was still missing and that Lily was their best hope of finding her. He estimated that there was time for one more call before Lily arrived and so he rang Cove Farm.

'Si?'

'Lucia you are back in Cornwall now.'

'Sorry Flip, force of habit. How are things, any news?'

'Yes some good news. Lily Warren has been released and she's on her way home. I'm still here waiting to speak with her. The other girl though is still missing. Hopefully Lily will be able to tell us something helpful. How is Sam?'

'She's clearly mortified but I'm keeping her busy. Something is troubling her and I think she needs to talk to you about it. I'll tell her your good news. Can you make it back here this evening?' Living in Spain ten o'clock at night was early for Lucia who rarely went to bed before the early hours.

'When I've finished here I'll come up. I expect Lily will want to get to bed, or her mother will want her to, so I shouldn't be late.'

'Your room is ready and waiting as always. Shall you have something to eat?'

'I'd love some of Bee's minestrone if there's any left over from the party.'

'Call me when you're leaving and I'll put some on the Aga. Mamá's just gone down to Zawn and Eva's putting the chickens away. Bee's at work. All's well here brother.'

At that he heard the sound of laughing voices from the hallway. 'I must go, Lily's here.'

'Later Flip,' Lucia said and hung up.

Lily Warren was tired but otherwise none the worse for her experience. Becky had quietly established that the man who had held them overnight had not touched them inappropriately or harmed or frightened them in any way. Lily confirmed Rick and Moonsong's account of their departure from the Island Park and their meeting with Willy at the car park.

When she was asked if she would be able to describe Willy for an efit, Becky had suggested that it would be much more effective if Lily were allowed to sit with her father and Guy would make a sketch for them. Treloar agreed. It was apparent to everyone that Lily, who was a quiet, serious child unlike the outgoing, precocious Tamsin, had actually enjoyed the adventure with Willy but had decided it was time to come home. When she had expressed that desire he had immediately agreed she should leave at once and had dropped her off near the police station. He was certainly the most considerate and obliging kidnapper Treloar and Grigg had come across.

Nineteen

Whilst Sam drove back from her home in Truro in fresh clothes, considering her imminent future, Amy Angove was reflecting on a distant past. Since the party she had been unable to get the tragic story of the Pitt-Townsend family out of her mind. At least it made a refreshing change from dwelling on the stalking business. She had asked her parents what they knew about it but they had nothing to tell her. They were aware of the story but had fewer details than Ochre Pengelly. So that morning, determined to confront the ghosts in her mind, Amy resolved to visit the old mine workings where the hangings had taken place.

She had a vague idea where the workings were from playing with the Maddox children, but that was years ago. But she knew they were on Lower Farm land and if she got lost she could always see if Phil could help her. It did not occur to her that with two missing girls he would be not be at home; it was Sunday after all. At eleven o'clock she bade farewell to her parents promising to be back for lunch and set off for Lost Farm estate in her custom-built Mini Cooper S convertible with its shocking pink paintwork and violet leather upholstery and roof. She loved this car: it was fast and it was pretty.

She drove down the lane from her parents' cottage to join the main road between St Just and St Ives. Turning right onto the B3306 she headed eastwards through Morvah, passing the lane which led to Cove Farm and on towards Zennor. Just after The Gurnard's Head she turned off, heading uphill towards the Lost Farm estate.

From this road she could make out the looming walls and chimneys of Radgell House - home to the dreaded and dreadful Ochre Pengelly - standing on the carn top glowering down towards the sea. Amy knew that Ochre despised her; she had known this from their first encounter all those years ago, even before she had married Pippit.

Over time Amy had grown inured to the envy, disdain and resentment of other women, but Ochre had been the first to hold her in such contempt, and not to try to disguise the fact in any way. Some people, she knew, hated her because she was beautiful, rich and successful and famous. But with Ochre it was something else: Ochre despised her because she wasn't clever. Ochre considered her irrelevant, "decorative but not functional" as she had heard her say at her wedding to Pippit. She knew that Pippit's sisters didn't like her, well, hated her to be fair in the case of Lucia and Beatriz.

She understood that it was because she had hurt their brother, but she did feel strongly that if he could get over it then they bloody well should be able to. And what was more they both had careers, Beatriz with her cooking and Lucia with her photos, so why couldn't they understand that she had had to take her chance when it came along?

It really was unreasonable of them and it just wasn't fair. And after all it was all so long ago. Really they were too mean. Still sod them all. Pippit had forgiven her and now he was going to help with this horrid business in London. Perhaps he still cared; perhaps there was still something there? Perhaps she should find out? That would certainly piss off the precious sisters, Ochre bloody Pengelly and that poxy police bitch who was drooling after her Pippit.

As she crested the hill she could see the standing stones above Lost Farm Barn off to her right. She smiled remembering her first time with Pippit, when they had made love in the centre of the ring on the flat stone. Afterwards he had made her promise never to tell anyone. He had thought it sacrilegious or some such nonsense. She had believed, still believed, that the pagan spirits of the place would have heartily approved and looked on in delight. She had not been in the slightest ashamed and she still felt pride and some awe to have lost her virginity in such a wild and beautiful place, a fitting location for such a sacrifice.

She sped down the hill to join the road between St Ives and Penzance. Turning right she drove along to the turn off to Lower Farm. In the daylight she noticed the new signage heralding Dylan's burgeoning empire. Poor Dylan, she thought, still trying too hard, still hoping to impress despite the pretty young wife. She recalled how he had lusted after her when they were in their teens; he had tried to hide it but it had been obvious to everyone. He had been absolutely furious when she'd chosen Pippit. God that awful night in Zennor when he'd found out. She thought he was going to burst into tears. He was so mad he couldn't speak; he just leapt onto his mountain bike and stormed off. Nobody had even noticed that he'd gone.

Poor Dylan. Still he had the lovely Hope now and a new

baby so he must be well over her surely? Perhaps she should test the water and find out? That would be fun. All the horrid business in London had got her down and she had been so right to get away, back home, back amongst her friends and people who love her. As Dr. Tremayne would later comment: 'Amy obviously didn't know her Horace: "They change their sky but not their soul, who run across the sea." You cannot outrun your true self.'

Amy had driven on past Lower Farm with its chocolate box rose trellis and up past the turn to Higher Farm and Lost Farm, before turning onto the track to Lost Farm Barn. Pulling up behind the derelict stable she noticed with disappointment that Pippit's Land Rover wasn't there. Oh well, she would still explore; it was such a lovely day. She stood by her car, facing south, and got her bearings. The stones were uphill to her right, therefore the abandoned mine workings must be down to her left beyond that small copse. She opened the boot of the mini, pulled out an old, battered pair of deck shoes and slipped them onto her bare feet, locked the car and put the keys in her shorts' pocket. Then, on a whim, walking into the courtyard, she decided to double check whether Pippit was definitely not at home.

The night of the party it had been dark when she had arrived and she hadn't been able to see much of the barn conversion. The next morning there hadn't been time to look around. Now as she stood at the entrance to the courtyard she couldn't help but admire the beauty of the house. It was not as impressive as Rosemergy, her house in Hampstead overlooking the heath of course, and obviously not worth half as much, but for down here it was certainly most attractive. Yes, she could picture herself living here. Not for ever of course, but for a few months over the summer whilst this horrid business was sorted out, and anyway, London was boring at this time of year. And who knew what might come of it? Yes this place had definite possibilities.

There was obviously nobody at home so Amy decided to visit the old mine as planned, and leaving the courtyard behind she set off down the hill. When she reached the copse she was glad of the shade offered by the trees. Looking out from the dappled light she spotted the ruined engine house amongst a cluster of dilapidated buildings a few hundred yards further down the hill. Beyond, on the horizon, she could see the shining waters of Mount's Bay and she could just make out the distant sound of children playing. There was not a soul in sight.

She emerged from the trees and started out across the meadow of wild grasses and flowers. As she progressed the terrain dipped and she lost sight of the mine buildings. It was hot and still, the air was dusty, and the going hard. As she climbed back up the incline she was forced to watch her footing on the uneven ground. Suddenly, looking up, the engine house was back in view and much nearer than she had expected.

The wall opposite the chimney stack was crumbling away and she could see exposed support beams. Hanging from the highest wooden strut was a swinging rope. Amy gasped and froze: surely this couldn't be the rope from the suicides, not after all these years? As she considered retracing her steps and abandoning her expedition she saw that the rope was swinging with greater force. She was rooted to the ground.

Then, after what felt to her like ages, she saw to her relief a black tyre attached to the end of the rope emerge from behind the engine house wall: it was a just makeshift children's swing. Amy giggled with a combination of relief and delight: she loved swings and wanted a go. As she approached the edge of the meadow she could hear a girl's voice singing softly: "there's a silver lining / through the dark clouds shining".

Amy pushed her way through the patchy hedge, snagging her cheesecloth shirt on the lichen-covered blackthorn. Swearing, she pulled herself free and made her way up onto the plateau and round the side of the engine house: nothing, no girl, no swing. Instead, lying on the ground amongst the broken brick and stonework, partially submerged in the ravening weeds, lay a narrow rubber-tyred wheel and a coil of hemp rope covered in black dust.

Amy was stunned. What the hell had happened to the girl she had heard singing and what had become of that swing? She was cross that she wouldn't be able to try it out. She pivoted surveying the land all around her, but there was nobody in sight. They must have heard her coming and run off. Perhaps they had heard about Dylan Maddox's reputation and his hostile attitude towards trespassers? Understandable then.

Looking around in the bright sunshine there was no sense of the sinister atmosphere she had anticipated. It was just a bunch of crumbling brick, stone and rusty iron. Nothing frightening or malevolent. She felt let down. But as she was here she might as well explore. Across the plateau from the engine house stood a second derelict building, smaller and square with a shorter chimney topped in black. As she approached she could see what looked to her like a series of wood-fired pizza ovens set in the brick. Perhaps this was part of Dylan's next enterprise: an outdoor pizza parlour?

Close up she could see greyish white deposits a bit like the lichen on the blackthorn but crystalline. She wrinkled her nose in distaste and took a step back. A wise decision since this was in fact a ruined arsenic calciner, where the tin ore was burned to release the impurities. Not nice, not nice at all. Fine. There was nothing for her here so she might as well head back and make a sentimental visit to the standing stones for old time's sake.

As she turned a dark figure emerged from the broken doorway of the engine house.

'What the hell do you think you're doing?' a rough male voice shouted.

The hunched man strode towards her intent on confrontation. His eyes were very dark, hooded and haunted, and a five o'clock shadow covered the lower half of his face, one side of which had slipped as if he had had a stroke. His hair was greying and dirty and he wore filthy old canvas trousers and a scruffy faded cotton granddad shirt. He was carrying a shotgun, broken over his crooked arm and Amy was scared shitless.

Unbelievable! There was someone up at the mine workings. It made him mad that people felt they could just wander at will over his land, ignoring the trespass signs. To hell with the right to roam. This was his property and they should keep the fuck off. And here, here of all places. He was increasingly spending more and more time at the mine workings, ostensibly exploring the feasibility of making the site into a tourist attraction, but he felt drawn here, pulled by something. Right, that was it; he was going to give them a piece of his mind. But as he drew closer to the solitary figure cowering in fright by the calciner, he realised with a flood of emotion that he recognised it: Amy Angove, his first love.

'Amy? It's Amy Angove isn't it?'

The transformation in the man was immediate and incredible. It was as if he grew several inches and lost several decades in age. He even looked cleaner, healthier, happier. But after her recent experiences in London Amy was very wary of strangers and she kept still and silent.

'It's me Amy, Dylan, Dylan Maddox. I heard you were back. How the hell are you? You look wonderful, as ever.'

Twenty

Amy was used to physical exercise. To do what she did, to keep her body supple and looking svelte, she regularly visited a private health club to lift weights; she regularly took advantage of the pool on the ground floor of a colleague's house in a gated community in Belsize Park; but the contrast of physical exertion in the open air, climbing the moorland up to the stones behind Pippit's barn was exhilarating. The encounter with Dylan Maddox had been a bit of a pain, it could have spoiled her day, but once she had recovered from her initial fear, she had soon relaxed and in no time at all he had been eating out of her hand. Poor Dylan, he hadn't changed at all, pretty wife or no pretty wife.

She'd forgotten how beautiful Cornwall was at this time of year, the air full of promise and light and warmth. The past few years she had rarely made it home: just the occasional Christmas. She loved this place. Oh she loved big cities: London, Paris, Milan, New York, especially New York. She loved the noise, the heat, the metal smell. She loved the busyness, the cinemas, the coffee shops, the shops! She loved the traffic, the buildings, the manicured parks.

Here, in her homeland, it was so very different, the antithesis of all that: the wildness, the quiet, the space, the open skies and the vast expanses of empty sea. She was getting old for her trade. Soon she would be past her sell by date. There was an endless queue of pretty young girls appearing over the horizon of her future, every single one of them eager to take her place.

Could she return to this world? Would she be happy? She would be rid of that awfulness that had been trekking her of late. Others had done it. The Shrimpton woman ran that hotel in Penzance, the blue place, didn't she? There was life after the catwalk. And think of all the upsides. She would be able to eat again, she would be able to drink beer again, schlep about in scruffy clothes. Maybe she could have a baby? She and Pippit would make beautiful babies, and with a beautiful baby, well everything would be forgiven and forgotten wouldn't it? There was a lot to think about.

When Amy reached the standing stones she was hot and breathless; the last part of the climb had proved far steeper than she remembered. But it was well worth it. This was the top of her world she thought as she looked all around her; the whole of Mount's Bay with its fairytale castle on St Michael's Mount to the south and the rugged coast disappearing into a boundless blue sea to the north.

This spot held a special place in her heart. She smiled as she ran her hand over the hot flat stone in the centre of the dancing circle. It was wonderful to be alone on such a day in such a place. It was such a luxury not to be on the lookout for paparazzi, not to be surrounded by crowds and constantly wondering if the horrid one was a face in that peering, leering mass. She shuddered, stamping her foot and shaking her head, determined to banish the ruinous thoughts spoiling the moment.

She felt a pang of hunger and looked at her watch. Shit, she was going to be late for lunch; her father would be mad. With a last lingering glance at St Michael's Mount she turned and hurried back down the hill towards Lost Farm Barn and her car. She didn't notice the figure that limped through the circle of stones to run his hand over the flat stone, raise it to his mouth and lick it slowly.

Mid October, the previous year

He was on his way to Totteridge on the tube, on the fucking Northern Line. How does that work, how do you get a fucking village in London? It had been all over the news and in the papers; he'd kept the best two stories, about the memorial for the lovely Melissa. It was today, in the church at Totteridge and he was on his way there.

He'd Googled it. Just a regular small village, with fucking fields, a village high street, cottages and everything, incredible! But Totteridge and Whetstone station was on the fucking underground, amazing! On his Northern Line, even more amazing, OK so it was twelve stations away from the Angel, and the train wasn't actually under the ground for the last six, which was well weird, quiet, unreal, seemed slow, light outside.

It was hard fucking work getting the right train because there were two branches going north and during the day they didn't run that often and you had to look carefully at the signs on the platform and the fronts of the trains to make sure you got the right one.

It was sunny, and hot by the window, the Indian summer was still happening, he remembered the Benetton window and the silver and gold mannequins and wondered if they had any shorts and bikinis left. Tripped off thinking about the first time, finding her outside the shop, following, the juggler, the ringmaster, the second time, the shop, following, the car park, Dan ……….

It had gone well at the crem. Seemed like ages ago, only a couple of weeks. Christ! They even called it the same, taxi driver had tried to explain why, but so what?! Early start, first one up, connected up the phone, nodded at the funeral director, she was quite sexy in the top hat and tails, like the ringmaster but older, low heels not high, no whip, he'd started to smile then seen the way she looked at him and stopped.

She pressed two buttons, curtain closed and playlist started, **The Tide is High,** he went over and turned it up, **Rapture Riders** (OK, only a mix but still fucking amazing!), **One Way or Another**. Round nearly three, or could have been four, or five times and half way through the last **One Way or Another** the funeral director came back, Christ he hadn't even seen her leave, and she was

137

signalling him out already, with her arm, hand out towards the door.

She looked nervous, he had waited for it to finish, unplugged his phone and followed her out, she looked back at him and was more nervous, there was a queue of people waiting and everyone looked at her, then they were looking at him, like he was fucking mad, and they walked in, glaring, past him, before he was properly out of their way. He tripped on a crack in a paving stone as he walked towards the taxi, which had waited, and the funeral director had said she would see him at the hotel in the afternoon.

The urn had been heavier than it looked, it still was even though it wasn't full; it was on the ground and it was bright, there was a full moon and no cloud, brighter than the gravestones around it; most looked grey, some were dark and nearly black, some were covered in moss. He was leaning against the outside wall of The Chapel, back in Islington. At the back, away from the street, in the old graveyard that had been kept but fenced off so people could still visit if they wanted to. He had never seen anyone there, hadn't really looked that closely, why would he.

What the fuck do you do with ashes, how should he know? He'd got the night boat back from the Hook of Holland after the funeral director had delivered the urn and his matching wrist pendant to him at the hotel, with a certificate for each and a lot of sympathetic smiling and kind words which he thought sounded real. The top hat and tails were gone, shame, but she wore a seriously smart dark grey men's suit, with the jacket unbuttoned and a pale pink shirt and red tie, black diagonal stripes sloped towards her heart, American he'd once heard, and tall, very tall, and spiky, black heels. Hmmmmmm.

He'd gone up to the top deck with the urn and was going to throw the ashes over the back of the boat. He'd taken a handful of the ashes and thrown them into the air over the railing, fucking cold it was, and windy, but it didn't seem right so he took the urn back to his cabin and thought about it and thought about it and then dropped off to sort of sleep that wasn't sleep because the fucking boat was moving all over the place.

So now ……… he still wasn't sure, what the fuck do you do with ashes? Didn't want anything official, organised, just to do the right thing for Dan. Behind him on the other side of the wall The Chapel was noisy, it was a Johnny Cash night, they were playing **Folsom Prison Blues** *and as he tapped his head back against the wall to the music, thinking, tripping off, he turned and looked at the wire mesh across the big stained glass window that Johnny Cash was blasting through and then the window ledge a couple of feet away at around the height of his head and underneath the stained glass picture of a blonde woman killing a dragon, and realised he was staring at a space underneath the window between the bricks and windowsill where the cement had fallen out. Fucking cracked it! Brilliant.*

Dan was standing the other side of the window, looking at him, wearing a grey, old fashioned but thin and modern trench coat, open, with a tight red T shirt and tight, short, yellow shorts, and red heels, the right one tapping in time with the Man in Black. Right hand on her side at her waist, with the coat bunched behind it, left hand in her coat pocket, leaning against the wall with her left shoulder.

He raised an eyebrow at her and she said, 'Right on cowboy,' and laughed, and he took a handful of ashes from the urn and carefully pushed them into the hole with a finger. They went right in, no problem, and he put another handful in and pushed them as far and as tightly as he could. He held up the urn and looked at her and said, 'Manchester', and she said, 'Why not?' and he put the lid back on the urn and weaved carefully round the headstones and gravelly squares and rectangles to the hole in the fence and squeezed back out and went home and got out a map to sort the best way to Manchester.

He left early the next day, dark for at least another hour, beat the traffic, at least London's, didn't have a fucking clue about Birmingham, music system loaded with Blondie, turned up loud, with Samuel (where the fuck do you think YOU'RE going motherfucker? Turn the fuck around NOW) L Jackson telling him how to get to the M1 from home, when to turn off the M1 and onto the M6 and used Dan's credit card to grab a burger and fill up the Fiesta at Hilton Park services, the first services on the M6 north of Birmingham, no problem, just needed the pin code, fucking brilliant!

He felt the wrist pendant every time he turned the steering wheel, it was still new, and the yellow cylinder was still catching his eye every time it moved, even though it wasn't that big or heavy. Didn't notice it so much on the motorways, apart from when he had reached to the passenger seat for his sunglasses and put them on, but getting to the M1 and driving to the services from the M6 .... saw it, felt it, thought of her lots ....

Boring or what? Fucking motorways! Off the M6, onto the M56, past the airport, Samuel L had told him to turn right just after the motorway ended, back into house-land, then he was amazed when he saw a sign saying River Mersey just before a bridge. There were signs to two golf courses on the other side of the bridge and he followed one of them and turned left and Samuel L asked him where the fuck he thought he was going and told him to turn the FUCK round right NOW! But he pulled left into a car park and parked up and sat there looking at the river.

Not high, running mostly a few metres away from the banks, over and round stones and through slower flowing pools, thinking, knowing that it went to Liverpool; The Cavern was there, Debbie played there as a warm up for the Dirty Harry tour, fucking amazing! **The Tide is High** *was near the end as Samuel L told him to stop fucking around man and turn the FUCK around and he reversed, and turned out of the car park and got back on the road.*

Two sets of lights, a right turn off the main road and ten minutes later Samuel L was telling him, 'You're there man, fucking stop right HERE, right NOW!' and he did and he was parked by a massive tree growing out of the pavement, which was outside a three storey house with a big garden. Cool. Next along was a big pub garden. Cooler, no wonder she had liked it!

Drove on slowly by the side of the garden and then the pub garden, to the end of the street, turned left onto a main road, past the front of the pub, the sign said 'The Didsbury Tales' then left again into the pub car park, took the phone from the music centre, put it in his pocket, took the urn from the back seat and went into the pub, asked for a double gin and orange and a pizza for the garden, paid for it all and went out and sat at the far end, next to the hedge bordering his new Manchester address, set the urn on the seat next to him and took the lid off, plugged his ear buds in and turned Blondie on then stood and took a handful of ash and threw it over the brown hedge. Again and again until he had thrown more

140

than half. He looked down and saw that some had gone down through the hedge and onto the ground, then he sat down, put the lid back on the urn, picked up the gin and orange and toasted the hedge and said, 'Cheers, nice one babe, good plan,' and turned round on the seat to wait for his pizza.

It was on the table and a waitress was walking away, quickly, looking back every few steps, wondering what the fuck he was doing.

He'd had a bottle of Bud and finished the pizza, gone back to the car and clicked on the Islington address on the SatNav menu, set off with Samuel L telling him how to get there, just in case, turned right into the golf club by the River Mersey when he got there, with Samuel L telling him to turn the fuck round, parked, reloaded the phone into the music centre and clicked on **The Tide is High** *and turned the volume up, took the urn from the back seat and took off the lid, got out of the car leaving the door open, walked to the riverside in the bright sunshine and down a rough path to the bottom of the bank and across to the stones at the edge of the river, kissed the urn then held it on its side, sloping downwards at the open end, and gently shook it, until it was empty.*

Twenty One

The mood that morning was very different from that at their first briefing. Whilst there was still an intense urgency and determination, the revelations of the previous evening had assuaged some of the fear. It now appeared that they were not looking for a typical predatory paedophile or a psychopath but for a man with mixed motives both personal and financial, and a disturbing obsession with Tamsin Thomas.

The previous evening when Treloar had finally reached Cove Farm he had found Sam and Lucia deep in conversation at the kitchen table. He could tell that there was something bothering them but before he could ask Lucia jumped up and pulled him across to a chair. She then looked across to Sam and shook her head quickly before turning to him with a smile.

'Sit and eat, you look exhausted and starved. I'll bring you a bowl of soup. Sam, cut him some bread. Do you want a drink? Here I think some of this Barolo will do you good. No argument.'

She brought him a steaming bowl of soup from the pan simmering on the Aga and a glass tumbler from a cupboard. Sam fetched a spoon from the dresser drawer and put it and a napkin from the pile on the table in front of him.

'Lucia told me the good news about Lily. How is she?'

'She seems fine, if a little tired. Fi Sinclair is still there with them but I've sent everyone else home for some rest. I don't think Tom has slept since the first call.'

'I'm going through to the sitting room to call Luca,' said Lucia making a discreet withdrawal.

Treloar rested his elbows on the table and rubbed his eyes with the palms of his hands. With a sigh he picked up the spoon and ate his soup. Neither he nor Sam spoke. When he had finished he pushed the bowl away and poured them both more wine.

'Right,' he said quietly, 'I want to know what is wrong with you. We've been in highly charged situations before but I've never seen you behave like this. First you lose it with Rick and Moonsong and then you physically attack the father of a missing child. You're bringing an attitude to this investigation that is totally unacceptable, totally inappropriate and totally out of character. What the fuck is going on Sam?'

As he spoke Sam had listened with her head down. When he had finished she took a deep, audible breath and looked at him.

'I'm sorry,' she said calmly. 'Everything you say is true. I have been irresponsible and selfish. I hope you will be able to forgive me.'

'Just tell me.'

'Do you remember the Alan Frobisher case in the nineties?'

Treloar frowned. 'Yes of course, who doesn't? Alan Frobisher abducted and murdered six children in Sussex. The press called him …'

'"The Down's Devil"'

'Yes. I remember. He dismembered the bodies and left them in shallow graves in woodland. But you must have been …'

'Ten. I was ten. And it wasn't only boys. There were six boys and one girl, Abigail Soames. She was my best friend.'

Treloar nodded but said nothing. Sam continued.

'We were living in Sussex then, in Lewes. My father was working in the legal department of American Express in Brighton. Abigail and I were at primary school together. We were very close; did everything together. Anyway, Frobisher snatched his victims from the street or parks or playgrounds. He took them up to the Devil's Dyke area above Brighton, abused, tortured and killed them, cut off their heads and took them away, buried their torsos in woodland at Northtimber Holt. Of course, the press needed a moniker, so they came up with "The Down's Devil".

There were shades of the Moors' Murderers, same alliteration; it made for a very catchy headline. And Newtimber Holt was next to a village called Saddlecombe, shades of Saddleworth Moor.' Sam spoke with no emotion. 'When they found the seventh body we were on holiday in France. I remember my parents' concern but also that slight relief: another boy, not me, not one of my friends.

But it wasn't a boy – it was Abby. She was obviously mutilated and headless and some village plod blabbed to the press on what he'd seen before any checks were made, just assuming it was another boy. After all paedophiles don't usually switch gender, not after six. I've never forgotten the horror and the guilt when we came home and found out that it was Abby. I'd been glad that it was another boy not her, glad that someone else was dead, and then the fact that it *was* her felt like a punishment'.

'Christ Sam, you were only ten.'

'They found the heads thanks to the IRA. He left all the heads, all seven, in a cool-box at the end of the Palace Pier in Brighton. It was the height of summer and he expected it to be far too busy for anyone to notice. But the year before, that same weekend, the IRA had left a bomb in a bicycle pannier chained to a lamppost near the pier entrance so security was on high alert. He was seen leaving the box by a vigilant member of the public who raised the alarm.

He confessed to everything immediately when they got him. When they asked why he took Abby he said he hadn't realised she was a girl: she was small, slender, short-haired. It wasn't until he got her clothes off that he realised his mistake. The disappointment stopped him, ruined it for him. She was his last victim. He's in Broadmoor now.'

'Why didn't you say something?'

'I thought I'd be OK. I've worked child abductions before; I thought I'd be fine. But something about this one brought it all back, all the anger, all the pain and the guilt. I don't know – the age of the girls I suppose – but I'm fine now. I've told you and I've never spoken to anyone about it before, not like this, not all of it. I've never admitted the guilt.

Oh a counsellor came to the school and spoke to everyone, especially Abby's friends, but I never spoke to her in confidence: I was too young, I realise that now. I used to wonder if I'd been with her instead of in France, well she would have lived. He would not have taken her if she'd been with a friend; she wouldn't have been in Brighton with her parents, she'd have stayed with me to play when her parents went shopping. But that way madness lies. It would have been someone else and he would have carried on and on. He wouldn't have stopped. It was just something terrible that happened.'

'And how do you feel about it now?'

'Normally I'm absolutely fine and I'm fine now I've spoken about it, exorcised the ghosts. I know I can help find Tamsin and I want to. It's important to me. You have my word that my behaviour and attitude will be exemplary from this moment. If there's any fallout from Sebastian Thomas I'll face that.'

'Well I think that's unlikely. If you are sure you want to continue and can do so objectively, of course I want you back onboard.'

He smiled at her and she smiled back.

'I'd better go tell Lucia it's safe to come back in. What have you two been up to anyway?'

He stood and walked across to the door which led from the kitchen to the sitting room corridor.

'Oh that can wait,' Sam answered, '… for now,' she added under her breath.

That morning Eva had taken Sam to Lost Farm Barn to collect her car before making her deliveries in Penzance. Sam had then driven home to Truro to shower and change before driving back for the briefing. It seemed to her like days rather than a matter of hours since she had set off in such an upbeat mood for the party. Treloar had headed to the Warren house where Becky Warren had answered the door, a woman transformed.

'The wonders of a good night's sleep and a shower,' she explained.

Her attitude towards the Thomases had also changed considerably, softening from her outrage of the previous evening.

'If the roles had been reversed and I thought I was protecting my daughter, I can't honestly say that I wouldn't have behaved in the same way,' she added as she preceded Treloar down the hallway.

'I expect you'd like to see Lily? She's in the conservatory with Fi.'

In the conservatory Fi Sinclair and Lily were sitting on the floor surrounded by piles of Lego; they were building a castle.

'Good morning Sir ... err, Phil,' said Fi standing.

'Good morning Fi. Hello Lily. Awesome castle, girls.' He angled head towards the open door, 'a word Fi.'

In the hallway they walked back towards the front door out of earshot.

'Well what more do we have?' he asked quietly.

'I think we can be pretty sure they were held on a boat in Penzance harbour.'

'Really?'

'Yes Lily describes a car journey and seeing "the castle on the island" – St Michael's Mount. Then they went along "supermarket alley", which Becky tells me is what her husband,

145

Guy calls the A30 heading into Penzance. After that they saw "the silly boat" – The Scillonian ferry, and they parked up and went aboard a "sailboat". That's where they stayed overnight Thursday, but they packed up and left before he dropped Lily off.'

'Tamsin left too?'

'Yes.'

'And it was just the three of them, all the time?'

'Yes.'

'And he didn't say where he and Tamsin were going next I suppose?'

'No such luck. But there is something strange about the whole business. Lily says the reason she was happy to stay overnight was because Tamsin told her it was OK with her mummy, both their mummies, and it was all part of her, Tamsin's, birthday surprise. What's more he was prepared for Tamsin's arrival.'

'In what way?'

'Well, when they left Island Park Lily had a bag with her clothes but Tamsin just had a towel – her clothes were in the chalet, she'd only taken a beach towel to the pool – but when they got to the boat there was a bag of clothes for her, right size and everything. And there was also an old stuffed toy: an octopus. Lily says Tamsin was delighted to see it, saying: "Look Lily it's Bubbles. I Thought I'd lost him." How can that be?'

'Well we know Tamsin was taken two years ago. She must have left it behind. Looks to me like this confirms it's the same guy. Do we have the sketch?'

'We do and it's brilliant. I mean it looks like a real person. Becky was right: it's loads better than any efit I've ever seen.'

'Were there any signs of sexual abuse or violence of any kind?'

'None. The family doctor was here last night and I was there when Becky asked her about it. No, from what Lily says they had a great time. They played games, watched DVDs and ate chocolate.'

'Chocolate?'

'Yes. Apparently there was nothing but chocolate and fresh fruit to eat. All kinds of chocolate, not just bars: cakes, puddings, biscuits, you name it, oh and hot chocolate and chocolate milkshake to drink. Apparently Tamsin loves chocolate so she was ecstatic. Lily less so; when she settled down last night all she wanted was cheese on toast. But Lily did say that Tamsin was the happiest she'd seen her when they were on that boat, much happier than at Island Park.'

'There's something very odd about all this.'

'Oh and Lily also says that "Willy" was great fun and very nice and very good at Lego. I don't know if it means anything but one of the videos they watched was "Charlie and the Chocolate Factory", you know, the film with Johnny Depp – Willy Wonka.'

'Yes I'd already made that connection. OK, I need to get to the briefing. You stay here with Lily. Call me if there's anything new.'

Treloar went back to the conservatory to make his farewells whilst Fi Sinclair fetched Guy Warren's sketch from the kitchen. She walked with him to the front door.

'You see what I mean about the sketch?' she asked.

Treloar studied the pastel drawing. It showed a man, probably in his thirties, with grey eyes and dirty blonde hair swept back from his face. Fi was right: it was very good. If you knew him, you'd recognise him.

At the Island Park briefing, as was her wont, Detective Superintendent Winters opened the proceedings and then left for a press conference. This suited Treloar who found that her presence inhibited the others especially when it came to throwing in ideas from 'left field'.

He was particularly pleased to have Sam back. Her absence, however brief, had reinforced his awareness of how he relied upon her for her incisive intuition and as a sounding board for his wilder ideas. He particularly valued her on high profile, high pressure cases like this one and those recent dreadful murders in Porthaven. She was the one who kept him in check when he was tempted to stretch the rules to breaking and beyond, so it had been deeply unsettling to him to see her behave so bizarrely. Still, she was here now and she looked great, back to her old self.

Assembled at the Island Park were the same officers who had attended the first briefing with the exception of Fi Sinclair who was staying with Lily Warren. As Sam handed out the photocopies of the likeness of "Willy", Treloar addressed the team.

'Right let's start with Lily Warren. As you know she's unharmed and untroubled by her experience and she's been very helpful. First off we have this realistic sketch of our man. Lily knew him as "Willy", but I don't think that's his real name. I think this is all part of his chocolate obsession and Tamsin Thomas has chosen to name him after Willy Wonka in the Roald Dahl story. We also now believe that he is the same man who abducted Tamsin from the pony trekking centre in the Lake District the year before last'.

As with Lily this time, he released Tamsin unharmed, but on that occasion, after the Thomases had paid a ransom. From what we can gather from the Thomases, confirmed by what Lily has said, Tamsin has formed an attachment to him and doesn't feel threatened or in any danger. In fact the opposite would appear to be true; she seemed to Lily to be delighted to see him and happy to be in his company. However it's not her choice and we need to find her. So, anything anyone? Luke what about the CCTV from Penzance last night?'

'Nada. Plenty of footage of traffic in the street but nothing showing Lily getting out of a car. Once you phoned through about the boat I called the Harbour Office. They have a number of boats that came in last week but one looks interesting. We have a name "William York", bloke on his own who paid in cash, but the boat's gone.'

'Gone when?' Treloar asked.

'Sometime overnight. He must have doubled back after he dropped off Lily. We have the boat details; it was hired from Fowey but apparently they know him well so they didn't take a deposit. They said he's a really great "American dude", he's always brought the boats back on time and he's always paid them in cash. They didn't think anything of it because a lot of foreign hirers pay them in cash. Boat's due back at the end of next week after a two week hire. I'll get this image of "Willy" in front of the boat hire guy to double check.'

'OK. If he confirms it's our man let's get the boat's details out to all the local agencies: harbours, marinas, coastguard, local fishermen, visiting yachts. And won't it have some kind of GPS? Luke can you organise that?'

'Sure. But there's no GPS on that boat, I asked Just VHF radio. It's not one they usually hire out and as they know him they weren't worried about having to trace it.'

'Winters has taken the image with her to the press conference so he'll be all over the TV news this evening.'

148

'So where's the car?' Sam asked. 'And how did he get a car and a boat to Penzance if he hired the boat in Fowey. He must have sailed to Penzance, and why Penzance anyway, why not just drive the girls from St Ives to Fowey? Col, you're the resident sailor what do you think?'

Colin Matthews was a keen sailor who kept a boat at Fowey.

'Well obviously Fowey's smaller so he'd be more noticeable especially with a child in just a swimsuit, because there's no beach at Fowey. If he's heading westwards out of Fowey then Penzance is an obvious port of call.'

'Where would he be heading, any ideas?'

'Well he's single-handed and that's a small boat. I wouldn't want to go too far, certainly not across to France or Ireland. But we don't know how experienced he is. He might just anchor up in some cove; plenty of deserted spots along the south coast.'

'And he won't want to go too far if he's planning on picking up a ransom,' Tom Grigg added.

'Exactly,' Sam said, 'so he'll be needing some way to contact the Thomases – instructions on the drop and Tamsin's release – and we're monitoring their phones so surely he won't risk a mobile call.'

'Why not?' Col asked. 'Pay as you go mobile, throw the chip overboard, hell throw the whole thing overboard, we've no hope of finding it.'

'Good point Col,' Treloar said although he was thinking of an alternative scenario he wanted to explore with the Thomases. 'OK what about the car? He probably wouldn't have wanted to walk too far with Tamsin at that time of night after dropping off Lily.'

'Oh come on Phil,' said Tom, 'this time of year, even at that time of night a man walking with a happy child wouldn't attract much attention – just another tourist family. It's not as if he were dragging her along screaming and kicking.'

'Yes I know Tom but he must have left it somewhere. Let's start with the Harbour car park. Perhaps Lily could help, she might recognise it if she saw it?'

'OK Phil', Tom said, 'I'll get Fi to broach it with Becky Warren. I'm heading back up there after this.'

'If we can find that car it might help. Either it's his and we'll get his details from DVLA; it's hired and he'll have to have shown a photo ID and a licence so ditto; it's borrowed so we'll find him through the owner; or it's stolen and we're fucked. But we might get prints and DNA for further down the line.'

'He doesn't strike me as a pro,' Sam commented. 'He's not doing this as a business - kidnapping children for money – we'd have heard something. And it's too buddy buddy with Tamsin. I don't think he'll have been covering his tracks. He didn't anticipate our involvement.'

'I think you're right Sam,' Treloar said. 'OK everyone let's go to it. Col and Luke, you get over to Penzance. Sam, you stay. I want us to have another word with Mr and Mrs Thomas.'

When the others had left Sam made coffee for herself and Treloar. She was feeling productive and useful for the first time on this case. She carried the coffees into the sitting room.

'Before we talk to the Thomases again, let's just run through what we're thinking and what we know for sure,' Treloar said taking the coffee from Sam. She was delighted. This was the way they usually worked together and a sure sign that she was forgiven for her recent aberrant behaviour.

'Let's start with the last time,' Treloar continued. 'Tamsin is with Kate Thomas away from home in the Lake District when she is taken. How did our man know that Tamsin was at the pony trekking centre, specifically there at that time and without Kate? That's our first question for the Thomases.'

Sam made a note.

'Then what about the ransom and the release of Tamsin? Who was involved in that?'

'Question number two.'

'Now come to this year. How did he know that Lily would be at the swimming complex at that exact time and again, on her own, well at least without either parent?'

'So if he knew where she was on both occasions when they were not at home but staying away, either he's a dedicated stalker or ...'

'Exactly. He was told where to find her.'

'Question number three.'

'Now we have Lily telling us that Tamsin told her that her mummy knew all about the little boat trip, her mummy not her mummy and daddy.'

'You're thinking Kate knew? What, on both occasions?'

'Sebastian wouldn't have known about the timing of the trip to the pony trekking centre. It would explain her attitude. Tom pointed it out. Becky Warren was distraught, out of her mind, but Kate was just concerned, troubled even. She wasn't expecting the complication of Lily being taken. The plan was going wrong.'

'But wouldn't it be a huge risk, letting your nine year old child go off with a stranger?'

'But what if he's not a stranger? What if he's someone Kate trusts to look after her daughter. From what Lily tells us, Tamsin adores him and he didn't harm or even scare Lily herself.'

'But why? I don't get it.'

'Well who's suffering in all of this? Who saw the blood in the pool, who was out searching, who is actually paying the money?'

'Sebastian.'

'Yes. I think this is all about hurting Sebastian.'

'Christ she must hate him.'

'Let's ask her.'

To reach the chalet where the Thomas family were staying, Sam and Treloar had to walk past the pool complex and The Island Park reception. As they approached the office Sam asked:

'I suppose we've been checking whether any calls have come in for Kate and Sebastian?'

'Yes of course. And screening out the media. No harm in asking as we're passing though.'

They walked into the reception area and approached the desk where a police constable was sitting with a staff member.

'Any calls for the Thomas family?' Sam asked.

'Nothing today Sarge,' the constable replied.

'So it's just been the press calling over the last two days?'

'Well there was that letter,' the young girl staffer piped up.

'What letter?' Treloar asked sharply.

'But that was before the girls were taken. I remember it because it was unusual for guests to receive post here. It came for Mrs Thomas. I just assumed it must be a birthday card or something.'

'And you haven't mentioned it before now?'

'Yes I told that tall bloke,' she was starting to look

concerned. 'It came before they were taken, so I didn't think it mattered to you lot, but I did tell him, honest. I handed it to Mrs Thomas when she came in to ask about the courtesy bus. It was when I was last on, it was Wednesday. I remember it was pay day. Oh and now I think about it again, it was weird.'

'What was weird?'

'Well it was scented. You know you can get cards and paper that smells like lavender or roses or whatever. Yeah I forgot about that, I should have told the other bloke.'

'It smelled of flowers?' Sam asked turning to look at Treloar as she spoke.

'Oh no. Nothing like that. It smelled of chocolate.'

He was jerked back to now-time by the train when it started moving again, suddenly. It had stopped between stations for some reason, not for long, probably. No announcements, so no-one knew why. It was still hot, the sun was still bright, crazy, he flashed back to Benetton's Indian summer signs and mannequins. His phone was still on Sky News, he'd turned it on as soon as the train was out of the tunnel, in case they showed the memorial, why wouldn't they? They'd been on about it for days - around reports and specials about builders and public safety, and how careful we need to be - and now here it was.

    His ear buds were in his lap next to the phone and he was staring through the screen, not seeing it at first, then he was looking down at Totteridge church and loads of people, everywhere, and the reporter was still going on, and then she was talking to red top, Melissa's very best friend, Trudy Parker, still blonde.

    He held the phone up closer to his face, plugged the ear buds in and listened to the dear Trudy saying how incredible it was that all these people had come to say goodbye to the wonderful Melissa, then struggle to speak, and then the camera started panning round the crowd.

    They were in small groups, twos, threes, fours, mostly, then a bigger group that Trudy was walking back to, all young, all blonde, all women, some with shoulder bags, some Gucci. He smiled. Then he noticed a young brown haired guy in a black suit on his own, near the church door, turning his head, looking at everyone else, then a woman in a black skirt and black jacket, standing on her own, under a big tree, looking at everyone else. Then he saw her look over to where the camera had seen the young guy by the church door, and gently shake her head.

    'WHAT!' he thought. He paused the programme, rewound it until he saw the guy by the church door again, zoomed in, finger flicked him to the centre of the screen and restarted it. When the camera panned round to the woman he paused again and zoomed in even closer and restarted again and saw her clear as day, mouth moving and speaking down to her shoulder, a mike, 'must be', he said to himself, 'Christ! Like the cops on the fucking TV', just after she had shaken her head in the direction of the guy by the church

door. 'FUCK!'

'Bastards!' he thought, 'they were looking for him, couldn't be, they didn't know, did they? NO fucking way, NO! No way, he was clear, he fucking KNEW; so they were there just in case. Just in case somebody, whoever had made the death 'unusual' like the papers had said way-back, turned up. Or maybe ..... maybe they were about to light up and they were trying to change each others' minds, yeah right!'

'Well fuck that, he'd dressed smart, well nearly; black 501s, black plimsolls, black socks, black leather jacket, zipped, plain white T shirt, but the crowd were all top smart, so he'd stand out so he wouldn't get off at Totteridge and fucking Whetstone just in case. Fuck, bloody waste,' he'd figured they would be there, the blondes, 'and they'll be well into Gucci like their darling fucking Melissa, smart heels, high, and that it wouldn't be hard to get into it - find loads, follow one, how hard could THAT be? Shit.'

He stayed on the train, looking at the phone; it was still showing the crowd, the reporter was still going on, and every couple of minutes he saw the guy by the church door and the woman by the tree crowd-watching, and looking at each other. Then the train stopped at High Barnet, the end of the line. 'Bastards!' he thought and got off, touched out with his travel card and went to the boards to see which platform he needed to get back home.

Sussed it was platform three, that it was going in one minute, touched in with his travel card and was nearly knocked flying by a blonde rushing past him for the same train, nearly got taken out by her briefcase; the sharp corner clattered the side of his knee. She got in the nearest carriage and he followed her on, and she went left and so did he, but not as far, and he stood not far from the door until she sat down, just as the doors closed, then he sat, on the other side, six seats away.

He got out the phone which was still switched on, plugged in the buds, and watched a vicar talking to the reporter about fate and belief and Melissa's parents and brother, and he couldn't see what fate had to do with anything, and he zoned out, waiting for crowd scenes to come back, until he saw the blonde's legs out of the corner of his eye, and the shoulder strapped handbag on the floor between them, and he stopped looking at the screen.

It was plain light brown leather with criss-cross diagonal lines and GG at every place the lines would have crossed if they hadn't been left out at that point for the GGs. The lines and the GGs were in darker brown. 'It must be fucking well called something,' he thought, 'the GG diamonds? Something! What? You saw it everywhere!'

Her briefcase was wide open on her lap and the top was upright, held by straightened metal hinges, and she was looking through some papers. The top was battered and faded, the colour of dark red wine, looked like leather and had diagonal criss-crossed lines stamped into it.

'She looks good,' he thought, 'twenties probably, not teens, maybe thirty, orange jacket buttoned up to its round neck, nothing obvious underneath, orange skirt, couldn't tell how long, above the knee, covered by the brief case, couldn't see much leg so not that short. Wooden style wedges, dark and light brown stripes, four inches, with orange straps, maybe four and a half, could be Jimmy Choo, classy, hard to tell. Nice!'

By the time the train was jerking south out of Totteridge and Whetstone he had decided he HAD found after all and when he looked at the phone and saw that the crowd had gone in and heard them in church singing he decided he didn't give a shit anyway and was well chuffed he'd come.

He looked back at her, turned down the TV volume but left the programme on and the buds in; he could be watching a film, listening to music, or skyping a mate, 'she's fucking miles away,' he thought, 'she won't see me looking anyway.' She was going through papers, putting some on the seat next to her, not many people on the train, not mid pm yet, only seven in the whole carriage, picking them up again, reading them, making notes on a pad inside the briefcase, putting them down again. Didn't look up when the train went underground and it got noisier, and the sudden rush of air through the carriage blew some papers from the seat to the floor.

Didn't see her look up or around until the train jerked out of the Angel when she suddenly picked up the papers on the next seat, put them in her briefcase with the pad on top and closed the briefcase, sat with it on her lap until they'd gone through the next station then stood up as the train braked into Moorgate.

He got up just after she got up. Picked up the papers from

155

the floor, folded them and put them in his inside pocket and was two people behind her out of the door and onto the platform, and was still two people behind her at the top of the escalator and three when he touched out with his travel card before going outside, turning right and back into the real world, on the follow, and wondered, 'where the fuck will we end up?! Brilliant! And when? ...... later than last time, that's for sure, don't get fucking seen, ha!'

There were buildings all over, old, new, big, small, didn't know the area, never really been there, not far from home, incredible, 'where is it?' he wondered. Lots of people, tall buildings, red buses, black taxis, loads of building work, big cranes, roadworks, noisy. They crossed the road at a zebra crossing, with lots of other people, when the light said they could. He was still three people behind. She turned right after crossing the road, half the people turned left so there were fewer now so he dropped further back.

She turned left, he turned left, ten metres behind, she was still there, even taller buildings in the distance, tower blocks, grey, she was walking quickly, but not in a rush, couldn't in those shoes anyway, briefcase swinging, not so many people about now, let her get further in front, twenty metres, she turned right at a T junction and he sped up and when he went round the corner he saw her turn left ten metres away and he crossed the narrow street and when he stepped up from the road to the pavement his foot trailed on the edge of the kerb and he tripped.

She walked past a long dark red brick car park with signs at entrances saying 'Barbican Centre Parking,' then just past one of the car park signs the same building turned into Guildhall School of Music and Drama whatever that was, then past another car park entrance then a grey concrete building with a sign going on about music and drama and bars and restaurants and then she turned left and he hoped he hadn't lost her and was speeding up and he saw another sign on the wall, a bright orange circle with white letters saying 'Barbican Centre ...'

He slowed down as he came to the corner, looked left and saw her turn right, about fifteen metres in front, on a wide footpath and sped up again, slowed again just before he turned right after her and saw that the footpath was by the side of a road now and that it would take them between two buildings. The one on the right was dark brown brick, with balconies with glass fronts and was

*curved, inwards away from the path and road, and the one on the
left was dark grey, bigger and longer, and weird looking with bits
sticking out and on top. Both, three or four storeys high. Behind the
two buildings was a massive grey tower block, triangular, weird. A
turn off the road ran in front of the side of the one on the right and
turned into a ramp sloping down, and there was a red and white
pole at the top of the slope with a private parking sign fixed to it.*

*She walked towards a glass door in the nearest end of the
front of the curved building, past a white sign low to the ground on
metal poles, with black letters saying Collingwood Crescent and
went in the door after swiping a card through a reader fixed to the
wall. 'Fuck,' he said and sped up and got to the door after it had
closed but in time to see her talking to a guy in uniform behind a
desk then go down some stairs.*

*He turned round and ran back and round the side of the
building, ducked under the red and white pole and went down the
ramp and saw her walking with another guy in uniform away from
a kiosk towards a door between two lifts, and he walked quickly
behind a parking row, not many cars, and hid behind a big square
concrete pillar and looked round it towards the door, on the other
side of a car lane.*

*Uniform guy pulled the door open after pressing on a key
pad four times and picked up a parcel from a shelf and passed it to
her and she tucked it under her arm and picked up her briefcase
with the other hand. They talked and then walked to the lift on the
right together, and the guy pressed the lift call button. She said,
'Thanks Pete,' and Uniform guy said, 'No worries Chris,' and
started walking back to the kiosk and when the lift's doors opened
Chris stepped into it, then they closed.*

*He ducked out from the pillar and ran across the car lane to
the lift on the left and called it, watching the floor number lights
above the other one to see where it stopped and just as his doors
opened he saw that it had stopped on floor three, top floor, three
storeys after all. He got into the lift and pressed the three button,
thinking, 'shit, maybe, maybe not, at least she hasn't seen me ....
yet!'*

*When the lift stopped he was seriously nervous as he put his
head slowly round the edge of the lift door and saw her about
twenty metres down the curved corridor, with her briefcase end on
to a door holding it open. The parcel was on the floor, and a pale*

coloured cat was rubbing its head against it, and not going back in as she was telling it to, loudly. Eventually she picked up the cat, put it under an arm, picked up the parcel awkwardly with the other hand, trying to stop the shoulder strapped hand bag sliding down, 'Shit,' she said when it hit the floor, then she gently threw the cat through the gap in the doorway, held the door open with a foot, grabbed the briefcase and went through the door and it closed behind her.

He walked down the pale brown tiled corridor, it had a white ceiling and light blue walls, to the door; it was painted dark blue, with a brass letter box, and the number 315 was painted onto a wooden square that was screwed to the door. There was a pottery sign with a picture of two cream and brown cats on it, and a speech bubble from the biggest one said, 'Please don't let us out, even if we ask nicely.'

Twenty Two

Sebastian Thomas was extremely unhappy. The police were back at their chalet to talk to him and Kate again. Why the hell weren't they out looking for Tammy, and more frighteningly why was that other girl free and his Tammy still held?

'We're not under house arrest surely? What has the other girl said? Does she know where Tammy is?'

'We'll get to that Mr Thomas, but first of all we have some questions for you and particularly, for your wife. Where is she?' Treloar said.

'Your guess is as good as mine Inspector. If I were you I'd check out the local bars; wherever she is I'm sure she has a glass in her hand.'

'Did you know that your wife received a letter, delivered here, the day before your daughter and Lily were taken?'

'No I did not. Are you sure? It seems most unlikely.'

'Yes we are sure. You didn't see a letter?'

'No I did not. What's its significance?'

'We need to ask your wife that Mr Thomas.'

'Well I'm afraid you'll just have to wait to do that. I can't help you. She'll be back when she's ready. It has been … well … very oppressive. Kate just needs some space.'

When Kate had wandered out of the deli with her croissants, she had spied the small line of people waiting for the courtesy shuttle bus to St Ives. Freedom and some time to think, she thought as she joined the queue. She had no phone, no bag, no coat, but she had money. Yes why not? When the minivan drew up she leapt aboard.

As with many Cornish coastal towns, the only way into St Ives was down. As the shuttle dawdled downhill through the traffic she felt tremendous relief to be on the move and away from the suffocation of Sebastian. She smiled as she thought of the previous evening and the policewoman hitting him. The sheer bravura of the woman and the utter shock on Sebastian's face: priceless. She would relish that moment for a long time. He was nothing to her now, less than nothing. And he had been so much, he had been everything. She hadn't been able to see beyond him; she hadn't been able to see herself. He had filled her horizon like spilled ink, blotting out everything, smothering her in darkness. And now?

Now she despised him.

Kate was exhilarated. For the first time in a long time she was doing something by herself, for herself. Nobody knew where she was; nobody could contact her. She had left her phone in the chalet when she went to the deli with no intention of leaving the Island Park site but then she had acted on impulse seeing her chance for escape. She had money, what more did she need?

As they drew up outside a small Cooperative supermarket the driver spoke.

'Right this is Royal Square. If you get lost ask for the Western Hotel or the Coop. I'll be back at four o'clock. Enjoy your day everyone.'

And with that, the passengers stood, collecting their bags, and headed for the door. Kate left the bag of croissants on the seat. She was the last off the bus. It was 10:45.

Kate followed the other passengers as they joined the throng of people heading downhill into the small town. She followed the flow as it dog-legged through the narrow shopping streets to emerge on a quayside by a lifeboat station. She stopped only to buy a baseball cap sporting the 'I ♥ St Ives' logo. Although she was not strictly speaking 'on the run' she felt a need for some small measure of disguise and the yellow cap was very much 'not her sort of thing'. Besides, it was very warm and she had not brought her sunglasses. Perhaps she should buy a new pair? Large dark ones as favoured by Bono. Perhaps.

The wharf was lined with restaurants and cafés and she strolled along idly checking out the menus. Early lunch? Perhaps. Oh the joy of not having to cater to the others' tastes. Soon she reached a crossroads. Ahead and to her right she could see the harbour curving round onto the pier and its iconic lighthouse. To the left a cobbled shopping street veered away up a shallow slope. But straight in front of her people were sitting on picnic tables outside a classic old seaside pub. Most had coffees and pots of tea, but several had pint glasses of beer. Time for a drink.

But before she went into the pub she needed some basic supplies: a pen, a notepad and a book of some description. She spotted a small post office at the end of the cobbled street where she purchased the necessities for a lone woman venturing into a bar. Normally she could play with her mobile phone but obviously not today.

She would have to resort to the old fashioned props for a woman looking to avoid unwanted attention and eye contact. The book she chose was the latest edition of the Cornish Cove Guide; perfect for her to blend in as a typical tourist.

Inside, the Sloop Inn was wonderfully dark and cool with its wood panelling; a very old-fashioned, traditional, unspoiled British public house with a great smell of beer. At 11:15 it was already getting busy. She bought a large glass of the house dry white wine, Spanish, and opted for a small table opposite the bar, positioning herself at the end of a long cushioned seat so that she couldn't be boxed in by other people.

Once seated, looking up from under the peak of her cap she surveyed the clientele and her surroundings. To the left of the entrance an elderly couple accompanied by a huge shaggy dog were sitting in a small nook with the comfortable, relaxed look of regulars in their usual spot. On the other side of the door a group of surfer dudes were sprawled around two tables littered with bottles of beer and Coke. They were laughing and glowing with that sun-kissed, bronzed skin that made young men so sexy at that age to Kate's mind.

One of them caught her appraising look and offered a broad smile which she returned briefly before opening the guide in front of her on the table. Steady girl, she thought. When she looked up again he had turned his attention back to his companions. To her left, deeper into the gloom, there were two couples, overweight Northerners, who she dismissed completely.

Turning her gaze back towards the light coming through the open door, her eye fell on a newspaper abandoned on the table next to hers. Poking out from its folds was one of the flyers bearing the pictures of the missing girls and the smiling face of her daughter. Fuck it, she thought, trust her to intrude on my day. Well at least the other one was home safe and sound in the bosom of her precious family and her ghastly mother would be happy now. Lifting her glass she found it was empty. She took off her cap and placed it on top of the guide and carrier bag on the table to secure her place, then stood and approached the bar.

'Another?' asked the pretty young barmaid.

'Please,' she replied, 'it was the dry white. A large one.'

The girl placed a fresh glass in front of her on the bar.

'Anything else?'

'No, that's it thanks,' Kate said handing over a twenty pound note. She took her change and pocketed it, then took her glass and returned to her table.

By 13:30 Kate was finishing her third large glass of wine and the Sloop Inn was bursting with people and noise. Kate now considered herself an expert on the relative merits of Cornish coastal venues having read the Cove Guide from cover to cover. Time to move on. But where? She still had over two hours to kill before the courtesy bus. Another bar? Yes why not? Somewhere where she could sit outside and watch the world go by.

She gathered up her books and stuffed them into the carrier bag, positioned her cap on her head and moved toward the light coming through the open door. Onwards and upwards. As she stumbled out into the blinding light she fell into the arms of a tall, very strong and sexy dark-skinned man who was approaching the door. Kate smiled up at him from under her baseball cap, grasping his shirt.

'Oh thank you, it's so bright out here after the bar.'

'My pleasure Mrs Thomas. I've been looking for you,' said DC Luke Calloway.

When they found out that Kate Thomas was missing, Treloar had called Colin Matthews and Luke Calloway back to Island Park. Colin had established that she had taken the courtesy bus into St Ives and the search was started. Whilst they waited for her to be located Sam and Treloar sat with Sebastian Thomas. He was still wary of Sam but had made it clear that he had no intention of filing a complaint about the assault. He did not want the matter taken further after accepting her apology. Treloar thought that Thomas believed any publicity of the incident would not reflect well on him or his business.

'Tell us again about the last time when Tamsin was taken,' Treloar said.

'Well I wasn't there so I don't quite see what I can tell you,' Sebastian replied tetchily.

'Yes we appreciate that, but whilst we wait for your wife, humour me, please.'

'Well as I told you yesterday Kate dealt with everything. I

organised the money and had it delivered to Kate at the hotel in the Lake District. She left it as instructed, as she told you, and Tamsin was released.'

'So all contact with the kidnapper was in fact through Kate. You didn't see the note.'

'No,' Sebastian sighed, 'Kate handled everything. She can be competent when she puts her mind to it and leaves the bottle alone.'

When you saw Tamsin afterwards how was she?'

'She was an absolute pain to be honest. You'd think she'd come back from a planned trip; it was Willy this and Willy that. I got sick of hearing about precious Willy and how much fun she'd had with him.'

'Did she mention chocolate at all?'

'What? I don't know Inspector, I didn't want to know; I didn't want to hear. She was back and she was unharmed and that's all I cared about. We all agreed never to mention it again. Tammy got a new pony and that distracted her. She hasn't mentioned him since, at least not to me,' Sebastian paused and rubbed his eyes. 'You think it's him again don't you?'

'From what we've learned from Lily Warren, it's a very strong possibility.'

'God I don't believe it! Why? How did he know where to find her?'

'Well, your holiday plans are on your wife's Facebook page, although that doesn't explain how he knew she'd be at the pool. You could have been out for the day, he was very lucky.'

Yes or somebody told him she was there, Sam thought.

Treloar continued: 'What brought you to Cornwall and here to Island Park specifically?'

'Well, it's somewhere we both used to spend childhood holidays. Kate suggested it and found this place on the Internet. It seemed ideal for a short break.'

'So Kate organised everything?' Sam asked.

'Yes, she always does. I'm always too busy to get involved and Kate enjoys the research, the planning, all of it.'

Treloar and Sam exchanged a glance. They were both more and more convinced that Kate Thomas was involved.

'Going back to your question why – well you paid up last time.'

163

Sebastian looked at him in despair, 'Then why hasn't he contacted us this time?'

Good question Sam thought. Perhaps he has contacted Kate. There was a knocking and Luke Calloway poked his head around the door.

'We've found Mrs Thomas, shall I bring her in?'

'Just a minute Luke,' Treloar said, crossing to join him at the door and leaving the room closing the door behind them. They stood outside.

'Did she say anything on the way up here?'

'No. Well other than asking if I'd like to try out my handcuffs on her and repeating how she'd come quietly if she could control herself with me. Christ what a bloody handful, I pity that poor sod of a husband.'

'Is she drunk?'

'No, not drunk. She wouldn't pass a breathalyser though, so I'd rustle up some coffee if I were you. She seems pretty relaxed about everything. She's a weird one.'

'OK. Take her to the chalet we're using, not up here,' and with that Treloar went back inside the chalet.

Sebastian and Sam were sitting in silence as he scrolled through something on his mobile.

'If my wife is here now perhaps you could spare me Inspector? I still have a business to run and I need to make some calls.' Treloar nodded. 'I'll be in the other room if you need me.'

'It's OK Mr Warren, we're going to be talking to your wife in the chalet we're using. We'll leave you in peace, for now.'

At 15:00 Kate Thomas was back at Island Park but not in her family's chalet. She had been taken by the sexy black cop to the temporary police accommodation. He had made her some coffee and left her alone and she was starting to feel concerned. What did they know, what had the other girl said? What a bloody mess. After twenty minutes the Inspector and the mad policewoman walked into the room.

'Right Mrs Thomas we need you to tell us the truth now and to stop fucking around,' Treloar said.

'Which truth would that be Inspector?' Kate asked with a smile.

'The one where you tell us all about your involvement in the

164

kidnapping of your daughter Tamsin, and most importantly, where she is now.'

'I don't know where she is now,' Kate said with a sigh.

'But you know who she is with, don't you?'

'Yes Inspector, I do. And she is perfectly safe with him.'

'You'd better start at the beginning.'

'Which beginning would that be Inspector?'

'Stop fucking about you precious bitch,' Sam snarled, 'who is he, how do you know him and how does he know how to find Tamsin so easily, twice?'

'It's OK Sam,' said Treloar quietly, 'Mrs Thomas knows it's time to talk.'

'Don't call me that, call me Kate,' she snapped.

'OK Kate. Why don't you start from the beginning; how you know Willy.' Treloar continued.

'His name is not "Willy". His name is Henry York and he's known as Hal like in the Henry IV Shakespeare plays - his mother was an English Literature professor at Stanford. He's American, he grew up in San Francisco, and I met him when I was at Art School in London years ago.'

'So why, all these years later, would he take your daughter?' Sam asked.

'I don't know, perhaps he needed the money. Everyone knows Sebastian is rich.'

'I don't think it can be as simple as that Kate,' Treloar said.

'I don't know why, but I knew it was him, I knew it after the first time, that's how I know she'll be fine. He loves her and she loves him.'

'How can you possibly say that?' Sam asked.

'Because I know that Sergeant,' she shouted, 'All right, all right! I had an abortion all right? When I was at Art School. Hal was the father but I didn't tell him, he found out somehow and he took Tamsin, the first time, to punish me.'

'How did he find you?' Treloar asked.

'He's always known where I was, through mutual friends, social media, Art School publications – you know the sort of thing, "Where are they now?". I've scarcely been hiding. The trip to the Lake District was pre-announced on our Facebook page, I was sending tweets from the hotel. As soon as he rang I recognised his voice even after all these years,' she said with a wistful smile.

165

'So he took your daughter for money, twice, and you smile at the thought of him,' Sam said in outrage.

'Of course he didn't take her for money. He has loads of money. I told you he took her to punish me.'

'But the money … ' Sam was interrupted.

'The money was my idea, my idea,' Kate shouted, 'I wanted to punish Sebastian. Take his precious Tammy and his precious money. Why do you think we didn't tell the police the first time? Sebastian just wanted to forget all about it when it was obvious to him that Tamsin had had a great time with her new pal "Willy", and I didn't want my past dredged up. I kept the money. Hal knew nothing about it.'

'And this time?'

'Well this time is a total fuck up isn't it? I told him where she'd be, there was no need to involve those dopeheads, and why the hell Tamsin had to drag that girl Lily along?'

'Did she know it was going to happen again, Tamsin I mean?' Treloar asked.

'Christ no, she'd never have been able to keep her mouth shut. No it was all a birthday surprise for her. Hal wrote to me with the date and time for the collection. He couldn't ring in case Sebastian took the call or involved you lot, what with phone traces and everything, so he sent a note in the post.'

'So now what is supposed to happen?'

'Fuck knows. I told you it's all fucked up. He'll let Tamsin go like he let Lily go and that will be that.'

'And what about Sebastian, what were you going to tell him?' Treloar asked.

'Well obviously the plan was to get some more money out of him and to make him suffer by taking his precious "Tammy". You should have seen his face when they saw the blood in the pool. That was my idea. God knows where Hal got the blood. Anyway, she's always been Daddy's girl. He took her from me like he takes everything: my independence, my career, my looks, my future, my life.

I became completely subsumed by him. I'm like some monstrous parasitic growth on his neck; something irritating, embarrassing and unsightly; something he wants rid of but is stuck with because if he cut it out he'd bleed, bleed those things more precious to him than blood: money, prestige, approval, admiration,

166

envy. Tamsin is his, just like everything is his: his company, his house, his cars, his friends, his whores!' Kate spat the last words out.

'But she's your daughter too,' Sam said.

'I hate her don't you understand? Oh I've lost Sebastian to other women, I know that, but she was the first. She stole him from me before she was even born. As soon as he knew I was pregnant he didn't want me anymore. Ours had been a passionate, physical relationship, all consuming, intense, wonderful. My pregnancy repulsed him. He no longer wanted to touch me. It was devastating, heart-breaking. I thought about abortion but … well I couldn't do that, not again.

When she was born he fell in love with her; he was besotted and she returned that adoration. I was superfluous. He didn't want me to breastfeed so I didn't. Foolishly I thought that my physically distancing myself from her like that would bring him back to me. Another self delusion, one of many over the years. They had each other and I was on the outside of their world. They didn't need or want me.'

'Didn't things change over time?' Sam asked quietly.

'Lord no. If anything as she grew, learned to walk, to speak, they forced me further and further away. And she loved it, loved it, I could see that and I was powerless. She relished my misery,' Kate spoke with venom and Sam was astonished by the blazing fury in her eyes. 'So when she came back with her obvious adoration of the wonderful "Willy" it was poetic justice. At last I could see him suffering as I have suffered all these years, knowing that his beloved daughter only had eyes and thoughts for someone else. You cannot begin to imagine the satisfaction that gave me. So, I thought why not again, why not make him suffer again?'

'But what's in it for Hal?' Treloar asked.

'Oh he's still in love with me. He's doing it for me. And if you think about it, what has he done wrong this time? OK the first time was a kidnapping, technically I suppose, but this time he has my permission and Tamsin is a willing guest on his boat. She's having an extra birthday treat. No money has been handed over, there's no extortion or menace on his part.'

'But what about Lily Warren?' Sam asked.

'Yes, well that was unfortunate but she came to no harm. He could hardly have just abandoned her in town when those idiots pitched up with both girls. God knows what he was thinking involving them.'

'You haven't spoken to him?' Treloar asked.

'No. I was waiting for him to contact me. But now, well, I suppose the game is up so I might as well arrange for him to drop Tamsin off somewhere when he calls.'

'You sound disappointed,' Sam said.

'Of course. No doubt you'll try to charge me with conspiracy to waste police time or something, and Sebastian will find out and be a pain about it all. It's all very tiresome really.'

'Oh I think it will be more serious than wasting police time Mrs Thomas,' Treloar said although he was so amazed that he hadn't thought about charges. That would be for the CPS. 'I think you should make sure that Tamsin gets back safely. It would also be better for Mr York to hand himself in now we know who he is.'

'Very well. But you'll have to wait for him to contact me. We had no arrangement for me to call him obviously, that would have given the game away. And before you ask I don't have a number or any means to reach him. We'll all just have to wait. Could I get some more coffee?'

'That woman is unbelievable, monstrous. Never mind Henry IV she's like Lady Macbeth,' Sam was still venting. They had left Kate Thomas going over her statement with Luke Calloway and were sitting in the deserted Island Park bar. 'What in God's name are we going to tell Sebastian Thomas?'

'Well, the first thing we tell him is that we believe Tamsin is safe and well and being cared for. Then we'll touch on Kate's involvement but we won't go into any detail. We need to tell Frosty and the others what's happened and update the alert for Tamsin. I'm going to let Frosty decide how to proceed with charges. She likes talking to the CPS.'

'Who would believe that a woman could be so hateful towards her own daughter? I can sort of understand her feelings towards Sebastian, but Tamsin? She's only nine for Christ's sake and her mother talks about her as if she were her husband's mistress.'

'Yeah. That woman has some serious issues. But that's not our concern now. We just need to make sure that York doesn't panic and dump the child.'

'From what Kate says that's not likely. He was responsible when it came to letting Lily go and he seems to be genuinely fond of Tamsin from what we've heard from both her parents.'

'Yes but that was when he was in control and unknown to us. Things have moved beyond that now. I just hope to God that this all ends well, and soon.'

Still mid October, the previous year

'Wow! Found, followed .... brilliant ...... now just need to get out!' he had said to himself as he got back in the lift. Got out on the ground floor, straight past the uniform guy still at the desk, straight out the door. No problem. Took her papers that he'd picked up on the train from his pocket and started looking through them; three pages - two letters, one from her and one from a customer company to her, and a print of an email.

He read as he walked, but couldn't take it in except that she was an account manager, whatever that was, it said so underneath her signature on one of the letters, and that the firm she worked for, which had offices all over the place, had people working in it that the customer company wasn't happy with, that some software that had been installed wasn't working properly, and that she was going to Newcastle to sort it out once she knew what needed doing, and maybe to Rome. Once she'd spoken to the software people in her company.

'Christ, brainy, boss, wonder how many people she's got working for her,' he had almost thought to himself when there was an incredibly loud 'PAAAARP!!' as he went to step off the pavement without looking and realised he had nearly been run down by a bicycle courier who had blasted an air horn at him. 'Fuck!' he said. He had been miles away, reading the papers, trying to understand them, decided to put them back in his pocket until he was home.

It was Wednesday, he'd gone home, seen from the letters that she worked in Barnet, in an office in a business park, just south of Barnet High Street, and seen from the directions on the Contact Us page on the company web site that it wasn't a long walk from High Barnet underground station. He Googled the business park and saw from Google Earth that it was on the edge of a proper park with grass, tennis courts, a bowling green, a building with changing rooms a café and a kiosk, trees, paths, and seats. By the time he'd gone to bed he'd made a plan.

Easy - buy a bike; get the lycra and a shoulder bag, good to go! Spooky, turned out there was a bike shop less than half a mile away, just the other side of the next square north from where he lived, sold really good bikes - 'Bianchi, whatever they were! Never

170

heard of them,' he was thinking as he went to sleep. They had loads in stock, he'd phoned to check, in a warehouse, only six in the shop though, he could take one of those if he wanted but they might not be right for him, he'd have to take it as is, no mods possible, unless he wanted to wait ten days, he didn't. They sold all the lycra stuff, if he wanted it, and all the bags for couriers, and map holders and racks and panniers, whatever they were.

Back home by mid-morning, new bike outside, locked to the railing, looked good even if he hadn't had much choice. His eyes had gone straight to it when he walked into the shop. Sky blue frame, everything else black, strong, seriously cool, nearly nine thousand pounds, 'eight thousand five hundred for cash …… well, or card,' the guy had said, looking smugly at him. 'Got all the bells and whistles so we can talk to customers about them and show them exactly what we're on about,' the guy had said, looking him up and down, taking in the scruffy jeans, faded hoodie and old hi-tops. 'It's a twenty two speed with electronic gears,' he'd said, 'upshift on the right, finger push lever, down shift on the left, thumb controller. Pedals are included and there's the disc brakes too.'

There were only six road bikes in the shop, Bianchis anyway, three men's, three women's; and the other two men's were lower range and not fully kitted up - racks, high security reinforced aluminium panniers, locking wheel nuts and saddle and handlebar mounts, integral lights, mudguards. The XR.2 was a no brainer, even if he didn't believe he'd find twenty two wireless electronic gears really useful; three had been enough when he was a kid, and they didn't always work anyway. They taught him how to use the gears in the square behind the shop, threw in two black drinks holders with black bottles, and a map holder; fitted them in ten minutes, and a shoulder bag.

He wasn't worried about the money, just gobsmacked, but not as gobsmacked as the guy, when he had said OK, and got his card out. Decided to come back later for the clothes, too complicated, apart from a neat blue jacket, long black lycra leggings, thin black leather gloves because the guy said his hands would get sore, and waterproof cycling shoes. Then they'd asked him about a helmet, so he took the first black one that fitted.

He'd Googled The Barbican Centre and Collingwood Crescent yesterday and set off via the Angel, the Northern Line and

Moorgate, and was looking up at the conservatory on top of the Centre not much more than half an hour after putting his bike in the hall before picking up his prepped camera bag and leaving home. He was wearing faded old black 501s, with matching scruffy black hi-tops, a plain yellow T shirt, the new blue cycling jacket, and a faded grey Blondie baseball cap.

Looking like a photographer, and exactly like he knew where he was going, because he did, he walked straight to the lifts avoiding the ticket counter, straight into a lift that was open and waiting and pressed 'ROOF.' He got out opposite two glass doors which he could see led through to the conservatory, which even he thought looked pretty amazing on-line; second biggest roof garden in London. 'No entry to the public until Sunday' was on a notice hung from the door on the left, marked, 'IN' which he was expecting, because it was only open to the public on Sundays. At this time of year.

He tried the handle anyway and pulled it open, which he thought would work because he had read that at this time of year there was a lot going on behind the scenes on the roof, to do with trimming and pruning and planting, that they couldn't do when it was open. On Sundays.

As soon as he was inside he heard the gardeners talking, not close, he couldn't hear what they were saying, or see them. There was a path to the left which went to the wall of the conservatory, which he followed until it turned right at the wall and ran along it on the one side and past all kinds of trees and bushes on the other. Through the conservatory's glass wall he saw Collingwood Crescent.

'Bloody brilliant or what?' he said under his breath, and quickly counted eight balconies in from the right; one, three, five, seven, nine, eleven, thirteen, fifteen - the even numbers faced the other way, and walked until he was almost directly opposite 315, and leaned backwards against a pillar holding up the roof. He checked ahead on the path and saw no-one else but still heard the gardeners talking, took out and switched on the camera with the long zoom lens and 2x tele-plus converter already fitted, and looked across to see what he could see.

'Christ, fucking amazing,' he said when what he saw was way better than he had hoped. He had a clear view through the glass front of the balcony which had been extended upwards by at *least an extra metre, for the cats according to the resident meeting notes he'd found online, and into the flat; bedroom on one side and sitting room on the other, both with full-height full-width glass sliding doors, just like in the estate agent's details he had found on-line, and he saw that one of the doors to the sitting room had a cat flap. Inside there was the usual stuff - chairs, sofa, low table, TV, speakers, and a cupboard, with a picture above it; a middle aged woman and a man, standing next to her, on a harbourside, in front of a boat.*

The man and the woman were holding hands and waving at the camera, and laughing. They both wore white floppy sun hats, T shirts and shorts. She was standing just to one side of the woman; hand held up in a 'Hi' gesture, and her tongue was sticking out. She was wearing a flimsy strappy red top, cut low, short red shorts, and wedge sandals with white straps. He zoomed in as far as he could and took a picture.

He zoomed back out and panned across to the bedroom but suddenly stopped in his tracks, 'Fuck!' he said, 'incredible.' The two cats from the front door sign were on the balcony, sitting upright, looking straight at him; brownish heads and feet, bright blue eyes, and creamy bodies. There was a short-sided blue box with small grey stones in it behind them to the right. Didn't want that in shot whatever it was, and moved the camera to the left, zoomed in and altered the focus, got rid of it apart from a corner; he could deal with that later, turned the camera ninety degrees to make it a portrait shot. They almost filled the frame, and he took their picture. Took four more on different shutter speeds to make sure, then checked on the screen to see what he'd got and smiled.

Getting out of the conservatory and the Centre was a non-event and he was back home again by mid afternoon. By early evening he was sitting in the kitchen in front of his laptop and Photoshop, congratulating himself, 'not bad for a fucking amateur eh?' he said. He was looking at the image of her; hand raised in a 'Hi' gesture, her tongue was out with the tip curled seductively upwards. He'd also changed the image so that she now wore a low cut baggy black blouse tucked into a short flared yellow skirt; the wind was blowing it up to her thigh on the right, and high heeled wedge sandals with bright red straps.

173

'Really good, well good …….. pro,' said Dan. Then she smiled, stuck the tip of her tongue out, tip curled up, and moved it quickly from side to side between dark red lips. She was leaning against the kitchen counter, blonde hair short all over, wearing a long, tight all over, pink grand-dad vest, top five buttons undone, and high heeled black strappy slippers. 'But which one are you going with?' she asked, and tapped the keyboard to get the slide show running again - mum and dad cropped out from the original, the cats, full frame, with what he now knew was the litter tray cropped out, mum and dad cropped out again but separated by a ragged tear in the picture, wide at the top and narrow at the bottom, big cat separated from little cat by the same ragged tear, then her, just her, magically cropped out of the original, onto a plain white background, then the new her, sexy and seductive.

The printer was already loaded with glossy postcard-ready photocard and he clicked on 'print all' then went upstairs to get them, still wearing the electronics insulating gloves he'd put on before loading it, picked up a handful of brown envelopes, a blue ballpoint pen, a thick red felt-tip and a bag of The Bulldog's tulip petals from the desk. Back in the kitchen he sorted the postcards, chose one and laid it on the counter, then wrote 'Chris Trent' on the top address line with the ballpoint. In the message space using the felt-tip he wrote 'TELL NO-ONE!'

Twenty Three

After the mad intensity of the last few days Treloar was content to sit alone outside his kitchen in the early morning sunshine. Two of his three cats, Messi and Cruyff, named and given to him by his mother, the FC Barcelona fan, were stretched at his feet. The third, the youngest, Pep, was chasing some flying creature through the long grass beyond the flagstones.

People, even his friends and family, thought he was insensitive, blind to Sam's feelings towards him. But this was far from the truth. He was keenly aware of her strong attraction, her clear concern for his well being and her terrible uncertainty of how to deal with the situation. Christ, he was deeply attracted to her, but Superintendent Winters would crucify her, crucify them both; she was a stickler for the rules when it came to 'fraternisation' - ironic really given her clumsy drunken passes towards female staff, including Sam, at various gatherings.

It was not possible for them to have both the professional and the personal, not to the degree that they would both want, and not openly. Something would have to give; someone would have to move on. And after Amy he had turned his back on personal relationships. He had exposed himself once and he had been flayed. Her being here had brought it all back in blinding clarity. It wasn't that he still had any feelings for her, well a certain fondness perhaps, but he did recall the ferocious passion he had once felt and the wretchedness and pain of her leaving him.

Looking at the lives of the people he had met recently, he couldn't help but think that the bachelor existence had a lot to offer. But enough of all that. He would put the whole business out of his mind with his customary self discipline. It was a calm, peaceful morning, just him and the cats.

He loved this time of year. The air was warm and the light was fresh and clean. Everything felt new and unsullied. On such a day anything seemed achievable. It was Sunday and his mother and Eva would be attending mass at The Sacred Heart and St Ia Catholic church in St Ives but they would be home to cook lunch and he was expected.

As a vegetarian he found it challenging to find decent food when he was out, especially since his mother was such a phenomenal cook and most 'V' marked options on menus were severely wanting in comparison with her food, so Sunday lunch at Cove Farm was to be anticipated with relish.

As he stood to clear the table of his breakfast remains he was startled by a sudden shriek coming from somewhere to his left on Lower Farm land, but as he focused his attention it stopped. He stood and scanned the horizon in the direction of the noise, concentrating, but all he could hear was the faint drone of insects and the snuffling snores of the elderly Cruyff. Probably some of the campers on Dylan's newly opened site.

He collected his coffee mug and plate and walked into the kitchen. As he ran the cold tap to rinse the dishes the phone rang. He crossed the kitchen to answer it with a growing sense of disquiet mixed with anger. He was not expecting any calls, he was back on leave, just for the day, and Winters had promised they could do without him. It was a matter of waiting and searching now and his personal involvement was deemed unnecessary.

'Treloar,' he barked into the handset.

'Pippit sweetie what's wrong?' It was Amy. Well it wasn't Winters, but it still wasn't welcome.

'What do you want Amy?'

'Oh don't be such a grump. I wanted to ask if we could meet up and talk some more about my problem. I came over yesterday hoping to see you but you were out,' she said sulkily.

'Amy, I don't know if you've been hiding since you got back but there have been two little girls missing and I have been rather busy.'

'Oh yes I know about that,' she said dismissively, 'but one of them's back now and she's not been raped or anything. Anyway you're there now so I can come straight over.'

He sighed inwardly, but Amy was impossible to dissuade from a course once she had her mind set, and other than lying to her, he couldn't see a way out. And he had to admit that he was concerned by what she had told him the morning after the party. 'OK, fine, come over now. But I have to leave at one because I'm going to lunch at Cove Farm.' Even as he spoke the words he regretted them.

'Oh great, I'll come too. It's ages since I've been over.'

Christ no, he thought. Not his sisters and Amy. 'Amy, I don't think ...'

'Oh damn I can't,' she interrupted, 'I have to go to some

176

wretched local thing with Mumsie. Never mind, there'll be another chance whilst I'm down. Right, I'm on my way,' and with that she hung up.

Small mercies, he thought.

Thirty minutes later she walked into the kitchen. She was wearing a pair of faded cut-off jeans with fashionable rips and a bright yellow cotton vest. A large scarlet leather bag was slung over one shoulder. She looked beautiful. Treloar opened a drawer and pulled out an A4 pad and a pen.

'I've made some coffee,' he said, 'shall we sit outside?'

He led the way outside to the table on the patio where the coffee awaited. Amy followed him and sat down.

'When I was over here yesterday,' she said, 'I saw Dylan Maddox. I haven't seen him for years and years. He looked so old and grey and his behaviour …. well I just thought he was really creepy.'

'Hang on a minute. Are you saying Dylan was here at the barn yesterday?'

'No of course not silly, he was over at those old mine buildings.'

'What were you doing there?'

'I wanted to have a look at the place after hearing that story Ochre told, you know, that awful, sad story of the sister and brother who were hanged there.'

'Why on earth would you want to do that?'

Amy was quiet for a moment gazing at her hands outstretched in front of her. 'I don't know really. I was here and I just felt that I had to go and look. There was nothing to see really and just after I got there this mad man came storming up to me shouting and swearing. It was totally horrid and well over the top. And then it turned out to be Dylan Maddox, little Dylan. I would so not have recognised him if he hadn't told me who he was.'

'Amy listen to me. Dylan gets very unhappy about people wandering about on his land. I really don't think you should do it again. Plus it's dangerous: the ground is very uneven, the buildings are unstable and God knows what noxious substances are lying around. The whole place should be closed off and cleaned up; it's hazardous.'

'Oh Pippit don't be such a bore. Once he saw it was me he

was completely different; all smiles and a total delight. You know I had totally forgotten how much he used to like me. I think he still has a bit of a crush,' she added giggling.

'Amy I want you to promise me that you will keep away from Dylan Maddox. He's married now as you well know, and he has a baby. He doesn't need you messing with his head.'

'Pippit really, I was only teasing. I don't suppose I'll see him again; I have no plans to go back to his precious mine.'

'Good.'

'Anyway, I only mentioned it because he made me think that he was the kind of person who could be sending me all these nasty things. You know somebody creepy.'

'Right then. Did you bring the diary?'

'Yes it's here,' she said hauling the soft leather bag onto her lap and rummaging around inside it. Eventually she pulled out a bright pink A5 sized Filofax. 'I wrote down every time something happened. I made up a code so I can tell you what happened each time, you know: mobile call, email, letter, parcel. I thought that was best.'

'Well done. This could prove very useful.'

She beamed at him, and he could see again why he had fallen so badly for her all those years ago: she was a magical creature at times. But he also saw with blinding clarity, how over the intervening years he had matured, grown older and wiser, whilst she had remained the dazzling, intoxicating, infuriating creature of their youth, and he recognised with a certain sadness, but mostly relief, that their marriage would never have lasted and that its failure had been as inevitable as death. Swept up in her enthusiasm and pride at his praise, Amy didn't notice his wistful expression.

'Right then,' she declared opening the Filofax, 'pink dot means a mobile call, green means a mobile message, blue is an email, red is a package at home, black is a package at the agency. There were no calls to my home 'cos I don't have a landline for the phone, just the Internet. Well I expect there is a line, but I don't use it so there's no number.'

'Did you make a note of every call and keep every package?'

'Well no. At first I didn't twig that it was all the same creep. I get fan stuff: photos, selfies all the time and I didn't think anything of the first package; the photo of me at Selfridges and a load of dried tulip petals. Though looking back, I should have thought it odd, when it came to the house not the agency. But once I did, yes I kept all the packages and I printed all the emails. I didn't keep the mobile messages 'cos he didn't say anything: they were all pauses then hang-ups, or weird music.'

'So you've never actually spoken to him so you can't be sure it's a man?'

'No. I suppose not. I just assumed. It normally is, isn't it?'

'Who knows about this?'

'Well everyone in London: friends, other girls at the agency and my immediate neighbour.'

'Family?'

'Oh no. I didn't want to worry them and they've not received anything: no calls, no parcels. I really don't want to tell them Pippit, not 'till it's over and maybe not even then.'

He nodded, 'All right, for now, unless anything changes and they have to know. Let's start at the beginning. What made you think it was somebody obsessive, not just random, not just fan mail.'

'It was the first package. It came to the house in the morning post early in February; just an ordinary looking Jiffy bag.'

Treloar was taking notes. 'So it wasn't hand delivered; it came via Royal Mail?'

'Yes. Or one of those private companies that deliver post.'

'And what was in it?'

'Pressed dried flowers. Red tulips actually.'

'And anything else; a note?'

'No nothing. Just the flowers.'

'Anything on the outside of the bag: a return address, anything at all other than your address?'

'Nothing.'

'Fine. So what was it about this package that made you single it out as odd, other than the fact that it was a curious choice of gift?'

'Well, that same week I'd had two hang-ups on my mobile – you know, just silence then the tone. Anyway, I just happened to mention it on the shoot - cameras not guns,' she added with a grin, 'and so Immy says ...'

Treloar interrupted, 'Immy?'

'Immy is my boss at the agency, she owns it: Imogen Jordan. She used to be a model you know. You must remember her, she was the face of Calvin Klein perfume in the nineties and she was in that famous campaign for Levis, the one filmed in Nevada with the white horses ...' Amy trailed off noticing that Treloar had stopped taking notes and had fixed her with a stare. '... sorry Pippit, anyway as I was saying, Immy says it might be trouble. So I say "what sort of trouble?" and she says a dodgy fan and that I should start to keep a record of anything weird just in case we needed to report it to you guys. So I went out and bought this dear little book.'

'Sounds like a sensible woman.'

'Yes, well, we're not all bimbos just because we're beautiful,' she said with a pout and no conception of the arrogance of her words, 'and here it is: my stalker journal.'

'Do tulips hold any significance for you? Have you mentioned them to anyone, in person or on social media?'

'No I've never talked about tulips, and we're not allowed on social media: no Twitter, no Facebook, no nothing.'

'Really?' Treloar asked in surprise thinking all publicity; good publicity.

'Oh no. Absolutely forbidden. In our contracts we have to promise that. Immy has total control over our images you see; nothing unauthorised goes out. We're not even allowed to send selfies. Well, actually, I do have a Facebook page and a Twitter thing but it's all done by the agency. I mean I don't get to put anything out there, they do it all. But they haven't said anything odd has turned up on either and they would've let me know, wouldn't they?'

'OK, so no personal social media,' he made a note and underlined it, 'but back to tulips, have you ever appeared in any ad campaigns where they featured or bought them on a regular basis? I seem to recall your favourite flowers were freesia.'

'Oh Pippit darling, you remember!'

'Well ... yes ... I bought enough of the bloody things,' he flustered.

Amy frowned. 'Actually, I've grown out of freesias now, they're a little ... simple. No now I love ranuncula and gerbera - though you do see gerbera on every restaurant table – they're far more sophisticated – bold and vivid – much more my style. Did you want to note that down, just in case?'

Treloar smiled. She really hadn't changed. 'Back to the

tulips. They mean nothing special to you?'

'No nothing …. Oh and I do love white lilies and white roses, especially old-fashioned, blowsy, scented English ones like you see in cottage gardens in Agatha Christie, you know …' seeing the look on Treloar's face she looked down at her hands, chastised, and mumbled, 'enough of the flowers.'

'Did you note the number or numbers of the hang-ups?'

'All withheld.'

'So what happened next?'

'Let me see,' she said furrowing her brow and turning the pages of the Filofax. 'So that was the first package: the tulips on the Saturday. On the Tuesday I got the first recorded message on my mobile.'

'What was said?'

'Nothing was said, it was just awful music, ghastly stuff like you get at fairgrounds and before you ask, the number was withheld, again, and I deleted it.'

'Why?'

'Well nothing was said. What point was there in keeping it? But before you tell me off, I told Immy and she told me I should keep everything even silence and crappy music. So I have. Oh and I went out and bought a new phone with a new number for friends and family and there's been nothing creepy on that … I wonder if I can claim that as an expense?'

'Next event,' Treloar said.

'Next "event" as you put it, that would have been the following Saturday – another parcel, same as before in a Jiffy bag, in the post.'

'And what was in this one?'

'A small shiny plastic windmill. You know, the sort you buy for kids at the beach.'

Or like the ones Ochre has in her herb gardens at Radgell. Interesting, he thought making a note. 'Next,' he said.

'Oh really Pippit,' Amy said with a sigh pushing her long hair back from her face with her hands in a gesture he remembered so well. 'this is totally boring. Can't we have a break, get a nice glass of something?'

'Do you want my help or not Amy?'

She sighed dramatically. 'Yes I do and I do appreciate you're doing this, really I do. Let's just get on with it and get it over with. I hate even thinking about it, especially down here, but I know I can't ignore it – Immy says so.'

Good for Immy, Treloar thought.

Over the course of the next two hours they went through Amy's Filofax, Treloar taking notes. In essence, the pattern which emerged was of small packages, all posted in London, delivered by Royal Mail mostly at weekends, and calls to her original mobile which were all hang-ups or music; no speaking, all numbers withheld. None of the package contents and none of the music held any significance for Amy. He had made general notes but he had not listened to the messages because Amy had left the phone at home in London. In addition to the tulips and the windmill the "gifts" had been a packet of liquorice, some chocolate, more dried tulips – yellow this time, a velvet ribbon, a string of beads and a bag of coffee beans.

By the time they had finished with the arrival of the coffee beans the previous Saturday it was time for Treloar to leave for lunch at Cove Farm.

'Right Amy. Leave this with me and I'll have a word with a few colleagues who have experience in this area. And try not to worry. You're keeping a record and that's exactly the right thing to do.'

'Oh thank you Pippit darling. I so didn't want to talk to strangers. I've had similar problems before, we all have it goes with the territory, being in the public eye, but this time it's … well it's just creepier and it's going on and on. Before it's just been the odd call or unwanted gift, a bunch of flowers left on the doorstep, never a … campaign like this.'

'Well as soon as I know what's best to do we'll make a plan. You know it probably is just a devoted fan with weird tastes and if he or she, but let's say he, is posting all his parcels in London he's probably there and you're here. I don't think you'll hear from him whilst you're in Cornwall. How long are you staying?'

'Just till the weekend; I have to be back on Monday; I'm off to Milan to do a second ad campaign shoot for Bianchi. They loved the first one. Apparently, it was very, very sexy.' She reached up and gently touched the side of his face in another familiar gesture. 'Thank you Pippit, I must let you go. You mustn't be late for your mother, not on a Sunday. Promise me you'll find him Pippit, promise me you'll find him and stop him.'

'I promise Amy,' he said softly, and with that reassurance she picked up her bag and keys from the table and walked out.

Treloar watched her cross the courtyard. She had changed so little over the years it was disturbing; the same beautiful, infuriating, exasperating creature he had fallen for all those years earlier. And still so fragile, so delicate. He hadn't wanted to worry her, but this stalker, and he was sure that's what this was, this behaviour was sinister and he was concerned from the pattern that it was escalating. He needed to talk to Priss Forbes and he wanted to talk to Doc Tremayne. But now he was running late and he rushed to close the patio doors, grab his car keys, lock the kitchen door and run to his land Rover.

If he hadn't been preoccupied and in a hurry he would have taken the time to scan the land around his property as was his habit, and then he would probably have spotted the glint of sunlight on glass as the watcher in the copse lowered his binoculars, but as it was, he just shouted a further goodbye to Amy, who was standing by her open car door changing her shoes, and drove away.

Had he not been running late, he would have waited and followed her down the lane back to the St Ives road. As it was, to save time he headed up the lane to cut across Higher Farm land to join the main road near Zennor. If only.

Mid to late October, the previous year

No drama getting up to Barnet by mid morning. Still warm and sunny, the envelope was in his shoulder bag. A big printed label on it said, 'Private & Confidential. For the personal attention of Chris Trent, Account Manager, GoHR Systems.' He had cycled past the bricked drive down to the firm's car park on his right and on to a park entrance so he could go right around the building.

It was rectangular, single storey, fifty metres by twenty, old slate roof, mossy; he also knew from the GoHr website that the security was amazing even though there was only a one metre recycled brick wall separating it from the park. The company had agreed to this and other conditions forced by the council when it sold the corner of the park to raise money in the face of loads of objections from all over the place. There were security beams and guards and dogs at night and hidden CCTV cameras all over, and other stuff mentioned to put burglars off, but not described in detail. The windows and doors were fitted with 'president grade glass .... also eliminating damage from thrown bricks and stones,' the manufacturer's website said.

He cycled slowly, but not too slowly, looking to his right at the French doors, some were open, most weren't. The patios they opened onto were in the shade and no-one was sitting outside; one man stood outside smoking. As he cycled past occasional big old trees he could see people sitting in their offices, most worked at computers, some sat at tables writing, others were on the phone. He didn't see her and wasn't happy when he turned right, along the short side of the building, at the back, where two people were outside at their bench seats, and it was sunny.

He was cycling just inside a line of big old trees and got so excited he nearly fell off his bike when he saw her stepping down to the patio from an office with her briefcase, which she put on the bench table then sat down, and opened it. She was wearing a mid blue dress, high neck, above the knee, not far when she was standing but showed good thigh when she sat down, couldn't see the heels, and a dark blue jacket. 'Fucking ace,' he said to himself as he cycled past. Then carried on cycling, and thinking as he went round the corner, 'fifty metres down to reception, fifty back, maybe .... hopefully .... let's do it.'

He turned right again down the other long side of the

building and back to the road, then right and right again down the brick drive and straight through the car park and to the right of the main reception door where he leaned his bike against a thick, dark, wooden post holding up a wooden roof over the doors, which were open. He took off his new jacket and hung it over the crossbar and walked in and straight up to the reception counter and said, 'Good morning,' to the middle aged but good looking brown haired woman behind it, reached into his shoulder bag and pulled out the envelope. He looked at it and smiled, and said, 'Special delivery for Chris Trent,' handed over the envelope, said, 'Cheers,' walked back out, stuffed his jacket into the shoulder bag, got on his bike and cycled back to the road, then to the right and back to the park, then right again, to start another ride around the building.

When he was half-way down the first long side of the building he thought, 'Shit, should I have asked for a signature?' By the time he had turned right, to go along the back, to her office, this time behind the row of big old trees, he was too hyped to think about it anymore and stopped so he was hidden behind a tree and hoped she wouldn't see the bike sticking out.

Her briefcase was still on the table, she wasn't there. He got his phone out, started the camera app and put it on zoom so he could see the table and the inside of the office clearly and waited. Not for long. On the screen display he could see her holding the envelope as she came into the office looking puzzled, and ripping it open as she walked down the step to the patio, then she stopped and pulled out the postcard, picture side towards her, saw the cats separated by the tear, and jerked her head back as the colourful petal shapes flew out after the card, she batted some away from her face, some fell on the floor and some into the briefcase, and frowned, then opened her mouth, then closed it again, then shrieked. Then she turned it over, and almost fell onto the seat by the briefcase as she read and re-read the message and just sat there staring at the card, turning it over and over then back again and over and back again.

She kept opening and closing her mouth, to start talking, didn't speak, reached into her jacket pocket for her phone, looked at it and put it down on the table, frowned, kept on opening and closing her mouth. Kept on looking at the card and turning it. Thinking, then looking scared. He took pictures, lots. Then she stood up suddenly, threw the card and envelope into the briefcase, slammed it shut, went inside and closed the doors to the patio then stormed out of her office.

'Now what?' He asked himself as he cycled behind as many trees as he could back towards the front of the building. He saw her, through the glass wall, from behind a tree on the edge of the car park, talking to the receptionist who was shaking her head, 'don't know,' she could have been saying, 'didn't see any names or logos .... why? Is everything alright?' she could have asked. She nodded, looked at her watch, said something to the receptionist, who nodded then wrote something in a book on the counter, then pressed a button on her flash looking phone system.

He hoped she was going home and waited until she was a minute down the road from the car park before getting back to the road himself and going quickly past her without looking and on to the new park and ride cycle lockers built into the steep hill that High Barnet underground station was at the top of. She would be about ten minutes behind if he was right.

He quickly took off his helmet and put it in a pannier, took his jeans out of the other pannier and pulled them on over his cycling shoes and leggings, took his jacket out of the shoulder bag and put it on before putting the shoulder bag in the other pannier and using Dan's credit card in one of the two empty locker doors to pay two pounds for two days after entering Dan's PIN code, then opening the door and standing the bike on its rear wheel and pushing the front wheel into the clip high up on the back wall of the locker, then shutting the door and running up the steps to the station.

He saw from the boards that the next train through Moorgate would leave in eight minutes from platform two and that it was already waiting, then walked over to the small station shop and bought a newspaper, a Mars bar, and a large black coffee to go. As he came out of the shop he saw her walking alongside the train then getting into the second carriage. He touched his travel card in and followed her, sitting six or seven metres away; they were the only two people in the carriage and only one other, a big young guy wearing grey overalls with white and yellow paint splashed all over them and a matching baseball cap, got on before the train jerked away. Paint splash guy had sat between them, looking at her, and blocked his view.

Twenty Four

The Tremaynes lived in the centre of Lostwithiel, ancient capital of Cornwall on the River Fowey, some five miles from Bodmin. The glorious name comes from the Old Cornish, 'Lostgwydeyel', meaning 'the place at the tail of the forest'. Their beautiful old house stood behind a walled garden, with their upper rooms overlooking the river, and that afternoon Dr. Tremayne and Molly were sitting in that garden discussing Phil Treloar.

'Well I'll tell you one thing; Sam will be watching him like a hawk now that Amy has reappeared in his life,' Molly said as she poured from a jug of homemade lemonade.

'Yes, there's that. Perhaps this might finally bring that to a head,' her husband replied.

'I feel for Sam, but I don't know why she doesn't just tell him how she feels.'

'Propriety my love, probably something in police regulations, and a little fear I imagine.'

'Well it will have to be resolved soon; she can't go on with this silent adoration. I'm sure she must be finding the situation humiliating. By the way, what were you and Sam looking for in those photos at the party?'

'Oh she was just asking me about Jago.'

'What about him, surely she knows the story?'

'Yes she does.'

'Out with it man. What aren't you telling me?'

'Molly this must absolutely go no further.'

'You have my word.'

'Charlie Hendra, a sergeant, was telling me that he would swear that he saw Jago in Union Street in Plymouth the other night.'

'What? He must be mistaken.'

'I don't know; he knew Jago well and he's convinced. Anyway, I was pointing him out to Sam. She's going to try to get a look at any CCTV coverage when she gets a minute. Obviously this child abduction is taking all their time at the moment.'

'Tremayne, Tremayne, it's Phil,' Molly called from the dining room French windows, 'hurry up man, he's at Cove Farm about to sit down for lunch.'

Dr. Tremayne put down his newspaper and walked across the lawn to take the phone from his wife. 'Hello Félipe, what can I do for you this fine day?'

'Hi Doc. I just wanted to bounce something off you,' and he went on to describe his conversation with Amy detailing the parcel contents. When he had finished Dr. Tremayne was silent for a while.

'What did she say about the music?'

'Something you'd hear at a fairground, something operatic, some Queen song and something in French with a bloke shouting about a 'femme infidèle.'

'And did she say what colour the ribbon and the beads were?'

'No. Well she said the beads were amber.'

'Well I wouldn't take this to court, and I know you said the parcels were all posted in London, but I think your link, the commonality here is The Netherlands, Holland.'

'Really?'

'Yes think about it. All the "gifts" have Dutch associations: tulips, windmills, liquorice, and amber beads which are a shade of orange. Check if the ribbon was orange. Then the music. Well, traditional fairground music is from barrel organs and they are still popular in the Low Countries. The opera segment could be Wagner, the Flying Dutchman, and the French bloke, well that's actually a Belgian, Jacques Brel, one of Molly's youthful heartthrobs, but it's from a song about the port of Amsterdam. I wouldn't be surprised to see little wooden clogs and toy bicycles turning up. Ask Amy about Holland. Does she know any Dutchmen, flying or otherwise?'

'Thanks Doc, you're a mastermind. Oh and there's a Queen song that starts "I want to ride my bicycle".'

'Ah Queen. Molly didn't favour Queen. Couldn't stand that nonsense about Galileo.'

The Pengelly family home was a huge grim granite house looming on the carn above Cove Farm. One incongruous pinnacled round tower, like something from a French chateau, dominated the skyline at its southern end, offering panoramic views of the coast. Radgell was surrounded by high stone walls; very bleak, very austere, but once through the gates the atmosphere in the sheltered gardens was a complete contrast. Here Ochre Pengelly had planted riotous flowerbeds and hundreds of windmills in various materials, colours and sizes. Beatriz described it as magical, like something in a children's fairy story picture book.

That morning Ochre was in the front sitting room with her older brother Orlando. The room faced north, looking out over the gardens, but its cool aspect was tempered by the amber papered walls and the rich brocade of the curtains. The furnishings were also in warm shades of crimson and gold. Orlando was standing in front of the stone fireplace, his back to the hearth; Ochre was perched, improbably, on a delicate Queen Anne wing-back chair at a small table. She was studying a pink Moleskine notebook.

'How does this sound? "It's easy to believe that bad things happen to bad people, easy and lazy. Bad things also happen in paradise and even angels fall prey to evil",' Ochre declared dramatically.

'My God sister dear, you sound like the voiceover introduction to a third rate American television programme,' Orlando said.

'Splendid! That audience is our customer base. We want the little man or woman, the bitter soul, powerless, disenfranchised, vengeful, wronged. He, or she, is our prospect and we will help to release their pain.'

'Listen to yourself woman. You are pandering to the base instincts of desperate people. I doubt what you're doing is illegal, but it is most definitely immoral. How can you justify such a tawdry enterprise?'

'Oh calm yourself brother dearest, your pomposity's showing. It's not illegal and as for morality, well I see it as a form of therapy. We bring people comfort. If one recognises oneself in a character well then there is the justification, and if one doesn't, well no harm, no foul. Look at Ian Fleming. He used real names for both Goldfinger and Blofeld, names of people he knew: Goldfinger, an architect who built a house he disliked near his home in Hampstead, and Blofeld, a contemporary at Eton. We are offering a valuable service: allowing people to express their feelings, allowing them to "vent" you might say.'

'I would not so say.' Orlando muttered. 'A valuable service; valuable to your business empire no doubt? I'm sure payday lenders comfort themselves with similar thoughts. It's exploitative, however you dress it up. You don't fool me and you don't fool yourself.'

'Well … we must just agree to disagree.'

'So be it.'

Ochre and Orlando Pengelly were talking about the latest addition to Ochre's commercial portfolio: www.loathinc.com. For a fee, *loathing incorporated* allowed people the opportunity to provide the basis for a character or organisation in a work of fiction. Ochre had assembled a group of writers who would incorporate a suggested character into their work.

Say you hate your boss; www.loathinc.com offered a means for you to post a description of that boss as you see them, and have that portrayed in fiction. No actual names. As the book blurbs say: 'any resemblance to real persons is entirely coincidental'. No libel. And in the site Terms and Conditions the company reserved the right to reject any submission it considered inappropriate.

It was proving very popular and highly lucrative. Ochre had first thought of the concept when she had had a falling out with a local brewery and decided to boycott their establishments. Not satisfied with this redress, she had approached a writer acquaintance who had agreed to incorporate a ruthless, money-grabbing, family brewery in his next novel. The fictional demise of the brewery's managing director had brought Ochre much satisfaction.

Ochre's other business interests included *Zennor Aromatics,* which made soaps, scented candles, diffusers and room sprays; her series of highly successful adolescent historical novels set in Cornwall – 'think *Jamaica Inn* with vampires and teenage hormones', to quote Dr. Tremayne; and the considerable revenue from the sale of her paintings.

To Orlando, who taught Philosophy at the University of Exeter, it was all rather grubby. Still, he did like the scented candles, and took a secret delight in his involvement in the naming of the new fragrances, so when Ochre opened the box of Christmas samples that had arrived that morning and were sitting in their box on the rosewood table, his mood lightened considerably.

'Why don't you write another teenage smuggler saga? Harmless escapism.'

'People don't want escapism nowadays; they want comfort. They want chocolate box, jigsaw puzzle England: snowy Christmas scenes in Victorian churchyards, stew and dumplings, apple crumble and custard; Miss Marpleland.'

'What's for lunch?' he asked, their previous argument dismissed from his mind. Their disagreements were like summer storms: intense but short-lived and quickly forgotten.

'Crab couscous,' Ochre replied, and crossing the room she handed him a small block of mottled orange wax. 'What do you make of this? It's one of the new Christmas range.'

He sniffed the wax. 'Well, cinnamon and orange, mandarin I think, but something else I can't quite place.'

'Cardamom,' she whispered with a smile.

'Of course! You clever beast. What shall we call it?'

'I was thinking: *Ding Dong Merrily.*'

'Please tell me that's a joke.'

'Ho, ho, ho,' she huffed in a deep voice and kissed him on the cheek.

After lunch Ochre drove down to the coast just along from Cove Farm. It was a favourite place where she used to walk with Beatriz Treloar after her father Jago's disappearance. As she looked down into the small cove, or zawn as it was called in Cornwall, she was troubled. The water below her was teeming and churning, unwholesome and uninviting, as if a host of small angry creatures thrashed, trapped, just below the surface. Something was stirring.

What Ochre hadn't mentioned to Orlando was that she had recently received a submission on *loathinc.com* which she recognised as a description of Amy Angove in her Lamorna Rain persona. Clearly the person who had made the posting shared Ochre's view of the woman as vain, superficial and pointless but there was a deeply unpleasant and menacing element which disturbed her and she was considering rejection.

She was disturbed by Amy's appearance at the Treloar party. Ochre made no secret of her contempt for Amy; she considered the creature dangerous. Phil was long over her, but Amy had an insidious way of strolling into people's lives and wrecking them with casual cruelty. Ochre despised her for it. She had also been giving some thought to the gas mask business at the Treloar party. It had certainly had a dramatic effect which she would have found satisfying had she been involved, but she hadn't, and she had an uneasy feeling who had, and it did not bode well. Somebody out there had it in for Amy Angove.

She would just have to find out what Amy was up to. Bee might know; she had stayed that night.

Ochre liked all the Treloar sisters. They shared qualities she valued: self-reliance, strength of character, open-mindedness and generosity of spirit, But she truly loved Beatriz.

Twenty Five

Pixie had wanted to go to Turkey. All her friends were going to Turkey but here she was stuck in a frigging tent in Cornwall, and all because Robbie wanted to go surfing. Well she now knew that she hated camping, she hated Cornwall, and she was beginning to have mixed feelings about Robbie. Here she was, miles from anywhere in a frigging field, and there wasn't even any phone signal. What a shit holiday. Still, the weather was good, and she did like the pool at the Leisure Centre. Oh, and she'd had some great burgers in St Ives and there was that cute chocolate shop.

That morning Robbie had gone off early to catch some waves so she was left to her own devices. So at 11:00 that morning she emerged from the tent into bright sunshine intent on exploration. The nice woman in the farm shop had told her there was a circle of standing stones up behind the campsite, and apparently, from up there in clear weather, she would be able to see the north and the south coasts which would be kind of cool and make a good video to show the gang. But first she needed to collect her phone from the farm shop where the woman, called Hope, cool name, had let her leave it on charge. Robbie had been playing Candy Crush Saga on it, again, she just knew it.

She had been told it was quite a climb up to the stones so she had put on shorts, a T shirt and her trainers rather than the flip flops she had been living in since they had arrived. She had her sunglasses, her new straw hat and her small backpack. As she emerged from the gate to Lower Farm into the lane and walked up towards the farm shop she could hear raised voices, well one raised voice: a man's.

'I've told you a thousand times I don't care that we were friends at school. He's stolen my land and I don't want you setting foot up there, let alone going to his fucking party.'

There was a pause, presumably a response which she couldn't make out, and then he continued:

'I don't care what my father says, you're my wife, the mother of my child and I don't want you or her visiting Lost Farm Barn again. Never.'

Pixie froze in her tracks. For all her bravado she hated confrontation. Now what to do? She didn't want to get involved but she needed to get her phone. As she stood considering her options, the dilemma was resolved for her as a battered Ford pickup tore out of the farm shop car park and hurtled up the lane away from her throwing up a cloud of dust. She continued up the lane and turned into the farm shop car park. It was empty. The shop was a modern brick and timber building with double glass doors. Both were shut and the 'CLOSED' sign was up, but Pixie tried a handle and the door was open so she went in.

'Hi! Hope? Are you there? It's just me, Pixie. I've come for my phone.'

Lost Farm Estate farm shop primarily sold local produce: meat from the estate farms, fruit and vegetables - some from the Treloar family's Cove Farm, bread and baked goods from an artisan baker in St Just, chocolate and confectionery from St Ives. Much to Dylan's disgust Hope had also insisted on stocking a few basics like tea, instant coffee and baked beans for the holiday cottage and camping customers. As Pixie advanced down the aisle she could see Hope behind the delicatessen counter putting out cheese.

'Oh hi Pixie, I was just about to open up; I'm running late today: Bethan had a bad night.'

She smiled broadly, and Pixie could see no trace of anxiety on her pretty face. Perhaps Dylan was one of those volatile types like Robbie's dad: quick to anger, quick to calm.

'Just came for my phone.'

'Yes of course, I'll fetch it,' and with that Hope disappeared through the back to the office, retuning to hand Pixie her phone, 'there you go: fully charged. So what are you guys up to today?'

'Robbie's gone surfing, again, so I thought I'd walk up to those stones you told me about.'

'Yes: The Dancers. You could go up the lane and cut across by Lost Farm Barn or go straight across the lane from here and up past the old mine. That's a nicer walk. You can't see much going up the lane because you're rather boxed in by the hedges. I'd go via the mine, but don't go onto the mine site itself; it's dangerous and the ground is unstable. You'll see that it's fenced off and there are warning and 'keep out' signs everywhere; Dylan hates people trespassing up there. Once you get to the fence just follow the edge of the field to the right and you'll reach a stile. You can see the mine workings from the gate opposite and then you can see the stones from the mine, so you can't get lost.'

'OK, thanks. I'll go that way. Can I grab a piece of the

asparagus quiche and a couple of apples to take? Oh, and do you have any bottled water?'

'Back by the entrance in the fridge cabinet to the left,' she replied handing over a generous slice of the quiche double-bagged. Help yourself to apples. You can pay me later; I haven't done the till yet.'

'Thanks Hope. See you later,' and with that she pocketed her phone, grabbed a small bottle of water and headed outside.

Across the lane from the farm shop was a gate into a field. Pixie rested her arms on the top and stood looking up to where she could see the chimney of the engine house silhouetted against the blue sky. With a last look behind her and a wave to Hope who was propping open the shop doors, she climbed over the gate and started out across the meadow. It was going to be a lovely day.

As she made her way through the long grasses and wild flowers Pixie thought how glad she was that Robbie had gone surfing. It was good to be alone for once. Had Robbie been there he would have been jabbering on about his new surf pals. She'd met them down at the beach opposite the Tate gallery and they seemed OK but she really didn't need Robbie going on and on about their exploits … boring or what? She stopped to take a swig of water and check her bearings.

She was on a path of sorts, more a trampled gap in the long grass, heading across the fields towards the mine. She could see more of the derelict workings now and the engine house chimney looming up into the clear pale blue sky. It struck her again how the sky here seemed higher, bigger somehow than at home in Reading. And at night, well it was dark, really dark and starry. Dark, deep blue-black blue, not the sludgy orange grey it was at home, like the colour of melting gritted snow. Robbie had told her that it was because of the difference in the ambient light and that in built-up areas all the light from streetlights and housing and other buildings was reflected and made the sky look grubby. Whatever, it was so lovely and clear and shiny here.

She liked to be out in the open. Often she would cross Reading Bridge to walk along the Thames to Caversham and the water meadows. But here everything was so much …. wilder, timeless – no houses, no cars, no people. In fact she couldn't see another living soul. It was really cool. Occasionally, she could hear the distant cries of playing children drifting across on the warm breeze. There was also a constant low chirruping sound which she took for a small bird, or maybe insects.

Swinging her gaze uphill to the right she could see a small copse of trees and behind it, up on the barren moorland in the far distance right on the horizon, a large dark foreboding house like something out of a horror flick. She must remember to ask Hope about it. Further to the right she could see farm buildings which must be Lost Farm where Hope's father-in-law lived. She held up her phone and panned the camera around. Right: onwards and upwards she thought walking on.

It was easier going in this field. The grass was cropped and there was a well trodden path running around the edge. Looking down the slope to her left Pixie could see small brown cows the colour of her friend Suzie's Labrador and beyond them more fields and the distant sparkling sea. She wasn't afraid of cows, in fact she rather liked their slow, docile nature, and anyway these were a long way off. Although she no longer had to push her way through long grass, there was a steep incline and she soon found herself puffing. To her right behind the fence the small wood was rustling in the strengthening breeze. Through the trees she could just make out a long low house with a glassed section of roof glinting in the sunlight. Nice place to live she thought.

At the end of the long field was a further gate. Looking over it she could see barren moorland and way up ahead, the standing stones rising into the shimmering sky. She took a swig of water and climbed over the gate.

Since leaving Hope in the farm shop Pixie hadn't seen another living soul - well assuming you excluded the cows. She was used to being among people; she worked as a receptionist at the headquarters of an insurance company in Reading and she couldn't remember the last time she had been totally alone for such a long time in daylight hours. It was strange, but kind of exciting too.

Finally she reached the stones. They stood on a plateau with the only higher ground in sight the rising moorland further to the west. In all other directions she could see to the horizon, the sea to the north and to the south and the rolling farmland to the east. It was wonderful. She stretched out her arms and twirled on the spot, laughing.

The stones, there were ten of them standing and a central one lying almost flat in the centre, formed a rough circle. She could understand why they were known as The Dancers, she could picture a group of girls dancing here on a day such as this. Perhaps the flat stone represented a boy or two with musical instruments; a pipe and a drum? She was so pleased that Robbie wasn't there. He would be going on about Druids and pagan sacrifices on the central stone altar, blood soaking into the ground, burning torches and chanting, naked virgins. She dismissed the thoughts from her mind but did resolve that this was not a place she would ever visit at night. Shivering, she turned and headed back down the way she had come.

She could hear a noise coming from the mine workings. It was a steady creaking. The wind had picked up since she had passed earlier and her attention was drawn to the gaping doorway of the building. There, lying on the ground was a large scarlet leather tote bag gaping open, its contents strewn across the rough ground: a mobile phone, a notebook, a hairbrush and, incongruously, a banana.

'Hello,' she called out, 'hello is there anyone there?'

There was no sound but the steady creaking. Something wasn't right. Perhaps someone was hurt? Warnings or no warnings Pixie was going to find out; she climbed over the gate and headed towards the mine.

Late October, the previous year

She was just staring, out the window, at nothing; the camera app was on and he had the phone on his knee, camera pointing at her, past paint splash guy, taking pictures then looking at them to see what she was doing, and he had an idea as they jerked into Totteridge and Whetstone station and stopped. No-one got in.

By the time they were moving again he'd cleaned all the source data off his favourite picture of her, mouth open, batting away a tulip petal and looking well-freaked, and emailed it to the prepaid phone he'd got with him, one of the four he'd bought for cash at The Phone Place in Islington after getting the bike; set up to use one of his new gmail addresses. Then he emailed it from the prepaid to her at Chris.T@GoHR.co.uk. It would go to her phone because the letter he had picked up said it would - 'all emails sent to me go to my mobile as well as the computer, so I'm always in even when I'm out'; her email address was on the letter, underneath her name. Before pressing send he added, 'See you Chris,' as the subject and 'xx' in the text.

Paint splash guy was still in the way so he held his phone on his knee with the camera app still on and waited. When he heard an old fashioned cartoonish 'bloop,' noise come from her direction he guessed that the email had arrived and started taking pictures, every few seconds, and he carried on until paint splash guy was out of the picture.

She had gasped loudly with a sharp intake of breath when she saw the photo and looked scared, he knew later after looking at his pictures, and then she stared with her mouth open looking at her phone, and started crying. Paint splash guy had stood and gone over to her and sat next to her and looked at her and said something and she looked even more scared and shook her head.

Paint splash guy raised both hands, one round her neck and onto her right shoulder and one on to her left shoulder and she shook her head even more strongly and shouted, 'Leave me alone bastard!' then jerked her elbow up hard, into his throat. Paint splash guy got up and staggered to the back of the carriage, struggling to breathe, his left hand rubbing his throat, and stared at her. He got off at the next station.

'Christ!' he said to himself, 'Need to be careful with this one.' By *the time he was following her off the train at Moorgate he'd sorted through the pictures he'd just taken, found one that worked well and cleared the source data from it and emailed it to the prepaid. In it she was looking at the phone which was in her right hand and level with her face, her mouth was open wide and her left hand was just coming up to her mouth and her eyes were open wide. He was well chuffed; she was well freaked.*

He was ten metres behind her off the train, up the escalators, through the travel card readers where he used the card he'd bought using cash to touch out, and across the road, which wasn't very busy. Weird. Instead of turning right behind her, he turned left and ran to the next right turn and right again at the end of the block and then to the end of the road he knew she would be coming down, where he slowed down and looked right and sure enough she was about thirty metres away from the corner, walking towards him, not too quickly.

He crossed the road then started running again and turned left and on the left-hand pavement trotted up as far as the first Barbican car park entrance and ducked round the corner. It was dark, there was no kiosk, no cars coming in, no-one walking about inside. He switched on his phone's video app and held it so that the lens pointed back down the road, with the zoom on, and was standing so that he was inside the car park entrance but could still see down the road on the angled screen.

Twelve seconds later, he counted them, she walked round the corner and he emailed her picture from the prepaid with 'nice one Chris,' as the subject and, 'but not paint splash guy :-)' as the text and started the video, her head and shoulders filled the screen. Five seconds after that, she took her phone out of her pocket, looked at the screen, said something that could have been, 'Fuck,' looked scared, stopped walking, tapped the phone, saw the picture, looked even more scared, dropped her briefcase and held her mouth with the hand that had been carrying it, turned and looked behind her then back to the front, blonde hair covering her face, shook her head and got most of it off, pushed the rest off with her hand, picked up the briefcase, stuffed her phone into her pocket and started running, scared, towards him. He looked round and it was still dark and there was still no-one around. He looked back to the screen and she was still running, still scared, straight towards him. He smiled and pulled his phone towards him, out of her sight.

Twenty Six

One of Dylan Maddox's grand schemes for his Lower Farm empire was to open a café/bar next to the farm shop. Much to Hope's embarrassment he had approached Beatrix Treloar about running it, but she had politely and understandably declined as Hope had predicted. So at this stage the café consisted of some picnic tables and parasol umbrellas at the rear of the car park. This was where Pixie Armstrong was sitting with DS Sam Scott and DS Tom Grigg in the early evening sunshine, drinking tea.

'Did you see anyone whilst you were walking?' Sam asked. She was still shaken by the discovery at the mine, but she was not going to let her emotions get the better of her again.

'No, nobody.'

'You're sure?'

'Absolutely certain. I remember thinking how it was ages since I'd been on my own for so long. I didn't see anyone. Nobody. The last person I saw was Hope when I went to get my phone from the farm shop and I heard ...,' Pixie hesitated.

'You heard someone?' Sam asked.

'Well ... it was just ...,' she took a deep breath and exhaled, 'before I reached the shop I heard raised voices, well just one raised voice: a man's. I think it must have been Hope's husband, but I didn't see him. I just saw a pickup leaving the car park.'

'Did you recognise the driver?'

'No, I didn't really see him, but I know that's Hope's car, I've seen her driving it.'

'Where did it go?'

'It headed up the lane away from the shop. It was going real fast.'

'You didn't see Amy, Lamorna Rain's car at all? You would have noticed it: she drove a shocking pink Mini Cooper.'

'No, the only car I saw was the pickup.'

'Did you hear anything else: shouting, screaming, talking, anything?'

'I heard voices when I was crossing the first field, but it sounded like children playing and it was coming from behind me. I just assumed it was some kids back at the camp site or by the holiday cottages.'

'Right Pixie, you're doing really well, just carry on telling us what you did and what you saw,' said Tom Grigg with a reassuring smile.

'Well I just carried on across the field until I reached the end next to the mine. Then I turned and went along the edge of the field, like Hope told me, and across more fields up to the stones.'

'Did you see anything or hear anything when you were by the mine the first time?' Sam asked.

'No. Hey, that's a good point. The bag wasn't there! When I was on my way up to the stones I looked across the fence and I could see the ground in front of that building and the bag was not there, definitely not, I would have seen it.'

'Right, good,' Tom said, 'and what time was that?'

'It must have been about half eleven.'

'OK, carry on,' Sam said.

'So I went through the field past the wood, the one with the brown cows in it. I could just make out a house through the trees, nice place, but I didn't see anyone there.'

That would have been Lost Farm Barn Sam thought, picturing Pixie's route as she told her story.

'Right, well at the end of that field I climbed the gate and stopped for a drink. I could see that great big gloomy place up on the hill ahead of me, right up on the horizon. What is that anyway, looks like a prison or a nuthouse or something?'

'You must mean Radgell,' Tom said, 'it's a private house. Did you look back towards the mine at all?'

'Yeah, I looked all around but I didn't see anybody, no cars either, just the lovely cows.'

'Carry on,' said Sam.

'Well, after that I just headed up across the moorland to the stones. I took some photos and videos and had my lunch. You lot took my phone to look at the footage, but I know I didn't see anybody because it would have registered with me. Anyway after lunch, it must have been about half two by then, I started back the way I came and … well you know what I found.'

'This is important Pixie,' said Tom in a serious tone, 'did you hear or see anyone or anything on your way back? You would have had a good view of the mine workings at various points on your route.'

'No, I promise. Nothing, nothing at all. And you're right I could see the mine some of the time but there was nothing.'

'That's fine Pixie, you can't tell us what you didn't see. Let's talk about what happened when you got back to the mine site. You followed the field edge again?' Tom asked encouragingly.

'Yeah, exactly like on the way up. I went along the edge of the field to where all the no trespass and warning signs are, where you cut across back to the lane and the farm shop. I just happened to glance over the fence towards that chimney and that's when I saw the bag.'

'Tell me exactly where it was and how it looked,' Sam said.

'Well, it was lying on the rough ground just outside the chimney building …,'

'The engine house,' Sam said.

'Yes. The engine house. Anyway, I could see that it was a nice bag and I could see all the stuff lying around it so I knew someone had dropped it and that seemed odd. You don't just drop a bag like that and leave it. So I called out, but nobody answered. Well I know Hope had said it's dangerous and all that, and not to go in, but I just knew something was wrong so I climbed over the gate. I thought if it's dangerous someone might have fallen over or down a hole or something and be hurt or even unconscious.'

'You did the right thing,' Tom said and Pixie smiled at him.

'Could you hear anything?' Sam asked.

'Just birds, and the kids' voices again in the distance, oh and the squeaking, but I didn't know what it was, not then.'

'So you walked across and picked up the bag,' Tom said.

'Yes of course I picked it up; anyone would have. I didn't take anything, I just shovelled all the spilled contents back inside and slung it over my shoulder. It was Gucci, I could see that, probably worth more than Robbie's car. Then I walked across to that awful dark place. I was still calling out.'

'What did you see?' Sam asked softly.

'Well it was really dark inside coming in out of the sun. What with all the rocks and bits of wood on the ground I was watching my footing, but I could hear the squeaking, getting louder now, so as soon as my eyes adjusted I looked to see what was making the noise. And there she was. I could see the rope was tied to the wooden beam in the roof and she was just hanging there,' Pixie faltered.

'You're doing really well Pixie,' Sam encouraged gently.

'I walked towards the body, I don't know why, it was like I

was drawn to it, and when I got closer I could see her clearly because behind me there was a huge open space where there must have been a window or door or something and the sunlight was streaming through it straight onto her like a spotlight. It was really creepy. I looked up and I could see her face clearly, her hair was all hacked off lying on the floor, and I knew her at once: it was Lamorna Rain. She was dead, I could just tell.'

'Did you touch anything?' Sam asked.

'Fuck no. I dropped her bag and ran. I knew there was no signal so I ran like hell back across the field to Hope in the farm shop and she called you lot. Well, you know the rest.'

'So you just ran, you didn't touch anything or pick anything up?' Sam asked again.

'No lady, I've told you,' Pixie said her voice raised in anger, 'I'm not a fucking ghoul, I didn't steal anything from her bag, I didn't sneak any photos to sell on the Internet and I didn't speak to the papers. I just ran for help. Not that anyone could help her poor cow … I wonder what made her do it? All that money, all that fame, just goes to show. And what a place for someone like her, middle of nowhere, what was she doing there? Weird.'

'We haven't established cause of death yet, we have to wait for the post mortem,' Sam said, 'but we are treating it as suspicious.'

'Well it weren't no accident, that's for sure,' Pixie said.

'Well I think that's all we need for now Pixie. Thank you very much,' Tom said. 'Will you be staying on for a while?'

'Well we were, but I'm not so sure now.'

'Well we have your details, so if we need you again we'll find you. The press will try to reach you but we would appreciate your not talking to them, at least until we have a clearer picture of what happened,' Tom said. Well it was worth a try.

'Oh don't worry. I really liked her; I'll keep quiet.'

'Thank you,' Sam said, 'I'm sure her family will appreciate it.'

Still late October, the previous year

Busy busy. That afternoon, after she had run straight past him, fast and close, he decided to join a courier firm as a freelance guy, tomorrow. So he could use the Company ID and sign sheet to get past the cats and into the flat. Leave the cameras. Then he decided he was going to speak to her on the phone, a few times, starting soon, and needed something to disguise his voice, scary maybe, then he decided to get back to Barnet on the tube, to get his bike, so he could go to Tottenham Court Road. He wanted to find something today and be set to get to the courier firm tomorrow, wherever it was.

As he walked into Moorgate tube station he saw a London Metro billboard that stopped him in his tracks - 'Melissa Killer, trial soon.' Couldn't believe it. Seemed like ages since he'd seen anything about it, just concentrating on the new one. 'Christ,' he thought when he realised it was only a few days since the memorial, seeing the police on the TV, not going. Getting smacked on the knee by the briefcase he'd just seen flying down the road, following her, freaking her, just a couple of days, but it seemed longer, ages.

He picked a copy off the pile and read the story way before the train came out of the tunnels. The trial had been listed to start at the Old Bailey at the end of November.

'Stan Briscova has been on remand and will stay in prison until the end of the trial at least,' The Metro said. The Company Briscova owned, or Briscova, or both, were charged with corporate manslaughter and he and the Company were charged with a shitload of other stuff that sounded seriously complicated. 'Christ!, he said, 'Fucking amazing,' and a woman sitting next to a small girl three seats away had turned and glared at him; he didn't notice. He decided he'd start getting all the papers again, to understand. Look at what he'd made happen ……… at what was happening. Busy busy.

He started Googling couriers when the train was out of the tunnel and by the time it jerked out of Totteridge and Whetstone he'd decided on Cavendish Cycle Couriers, based near Kensington High Street, 'run from the ground floor of a central London mews house,' the website said, not far from the Hyde Park end. They 'specialise in urgent deliveries for the rich and famous and their agents and managers, but are also used by many businesses for

*reliable and secure delivery of important documents and parcels,'
and were looking for part-time hard working freelancers to cover
the other side of Town. Perfect.*

*He got the bike from the Park and Ride lock up, jeans off and
into the pannier, jacket and helmet out of the pannier and on,
cycled to Eurospy in Tottenham Court Road and was back home by
five o'clock. It was getting dark; he was starving and stuck a pizza
in the oven. Got a Sol out of the fridge, plugged in the digital voice
changer to charge it up and started reading how to use it sitting at
the kitchen counter. He'd finished before the pizza was ready,
'nothing to it, bloody amazing,' he said to himself.*

*He decided on the 'older man with a cold,' voice; one of
twenty five that came with the changer and he could buy more
online if he wanted. Just had to plug its cable into the head phone
socket on the prepaid then use it like a phone itself, top up to his
ear, microphone towards his mouth. He'd call her in the morning
before going across Town to the couriers.*

*It had seemed like a good plan, sounded easy, talk about paint
splash man, freak her, wouldn't see it this time, but would hear it,
fear; the voice changer test had worked a treat last night, calling
himself on the home phone and leaving a message, but it all turned
to ratshit straight away. Just after nine in the morning he called
GoHR on the prepaid as 'the older man with a cold,' and asked for
her and was told, 'I'm sorry, but she won't be in the office today,
she's gone to Newcastle.'*

*'Shit!' he thought. Then quickly regrouped. 'Oh dear, I
wonder if you can help me?' he said. 'I'm Chris's father and I need
to speak to her quite urgently, when will she be back?'*

*'Oh, she'll be back tomorrow, but you could try the mobile.
It'll probably be off at the moment because she's still on the plane,
but give it an hour or so and try then.'*

*'Oh dear, we don't like calling the mobile during the day in
case she's with people, in meetings,' he replied.*

*'Ah, yes, I can see that .... hmmmmm. If you could wait
until later you could try her at the hotel. She'll be back there for a
couple of hours in the late afternoon before going out again.' The
receptionist laughed and said, 'she's taking the flack this morning
and afternoon - told her she should wear her asbestos knickers ...
oops, oh, sorry .... anyway she's schmoozing them tonight in*

China Town, table for eight at seven o'clock at the Royal Emperor, poor thing will be tired out after all that but she'll be back in the hotel for a couple of hours in between.'

'Ah, great, that's really helpful .... which hotel is it please?'

'No problem Mr Trent, it's the Malmaison, next to the river, and she'll be in room eight seventeen, I booked it all myself yesterday.'

'Ah, thanks very much, you've been really helpful,' he said.

'You're very welcome,' she replied, 'I hope your cold gets better soon.'

'Christ on a bike!' He said after he'd hung up, 'Now what?' He was buzzing, bad call turned good .... 'not so bad after all,' he was thinking as he Googled flights to Newcastle, and 'fucking ace,' when he discovered he could easily get there with British Airways by two o'clock from Heathrow Terminal Five. He booked and paid online for a seat, coming back in the morning on the nine thirty five. Then he called The Malmaison after Googling it for the number and booked a corner suite on the seventh floor, then the Royal Emperor and booked a table for one at six thirty.

He'd allowed an hour and a quarter to get to the airport, just in case; didn't know what the traffic would be like, didn't want the tube this time. It could take longer than driving, more than twenty stations, 'No way,' he thought and booked a taxi. He re-dressed, smarter, including black 501s with a black carbon-buckled belt, and packed, didn't really need anything, just a change of shirt, boxers and socks, Blondie baseball cap, laptop, unused prepaid, gloves, and chargers. And voice changer. And selfie-stick. Then he went to the Newsagent in Upper Street to get the papers and they went into the small grey leather holdall with everything else.

He was at the hotel by three o'clock and it had been straightforward, clockwork. Taxi, read papers, marked stories, airport, checked in, picked up The Metro and Standard, got a beer, got on plane, read papers, got a gin and tonic, marked stories, got off plane, got in taxi, checked in to hotel, went to room, left bag on bed. Then he went to find the fire door and stairs up to the eighth floor to see where eight seventeen was. Not far, next but one to the fire door, looking over the river, just about above his own.

Then he went back to his room and used the scissors on the key ring that had been in the holdall and that shouldn't have been taken onto the plane to cut out the stories that he'd marked up and put them in the bag. They didn't say much new, mostly what he'd read in The Metro yesterday, more detail, but it had taken him nearly two hours to go through them all and check who was charged with what, and why the case was being heard so soon.

Turned out that there weren't many witnesses, a lot of very clear evidence, and not many charges. The Company was being charged with corporate manslaughter and the owner with four breaches of health and safety regulations with another seven to be taken into consideration. Some papers said it should be cut and dried with sentencing within two to three weeks, and some were quoting other cases and saying it could go on until the end of January; they also went on about jail sentences and unlimited fines and compensation, and who could be entitled to it. 'Who the fuck knows then?' he said as he started dumping the papers into a bin under the desk. When he realised they'd never all fit he put the rest on the floor next to it.

The mini bar was next and he took out a half bottle of Bombay Sapphire, a bottle of tonic and an ice-cube tray, and made himself a drink before calling room service and complaining there was no lemon in the fridge. One arrived four minutes later with apologies and a knife to cut it with. He got the stories back from the bag, took them to the desk and sat in the leather chair with his drink and read and re-read them until six o'clock when he called down to reception to book a taxi.

They said there was always at least one waiting outside so he put the stories back in the holdall, took out the prepaid, the selfie stick and the gloves and put them in his shoulder bag. His phone was already in his pocket, then he zipped the holdall and went down to the taxis and straight to The Royal Emperor. It took five minutes.

He was early so he asked the driver to drop him at the end of the street so he could walk back down and look at other restaurants and the other places in the street that was most of Newcastle's China Town. It was already pretty busy so he walked quickly, didn't want to be late. He was surprised by how many Chinese places there were, shops as well, and how full they were. 'They must go straight from work,' he thought.

When he walked in there was already a buzz in the air and he was met quickly and taken straight past full tables and up some stairs, to a table big enough for four in a corner, and noticed on the way over some more stairs leading up to yet another floor, 'Oh fuck,' he thought. As he sat, he told the waiter he might be joined by someone and asked if that was OK and would he mind if he waited to see if they were coming before he ordered, but asked for something small to be going on with, and a beer. He was starving, 'Only had a bag of nuts since breakfast, on the plane,' he said.

'No problem,' the waiter said, 'I'll bring you a selection, anything you don't like? he asked.

'No, just whatever,' he replied, 'Cheers.' On the way to the table he had seen a table set for eight in the window and hoped his luck would hold.

It did. Just as he was dipping a small duck spring roll into a bowl of hoisin sauce she came up the stairs and sat at the window table, side on to him. She wore the orange jacket she'd had on when he first saw her, or one like it, it was open, white blouse underneath, a matching just above the knee orange skirt, and very high orange, spiky heeled shoes. The skirt showed good leg, lots, when she sat down. He smiled.

Ten minutes later her table was full and she had shaken hands with everyone before they sat down; one more woman and six men. Two were foreign, Italian he guessed; he heard one being called Luigi, and she said, 'Chow,' when she shook his hand. Luigi had introduced the other one, he didn't catch the name, she had laughed, and said 'Chow,' again.

He had nearly finished his sweet and sour pork with chips and had taken a few phone pictures when Dan came up the stairs. Short hair still, just above knee length red silk dress, high round neck, red strappy high heels. When she leaned against the wall next to him a slit in the side of the dress opened, showing the top of a hold up. 'Cool,' he said. 'Glad you like it,' Dan replied.

They looked at the table for eight when it suddenly got even louder; they'd got louder as more and more drinks had been drunk, and Luigi was shouting now and the others were trying to shut him up. 'I am not a thief, I am not a thief!' Luigi shouted, then started ranting in Italian. The others couldn't shut him up.

She was talking, loudly, to the other Italian, 'I didn't say

208

that, not at all, why would I? I was joking, all I said was it was good to meet him and I was glad he'd managed to sneak in to the meetings and the dinner. I thought it was funny. Then he went ape! Now look, what's he fucking doing?'

'So,' he heard Luigi's pal say while Luigi ranted, 'Explains it. You don't know. Italian for 'sneak' means same as thief, and coward. He thinks you call him these.' Luigi was suddenly on his feet, pointing at her saying, 'insulting, you are saying, I am not a thief!' Then he walked round to the back of her chair, ranting again in Italian and put his hands around her neck.

She pushed her chair back hard, her hands on his hands trying to get her fingers under them, stood up quickly, almost screamed, 'for fuck's sake get off!' turned round quickly and walked around the chair, her hands were still on his hands which were still around her neck and he was still ranting and her eyes were level with his mouth, and nearly closed, she squinted, spit flew in her face.

Everyone else at the table was staring at them, so was the whole restaurant including waiters, and she drew her head back quickly, then forward even more quickly and smashed her forehead as hard as she could into his nose, which crunched then flattened just before Luigi's hands came loose and he fell straight to the floor. He was shooting video by that time and when he played it back later, he heard it and saw it in slow motion in full HD. 'Incredible!' he thought.

She put both hands to her neck and rubbed it, then walked round to his head, lifted her left foot and rested the heel on his neck, next to his Adam's apple, glared round the table, then pressed her heel down harder.

She looked down. Pushed her heel further into Luigi's neck, stretching the skin, she looked round the table, then pressed even harder for a couple of seconds before grabbing her shoulder bag from the back of her chair, walking over to the waiters' desk and paying using a credit card, apologising to the waiter, then walking down the stairs still rubbing her neck, at the sides and front, with both hands. 'Wow!' Dan said, 'Schmooze on that!'

Twenty Seven

'I told her not to go back there, I told her!'

'Why?'

'What does it matter now?' he asked bitterly.

Sam was sitting in the kitchen at Lost Farm Barn. She had driven over first thing that morning. She was going to revisit the mine where Colin Mathews and Luke Galloway had been working since daybreak, combing the site for anything missed the day before.

'Well it would be useful to know if she went there of her own accord or whether she was taken there against her will,' Sam said gently.

Phil sighed and rubbed his hands across his eyes. 'The mine is dangerous. The ground is polluted and riddled with pits, the buildings unstable and then there's Dylan Maddox. He hates trespassers, threatens anyone on his land without express permission.'

'Would he have hurt Amy?'

'No. No way. He worshiped Amy. She told me that once he recognised her yesterday he was really pleased to see her. He may have been acting strangely recently, he may hate me and half the world for all I know, but he loves Amy, always has, since we were children. It's not Dylan Maddox. No it's this bastard stalker and I told her she was safe down here. I promised her I'd find him Sam, I promised her. Christ I can't believe this. She was sitting where you are only hours ago. I failed her Sam, I failed her.'

'Let me make us some coffee. Why don't you go and sit outside? It's good to be in the fresh air.'

Treloar stood slowly and walked across the kitchen and out through the French windows. As Sam went to fill the kettle her phone rang. It was Dr. Tremayne.

'Hi Doc.'

'Sam, I just spoke to John Forbes. He hasn't started the post mortem yet but he has examined the body and confirmed that cause of death was probably the blow to the head as we suspected.'

'Well at least she didn't suffer; it wasn't a slow strangulation from the hanging.'

'No, but she wasn't taken by surprise, well John doesn't think so.'

210

'What do you mean Doc?'

'John says there were dried tears on her face. He thinks she must have known something was wrong. Perhaps she tried to run and he caught her and struck the blow. But I don't think you need to tell Phil that detail.'

'He'll find out.'

'Yes but let some time pass and he'll be less raw. How is he?'

'He's beating himself up because he told her she was safe down here. Apparently there's been a problem with some sort of stalker in London. He thinks it was him; followed her down here and waited for an opportunity to get her on her own.'

'That's certainly a possibility.'

'Phil doesn't think its Dylan Maddox, you know the guy that owns the land, but I'm not so sure we can just write him off. Anyway Doc, I must go, he's waiting outside for coffee.'

'OK Sam, bye'

'Cheers Doc,' as Sam ended the call her phone rang again.

'Sam Scott.'

'Hi Sam it's Colin.'

'News?'

'Yes. We've found Amy Angove's car. It was parked on a garage forecourt just down the main road to Penzance, stuck on the end of a row of cars for sale.'

'OK. Any CCTV?'

'I'm checking. It's walk-able from the mine. Perhaps he dropped it off and went back for his own vehicle. I'm betting he was watching when she was at Phil's; waited for him to leave and snatched her. Took her to the mine; did her; then moved her car and went back for his own. Unless he had an accomplice of course?'

'Whoah Col. Don't let's get ahead of ourselves. I need to go. You can tell us all your theories at the briefing.'

'See you there. Frosty must be loving all this. First a child abduction, now a celebrity killing, all that press exposure and the season's barely started. She's probably out having her hair done. See you later,' and with that he was gone. He had a point Sam thought. Superintendent Winters did relish the high profile cases. She had called a briefing for noon. They were still using the chalet at the Island Park. Phil had not been invited. Winters had made it clear that he was not to be involved as he was a witness to Amy's last known movements and he was obviously her ex-husband. He understood but he was not happy. Sam could see that he was upset, of course he was, but he was plotting something, she was sure of it, and it wasn't something Winters would condone, she was sure of that too.

Twenty Eight

It was with a sense of déjà vu that Sam drove into the Island Park resort. Was it only four days since she had first visited this place? It seemed like weeks. A few members of the press were hanging around at the entrance. Sam wondered idly whether they were here for Tamsin Thomas or Amy Angove. In the chalet someone had been busy moving all the paperwork associated with the missing girls. The place was crowded with officers Sam vaguely recognised and a few she knew, including Tom Grigg, Colin and Luke. She pushed her way through the crowd to join Tom who was standing by the window talking on his phone.

'I understand Ma'am. Yes of course I'll ask. That will be my first question and I'll get back to you.' He paused to listen. 'Oh OK, right you are then, I'll wait for your call.'

'Our esteemed leader?' Sam asked.

'Oh yeah and she's after blood. Some woman from Amy Angove's model agency in London's been on to her about a stalker, and she seems to think we should know all about it. News to me.'

'I know about it. I found out this morning from Phil and he found out yesterday from Amy Angove. Nobody else down here knows a thing about it, not even Amy's parents, so Frosty needs to back off. The last thing Phil needs is her on his back; he'd blow, the mood he's in at the moment.'

'Right. You'd better fill us all in now,' Tom said clapping his hands loudly. 'OK everybody settle down, settle down! We're going to start in two minutes so put those phones away and get your notepads out.' He turned back to Sam.

'How is Phil?'

'Blaming himself because she had been at his place. Ridiculous I know but you know what he's like at the best of times; he does get so involved.'

'Yeah well it's understandable this time mate.'

'I know. I know. I just hope he won't do anything stupid. Frosty's already told him to keep out of it. Hope in hell.'

'Right. I'll summarise what we have, then you tell us about this stalker.' He clapped his hands again, 'OK everyone, let's make a start! As you all know, yesterday afternoon the body of Amy Angove whose professional name was Lamorna Rain, was found in the engine house of the old mine above Lower Farm on the Lost

213

Farm estate. It has been confirmed that she died from blunt force trauma to the back of the head. Her body was then strung up from the rafters.

There are no signs of sexual assault; her clothing was undisturbed, but her hair had been cut short and most was left at the scene but we believe from the quantity found, that some was taken, presumably by her killer. As some of you know, she was the former wife of DI Phil Treloar and, to our knowledge, she was last seen alive by him as he was leaving his property, a converted barn on the estate, at 13:15. That property is approximately a mile and a half from the mine. She had visited him driving her Mini Cooper which was found this morning at a garage on the B3311 just north of Gulval.

She had been staying with her parents who have a cottage near Morvah. Again, most of you know that Amy was a highly successful international model who lived in Hampstead. We understand that she had been receiving disturbing calls and packages recently in London. Yesterday she told Phil Treloar about it and this morning he gave Sam here the details. Sam, over to you.'

'Well it seems that Amy had a stalker. She had been receiving hang-up calls, recorded snippets of music, and strange objects delivered to her house, all posted in London, for about twelve weeks. So it's a possibility that she was followed or traced here from London and confronted yesterday for whatever reason.'

'What about other possibilities?' asked Colin Matthews.

'Well,' said Tom, 'obviously there's the landowner Edmund Maddox, his son Dylan who has been working at the mine site, or someone staying at the Lower Farm campsite or holiday cottages, a local or passing stranger. Early days Col.'

'What about the DI?' piped up a voice from the back. Sam glared at the offender.

'Well apart from the fact that he is a fellow officer and a good friend,' said Tom, 'he was with family at the time of death, several miles away from the crime scene.'

'How about someone else she knew down here?' asked Colin, 'she grew up down here as I recall. Could it be someone from the past with a grudge?'

'Well I'll be checking with her parents to see if she mentioned anybody who falls into that category. You and Luke have been back up at the mine this morning Col, anything new?'

'Well I think we can minimize the chance of a random encounter. It's very remote up there and well fenced off with tons of warning signs about trespass and unstable buildings. It seems highly unlikely some wandering psychopath just happened by.'

'I agree,' said Sam, 'and Phil says he had warned her about visiting the place. She had been there on Saturday and she had encountered Dylan Maddox. Phil told her to keep away because Maddox doesn't like people on his land. Sorry Col, I interrupted, you carry on.'

'Thanks Sam. Right, the rope was standard stuff you could by in any DIY, but it was new, it hadn't been lying around up there for months so somebody took it there on purpose. We found Amy's bag on the ground where the witness Pixie Armstrong says she left it. Everything you'd expect: cards, money, phone, girl stuff. No keys; her keys were left in the ignition of the Mini. But we've only scratched the surface, excuse the pun. It's a huge site: uneven ground, pits and shafts, collapsed buildings, piles of rubble, building supplies, we've left a team up there and Luke and I are heading back after this.'

'What about these Maddox blokes?' asked a new voice.

'Sam?' Tom said.

'Yes, I spoke Edmund and Dylan this morning. There's also a third Maddox: son Rees, but he's away in Norfolk at the moment and that's been confirmed by the local force who spoke to him in person. I spoke with Edmund and Dylan at Lost Farm which is Edmund's home. Edmund was alone at the farm with just his dog at the time, but he did receive a call from a neighbouring farmer on the landline and he was talking to him at the relevant time; I confirmed it. He seems genuinely upset and a really nice man. Dylan, the son however, was very strange. He was extremely, disproportionately upset, kept veering from tears to anger. But he has a firm alibi: he was in the Morvah Arms all afternoon playing darts. I think he's weird but I don't think he killed Amy.'

'With them standing stones, The Dancers, so close, maybe it was some sort of occult, ritual sacrifice by Satanists, what with cutting her hair of an' all,' said a young local PC.

'You've been reading too many Ochre Pengelly novels mate,' said Tom to general laughter. One of Ochre's most successful teen novels, a tale of vampire, smuggler pirates pitted against a virginal, pagan sect had featured much steamy action at a stone circle.

'Well, could be something like that,' the blushing PC insisted, 'only it's too open and exposed up at the stones and they wanted a hidden place.'

'Enough already Vyvyan, it'll be werewolf aliens next, let's stay focused.' Tom said to more laughter.

'Could it have been a woman?' asked Luke Calloway.

'Now that is a very good question Luke,' said Tom, 'and yes, physically, it could have been a woman. Amy didn't weigh much. The only local Maddox woman is Hope, Dylan's wife, but she couldn't have done it; she was working in the farm shop all afternoon. Could have been Pixie Armstrong, but Sam and I don't think so. No reason this stalker couldn't be a woman either, but I think we're looking at a man for the stalking and the killing. Gut feeling to be honest but the stats back it up. Chances are it's a man. Sam do you want to run through what Amy told Phil about the business in London?'

So Sam relayed the story of the unsolicited parcels and the phone messages as Amy had told to Phil. The meeting broke up with actions allocated and people headed out leaving Sam and Tom the last in the room.

'Do you think this is a one off Tom, do you think it was all about Amy?' Sam asked.

'Yes Sam I do. I think it's the bloke from London who followed her or found her down here and took his chance. How likely is it that she'd have a stalker and a separate killer on her case at the same time? No I think it's one man and so does Frosty. She's going through the proper channels with the Met … ' he paused then added, 'Phil thinks it's one man too.'

'You've spoken to him?'

'Yeah …' Tom busied himself packing his briefcase.

'Tom is there something you're not telling me?' Sam asked slowly.

'As if Sam, as if,' he replied with a smile.

As they walked together to their cars, Sam's attention was drawn to the cries, laughter and splashing coming from the open glass doors to the swimming pool.

'I don't suppose there's any news on Tamsin?' she asked.

'No nothing. It's just a waiting game I reckon. Unless

someone spots the boat or sees York and the girl somewhere, we'll just have to wait for him to bring her back.'

'I heard Winters let the Thomases go home.'

'Well he'd done nothing much wrong and she's guilty of being a crap mother and a bitter wife so what could Frosty do? I doubt the CPS will go for much beyond wasting police time. The Warrens don't want to pursue it.'

'Why ever not, I don't get it?'

'In their minds Lily wasn't harmed; in fact she had a good time and he left her safe when she said she wanted to go home. They don't want to put Lily through a court case, they just want to forget it and move on. I can understand that.'

'But Kate Thomas will get away with it if nobody presses charges.'

'Yes but her husband is onto her now so I reckon she'll pay one way or another.'

'I suppose so. I just feel sorry for Tamsin.'

'Well she's still got doting daddy.'

'Yes I suppose … OK we've got Amy's killer to catch now. Do you want me to come with you to see the Angoves?'

'Yes I think that's a great idea. We can call in at Cove Farm on the way.'

'What, to check Phil's alibi?' Sam asked aghast.

'Shit no. I want to buy some herb plants for my greenhouse.'

Twenty Nine

When Edmund and Tegwen Maddox had bought Lost Farm Estate in the early eighties it had been a run down, neglected collection of buildings, fields and moorland grazing with the main farm and two smaller farm holdings: Lower and Higher Farms. They had moved from a farm in the Black Mountains near Crickhowell in Wales which had been in Tegwen's family for five generations, but she had decided she wanted to be near the sea and somewhere less spartan and warmer.

Unlike the warm and colourful kitchen at Cove Farm, the large kitchen at Lost Farm was gloomy and chilly even on this bright early summer's day. The walls were painted an unfortunate pale green, almost institutional, and the furniture was heavy dark wood brought from the Welsh Black Mountain properties of Tegwen's childhood. Since his wife's death from cancer some fifteen years previously little effort had been made to decorate or garnish the house. Tegwen herself, with her chapel roots, had had simple, austere tastes; she had not been one for frivolous ornament and the room had remained much as when she had died.

That lunchtime Edmund was sitting at the table with a solitary lunch of bread and cheese. Owain, the large mongrel dog, his constant companion, was stretched out in front of the range sleeping and the room, indeed the entire house, was silent apart from the ticking of the grandfather clock.

Edmund was thinking about this dreadful business with Amy Angove. He had never particularly liked the girl but she had been harmless. But Dylan … well Dylan had been obsessed with her when they were all in their teens. He had a breakdown of sorts and had to go into residential therapy for a while. Edmund was thinking about Dylan a lot recently.

When the boys had reached their twenties, Edmund had handed control, but critically not ownership, of the two smaller holdings on the estate to his sons Dylan and Rees. It was understood that they would inherit the land and buildings on his death, with daughter Megan inheriting the larger Lost Farm house itself. As she had no interest whatsoever in farming, the land associated with Lost Farm was to be split between the boys.

But Edmund was beginning to regret giving his sons control over the farms. Not Rees, Rees was thriving at Higher Farm, following in his father's footsteps with his love of cattle and his prize Devon herd, but Dylan, what to do about Dylan? What was wrong with the boy? He was increasingly spending all his time at the derelict mine leaving Hope to deal with the holiday lettings, the campsite and the farm shop, never mind baby Bethan. Even this new café project had fallen by the wayside. He would have to speak to Dylan … again. Perhaps it was time to get him some help … again.

He couldn't understand why Dylan was so angry about the Lost Farm Barn sale. It wasn't as if the barn had formed part of the Lower Farm holdings, if anything, it was adjacent to Higher Farm land and would eventually have gone to Rees. It would never have been Dylan's. Why was the boy so mad? He never used to be so … bitter and hateful. He had taken his mother's death badly but so had they all. Megan and Rees had grieved but they had got beyond it. Why couldn't Dylan?

Was it even that? It seemed to be getting worse and the business over the barn sale To Phil Treloar was an obsession with him. Edmund needed to speak to Hope. Perhaps it was time to consider some sort of counselling. The situation was becoming a real concern and Edmund was starting to harbour fears for Hope and Bethan. Surely he wouldn't harm them.

Edmund had seen the gas mask at Phil's party; he knew it must have been Dylan who had left it there, he himself had been with the boy when he found it in an outbuilding years before. What had possessed him to keep it for all this time? What had possessed him to leave it in the courtyard, but worse still, what had possessed him to leave Bethan alone to do it? God almighty.

It had been such a lovely evening. He had offered to babysit so Dylan could go, but he had known that was a vain hope on his part. Once he had arrived he was secretly glad at his son's obstinacy. She had been there and she had been smiling: his Inés.

He had loved her at first sight: a hot Friday lunchtime in June that first year they had been in Cornwall. It was in the courtyard at the Tinner's Arms in Zennor. He had met Jago Treloar at a farmer's get together of some sort, he had long forgotten what, and Jago had invited him to meet for a drink in the pub. He would never forget walking round from the car park and seeing Jago with this small, delicate, exotic creature.

His Tegwen had been a large woman with a broad open face and a buck-toothed smile. She favoured floral cotton dresses in the summer and chunky cork sandals; she wore heavy perfume and her long blonde hair in ponytails. Inés was dressed in a plain navy blue sleeveless dress and cream espadrilles; her black hair was swept back in an elegant chignon and she smelled of pepper, a natural, earthy, sensuous smell he could still recapture. He was smitten.

Nobody knew: not Tegwen, not Jago, especially not Inés. Oh, they were great friends, more than friends, both she and Jago. She had been a tremendous support when Tegwen was dying and afterwards when the guilt and grief had overwhelmed him for months, and he in turn had been supporting her since Jago had gone. He could speak with her about anything, anything except his true feelings and the heavy burden of the secret he kept for his best friend: Jago Treloar was alive and Edmund knew where he was.

End of October, the previous year

On the plane back he was down. At least they were on the same flight, wasn't expecting that. Hadn't seen her since the Chinese. He'd left just after her, didn't see her outside, couldn't find her in the hotel bars. No chance for anything and couldn't think of a way to get in to her room. Spent a couple of hours going through the pics and video from the Chinese, cutting, cropping, taking out source data. Best three were ready to go. Wanted to see her face when she got them; they were loaded and ready on the prepaid. She was right at the front and he was near the back.

He'd got some good pictures of her in the check-in queue though. Was chuffed about that, went through them on the plane. Used the selfie stick, standing by the Birmingham check in queue. She wore a scarf, long, black and white stripes, NUFC in black on the white bits, wondered how she'd got it. Didn't match the yellow dress, or jacket, or bright yellow high heels, or her, she looked knackered.

He was way behind her off the plane; she hadn't checked anything in so she wasn't at the carousel waiting, so he went straight out. Saw her climb into a taxi just as he came out the doors to get one for himself. 'Shit,' he said, 'Fuck,' stood there wondering if he should run to the taxi rank, jump in and say, 'Follow that cab,' but by then it had gone. Decided to go home and find out where to.

Tripping off in the back of the taxi, he was miles away, and brought back when the taxi went over rumble strips in the road, on a bridge. A big blue on yellow sign caught his eye, rotating, on the left in the distance, he realised it was an IKEA shop, 'Quick, over there, that way,' he said pointing, and the car veered and turned off what he realised must have been the A4 coming up to the Hammersmith Flyover.

The driver had found it easily enough, it was massive, but had taken a bit of persuading to wait, a £50 note grabbed his attention and the taxi was still there when he came back half an hour later, smiling, and said, 'Right, now Tottenham Court Road please.'

The driver was well pleased an hour after that when he'd got out in Islington and handed over six more £50 notes and told him to keep the change. 'Only after he'd scanned them to check though,' *he thought as he walked to his front door.*

The plan was coming together, 'Just hope the fucking wheels don't come off like last time,' he thought as he took his purchases out of their bags. Two picture frames from the white with yellow and blue logo IKEA bag. A bubble pack stuck to a card that had 'ultra thin, flat, solid-state data recorder complete with four input ports, transmitter and integral flat military-life battery,' printed on it, and an ID wallet pack from the plain brown Eurospy bag.

It took longer than he'd thought, but by nine o'clock he was ready to go, everything that needed testing was tested and working, everything that needed printing had been printed and looked good, and everything that needed assembling had been put together and looked the part.

The picture frame had kicked it off. He'd been thinking in the taxi about the images he'd made using the picture of mum and dad and her on the wall, whether or not he'd use them, and how and when. About getting cameras set up in her flat and where and how.

The rumble strips had bought him back and then he saw the IKEA sign and remembered seeing something like the mum and dad frame, plain, black, wood, on the IKEA website when Dan had been looking for a frame to put a picture of Jodi and her in, for a present. He knew he was right about the frame, he'd seen it often enough, close up, when he'd been working on the images, 'how different can picture frames be anyway?' he thought. He didn't know the size though.

The shop had four on display and he knew it couldn't have been either of the smallest two, so he'd bought the two biggest and reprinted the original picture in highest quality onto photo paper, in two sizes.

He had dismantled the motion activated mini camera kit he'd installed upstairs to get the bits he needed then drilled small holes, three, into each frame to take the pin-hole lenses he knew would be perfect. Then he fitted the lenses and smeared them with thin matt black varnish so they wouldn't show, three in each frame.

Finally he trimmed the lens cables so they'd fit to the camera, which he'd already fitted to the transmitter and mounted as an assembly onto thick card. The card would be fixed with glue to whichever frame was the right size, but for the test he connected it up to the smallest frame and stuck the card to it with Sellotape.

He switched the camera and data recorder on, stood the

frame up against the wall of the kitchen and walked in front of it three times at different distances, then went outside with his phone, to the other side of the park, over two hundred metres away.

He switched his phone on, loaded the transmitter receive app and twenty seconds later pictures appeared as thumbnails on the screen. 'Jesus! Fucking brilliant,' he said, and, 'incredible,' as he started clicking on the thumbnails to enlarge the pictures. There were five. He'd set the camera to decide automatically when to take the pictures and which ones to take, depending on distance and which lens was in the best position when the motion was detected.

Then the transmitter had detected the app on the phone when it was switched on and sent the pictures to it. 'Brilliant, just don't forget the superglue to fix the card once you know which frame you need,' he was thinking as he walked back to the house.

The ID had been easy. Just copied the logo from the Cavendish Cycle Courier's website onto card, cut it out and pushed it behind the clear plastic front of the ID wallet. Then he'd stuck a passport sized picture of himself near the top of a licence he'd designed with the crest of the Royal Borough of Kensington and Chelsea at the top, and a courier number and the firm's name underneath. It was signed by himself and Malcolm Cavendish, the owner, confirming that he worked for the firm; he pushed it behind the plastic cover inside the wallet, and there it was.

A small clipboard with a printed form with the Cavendish Cycle Courier logo and address across the top, and names and addresses and dates in columns, with receipt signatures in the received column of some of them had been next. Her name and address was third from the bottom. Last was the card that he was delivering, from the Rome office that Luigi worked in, apologising for his behaviour and thanking her for resolving their problems, and hoping they would see her soon.

It was in a white A4 envelope with a picture of the Coliseum in the top left corner, the green white and red striped Italian flag in the top right, the Company name and logo in the bottom right corner, and her name and home address in the middle of the envelope on a label.

Just needed to know when he could take it. Probably an evening, maybe the weekend, soon. In the morning he rang her office with the voice changer on the 'posh woman,' setting, asked for Chris

Trent. The receptionist said 'I'm sorry but she's off sick today.' He told her he would call back tomorrow, ended the call, pumped the air and shouted 'YES!'

He was already dressed in the courier kit, good to go, either to her place or to the courier place. He got everything together, got on his bike, went to Collingwood Crescent and cycled round it. Saw uniform guy behind the desk through the glass door, but not uniform guy in the kiosk. Cycled past the gap at the end of the red and white pole and down the car park entry ramp, past the empty kiosk and leaned the bike behind the pillar near the lifts, between two cars.

He walked to the lift on the left because the 'CP' car park sign above the door was lit up, taking the clipboard and ID out of his shoulder bag on the way, pressed the call button which opened the doors and pressed 3 when he was inside and a minute later we was outside 315, heart thumping, stomach churning, waiting for the doorbell to be answered, with his ID at the ready.

'Who's there, what do you want?' she asked. Sounded as though she was struggling to speak. 'Delivery,' he said, and held the ID wallet, up to the spy hole. 'Hang on,' she said, ' Oh get back you little .....' then, 'Oh bloody hell, what a fucking nightmare,' he heard from inside the door just before it opened slightly.

'Hang on, I'll put the cats outside,' she said, and he walked quietly in. She wore a grey sweat shirt, he could see finger marks on her neck, jeans and pink slippers; her hair was tied back and she had the little cat under an arm and was moving the big one towards the slightly open balcony door with her feet, slowly.

He quickly sussed it was the small frame he needed once he got to the living room. There wasn't time to use the superglue and he hoped the Sellotape would hold as he quickly swapped the picture from his bag with the one on the wall, switching it on before he hung it up. Then he took the card and the clipboard out of the shoulder bag. She closed the door when the cats were on the balcony.

'CHRIST what are you doing? I said wait!' she croaked when she had turned round, and, 'Jesus, you made me jump,' as he took out the card and showed it to her. 'Bastards,' she whispered to herself. He was looking at the cats on the balcony and she was opening the card when he said, 'Can you sign for it please and I'll leave you to it?'

She ignored him, was staring at the card, opening then closing it, looking at the inside then the outside, inside, outside. 'What ...?' she said. He was holding out the clipboard with a pen. 'I don't believe it, they wouldn't do ...... never!' she said, 'that's not ...... don't believe it ... must be the Newcastle bunch... haven't even started on THEIR shit yet.' She was struggling to speak, 'Look!' she said, holding the envelope towards him, 'fucking flag's the wrong way round ...... THEY wouldn't do that, and this envelope ......'

'Shit,' he was thinking as he saw her staring at him. Did she recognize him? He moved towards her, held up the clipboard again, quickly, he wanted her signature, he wanted to get out, and she took two steps back, eyes scared, and walked backwards into the low table, hitting it with one calf then the other. She sat quickly, it was a narrow table, only a small apartment, and the momentum took her further backwards and her feet lifted up and she rolled over the table and onto the floor, back of her head first, it was loud. Legs stayed on the table. Still.

'Jesus! Now what?' he asked. 'Fuck!' Her eyes were shut, she wasn't moving, didn't know how to check for a pulse, saw a cushion on the sofa and grabbed it and put it over her nose and mouth, after a while her left foot moved, her hands flapped and he felt her head shake, for a few seconds, then nothing.

He put the clipboard and pen back in his shoulder bag, the cushion back on the sofa, picked up the card and envelope and put them in his bag, swapped the picture frames again, looked round, looked at her then his black gloves and went, 'Yeah! Right. Christ!'

He stood and stared at her, at the pony tail, thinking. A thought came to him and he rushed to the open-plan kitchen at the end of the room, looked through drawers until he found some scissors, rushed back to her and cut off the pony tail, just above the band. Looked at it, thinking, was about to put it in his shoulder bag, thought again, went to the bathroom and pushed it through the lid of a small red swing bin. Put the scissors back in the drawer, went back to her and took a photo with his phone, head shot.

Then he looked at the balcony doors, looked at the cat flap and didn't understand why they hadn't used it, then went quickly to the front door and let himself out. He got the lift down to the car park, onto his bike and cycled past the kiosk, waved to the reappeared uniform guy, up the out-ramp and past the end of the red and white pole and was back home in less than thirty minutes.

Thirty

Peter and Susannah Angove lived in a small cottage just off the B3306 between Morvah and Pendeen. They had moved to Holly Cottage when Peter had given up both working on a farm near St Just and the tied cottage that went with the job. Amy had bought it for them. It was a pretty little place with a large specimen of the eponymous tree in the front garden. As Sam and Tom Grigg walked up the path to the front door she reflected on how the Angoves would be glad of the shelter that tree offered from the prying eyes camped out in a lay-by just back down the main road.

'Hello Sarge,' the door was opened by DC Fiona Sinclair, acting as liaison officer again.

'Hello Fi. Everything OK here?' Sam said.

'Yes everything's quiet. Mark Angove, Amy's younger brother has just arrived from Plymouth and her other brother, Matthew, has just popped home to change; he's local, lives in Pendeen and he's been here all night.'

'And you?'

'Oh I went home about eleven and got back just after eight. They're all at a loss. They didn't know anybody who would want to harm Amy and they're horrified that it should happen down here. Shall I make some tea?'

'That would be great Fi,' said Tom, 'could you just do the introductions first?'

'Of course, it's this way.'

The small sitting room was filled with floral prints: wallpaper, curtains, cushions, paintings, baskets of dried flowers; it was overpowering to Sam who favoured simplicity on décor. A miniature, older version of Amy Angove, with huge blue eyes and glossy blonde curls, was sitting on a sofa beside a good looking young man who was obviously brother Mark. Peter Angove was standing with his back to the fireplace. He was a tall, hefty man with the weather-beaten face of one who has spent much of his life outdoors, he looked physically powerful but his eyes were puffy and red-rimmed and his hands were trembling slightly. Fi Sinclair made the introductions and withdrew to make tea.

'Is there any news?' Mark asked.

'No, nothing I'm afraid,' said Tom quietly, 'we just wanted to say how very sorry we all are, and to have a chat to get a picture of how Amy's been spending her time down here the last few days. That's all we're here for, we don't want to intrude.'

'Where's Félipe?' asked Mrs Angove, 'why isn't he here? Félipe will find this monster, I know it.'

'Hush now Mum, Phil can't be involved, you know he told dad that last night on the phone. He's a witness. He knew Amy and he was with her yesterday.'

'Félipe wouldn't hurt her!' his mother cried out in anguish and burst into tears.

Peter Angove moved to kneel at his wife's feet and wiped the tears from her face.

'Nobody thinks Phil's hurt her Susie, nobody thinks that, do they?' he turned to stare hard at Tom and Sam wanting confirmation.

'Absolutely not Mrs Angove,' Sam said firmly, 'but your son is right that DI Treloar has to stand back from the investigation. But I can assure you that his team, the Major Crime Team, is working day and night to find out what happened to Amy and who hurt her.'

'Are you in that team then?' Peter asked.

'Yes Mr Angove I am,' Sam replied, 'and Sergeant Grigg is seconded to us for his expert local knowledge.'

Tom Grigg looked at Sam with a raised eyebrow but turned to nod solemnly at the Angoves.

'Please find a seat won't you?' said Mark getting up to move two wheelback chairs from the gate-legged table and face them towards the sofa. Sam and Tom sat down.

'She should never have left Félipe, she should never have gone to London, she should be living down here with beautiful babies, happy and safe. I rue the day she met that wretched man from the agency; I knew no good would come of it, I knew it …' she tailed off, wringing the floral handkerchief in her hands.

'Now Susannah you must stop all that. Amy loved her job, she loved her life. You must help these good people now,' he added softly, 'can you do that my angel, can you do that for our girl?'

'Yes of course Pete; I'll try,' she replied with a deep sigh.

At that moment Fi appeared in the doorway with a loaded tea tray which she placed on the table before leaving again.

After Susannah Angove had served everybody and taken her seat Tom opened his notebook.

'Perhaps we could start with a picture of the last few days? I understand Amy arrived on Thursday evening?'

'Yes,' said Susannah breaking into a beautiful smile, her face the image of her daughter, 'yes it was lovely and a complete surprise. We were at the Treloar party up at Félipe's. We weren't expecting her at all, but I'd told her we were going as usual and I mentioned that it was going to be at Félipe's this year and she knew where that was. Didn't I see you there?' she looked sharply at Sam who nodded. 'Well, we were as surprised as anyone when she burst in dripping wet; always one for an entrance our Amy!' she stopped speaking and a single tear rolled down her face. Peter took over.

'Yes well, we left about half past ten and Amy was still there. She rang the next morning to say she'd stayed over and that she'd be back for lunch.' He looked at his wife. 'Susie thought perhaps she was getting back with Phil but I told her not to get her hopes up.'

Sam cleared her throat feeling, absurdly, uncomfortable. Luckily Mark spoke up:

'No Mum, that was never going to happen, it was long in the past between them.'

Susannah frowned at her son and spoke again.

'Anyway, she was back for lunch as promised and we had a lovely time: she told me all about her last trip to New York and how she was off to Italy. It was just lovely,' she stared into the distance.

'I understand she went back up to Lost Farm Barn on Saturday,' Sam said.

'Yes that's right. I told her it was a waste of time; I told her Félipe would be busy with those missing girls; I said you'd want your best people on something like that, but she insisted. She could be very determined.'

It was clear to Sam that Susannah Angove still carried a torch for her former son-in-law.

'So when she was gone so long I thought perhaps I was wrong and Félipe was there after all, but when she did get back, she told me he was out and she'd gone for a walk; it is lovely up there, and she'd bumped into that Dylan Maddox.'

It was clear from her words and her tone that she did not

hold Dylan Maddox in the same high esteem as Treloar; everyone noticed and Mark spoke up:

'Dylan's all right Mum, once you get to know him, he's just a bit ... intense. Good darts' player.'

'Oh for heaven's sake Mark, you don't remember what he was like when they were all at school, you were too young.'

'Was there a problem Mrs Angove?' Sam asked.

'Yes Sergeant there was a problem. Dylan Maddox was obsessed with Amy; he mooned around her, sent her presents and cards, hung around at the farm where we lived then. It was very disturbing. Amy just laughed about it, but we were concerned.'

'Did you speak to anyone about this?' Tom asked.

'We didn't have to in the end,' Peter replied, 'she took up with Phil and it all stopped.'

Susannah snorted: 'At least he had the sense to realise that he didn't stand a chance against Félipe. But for a while we were worried where it was heading. It was getting ... scary. You'd call it stalking now and he'd be put away for it.'

'Now then Susie,' Peter said, 'I admit it was a bit strange, but the boy's mother was ill remember. It can't have been an easy time for the lad at home.'

'Yes, I admit it was hard for him but it still wasn't ... healthy. And I'll tell you another thing; I never understood why a lovely, sensible girl like Hope Pascoe would want to marry him. Still, they do have a lovely baby, that Bethan.'

Everyone was quiet for a moment and Sam wondered at the ways in which grief affects people. Peter was sad, calm and dignified; Mark looked awkward and uncomfortable and Susannah, well she was veering from one extreme emotion to the next, almost manic.

Tom broke the silence:

'So Amy went back to Lost Farm Barn yesterday morning to see Phil.'

'Yes she did,' said Susannah, 'and why would she keep going up there to see him if there was nothing between?'

Tom and Sam exchanged a look and Sam nodded almost imperceptibly to indicate that he should give them the true reason for Amy's persistence. They would find out soon enough and it was better that the truth of the matter came from them.

'We believe she wanted to talk to Phil about some problems

she'd been having in London,' he said.

'She had been receiving odd parcels through the post and troubling phone calls,' Sam explained.

'What, what?' Susannah cried, 'she's said nothing to us. It's that Maddox boy again, it must be.'

'No, no we don't believe it was anyone local because all the packages were posted in London. But we will be speaking to everyone of course including Mr Maddox.'

'But it must be him; she was found on his land, at his horrid mine.'

'Yes Mum but that's right next to Phil's place and Dad told me she was going on about that old story Ochre Pengelly told about the hangings there; she was fascinated by the place.'

'It wasn't Dylan Maddox who killed your daughter Mrs Angove,' Sam said gently, 'he was in the Morvah Arms playing darts yesterday afternoon. We've confirmed that. He didn't do it.' She needed Susannah Angove to move on from Dylan Maddox.

'Did Amy meet up with anyone else over the last few days?' Tom asked.

Susannah Angove was fighting with her emotions and her husband answered.

'Well she saw Matthew of course, our other son. He lives just down in Pendeen. He came over on Saturday evening with his girlfriend, Poppy. And of course she was going to see a lot of people at our neighbour's barbeque yesterday lunchtime, but ...' At that moment Susannah burst into tears and hurried from the room.

'Sorry about that,' Peter mumbled as Matthew chased after her.

'No need to be sorry Peter,' Tom said, 'naturally she's very upset, and I'm the one who's sorry that we have to trouble you at this bloody awful time for you all.'

'Thanks. We know you're only doing what you have to, to find the bastard who hurt our Amy, and we all want that. Can we help with anything else?'

The door opened and Mark walked back into the stuffy room and sat back down on the sofa without a word.

Sam was glad of the distraction. This was the part she hated; raking through the sad, abandoned belongings of the recently dead; things once treasured and valued, rendered meaningless, surplus and redundant.

'Would it be possible for us to see Amy's belongings, the things she brought with her, just in case there's anything at all that might help us?' she asked gently.

'Yes of course. I packed them all up this morning. I didn't want Susie upsetting herself looking at them, and well, we've only the one spare room and we'll need that for Mark now. Will I fetch the bags? You can take them with you; I'd prefer that, as long as we get them back.'

'Of course, of course,' said Sam trying not to sound too relieved. 'We'll take good care of them and get them back to you as soon as we can.'

'Mark, can you fetch those two bags out the back bedroom?' Peter said, and Mark left the room again.

'Do you think you'll get him? What are the chances if it's a total stranger, just some mad, evil bastard? At least he didn't touch her, you know what I mean, her mother's glad of that.'

'We will do our utmost Peter,' said Tom, 'and I am personally going to be speaking to an excellent senior officer in the Metropolitan force, a bloke I used to work with up there to get him on the case at that end. Don't worry, we'll not let up till we have him. I have daughters myself and I can only begin to imagine how you're feeling mate.'

Peter Angove's eyes filled with tears and he turned his back as Mark opened the door.

'I've left the bags by the front door,' he said holding the door open.

Sam and Tom stood up and shook hands with the two Angove men.

'Please say our goodbyes to your mother for us,' she said to Mark, 'we'll be off now but Fi will stay for a while. We'll just have a word with her and be on our way.' Sam studiously avoided the expression "leave you in peace" on these occasions recognising how trite and inappropriate it sounded. As they walked to the door Tom called Fi who emerged from a room at the back of the house, presumably the kitchen which was her room of choice when on family liaison duties.

They left the house, stepping into the warm, sunny garden with its neat flowerbeds. It felt to Sam as if they were breaking free from thick dusty cobwebs; it was good to be in the open air, able to

231

breathe freely again.

'Right Fi,' said Tom, 'keep your eyes and ears open, especially for any strange post or phone calls. Anything out of place, call me.

'OK Gov,' she said turning back into the cottage. And so they left heading back to Lost Farm estate to report back, albeit off the record, to Treloar.

Whilst Sam and Tom had been talking with the Angove family, Colin Mathews and Luke Calloway had indeed returned to the mine. They parked at the farm shop which was closed, much to Dylan's disgust. He had argued that there would be hordes of people coming to see where Amy had died so they might as well make some money out of them, but for once Hope had prevailed, and when Luke and Colin arrived, the only vehicles in the car park were those of the police and the forensics team who were gathered to discuss their progress.

Luke and Colin donned their protective suits, Colin lifted a Coast HP17 flashlight from the rear seat of the car, and they headed off across the field towards the mine. Dylan had reluctantly removed the padlock on the gate and the path to the engine house was now well-trodden and clearly visible from all the foot traffic of the past 24 hours.

As Colin stood in the opening to the engine house, gazing at the rafters, picturing the scene as Pixie Armstrong had come across it, Luke walked around the outside of the building. Colin heard him calling:

'Col, what's that place over there?'

Colin emerged from the gloom and walked round to join his colleague who was pointing across the open plateau to a smaller building.

'Looks like some kind of oven,' he added.

'That's because it is. It's a calciner. It's where they used to burn the ore to extract the impurities; mainly arsenic.'

'Has it been checked? Only it would be a good spot to spy on anyone visiting the engine house.'

'Well, it was on the plan, but no harm in us taking a look.'

The two men strolled across the open ground and climbed through an opening. Inside, all the workings and machinery had been removed and the place was a hollow shell. Luke clambered back out. Again, Colin heard him calling:

'Col, come out here a minute will you?'

Colin found him behind the calciner staring at the structure.

'What is it Luke?'

'What is wrong with this building?'

'Well it's falling down and contaminated with God knows what …'

'No. I mean the building itself. Look at it closely.'

Colin looked. The rear did look to be in better shape, the brickwork cleaner and more solid than the other walls.

'Well,' said Colin, 'I suppose it's not as derelict, but there are no openings, so it's not been so exposed to the elements. The weather hasn't eaten away at the fabric so much.'

'OK, follow me right round and back to the entrance, but keep an eye on the structure.'

Colin obliged and they found themselves back at the entrance.

'Right …' said Colin.

'OK, now back inside,' said Luke clambering through. Colin followed.

'Now, look around in here.'

Colin was losing patience. 'What's your point Luke?'

'It's too small,' Luke said with a grin, 'I know granite slabs are thick, but even so, this interior is just way too small for the size of this building.'

'Luke you're right,' said Colin, 'we're missing something. Let's check these walls.'

Treloar had wanted to go in to work, but Winters wouldn't let him near the Amy Angove investigation because of his personal relationship with the victim, so he was still on the leave he had arranged to take for the May Day party and the following two weeks. His plan had been to complete the decking and planting at the rear of Lost Farm Barn, and it was there, laying sand, that Sam and Tom Grigg found him that evening.

'Well mate,' said Tom as he and Sam walked out from the kitchen, 'you've certainly got a fan in Susannah Angove.'

Sam felt herself flush as she caught sight of Treloar, dressed only in cut-off Levi's and heavy workboots. He was sweating and dusty, but the physical effort of the construction work of the last few years was evident in his muscled torso. Get a grip woman, she thought. Treloar pushed his shovel into the pile of sand and removed his work gloves. He crossed to join them at the open kitchen door.

'Yeah, Susie always had a soft spot for me,' he said wistfully.

'But she sure as hell don't like Dylan Maddox,' Tom added.

'No. Dylan was a pain when we were younger. He had a massive crush on Amy and it was getting a bit out of hand, but when she and I got together all that stopped. He went away for a while; some residential course I think. Christ, it's years ago now, but Susie has a long memory.'

'She thinks Dylan killed Amy,' Sam said starkly.

'What?' Treloar laughed. 'Bollocks. No fucking way. The man still has a huge crush on Amy, even now, but he's happy with Hope and he adores Bethan. No, Susie's just distraught. It wasn't Dylan … I suppose you've checked?'

'Yes. He was playing darts in the pub apparently,' Sam said.

'Sounds likely. He's a star player at the Morvah Arms; team captain. How are the Angoves? I spoke to Peter last night. Is Mark down?'

'Yes. They're as you'd expect,' Sam replied.

'We've got Amy's stuff in the car,' said Tom to Treloar, 'do you want a look?'

'Sure. Bring it in the kitchen. I'll make coffee.'

'Tea for me please,' Tom called as he walked back through the kitchen to fetch the bags.

'Winters will go spare if she finds out you're involved in this Phil,' Sam said quietly.

'Tough,' he replied. 'Look Sam, if you don't want to be a part of this, why don't you wait for Tom in the sitting room?'

'For Christ' sake,' she cried out in anger, 'don't you know me at all? Of course I understand, I'm just chalking up a warning: we need to be careful.'

Treloar lifted a hand to punch her lightly on the shoulder. 'That's my girl,' he said with a broad smile.

Colin picked up the torch and turned it on. Switching the powerful beam from spot to flood, he illuminated the rear wall of the calciner. There were lengths of reclaimed timber stacked against the wall. Luke walked across and went to move a plank. It was heavier than expected and he repositioned his feet for extra purchase. To his astonishment, rather than a single length, a section of wood shifted.

'Here, Col, bring the torch.'

'What is it?'

Luke pulled at the wood and a panel of overlapping, nailed-together lengths moved away to reveal a roughly built wall inexpertly cobbled together from old brick, new brick and granite slabs.

'Help me shift this lot,' Luke said grabbing another section.

The two men moved four more rough wood panels to reveal more ugly brickwork and an old metal door.

'Jesus, what is this? Luke asked breathlessly.

'Let's find out,' Colin replied, grasping the door handle.

Behind the makeshift wall was a small room which stretched back to the true rear of the calciner. There was a camp bed with a folded single duvet and pillow in incongruous covers featuring cartoon ducks, obviously meant for a child; faded and worn; much washed, much loved. On the floor against the wall were two buckets: one large yellow plastic, one shiny zinc metal. Next to them was an orange rectangular plastic washing up bowl containing a beach towel. A well-used Tilley storm lamp stood on an upturned crate. A second crate contained assorted enamel plates and mugs, cheap cutlery and an Oral B toothbrush in its wrapping.

'Look,' said Luke pointing to a corner.

Colin turned to look and there on the ground was a coil of rope exactly like that used to hang Amy Angove.

'Fuck,' said Colin, a man not known to use such language. 'Run back and get the team. We need to process this place now. And find out who checked Dylan Maddox's alibi. And check it again, yourself.'

'What is this place?' Luke asked, looking around.

'Looks like a cell to me. I reckon Maddox was planning on holding someone captive in here. It's too grim to be a personal space. Would you want to hang out here? No, this is not a good place.'

'You think it's Maddox?'

Colin was examining the rear wall, where small scraps of

tape and white photo paper had been left behind when photographs had been torn down in a hurry. He picked up a photograph that had fallen behind a crate: Amy Angove. He held it out to Luke, 'Don't you?'

Luke nodded slowly. 'Should I call Sam and Sergeant Grigg?'

'Do it. And Luke?' he called to the retreating back.

'Yes Col?'

'Well done. Spotting that this building wasn't right was good work. You'll make a detective yet.'

'There's nothing here,' said Treloar.

'There's several thousand pounds worth of clothing and shoes here,' said Sam stunned, 'let alone this makeup. And all this was just for a long weekend.'

'Now then Sergeant,' said Tom grinning, 'we are looking at tools of the trade.'

'Fair point Tom,' Sam replied, 'but Phil's right; there's nothing here to help us find the stalker.'

'No,' said Treloar, 'she told me she'd left all the stuff he sent and the phone with the music recordings back in London. I really need to get up there.'

'Have you heard from John Forbes?' Tom asked gently.

'Not directly. But he spoke to Doc Tremayne after the post mortem and he called and filled me in. I know the details and I'm all right, just ... well I just feel a cold anger and I need to catch him. I need to do that. I promised her I'd find him and I need to keep that promise.'

As the conversation came to a halt the phone rang. Treloar walked to the worktop and answered.

'Treloar.'

'Phil, Phil! I don't understand what's going on. I can't help them, I've told them, but they won't listen.

'Whoa! Hope? What's wrong?'

'The police are here; that young black guy I saw at your party and a tall lanky one and some in uniform. They want Dylan but he's not here. I've no idea where he is.'

'Dylan?'

'Yes! They won't tell me why but they won't accept that I don't know where he is. Help me! Please Phil, help me.'

236

'Wait there Hope, wait by the phone. I'll find out what's going on and phone you back. I promise.'

'OK Phil thanks,' she hung up.

'What the hell was all that? I could hear her from over here,' said Sam.

'That was Hope Maddox. Colin and Luke are at Lower Farm looking for Dylan.'

'Let me call Colin,' she said pulling out her mobile.

'There's no signal,' Treloar said, 'and how would you know to call anyway? You're not supposed to be here. Let me think. You'll have to go down there. I'll call Hope and tell her you're on your way and to keep quiet about me organising it. Get the facts and get back here.'

'I'll go,' said Tom, 'they're expecting me to turn up at some point.'

'Thanks Tom,' said Treloar as Grigg headed for the door. 'I'll pack all this stuff away. Then you two had better make a move.'

'Yeah mate,' he grabbed his keys from the kitchen worktop, 'you can't be seen to be involved or Winters will have your arse – she's been after it long enough.'

As Tom dashed across the courtyard Sam and Treloar looked at each other in silence. Sam spoke:

'It's a slippery slope Phil, and we're already sliding.'

'I'm not backing off Sam.' He stared at her.

'What is Col up to? Dylan Maddox was in the pub,' she said.

'He must have found something at the mine. But whatever it is, it's something significant. Hope is scared and she doesn't scare easily. Let's get these bags packed ready for when Tom gets back. You need to move. Winters can't know you were here.'

They set about folding the clothes, replacing the toiletries and makeup in their bags and repacking the leather totes.

A long fifteen minutes later Tom was back.

'Well?' Treloar and Sam asked in unison.

'Luke spotted something odd about the calciner building. Short version: they found a secret room, a hidden cell ready and waiting for some unfortunate. They're thinking Amy. They reckon it must be Dylan Maddox's handiwork.'

'But he has an alibi,' Sam aid in exasperation. Tom shook his head.

'Ah … well … about that …'

237

Early November, the previous year

'You need to calm down a bit, take it easy,' Dan was saying. She stood, leaning against the wall by the TV; he muted it, left it on just in case. The BBC News was on, about to go to the lunchtime London news. 'It doesn't have to be full on. Make it last, slow down, enjoy. Take your time.' She was wearing a black suit jacket with fine yellow pin stripes, fitted and tight, two buttons done up, sheer yellow blouse, a black bootlace tie with yellow tips and a clasp shaped like a yellow sun, black skirt matching the jacket, short wide A line, and black high heeled cowboy boots with yellow twirls round the top. Her hair was still short, no side burns. He looked at her and smiled, then laughed, 'Yeah man, tell me about it!'

He was buzzing, excited. Sipped a bottle of Bud as he watched the London news. Nothing about Her, but he was gobsmacked when they talked about the Melissa trial, three weeks away they said, 'It has just been confirmed by the publication of the November court listings for the Old Bailey.'

Next morning there was still nothing on the news about Her and no mention of the trial and after a coffee and a bowl of chocolate Special K he went over to Kensington to Cavendish Cycle Couriers. Malcolm, 'call me Malc,' had seemed OK, was well impressed by his bike, and the gear, but not the wristband. 'Suggest you leave that at home man. Don't want it getting caught round a gear changer or brake lever at the wrong time. You'll be arse over tit with no notice and flat as a fucking pancake if a lorry trailer's wheels find you after you've hit the deck,' Malc said.

'Shit, didn't even think about that,' he replied, 'I'm so used to it now; don't even know it's there. Cheers.' They chatted some more. Malc explained how it all worked, how the despatcher decided who would pick up from where, how she knew who was free and when. He explained he didn't want full-time but would tell the despatcher what days and hours he wanted a week in advance. 'Yeah well, we'll see how it goes, but she decides what she decides, bit of a hard nut, needs to be with you guys, so good luck with that!' Malc said, 'I'll tell her you're part-time, twenty five to thirty hours a week, four days max. Work it out between you.'

He signed some papers, Malc took a picture of him for his

ID and told him to come back in an hour when the ID would be ready and he'd be able to meet Sylvie, the despatcher. 'Had to go to the dentist first thing, but she should be here soon.'

He'd done a few days, mostly mornings, not much work, business still building, new area for Malc, mostly running around the City and Canary Wharf with a couple of trips between Islington and some flash lawyers' offices in Fleet Street, and once even from Totteridge to the lawyers' offices. Fun even, seeing big names he recognised on packages and envelopes. Footballers, singers, tennis players, TV and movie stars, cricketers, athletes even; he'd been amazed when a couple had answered the door themselves, mostly it was cleaners or secretaries. Going through the papers in the afternoons and finding nothing.

But it was all good. He was laid back, the work was easy, he was getting around, into some pretty smart places, seeing loads of potential, taking it easy. Not rushing. Remembering where the good ones were, waiting for the ideal, the best. Could go back if he wanted. Was going back anyway, plenty of pick ups and deliveries for regulars.

After a couple of weeks, on a day off, he was going over to Oxford Street on the tube to pick up some more petals and see what else The Bulldog had, when he saw One, seemed like in every other ad frame on the wall as he went up past them on the Oxford Circus escalator. Gucci ad, sexy girl, yellow dress, red Gucci bag over her shoulder, pouting red lips, looking straight at him. Blonde hair in a pony tail, swishing to the left. 'Seen her before! Fuck. Looker. Where?' He was still wondering as he walked back to Oxford Circus from The Bulldog. He'd had a couple of large orange Gins and bought well from the gift list: petals, whole tulip flowers, a windmill, and two pairs of miniature clogs, one orange, one blue, all nicely wrapped by The Bulldog girl.

He was double-taking on the down escalator, couldn't believe it. Again on the platform. The Gucci ad was every fourth one in turn, coming up on the big display on the wall opposite the platform. At the Angel he picked up copies of The London Metro and Evening Standard and stayed on the station side of Upper Street waiting for a gap in the traffic to appear as he walked. It didn't arrive and he ran suddenly into the road between a taxi and a white transit van, stopped in the middle of the road, then ran suddenly between a white Mini Cooper with a Union Jack roof and a grey Audi, jumped up onto the pavement and jogged across to the Newsagent. Came out with all the Nationals and went home to go through all the papers and Google the Gucci girl.

He was pacing himself with Gucci girl, finding out, before finding. Buzzing, lots, from seeing stories about Her, Christiana Trent, Her death. The mystery surrounding it, another one, 'Brilliant,' he thought, in the papers at the same time as the Melissa trial. Not big, took some finding, had to be careful in case he missed them. Added them to his collection, he was going to need a bigger box.

Hadn't taken long to find out that Gucci girl was English, and based in London. 'Wow, spooky. Fucking brilliant,' he said to the screen when he saw it on the Agency web site, which he'd tracked down by looking at the ad archive on the Gucci website. The Agency was in Shoreditch of all places, on the High Street. Nearest tube station was Old Street, 'Weird,' he said, 'only one stop from The Angel, before Moorgate' but he'd never been there. Got her name, Lamorna Rain, Ha! 'But where do you live?' he said to the screen.

Didn't take long to find her Agency Facebook and Twitter pages. He opened new FB and Twitter accounts and re-friended and followed his usuals from them, then her at the Agency. Maybe they'd help, maybe she would. Knew he'd seen her, not sure where, all over probably. Seen her, not paid attention, blonde, Gucci, then he remembered. 'Schiphol.' He'd made a start. Maybe nothing would happen, maybe he'd get lucky.

He did. The Agency told her friends they were really looking forward to seeing her back at work next week after a month off. She had been staying with friends just outside Sydney, 'Relaxing and getting her energy back after a busy summer.' There was a picture of her in front of the Opera House with some mates, all jumping in the air at the same time and laughing.

He'd just finished a busy morning three days after friending and following the Agency profiles. Ended up near Canary Wharf after dropping off a package, at what the developer's hoarding described as, 'a luxury apartment near the river,' 'only 2nd floor, couldn't be that fucking great, must have been at least ten stories,' he'd thought, and decided he'd go back home via a stop at Shoreditch.

It was on the way and he fancied a coffee, and maybe a pizza. Found the Agency, on the High Street, no problem, there was a coffee shop nearly opposite, with a rack for bikes outside. He locked up his bike, went inside and was amazed to see an open kitchen on the right hand side and a repair shop with three mechanics working on bikes clamped onto benches at the back, on the other side of the tables and chairs.

'Help you?' said a woman with long red hair, wearing cycling lycra. She was carrying a tray of empty cups and plates. 'Hellooo,' she said after a while.

'Ah, yeah, thanks, sorry, I wanted a coffee and something to eat ……… what IS this place?' he eventually said.

'We're a cycle café,' she replied, 'sit where you like. Let me get rid of this and I'll come over, there are menus on the tables.'

'Right, OK, Cheers,' he said and walked over to a table by the window where he had a good view of the Agency on the other side of the road. The coffee menu was longer than the food menu. When she came over he asked for a pizza, 'nine inch spicy beef with green pepper special and a large coffee,' he said 'you choose, not too bitter, with the milk splash please.' Then he asked, 'What's a cycle café?'

'Well, we've got great food, mostly pizzas and burgers, great coffee and tea, to go or drink in, and beer, and a few good wines, and great mechanics. So, we fix bikes, sell a few, refurbs, give advice about bikes and London routes, and feed up cyclists. Guess you haven't been in a cycle café before. I'm surprised. You know, you look like you would've. I'll be right back with the coffee; the pizza will be around fifteen minutes.'

He put a twenty pound note on the table in case he needed to leave quickly, and looked out and over the road. The coffee came, then the pizza, he had seen it being spun, chef putting on a show, but he was too focused on looking over the road to watch for long. 'Might come back,' he thought …….. 'but I might still be looking over the road,' he said to himself and smiled.

He had two slices left when a bright orange sports car stopped in the middle of the road, indicating right, to cross it, and Gucci girl came out of the Agency doors. 'Shit,' he said, and got up and ran out to his bike. By the time he'd unlocked it and got his helmet on, the car had parked on the other side of the road, Gucci girl had swung up a gull-wing door and got in the passenger side and the car was indicating left to cross back to the proper side of the road. By the time it had crossed back over the road and was moving again he was twenty metres behind it, wondering if he could keep up. It was noisy, throaty. 'Not if we get on a clear road that's for fucking sure,' he thought.

But they didn't. They headed north and slightly west, and sometimes he thought he'd lost it. It was very low and when more than two cars were in between them he couldn't see it. Heard it but couldn't see it. Lights helped, bus and taxi and cycle lanes helped, the London traffic helped. 'What's the point of a fucking monster car like that in London?' he thought, and stayed with it until they'd gone up a steep hill; it was drawing away by then, the road was clearer and he was thinking he'd blown it, when it suddenly turned right and parked up. She got out, said something to the driver through the window before he revved off.

Then she walked through a wide gap in a low wall. He cycled slowly to where the car had been and had a good look round, as if looking for a house number, he hoped. He saw that she'd crossed a gravelly area with big stone troughs for flowers round the edges, in front of a tall semi-detached house; between a bright pink Mini and a small yellow van with 'Top Mrs Mop,' and a cartoon cleaning lady on the side in black outline, with a phone number.

There was a path up the left side of the house, with bushes and trees beside it. She got a key out of her bag and looked up as the big pink front door opened and a woman carrying a rucksack came out and started talking to her. He couldn't hear everything, but did catch the woman saying '...... wanted to see ...... ' and Gucci girl saying '........ .party!' then laughing, then, '........ time next week please,' then, 'Thanks,' and going inside.

Thirty One

'Who the hell checked Maddox's alibi?'

Detective Superintendent Winters was furious. She tolerated incompetence less than failure.

'It was one of the locals Ma'am,' said Tom Grigg, 'but don't be too hard on him. The landlord lied. Apparently it was a standard arrangement between him and Dylan Maddox. If anyone asked if Maddox was there at a certain time the bloke would say he was there playing darts. Nobody had ever called him out on it before. It was a nod, nod, wink, wink gentleman's agreement to cover for Maddox when he didn't want his wife, Hope, to know where he was. It's been going on for months; it wasn't something set up for that afternoon especially.'

'Well I suppose no harm was done. But only thanks to the excellent work of Sergeant Matthews and that new chap. I dread to think what would have happened if they hadn't found that secret room.' God forbid the press get wind of the alibi debacle.'

'Calloway, Ma'am; the new chap.'

'Yes, Luke Calloway. He seems a most promising addition to the team.'

'Indeed; bright lad.'

Winters was reflecting on how a new fresh face; a good looking young man and black to boot, would go a long way towards undermining Treloar's hallowed position as media darling.

'Anyway,' she roused herself from her musings, 'I understand that all Mr Maddox is saying is that he didn't kill Amy Angove. He refuses to say where he was at the time of her death and he refuses to say why he has that sinister room.'

'That's about it Ma'am.'

At Lost Farm Edmund Maddox was baking bread. Rees Maddox was driving down from Norwich where he'd been visiting his sister, Megan. When she had heard about Dylan's arrest she had called to say they wanted to come home from the University of East Anglia, where she was doing a doctorate in Environmental Sciences. She planned to work for UNICEF in disaster relief water and sanitation projects. As Edmund took the second loaf of seed bread, Megan's favourite, from the oven, he heard the back door open and the sound of voices.

'Hi Dad!' called a deep female voice.

'Hello my angel,' Edmund said as Megan burst into the kitchen, tossing a large rucksack to the floor by the table. She was a tall well built girl with brown curly hair, freckles and pale grey eyes. She looked entirely at home in a farm kitchen. Her brother Rees followed behind with more bags.

'Are you OK?' she asked with a frown.

'Yes, yes. It's all some horrible mistake.'

'Of course it is. Dylan wouldn't hurt Amy, everybody knows that. Rees tells me Phil is going up to London. He'll sort it, I know he will. He doesn't believe Dylan did it.'

Thirty Two

The next few days dragged for Treloar. He wanted to get on; he wanted to go to London to find the man, and he was convinced it was a man, who had been stalking Amy, the man he believed had killed her.

Everyone agreed to hold the funeral as soon as was feasible. The police and the local tourist industry wanted to bring a speedy end to the media circus which was choking the narrow roads of west Cornwall and the family wanted privacy and peace.

So, at the beginning of the second week in May the mourners gathered at Amy's parish church.

Amy Angove's funeral had just ended with a rendition of the traditional Cornish song '*The White Rose*', and people were gathering in small groups in the churchyard.

'I would never have thought she did it. I mean I understand she was worried and disturbed, so it's wasn't the motivation, it was the method. I don't think she could have fashioned that noose,' said Colin.

'No, she was more of a Pimms and paracetamol candidate I concede,' Dr. Tremayne agreed.

'You knew her Doc, did you ever think she could have tied that rope?'

'Well no. Women do not tend to hang themselves; mostly overdose. Amy was not a physical creature, not in the adventurous, energetic sense; I couldn't see her climbing up onto that machinery either. And she wouldn't have hacked off her hair like that. I can't understand how the suicide rumour started.'

'Of course! You weren't there; you'd left by then,' Colin exclaimed.

'Where?'

'At Phil's party, late on. Ochre Pengelly was telling the story of the family who used to own the Lost Farm Estate around the time of the First World War. Evidently, to keep it short, there were two hangings at the mine: one murder, one suicide. It's a local legend. Amy was really affected, really upset. I bet you that's where the suicide rumour has come from; some local gossiping.'

'Well, John Forbes has ruled out suicide categorically, so hopefully that should be the end of fanciful, distressing stories.'

'Still Doc, would you have put money on Dylan Maddox?'

'No Colin I would not. Oh I know Dylan's an odd fish; very moody and volatile, but he's always shown nothing but ... well love, adoration for Amy. I would never have thought him capable of this. I know Phil is adamant that it wasn't Dylan, absolutely convinced you've got the wrong man.'

'Maybe he's right. What about the three sisters? There was no love lost there.'

'Really Colin, for a measured man of science, you do sometimes spout the wildest speculations. Surely it's far more likely to be someone from London, from her new life; someone who followed her down here or perhaps some random encounter with a stranger in a lonely place?'

'OK I concede that idea about the Treloar women is a little far-fetched. Forget I said that.'

Sam came out of the church and walked over to them. She was with a tall thin girl dressed in a floor-length scarlet and purple dress and an enormous wide-brimmed black straw hat.

'Christ,' said Colin under his breath, 'she could give Ochre Pengelly a run for her money.'

'Dr. Tremayne, D S Colin Matthews, this is Amy's old housemate and colleague, Christabel Drax,' Sam introduced the startling looking girl.

'I just don't believe it. She was walking for Dolce & Gabanna next week. She was going to be the face of a new Chanel campaign. She was sooo happy. Who could have done this to her?'

'Walking?' Colin queried.

'Yes you know: modelling; walking on the catwalk. And look, look at this. I found this in the church,' she held out a headshot of Amy. 'It's one of her comp cards. What on earth was it doing there?'

Suddenly a voice, plaintive and beautiful, ethereal, drifted out across the gravestones. Everyone standing in the churchyard was transfixed. Sam shuddered as if the sun had gone behind a cloud, but the sky was completely clear. *I only have eyes for you* sung slowly with minimal accompaniment.

'What on earth is that?' Ochre asked emerging from the church in waves of black silk.

'Isn't it coming from the church?' asked Sam.

'No it is not. It seems to be coming through the church but no one in there is singing,' Ochre replied.

With that, as abruptly as it had started, the singing stopped.

'Well that was bloody weird,' said Treloar walking towards them down the path from the church door, 'Col, go and have a look around.' Colin Andrews walked back up the path towards the church.

'Perhaps it was a fan?' said Sam.

'Mmm, maybe,' Treloar replied, 'or a stalker.'

'No, I know what it is,' declared Tremayne who had been deep in thought, 'well, the singer at least, it's Art Garfunkel; it's a track from a solo album *Breakaway*. Molly played it endlessly. It must be … almost forty years old.'

'Jesus Christ it's fucking spooky,' Ochre said.

'Well come along everybody, let's adjourn to the pub; it's The Tinners Arms isn't it Phil?' Tremayne was keen to get away.

'Yeah that's right. I don't think the Angoves are coming but Peter did say we should go ahead; there's food laid on in a room apparently. Amy's brothers will drop their parents back home and come along. A lot of her childhood friends will be there. Luckily the misdirection seems to have worked: I've not seen a single camera or pushy journalist. They'll all be down in Penzance. No one from London was invited, apart from you Christabel, and your model agency boss, Imogen Jordan, and I haven't seen any gatecrashers, so let's hope it stays that way.'

'Look at this,' said Colin Andrews walking up holding out a small boom-box, its handle gripped in a white handkerchief, 'one of the mourners found it over there behind the church. I think this is the source of the mysterious singing. We might get something off it. I'll get it to the lab.'

'Do that,' said Treloar.

Tom Grigg had walked across the churchyard to join them.

'I'll be getting back to St Ives,' he said.

'Can I have a quick word before you go?' Treloar asked. 'I'll see you all at the pub. Sam can you take Christabel and Imogen?'

'Sure,' Sam replied, and with that the mourners moved away leaving Treloar and Tom Grigg standing by the gate.

'You OK Phil?' Grigg asked.

'Fine. I wanted to ask a favour. I've taken some leave and I'm off to London tomorrow. Peter Angove's let me have the keys to Amy's house and I'm going to take a look around. I want to get this bastard Tom, I need to get him. Winters is barking up the wrong tree with Dylan Maddox. He's up to something, I don't dispute that, but he didn't kill Amy. No fucking way.'

'I understand mate.'

'You used to be with the Met. Is there anybody you could put me in touch with who'd be willing to help me? I know it's a lot to ask, I know it's not our jurisdiction, I know it's not allowed, I know I could get in the shit, but I have to do this. Is there anyone who'd see that and take the risk?'

'Ben Fitzroy. He was a DCI when I left but he's now something hush hush with some secret squirrel squad. You'll like him. He doesn't give a fuck for the rules either. He's the black sheep of an old aristocratic family; the third son who should have gone into the clergy apparently but he joined the army - Sandhurst and the Guards, and then the Met. He's fearless; vicious in a fight and bloody clever. You'll love him. I'll make the call and get back to you. You're going to the Tinners I take it?'

'Yeah I'll show my face but then I need to pack. I want to leave early.'

'I'll call you once I've spoken to him.'

'I appreciate this Tom.'

'No worries.'

'I know she was vain and silly; I know she was selfish and tiresome and irritating. But I don't think she deserved this, I don't think she deserved to die,' Phil was anguished and his distress was deeply upsetting to Sam and not for noble reasons she recognised.

'Nobody deserves this end,' she said quietly.

'I know my sisters despised her and a lot of our neighbours and friends had not forgiven her for her behaviour when she left me, but I had, I had Sam. I didn't love her anymore, I hadn't for years. Oh don't get me wrong I was furious and desolate when she first went; mad at her for making me look a fool and desperately alone; I couldn't see a way forward, but I got over it. It was Ochre who helped me see that my life still had a purpose. I've never told anyone that and neither has she. God only made one Ochre Pengelly, more's the pity.'

'She is certainly an impressive woman,' Sam said thinking she sounded trite, which she did, but she was very uncomfortable with this conversation and not sure why.

'Well I'm going to find this bastard. It's not Dylan Maddox

for fuck's sake. It's someone in London. He put terror into her heart and then he broke her. She was a fragile thing Sam and he broke her like snapping the neck of a dove.'

In fact her neck hadn't been broken. John Forbes, the pathologist, had established that she had died from a massive blow to the back of the head. She had then been strung up. It would not have taken much strength. They believed her hair had been hacked off after death and some had been taken, presumably by the killer.

'Phil it's the Met's case, the stalking happened in London. If it's him, he'll be back in London.'

'Fuck that. She's dead. She died here. It's mine. Finding him is not going to be a priority for them; not now Dylan's been picked up. I'm going to find him. Winters won't let me anywhere near the case down here; I'm going to London. I bet that was him with the music in the churchyard, but you're right; the answer lies in London and he'll be on his way back there now she's buried. Tom used to work in the Met and he's given me a name; some guy who Tom rates who thinks like me, bit of a loose cannon apparently. I'm going to track that bastard down.'

'For Christ's sake Phil,' Sam whispered urgently, 'you can't be involved and you know it.'

'Well that's my choice Sam not yours. I'm taking my leave and I'm heading up to London tomorrow.'

And with that he drained his glass and strode over to the bar.

Pea and mint soup in teacups, miniature sandwiches and some of Inés Treloar's famous cakes, not the nut cake of the party but tiny individual chocolate, orange and almond cakes which had been Amy's favourite. Treloar was chatting with his sister Eva, Ochre Pengelly and Dr. Tremayne.

'Dear God look at that – a skull in a skirt. Who the hell is she?' asked Ochre pointing at the willowy girl in red and purple.

'That is Amy's former housemate and fellow model, Christabel Drax,' Eva answered.

'I dread to think of the state of these people's bathrooms; all that obsession with bodily functions,' she nibbled on a breadstick, 'when they hear the term 'five a day' they think bowel movements.'

'Ochre!' Eva exclaimed, a mixture of delight and disapproval crossing her face.

'Well honestly. I'm right aren't I Doc?' she continued,

turning to Dr. Tremayne for vindication, but he was choking on his red wine and couldn't speak. Treloar was laughing out loud for what seemed like the first time in days. Ochre Pengelly was truly a force of nature.

'Ochre,' said Dr. Tremayne regaining his composure, 'trust you to get to the bottom of the matter.'

At this, Eva burst into laughter and the entire company subsided into giggles. Something about death made the living feel alive and giddy. 'Shhh everyone, she's coming over,' she said.

'This is Christabel Drax,' said Dr. Tremayne to the others.

'And what is your real name?' Ochre asked.

'Christabel Drax,' she answered, 'Yes I know people always assume it's made up, like Amy used Lamorna Rain, but it's not. My father is very keen on Coleridge. He wrote a poem about the lady Christabel, Coleridge that is, not my father, Coleridge wrote the poem I mean.'

Sam was at a loss. She felt frantic and panicked and had no idea who to turn to. Her beloved was risking his career and his future and with that all her hopes. The bitterest irony was, that had this been an issue with anyone else, it was him she would have turned to for advice without thinking. She couldn't involve Luke or Colin, certainly not Colin who was a toadying stickler for the rules. She couldn't involve Doc Tremayne could she? His opinion was absolutely one she valued but would this compromise him? What to do, what to do? As her mind whirled the answer walked through from the pub yard; an answer dressed in chocolate linen and four inch heels: Lucia.

Lucia had been in the courtyard speaking to Imogen Jordan. Lucia and Imogen, although not friends were respected associates, known to each other through the fashion circuit.

'Sam I've just been talking to Immy Jordan, Amy's boss, and she said they have been receiving strange calls and parcels at the agency since Amy's death. I would tell Flip but I don't think he's in the right frame of mind to take it in at the moment.'

'No he's not. I wanted to talk to you about that, but tell me what Imogen Jordan said first.'

'As you know Amy had been receiving strange parcels and phone messages, well since her death the agency has had two huge bunches of red tulips tied with black net gauze and daily phone messages with snatches of Mozart's Requiem Mass. Imogen was going to call the police but she wanted to wait and ask Flip since she knew Amy had confided in him. What shall I tell her?'

'I'll speak to her. Tom Grigg and I are running the enquiry. Will you introduce us?'

'Of course, she's just outside.'

Imogen Jordan was sitting at a trestle table in the courtyard. She was an extraordinarily beautiful black woman, tall and lithe with close cropped hair, high cheek bones and deep brown eyes. She appeared to be wearing no makeup, but Sam thought it was probably just a case of expert application, and she was dressed in a plain black shift dress with a matching cropped jacket. The only bright colour was her scarlet leather clutch bag lying on the table.

'Immy this is Sam Scott. She works with my brother. I've told her about the tulips and the phone calls.'

Imogen Jordan rose to shake hands with Sam. Even in flat pumps she must have been over six foot five. Sam noticed her warm slender hand and her beautiful smile.

'Hello Ms Scott,' she said in a soft deep voice.

'Hello Ms Jordan, I understand you have some information about Amy's stalker.'

'Yes, he sent flowers and left that dreadful music overnight on the machine, but my main point is I think he spoke to our receptionist before Amy died.'

'Why do you say that?'

A man rang the agency. He asked for Amy and was told she was away. Apparently he was very charming; he spun some tale about a lost cat. All she said - Fleur, the girl who spoke to him – all she said was that Amy was with family; nothing more. He must have known where they live. It's not a secret of course. Amy made a lot of her Cornish roots; her childhood on the farm and why she chose the name Lamorna. It was all in the press.'

'So he could have located her parents and followed her down here,' Sam said.

'Yes I imagine so. Poor Fleur is devastated. I've told her she's in no way to blame but still …'

'Indeed. If it would help I'll speak to her to confirm that she did nothing wrong.'

'Oh would you? That would be so reassuring for her. It

251

would mean a lot. Thank you.'

'Just give me a number for her. How long ago did he call?'

'It was on Friday, May 1st. He said it was urgent that he find the cat because his family was going away for the bank holiday weekend and his daughter wouldn't leave without knowing that the cat was safe. He gave his address and it was in the same street as Amy and Fleur fell for it.'

'He could have been genuine,' Lucia said.

'Ah no, I thought of that and I checked. The house number he gave Fleur doesn't exist. And why would he call us rather than asking his neighbours? No it was him.'

'Yes I think you're right,' Sam said, 'let me talk to Fleur, see if she can remember any detail of the call which might help us.'

Back in the bar Sam saw Dr. Tremayne talking seriously with a small, rotund man with rosy cheeks and a shock of thick white hair. He looked like a lot like pictures of Einstein. As she watched them Eva approached her.

'Who is that talking to Doc Tremayne?' Sam asked.

'Where?' said Eva looking around, 'Oh that's Orlando. Orlando Pengelly, Ochre's older brother. I'm very surprised he's here. He doesn't do this sort of thing. I would have expected to see him at the church, but not here. He's a professor or something at Exeter University. He's nothing like Ochre: chalk and cheese. But they're very close. He's a dear really, just a little ... preoccupied. Thinks a lot I expect. Have you seen Lucia?'

'Yes, she's outside with Imogen Jordan, from Amy's agency.'

'Thanks. I'm taking Mamá home now; she hates this sort of thing too. I want Lucia to wait and bring Flip. He's not himself today. Even after her death that girl is causing trouble.'

Sam had never heard Eva speak of anyone with any kind of disapproval. Her shock showed in her face and her silence.

'Oh, ignore me; ill of the dead and all that, but really that girl could try the patience of a saint. Still she did not deserve that dreadful end, that fear and horror. I may have found her tiresome and I did not forgive the way she had treated my brother, but nobody deserves to die like that, nobody. And I feel so for her poor parents; they're good people. Anyway, goodbye Sam, I'm sure we'll see you again and do call in at Cove Farm anytime you're in the area.' And with that she flashed the dazzling Treloar smiled and walked out into the courtyard, leaving Sam to ponder again on how Amy Angove could inspire such strength of emotion, even in the quiet, placid Eva Treloar.

'There is something of the Grimm fairy tale about this,' said Doc Tremayne.

'Yes, it does seem rather a pathetic, senseless but cruel death. You knew her Doc; what did you think of her?' Sam asked.

'Amy was essentially a vain and shallow creature but she was beautiful and she once brought Phil great happiness. Lucia used to say if you wanted an accurate portrayal of Amy, just read Jane Austen's *Pride and Prejudice* and look at Lydia Bennet. But Phil did love her, once.'

'He described her as a broken dove,' she said sadly.

'Yes, I think that encapsulates the barbarity of her death. But she is gone now Sam and you must not let her shade cast a pall over the future. Neither you nor Phil,' he added solemnly.

Thirty Three

Samuel Johnson famously said that a man, 'tired of London, is tired of life' although of course London was different when he was alive, smaller, quieter, smellier no doubt, less exhausting. In the exhilaration versus exhaustion debate about London, Sam was firmly in the exhaustion camp. She hated the place; it was suffocating. It was one thing she found surprising about Treloar, that a son of Cornwall could actually like being in London. Variety she supposed. Sam was not a great fan of cities and was thinking about moving out of Truro, though it scarcely counted as one to her mind. No, Sam liked deserts and islands and yes, desert islands. She did appreciate cities with non-urban settings like Cape Town and Sydney and Barcelona. Perhaps she'd go to Barcelona later that year; visit Lucia perhaps?

But for London, Sam had to admit to herself, Hampstead was not too bad. She was reminded of Clifton in Bristol where she had lived whilst at university; similar houses, cafés and shops, and where Clifton had the downs, Hampstead had the heath. Sam had taken the tube from Paddington to Belsize Park, changing at Oxford Circus and Euston. It had taken a long thirty minutes; if Sam disliked London she loathed the Underground. Hampstead resembles a village but is located just four miles from central London. Its heath covers 300 hectares with ancient woodland and parkland. Once home to Sigmund Freud, John Keats and Ian Fleming it is a much sought after area to live, with its leafy lanes, smart shops and pavement cafés.

She had been despatched by Winters to liaise with the Metropolitan Police and to inform them of Dylan Maddox's arrest. Winters was handing over everything on the stalker. As far as she was concerned they had their murderer and the stalking had not taken place on their patch. Winters did not know of Phil's presence in London. She certainly didn't know he was staying at Amy's house.

Amy lived in a five floor 5 bedroom/4 bathroom semi just off East Heath Road. The windows above the rear walled garden overlooked Hampstead Heath and the front top stories overlooked central London. Very nice. Outside the lower ground floor window at the front, what had once been a small garden was now a brick inlaid parking space for her Mini Cooper; the double front door was painted shocking pink to match the car, and the former garden was lined with sandstone troughs of pink and white geraniums. Very Amy.

As Sam's train was pulling out of Reading, Treloar was searching Amy's house. The basement kitchen was very hi-tech: ice white walls, Delabole slate floor tiles, lots of glossy stainless steel. The only incongruous item was a large American style 50's retro fridge in primrose yellow. One wall was half-covered by a huge magnetic board with an integral day planner, the day marked by a moveable magnetic heart; it rested over the number 1. Other magnetic hearts and flowers held notes, photographs, flyers and brochures. A large space to the right held jottings, doodles and hand-written notes in black and red marker pen. "Pippit" was scrawled in red next to "May 1" and a pair of hearts.

The only sound in the room was the slow tick coming from an enormous daisy shaped wall-clock fixed on the wall between the two pairs of French windows which opened onto the patio and the rear walled garden. A large bunch of some sort of daisy drooped and withered in a Scandinavian glass bowl on a black marble worktop.

Absentmindedly, Treloar pulled open the fridge door to reveal a jumbo pot of Greek yoghurt, 4 Mars bars, 3 bottles of Chablis, loads of small bottles of Evian water, some bags of washed salad leaves, an assortment of cheese and a bag of sliced white bread. Typical of Amy to have hardly any food, he thought, but then he recalled that she should have been in Italy. He closed the fridge. A bunch of blackening bananas hung from a hook next to an orange Bugatti kettle and matching espresso machine. Where would she have put the jiffy bags?

He started to pull open drawers and cupboards to find the expected cutlery, crockery and saucepans, but no paperwork of any description. 'Think like Amy,' he said aloud. She wouldn't have wanted the packages near her daily life so what would she have done with them?

He retraced his steps back up the stairs to the ground floor hallway and walked along to the front door. Coloured shadows from the stained glass insets at the top of the door fell across the black and white chequered floor tiles. To the left of the front door stood a long old wooden chest beneath a Cornish seascape which looked suspiciously like Ochre Pengelly's work.

He lifted the lid and there they were: a pile of jiffy bags stacked next to phone directories, London guides, and more takeaway menus. 'Bingo'. He pulled a pair of latex gloves from his pocket, put them on and carefully lifted the bags from the chest. He carried them through to the front sitting room and placed them on the huge square glass coffee table. 'Coffee,' he said aloud and headed back down to the kitchen.

First he sorted them into date order by postmark, then picking each up in turn he examined the exterior. As Amy had said, the only markings on the outside were the postal label and the address of this house, printed in black on a white computer label in Arial font. Once he had listed the postage dates he compared them with the delivery dates supplied by Amy and saw that they had all arrived between two and four days after posting. Next he opened the first bag and, using a pair of giant tweezers he had found in a kitchen drawer, he gently extracted a small delicate package of orange tissue paper. He unwrapped it: a dried pressed tulip as anticipated.

Over the course of the next forty minutes he opened each bag in turn and noted that the contents corresponded exactly with the list he had taken during his conversation with Amy. Finally he picked up the jiffy bag he had found on the porch doormat on his arrival earlier. Carefully, he slit the top of the bag with his penknife, preserving the seal. He smiled as he thought how Sam would be protesting; he should be handing it straight to the proper authorities in the Met, but fate had brought it into his hands.

It had arrived very recently from its position in the pile of post on the mat and delivered by hand this time: no postal label. He wanted, he needed, to know what it contained. Afterwards it could go with the others for prints and DNA testing. He knew Sam was uncomfortable with his actions and the way he was behaving, but he had to do this, and anyway he hadn't gone completely rogue, he'd contacted Ben Fitzroy.

As Tom Grigg had suggested, Fitzroy had "acquired" the investigation from the London end. Treloar understood that the man had power and influence. Whatever, he had given Treloar carte blanche to run with it. They were meeting later. He held the bag over a cleared space on the table, tipping and shaking it gently until the contents fell onto the glass. He stood up sharply, banging his knee on the heavy glass. He gasped in horror at the golden strands: Amy's hair.

Early November to mid December, the previous year

After cycling off carefully, still looking as though he was looking for house numbers, but really counting the houses, he'd cycled round the block to see what it was like at the back of Her house. It was mid afternoon, there was nobody about, and after counting the houses carefully on the other side of a brick wall that was so high he could only see their top floors, he pulled up at the side of the tree-lined pavement and said, 'Bollocks!' and glared at the wall.

Then he had looked around, still nobody about, lifted the bike up the kerb and walked the bike to the wall and leant it carefully up against it. Tested it, pressed down hard on the saddle. All his weight. Then he surprised himself by lifting a foot up, standing on the bottom of the frame, jumping, leaning, and sort of pulling and scrabbling upwards and ending up standing with one foot on the saddle and the other on the cross bar, holding on to the top of the wall, and seeing into Her back garden.

She had just come out of a patio door and gone to a table where she wrinkled her nose and picked up an ash tray and emptied it into a plastic bag, zipped the top and shook her head. Then she took the bag to an orange wheelie bin and dropped it in before going back through the patio door and closing it. 'Cleaner,' he thought. He climbed down more slowly than he had climbed up, but still no accidents. 'Amazing,' he said to the bike as he got on to ride off. As he turned left at the end of the road and onto the main road he realised he was in Hampstead Heath from the shop names, and that it wouldn't take him too long to get back home.

'Cracked it,' he thought later. He was in the kitchen with the laptop on the counter, looking at the "Candids" pages of Lamorna Rain on the Agency website, and a plan was coming together. The Sydney holiday picture was there, but he was more interested in the 'At Home' section than the 'Friends' and was looking at a picture of the lovely Lamorna in her kitchen, standing next to a massive fridge with take away menus on the door, one Thai one Chinese, the restaurant names and numbers blurred out.

She was wearing a bright yellow apron over a white T shirt, hair tied back, holding a book up just under her chin with the cover open, smiling with her mouth wide open and eyebrows raised, and pointing to Jamie Oliver's signature. It had 'Happy Birthday

Lamorna from us all at 15 xxxx' written above it. Over her shoulder there was a book shelf with cookery books. Big, thick. 'Telly chefs,' he thought as he looked along the row. He'd heard of most of them, some he hadn't; Heston Blumenthal, Hugh Fernleigh-Whittingstall, Rick Stein, Ken Hom, Giorgio Locatelli, Tom Kerridge, Lorraine Pascal, James Martin, Elizabeth David, Delia Smith, Nigella Lawson, the shelf went on behind her head, couldn't see the rest. 'Probably all signed, doubt she uses them,' he thought, and smiled, and decided on one of the Rick Steins.

The next day he'd arranged with Sylvie the despatcher for his last drop of the day to be as close as possible to Oxford Street Plaza, and went there afterwards, to Waterstones, to pick up a hard cover copy of 'rick stein's seafood'. Then he called at Eurospy, then he went home. No rush, but by the time it was dark he'd got it all together.

One camera was inside the stuck together pages of the Rick Stein, lens seeing out from the white dot above the i on the spine, and he'd got two free-standing mini cams ready, mounted on heavy flat circular bases with matt black lenses in the ends of black fibre cables. All with transmitters. And a top of the range prepaid mobile phone with a receive and repeat app that would switch on automatically once a day to receive pictures from the cameras then send them to his server at home. All the kit had military life batteries and the prepaid was in a sealed heavy duty brown plastic bag.

The job helped. Learned to do what was needed, when it was needed, not to rush, to rush when he HAD to, be controlled. 'Would have gone mad without it, followed too close, been seen, got caught. Staying cool with this one,' he thought as he took a break from the papers a couple of days later. The Melissa trial was about to start and the police were now treating the Christiana death as suspicious. Small stories, Melissa's was in some of the nationals and both locals every few days, but Christiana's was only in the locals. He looked through them all to know, to be sure what was happening.

A week after he'd first followed Lamorna he'd got the day off work and was at the end of Her road by eight thirty in the morning. Propped his bike against a lamp-post, took a plastic box of cold

258

pizza slices out of his shoulder bag and a coffee flask from the drinks holder, sat on a street sign, had breakfast slowly, and waited.

Not for long. The orange sports car showed up, when it went past him he saw it was a McLaren. She got in, wearing ripped jeans and a jeans jacket over a white shirt with a collar, and white plimsolls with pink stripes, and it revved off. 'Fucking poser,' he thought, and 'right, rock and roll man,' about fifteen minutes later when Top Mrs Mop came round the corner and parked up next to the pink Mini. He gave it another fifteen minutes for her to get going, finishing off his breakfast, looked around, no-one about, cycled down to Her house and onto the gravel, leaned the bike against the wall and listened.

There was the loud buzz, of a Hoover somewhere high up in the house and he pretended to ring the doorbell in case anyone was watching. Gave it a minute, buzzy Hoover was still going and he walked quickly round to the back of the house, heart thumping, and nearly laughed out loud when he saw the ash tray on the table, one stub in it, and the patio doors open. Didn't stop walking and went straight into the kitchen, took the Rick Stein off the bookshelf, put it in his shoulder bag and replaced it with his own, after opening it and switching on the camera, exact fit, he nearly cheered out loud, he was cheering inside, could still hear the buzzy Hoover, loud.

Went up the stairs to the hall and across into a big room with a massive screen on the wall with big speakers at the sides and smaller ones all round the room, saw a DVD player in a unit in a corner and put one of the free standing mini cams, after switching it on, on top of it at the back of the cabinet so it couldn't be seen, made sure the lens was poking in the right direction.

Heart still thumping, buzzy Hoover still buzzing, went back out, back down into the kitchen where there was a seating area with a smaller screen on the wall, another DVD player in a cabinet in the corner, switched on the other minicam and put it at the back of the cabinet and made sure the lens was pointing in the right direction, checked it couldn't be seen, buzzy Hoover was STILL going, 'what the fuck does she DO up there?' he wondered, and went out through the patio door.

Took the repeater out of his shoulder bag and switched it on through the plastic bag before leaning over and gently putting it behind a tree trunk that was behind a bush at the side of the path then going back round to the front of the house, shaking his head and shrugging his shoulders in a 'What can you do if they can't hear you?' kind of way, and cycled back to the main road, heart still thumping.

Knowing there would be nothing for him to see until later, pictures would be sent to the server at 8.00 at night and 9.00 in the morning, he decided to ring the office and see if there was any work. There was. Sylvie the despatcher thanked him for calling and gave him three jobs. Then another four that kept him busy until mid afternoon and he'd ended up doing more hours than normal. 'Not bad for a day off,' he thought.

After a pizza and a few beers from the fridge he was looking at the laptop on the kitchen counter when the first pictures downloaded. 'Fucking amazing!' he shouted, then, 'Wow, how about THAT!' when he saw the cleaner carrying a red feather duster past the sofa in the sitting room. Next there was a series of pictures of her from the kitchen, by the seating area, then by the fridge. He was chuffed, seriously chuffed, proud. Set it all up himself. The kit all worked perfectly and the picture quality was great.

'Wow! THERE you are,' he said when suddenly the next picture was of Her walking into the kitchen, carrying some envelopes, 'the post,' he thought. Still in the jeans, but with a pink collared shirt and red plimsolls this time. Eight pictures later She had opened an envelope and was reading a letter. The cameras were triggered by motion sensors and didn't care what was moving. He'd also pre-programmed them to look for faces and take photographs when the faces were towards the camera as a priority. Didn't want to overfill the data storage, or have to sift through hundreds of photos he wasn't that bothered about. Faces mattered.

They took a picture every three seconds until there was no motion and he spent three hours looking at Her. Seeing, going back over the photos, looking, zooming in, thinking. There were still loads of them.

A few envelopes were left in a pile on the kitchen table, most went in the bin. She took it upstairs somewhere and came back. Made tea, fancy glass, no milk, heated stuff in the microwave, watched TV, eating from a tray, picked really, with a fork, looking at Her phone. Thumbed replies, one handed. Then She'd got an iPad out of a drawer and spent ages on it and he wished he'd put a camera behind the sofa somewhere so he could see what She'd been doing on the phone and the iPad.

After looking at the TV for a while, not many pictures, not moving much, She turned it off, switched off the light, went back to the kitchen and made another cup of tea, then walked up the stairs and turned out the light. Then nothing. He was working the next day so he set the server to automatically forward the next morning's photos to his mobile, didn't want to wait until he got home to see them.

It was nearly 8.30am and he was about to leave for Kensington to pick up some of the overnight drop-offs from Cavendish Couriers when his phone pinged and he thought his pictures might be arriving early. 'Couldn't be?' he thought, 'who the fuck's that?' He was gobsmacked to see emails from the Agency via Twitter and Facebook inviting him to an 'Impromptu 'try 'n buy' with Lamorna morning,' at Selfridges. She would be informally walking the Gucci floor and picking and choosing what to show on an informal catwalk every half hour from 10.00am until 1.00pm, today, and he would be welcome.

It was a no brainer. He called Sylvie in despatch, apologised, said he needed the day off, that he'd make it up another time, ran back upstairs seriously excited and changed. Plain grey hoodie, white T shirt, black jeans and black hi-tops, put his mobile and a prepaid and the selfie stick into his shoulder bag and practically ran all the way to the Angel, where the first train out got him to Oxford Circus by 9.15.

He got his first pictures as She got out of the orange McLaren. Close ups. He was just one of the crowd. She wore a yellow short skirted suit with light blue pin stripes and mid blue spiky heels. With a light blue shiny Gucci shoulder bag. Loads were taking pictures, some were going for selfies, as She went into the store, path cleared by poser driver. He followed, the crowd followed. It was noisy, it was mayhem.

Much later, he was back at home, waiting, for the 8.00pm pictures to arrive, hoping. Since getting back from Selfridges he'd been busy, mega busy, and he couldn't wait to see if it had been worth it. The morning pictures had been interesting, hoped the evening show would be better.

It was. She was still wearing the suit, looked a bit frazzled, came down the stairs, dumped a pile of post on the table and went straight to the fridge. Got a bottle of wine out, Chardonnay, a large glass from a cupboard, filled it, took a long sip. Then flicked through the post, stopping at the envelope he had pushed through the letterbox in the afternoon. It was brown, A4 size, plain white label addressed to Lamorna Rain, home address, no stamp.

She looked puzzled as She opened it and looked inside, more puzzled as She pulled out an A5 sized photo, and she laughed when She saw Herself trying to look cool as the end of the scarf She had tried to casually swing around Her neck that morning had somehow knocked the right arm of the big sunglasses She was wearing out from behind Her ear and left them hanging across Her face and the scarf had somehow landed on Her head and was looped down over Her left ear.

Then She saw the caption, 'Fun day! From your fan xxx.' The laugh became a smile, then a frown. She looked puzzled again and sat staring at it for a few seconds before putting it down on the table, stared some more and had another long sip of wine. Then She shook her head, opened the other envelopes, threw most of them and whatever had been inside in the bin, and went up the stairs with the photo and the rest of the unbinned post.

'Well cool man, good stuff there. Clever!' Dan said. She was looking at him as she spoke and he was impressed at how bright her red lipstick was. Her hair was still blonde and short, and she wore big round pale gold earrings. She was standing next to him with one high heeled red patent leather boot up on the bottom rung of his stool. She wore a pink long collared shirt, top three buttons undone and a short, tight white skirt with red polka dots. 'Stay cool. Don't rush. Fancy The Chapel tonight?' He didn't. She went out, he went to bed.

There were no photos the next morning, or the next night, or the next morning. Nothing.

Thirty Four

Sam stood on the pavement outside Amy Angove's London house. She noted the slate sign next to the brass door bell: *"ROSEMERGY"*. She smiled. It was the name of the parish where Amy's parents lived. As she admired the property an old green Morris Traveller in excellent condition drew up at the kerb beside her.

DCI Leo Benedict Julius Fitzroy, known as Ben, was in a bad mood. He'd just discovered that he needed a new electric windscreen washer pump for Emily and it was going to be costly, not in money but in time: time to source it, time to fit it, and he thought he'd repaired the old one - twice. Emily was his Almond Green 1969 Morris Traveller; his pride and joy. He maintained and serviced the vehicle himself. Still, he was intrigued by the business with Amy Angove.

When he had first taken the call from Tom Grigg he'd been hooked. Good man Grigg. They'd last worked together on a rather nasty double murder in the City and Grigg had been very … solid. Surprising that he had chosen to head off to the sticks, especially since he was a Londoner, man and boy, but he'd seemed happy enough on the phone; content with his lot. And of course Fitzroy remembered Félipe Treloar.

Several years previously he had been on the interview panel when Treloar had applied to join the Met. He remembered a good looking serious man of strong character; results driven, highly motivated but with a strong moral sense. He'd liked him and recommended they take him, but then he'd been seconded to a Europol team and lost track. He wondered why Treloar hadn't taken the transfer. The Met didn't like to be rejected and he doubted there would be a second chance.

Yeah he recalled a no bullshit kind of bloke; interesting. Grigg had told him that their boss was not aware of Treloar's investigation. Fair enough. The man had his reasons, Grigg was supporting him and that was good enough for him. As he pulled to the kerb in front of the Angove house he was eager to get involved.

Sam turned from her appraisal of Amy's house as she heard a car door slam and approaching footsteps, to find herself facing a man who resembled a younger Ralph Fiennes. He was dressed in jeans and a battered brown leather jacket over a white T shirt. He smiled, revealing even white teeth with one chipped upper incisor, and when he spoke he sounded like Ralph Fiennes too.

'A beautiful woman admiring the residence of another beautiful woman. A certain symmetry but I'm afraid I'm going to have to ask you to proceed on your way.'

'Oh really? And you are?'

He pulled his warrant card from an inside pocket: 'DCI Ben Fitzroy of the Metropolitan Police.'

Sam rummaged in her tote bag and extracted her own warrant card: 'Snap. DS Sam Scott of Devon & Cornwall Police.'

To her surprise he threw back his head and roared with laughter.'

'Touché, touché. Are you here for Phil Treloar?'

'Yes, Shall we?' And she spun on her heel and headed for the pink front door.

As soon as Fitzroy was made aware of Phil's discovery of the jiffy bags, he took possession of the evidence and headed off leaving Sam and Treloar alone in Amy's kitchen, promising to meet up with them that evening at a good eating pub just along the East Heath Road not far from Amy's house. Sam related the developments back in Cornwall.

'Sam. I am telling you. Again. It's not Dylan Maddox.'

'But …'

'Jesus! How many times do I have to say it? IT IS NOT DYLAN.'

'But Phil, listen to me. You haven't seen the … cell, dungeon, whatever you want to call it. It wasn't thrown up overnight. It must have taken weeks, months to build. The only DNA is Dylan's. It has to be him.'

'Fine. I agree he made the cell but he didn't make it for Amy and he didn't kill her. Think about it Sam. Amy hardly ever visited Cornwall and he couldn't have known she was coming that weekend, nobody knew. Dylan built that place for someone else, or for himself; somewhere to get away from Hope and the baby; somewhere near his precious mine.'

'Phil, I've seen it. He didn't make it for himself: it's a prison, built for containment. And he had photographs there taped on the wall. He'd torn them down, but he'd dropped one, and apparently it was of Amy.'

'OK, OK, I hear you. I know he had a thing for Amy, I've told you that. But we need to focus on the stalker. He left that bag of hair recently and it couldn't have been Dylan because we know where he was up until his arrest, albeit his alibi for the time of death is shot, but he sure as hell couldn't have made it to London and back in the time that's unaccounted for.'

'I agree. We need to tell Winters about the hair.'

'I've spoken to Tom and he's going to tell her without mentioning me. He'll say Fitzroy found it.'

'Christ Phil.'

'Look Sam. You and Ben arrived less than half an hour after I found it. Ben has taken all the bags in for testing. If Winters finds out I'm involved it'll just complicate everything, you know that.'

'I suppose,' she said grudgingly.

'Fitzroy is going to get someone to check CCTV but I don't hold out a lot of hope. If he's even on it, he'll be aware it's there and avoiding facial exposure. He's also getting someone to check for similar cases: harassment, stalking, abductions, murders, in London and countrywide and particularly anything in The Netherlands. He's got good contacts over there through his stint with Europol. He was based in The Hague and he lived in Amsterdam. There has to be a Dutch connection.'

'I agree,' Sam said. 'I was taking to the model agency boss at the funeral. Apparently, they've received bunches of red tulips and some idiot leaving snatches of Mozart's Requiem Mass on their phone. Sounds like our man.'

'Useful man, DCI Fitzroy.'

'Yes. Tom really rates him. I like him. I'd forgotten we'd met before when I was going to join the Met. I liked him then too.'

'Kindred spirits.'

'Sam. He can help us find this bastard. That's what matters.'

Mid December the previous year to mid February this year

'To South Africa, for a fucking car advert!' He shouted at the screen. 'Bastards.' No pictures for three days had been getting him more and more worried. 'Has the bloody kit stopped working or what?' he had wondered. 'Has She found it, taken it out or fucking what? Christ!'

Then he had looked at her Agency "Professional" page and seen that She had gone to South Africa to work on an ad campaign for BMW. 'To take advantage at this time of year of the superb weather and really striking locations available to show off the new BMW range at its perfect best,' the page had said.

Going through the papers helped. There were daily Melissa stories, trial updates, in most papers, and occasional Christiana stories, so that took care of three hours a day, made him feel good, bought some of the buzz back. Work was helping. There was as much of it as he wanted really, tried to keep it to four days a week six hours a day. Helped with pacing, planning, not rushing. Do a thing, then the next, then the next, learn the Knowledge, how to get around town quickly, look forward to the papers. Find a story, cut it out, date it.

There were two boxes now, a Melissa box, a Christiana box. He was chuffed he was keeping himself organised. Made it easier to find the stories and go through them.

Christmas stuff was everywhere, even trees were spread over the pavements in Upper Street. Didn't want one. Then one day he was almost home, cycling past the park, when he saw a branch that had broken off a tree, had to cycle round it and had a thought. Went back out again after stashing his bike, picked up the branch and took it home. Stood it in the corner of the sitting room and went straight back out to the Staples stationery store on Upper Street and bought a laminator and two packs each of A5 and A6 sized plastic laminating wallets. Stopped in a Pound store he'd passed on the way with white tree lights in the window, and bought them. And some tinsel and glue on the way back.

A few days later and he was happy that the kit was still working when pictures came in of the cleaner, and he was well chuffed with his tree. 'This tree's not just for Christmas, he laughed, 'it's for the whole fucking year.' The branch was about one third filled with laminated Melissa and Christiana stories and *some pictures of Her. They had tinsel round the sides that sparkled when the white lights were switched on. The best picture of Her, 'so far,' he thought, laughing with the scarf on Her head and sunglasses hanging by one ear was in a tinsel star on the very top of the tree.*

She came back, he got good pictures. Stories mostly dried up over Christmas with the court closed, nearly three weeks. He worked more hours, hardly any couriers around and private parcels and party invites to collect and deliver, watched more TV, went to The Chapel, made excuses to Jodi for Dan.

He still went through the papers though; there were a few stories, not many. Tinselled up one for Melissa, one for Christiana. The families were 'despondent,' and 'upset,' 'at this time of year.' 'Boo fucking hoo,' he thought when he'd found them. She had disappeared again, 'for a Christmas break,' the Agency website said.

She came back in January. 'Had a wonderful time with friends on the Austrian slopes near St Anton,' the website said. There were pictures of Her in the snow, loads; ditzy on skis going in different directions and about to fall over, ditzy throwing snowballs, happy wearing a bright coloured pom pom hat and striped jacket 'toasting three of Her best pals with Pear Schnapps,' the caption said. Loads more. He cut and pasted some, zoomed for close ups, printed and trimmed and tinselled them for the tree.

The trial started again, stories started again, he wondered about going to see, to the Old Bailey, and on a day off he did. Nearly. Carried on walking past, flagged and got in the first black cab he saw, went to Oxford Street, The Bulldog. Smiled to himself in the back of the cab when he realised he hadn't been serious, and thought of the cops outside the church at Totteridge. It was raining so he sat inside at The Bulldog, had two Orange gins, large, and bought more full tulip flowers, dried, red, yellow. More mixed petals, a small model of a black bicycle, and a small whole Gouda cheese, bright red rind.

He got another invitation. Tweeted and FB'd. 'Awesome. Fucking brilliant!' he said to his screen when he saw them. To two more 'try 'n buy' days with Lamorna at Gucci. 'Get ready for the new year, the Chinese new year!!' The invitation said. 'Only four weeks to go. Gucci is celebrating it's 76ᵗʰ store in China (2 x 38 for you that don't know your lucky Chinese numbers!!). Best wishes from all at Gucci to all of you for extra luck. Celebrate the New Year with us in fantastic and colourful Chinese style!'

Later, he tripped off on the sofa watching TV, waiting for the News. He'd take a camera this time, as well as the phone. Loads had before. The 'Powershot, better zoom,' he thought, 'maybe the D600, tilting screen, easier to see what you're shooting when it's above your head .... Maybe a new one, maybe look around?'

Trudy Parker, Melissa's best friend, red shirt, had been on the TV, picture in the papers again, and he'd wondered about following her, 'when She's out of town .... maybe.'

The cycle café was good. Fun. Had been back a couple of times, with the Powershot, bit hit and miss, just sitting there on the table pointing, zoom set, clicking the shutter button when he thought the time was right. 'Hope and shoot,' he'd thought, couldn't make it obvious. Red haired lycra girl didn't mind, didn't say anything, didn't ask.

He'd got some good photos of Her in and outing the McLaren, 'especially when She wasn't in the fucking jeans,' he thought, 'better outing,' he was thinking .... smiling, looked over to the tree, he'd tinselled one up, 'seriously good legs,' he thought, moving his head towards it near the top of the tree.

Thought about his stories, best yet were yesterday. 'Two on the same page. Fucking national! Brilliant,' he thought .... he already knew them inside out, pictured them, didn't need to go over to the tree.

MELISSA KILLER JAILED

Daily Mail 29 Jan. Thursday

Stanley Briscova, owner of the Company that was responsible for the death of Melissa Stanley-Beale was jailed today for seven years and eight months after being found guilty of gross negligence manslaughter and four major breaches of Health and Safety regulations.

Briscova was responsible in his Company, SB Brothers Builders, for Health and Safety and had repeatedly ignored risk assessments and advice from his staff working not only on the Oxford Street car park site but on other sites previously.

Briscova's company, SB Brothers Builders, has been found guilty of Corporate Manslaughter and has been fined £1.25m. The company's assets have been frozen until such time as the fine has been paid, and it is understood that the court has authorised the sale of any assets necessary to secure payment of the fine at the earliest opportunity.

Melissa Stanley-Beale died after falling through an unsecured plastic barrier on the roof of a car park in which SB Brothers Builders was carrying out building work. 'This was a death that should not have happened and was entirely preventable,' said a spokesman for the Health and Safety Executive (HSE) outside the Old Bailey after the sentence was announced.

'A number of employees had informed Mr Briscova, both verbally and formally in writing of the risks to themselves as well as the public on the car park site but the advice was ignored and this tragic death was the result.

We are delighted that the Court has taken this matter very seriously and very much hope that it will encourage other businesses to pay close attention to Health and Safety regulations and tighten up their application of these important rules wherever necessary.'

Harry Stanley-Beale,

Melissa's brother said after the sentence was handed down, 'Nothing will bring Melissa back, but I am glad, the whole family is glad, that this man will be jailed. It is a real shame he could not have been given longer, and I hope he suffers in there, and afterwards, the b*****d. It should be forever. We'll be suffering for the rest of our lives, why shouldn't he?'

The second story had been in the bottom right corner of the page. Near the front of the paper. The first had been at the top in the middle. The stories were still running, but two on one page brought the buzz back, big time.

CHRISTIANA DEATH, POLICE CALL IN INTERPOL

Daily Mail 29 Jan Thursday

Police looking into the suspicious death of Christiana Trent last November have asked Interpol to see if they can track down a man they wish to question in connection with the death. A recent picture of the man, Mr Luigi Crespattori, with police contact details is shown below this article.

'It seems clear that we need to extend our search for Luigi Crespattori, who was seen to assault Ms Trent in a restaurant in Newcastle the evening before she died, as he cannot be found in any of the locations he would normally be expected to be,' a Metropolitan Police spokesperson said yesterday. 'We have spoken informally to our law enforcement colleagues in the USA where Luigi Crespattori sometimes travelled for work as well as in Italy where he was based.

He was born in Naples which is where most of his family still lives and our officers have spoken to

them, as well as his work colleagues in Rome. They have also spoken to his colleagues in Newcastle which is where the assault took place but no-one appears to have seen or heard from him since the day following the assault.

It is not unusual in a case like this for us to formally ask Interpol to search for people of interest, as they have extensive and widespread databases and methods of helping spot people travelling and residing outside the United Kingdom.'

Christiana Trent, who worked in computer system sales and was aged 29 died at her home in The Barbican in November last year. The police have not revealed the cause of her death but our reporters have spoken to witnesses in Newcastle who say that Luigi Crespattori had appeared to try to strangle Christiana Trent, and other witnesses in London who said that when found in her flat, Christiana appeared to have red marks on her neck. It was Christiana's father who found her body. He then called for an ambulance and the police.

He had gone to Christiana's apartment to see how she was after trying to ring her at work to invite her back to the family home for a bonfire night party and was told by her work colleagues that she was not well and had taken the day off work. He had not been able to get an answer when trying to phone her home number.

After being told about the Interpol search Mr Trent said 'I just hope they can find him. I know the Met and the Newcastle police are doing all they can but this man has gone to ground somewhere. With Interpol helping now, his picture will be all over the place and we're hoping he will be found soon so we can find out what happened to Christiana and why.'

''Try 'n buy' days are brilliant,' he was thinking, still staring through the tree, not seeing, it. The Agency had even put out one of his photos, 'Best fan pic,' they said in the Tweet and on Her Facebook page. 'Fucking ace,' he had thought when he first saw them. He still did. Was still buzzed when he called them up, on his phone or the laptop. He'd sent them from one of the prepaids.

Best though was when he'd seen the photo of Her in the kitchen, taking the copy he'd put through Her letterbox out of the envelope. 'From your VERY best fan xxx' it said on the back of the photo. She hadn't seen that at the time, 'too busy being scared by the petals flying out of the envelope at Her face when she pulled it out, brilliant!' he was thinking as he walked over and looked at the photo in the tinsel star at the top of the tree.

Thirty Five

As Treloar and Fitzroy went to order drinks at the bar, Sam took in her surroundings: nice place; smart, cool and subtle; the kind of place Sam associated with big cities but which was increasingly springing up in Cornwall. Here however the prices were reasonable, presumably due to the level of competition, something which in Sam's view didn't bother many establishments in Cornwall, determined as they seemed to her to extract the last penny out of the season and the tourists, ignoring the fact that some people actually lived there throughout the year.

She made a mental note to visit *Seafood on Stilts* again when she got back. Perhaps she could persuade Treloar to go … perhaps. Through the open window she could hear the to and fro, near and far, droning of a lawnmower. The song *Summer in the City* came into her head and she was humming it when Treloar and Fitzroy returned with a bottle of white wine in an ice bucket and three glasses.

'You're a bit young for *The Lovin' Spoonful* Sergeant, that song must be fifty years old,' said Fitzroy with a dazzling smile.

'At least you can recognise it,' said Treloar, 'Sam is not famed for her choral abilities.'

'Thanks very much,' Sam said laughing.

'I'm sure with such a rich and resonant speaking voice Sam must sing beautifully,' Fitzroy purred.

'Oh it's not her voice,' Treloar added pouring the wine, 'it's her appalling taste in music. Christ, don't ever get in a car with her; she insists on playing Abba.

'That is so not true,' Sam insisted.

'Actually, I'm very partial to *Lay All Your Love On Me,*' Fitzroy said, gazing at Sam.

Treloar picked up a menu, 'Right, fish and chips for you I suppose,' he said of Sam.

'Actually, that is not on the menu. So I'm going to have the burger. Medium rare. Extra ketchup.'

'You'll have to excuse my Sergeant Ben, for an educated woman she has the most appalling taste in food.'

'Not at all Phil, Sam has made an inspired choice, the burgers here are famous. I shall also have one. I highly recommend them.'

'Phil's a vegetarian, he'll have something with goats' cheese,' Sam smiled at Fitzroy.

'Actually, I'm going with the roasted vegetable pancake.'

'Also an excellent choice, I understand this place has a good reputation amongst bean eaters.'

Sam choked on her mouthful of wine and sneaked a look at Treloar. His face was showing no emotion whatsoever. This could be an interesting collaboration she thought. But then Treloar burst out laughing and any strain in atmosphere was dispelled. One of the many things she loved about her boss was his total confidence in himself.

'How is Tom Grigg adjusting to life so very far away from the big city?' Fitzroy asked.

'Tom's ancestors are from Cornwall,' Treloar said, 'came up with Trelawny, to revolt against some king or other, way back.'

'1497,' Sam said, 'and it was Henry VII. They objected to his planned tax regime.'

The two men stared at her and Fitzroy grinned.

'Meet our very own Samba,' Treloar said, 'Sam B.A. History at Bristol.'

Sam blushed. 'Tom is doing very well and his wife loves St Ives, so I understand. He gets on very well with people; he's a natural.'

'So, anything yet?' Treloar asked as they ate their food.

Fitzroy finished a mouthful. 'I've got a guy looking into similar cases in London and calls in to a couple of old colleagues in The Hague and Amsterdam. I should hear something in the morning. As we expected there was nothing useful on CCTV. But coming here tonight I noticed a camera on the wall of a house down from Amy's. It's a kindergarten.'

'I can check that out tomorrow,' Sam said.

'Good,' Treloar said glumly. He was frustrated that he could not be more directly involved but he knew that if he was, Winters would have all the grounds she needed to take his job. Sam picked up on his mood and its cause.

'Perhaps you could have a thorough look around the house in case we missed anything?' she said gently.

'Yeah,' he replied.

At closing time Treloar made his farewells and headed back to Amy's on foot, leaving Sam and Fitzroy calling taxis outside the pub.

'Where are you staying?' Ben asked.

'The Premier Inn Haverstock Hill.'

'Let's share a cab; I'll drop you on my way home.'

'Where do you live?'

'Oh, a little place just south of the river. Not as smart as Hampstead. You must come for supper whilst you're up here.'

'Yes. I'm sure Phil would love that.'

'Oh of course, both of you are invited. I'll open a tin of beans.'

Thirty Six

At 08:00 that morning Treloar was sitting at the patio table in Amy's walled garden drinking coffee. He had just spoken on the phone to Tom Grigg for an update on the Tamsin Thomas situation. He had explained to Tom how frustrating it was being on the periphery of the London investigation because he was officially on leave. Tom had sympathised. He too was frustrated because Winters was allowing the Thomas family to control the investigation into their daughter.

'It's fucking insane. How the hell did that woman get to be Superintendent?' Grigg said.

'Politics my friend,' Treloar said into the phone.

'Well she is just letting this business slide. Apparently, Sebastian Thomas has spoken to Tamsin and she is perfectly happy and wants to stay a few more days with her pal Henry. He insists that both he and his wife are happy with the situation and they don't want us to continue the search and they don't want us to pursue Henry York. I can't prove anything but I'm convinced there's money changing hands here somewhere.'

'Well look on the bright side Tom. With parents like Sebastian and Kate Thomas the girl is probably better off with York. From what I learnt at least he seems to care for her.'

'I suppose,' said Grigg with a sigh. 'Anyway how's it going up there? Winters still has her sights set on Dylan Maddox.'

'It's not Maddox.'

'And how is the lovely Samba?'

'She's fine. Fitzroy seems to be a good bloke; has his priorities right.'

'I knew you two would hit it off: cast from the same mold. Let me know if you need anything at this end, or get Sam to do it. Frosty still has no idea you're up there.'

'Let's keep it like that.'

'Cheers Phil, I'd better get off. Will you update Sam for me on Tamsin?'

'Will do. Bye Tom.'

Fitzroy had spoken to a former associate in Amsterdam, Marieke van der Linden, a Superintendent in the National Crime Squad. He came straight from the office to update Sam and Treloar who were at Amy's.

'It was spooky. She said they had just been speaking in the office about the remarkable striking similarity in appearance between Lamorna Rain and the victim of a tragic fatal tram accident last year; a British girl, Daniele Beaumont, on a weekend break.'

'Was she with a boyfriend or husband?' Sam asked.

'No. That was the second thing that was strange about it, another reason it stuck in their memory. She was with her brother. He was absolutely … broken. Marieke said she had never seen a relative so distressed, not even in the death of a child. They were orphaned recently, evidently.'

'You say that was the second thing, was there something else odd?' Treloar asked.

'Yes. The brother's name: Daniel.'

'Both siblings had the same name?' asked Sam incredulously.

'Apparently. Anyway Marieke is sending me what she can.'

'How come the Dutch are so familiar with Amy?' Treloar asked.

'Last year there was a massive advertisement campaign for Bianchi; billboards everywhere with giant posters of Lamorna Rain in skin tight lycra …'

'Christ she told me!' Treloar interrupted. 'She told me about a campaign for Bianchi. She was going to Milan for a second shoot that very week. I didn't connect to Holland. I thought Bianci, Milan: fashion.'

'No mate,' said Fitzroy. 'not fashion, racing bikes. They supply a Dutch bike racing team. Tour de France and all that.'

At that moment Fitzroy's phone beeped. 'Incoming.' he said opening an image, 'Christ Marieke wasn't wrong,' he held out the phone to Sam and Treloar in turn. It showed a beautiful girl with long blonde hair who could have been Amy's twin. The phone beeped again.

'Oh God,' Fitzroy exclaimed. He held out the phone again. It was clearly a post mortem shot of the same girl but here her hair was cropped short. 'I think it's time we took a look at Daniel Beaumont.'

Fitzroy arranged to meet Daniel Beaumont on the pretext of following up on his sister's accident as part of a review of the collaboration between the British and Dutch authorities. He had suggested lunch in a pub asking Beaumont to choose a convenient time and location. He had selected the courtyard of the Punch & Judy in Covent Garden at 12:30; Fitzroy said he would carry the FT.

Covent Garden, London's first modern square, was designed by Inigo Jones and built for the Duke of Bedford in the early 1600s. Its famed 19th century fruit and vegetable market relocated in 1974 and now its piazza is surrounded by small shops, pubs and cafés, popular with tourists and Londoners alike.

As there was no legitimate reason for either Sam or Treloar to be involved they had decided to arrive early to occupy two tables next to each other so that Sam and Treloar could listen in to the conversation and form their own impressions of the man. At 12:25 Sam tapped Treloar on the shoulder and drew his attention to a slight figure carrying a cycling helmet limping towards them pushing a bright blue bike.

'Here's our man,' she said loud enough for Fitzroy to hear at the next table. Luckily they were close together as the place was filling rapidly.

'Chief Inspector Fitzroy I presume,' said Beaumont with a grin, pointing to the Financial Times on the table.

'Indeed Mr Beaumont,' Fitzroy said standing with his most charming smile. 'Thank you so much for taking the time to meet. What will you have?'

'Oh, just a sparkling water please.'

'And to eat?'

'I'm alright thanks; I've got sandwiches back at base.'

Fitzroy walked off to the bar and Sam took the opportunity to cast her eye over Beaumont as Treloar was seated with his back to him studying the menu.

'There we are,' said Fitzroy placing a glass of ice and a bottle of water on the table.

'So,' said Beaumont, 'you want to know about my experiences at the hands of the Dutch plods. Actually they were probably pretty good. Kind and helpful and they speak fucking brilliant English. I was well impressed.'

'It must have been an awful time for you,' said Fitzroy.

'Yeah well it ruined the weekend that's for sure. We were having a brilliant time then Dan runs straight out in front of the fucking tram. Bam!' he punched his hands together.

'Yes I understand it was a dreadful accident.'

'Yeah well only the good die young, the good and the beautiful someone said. Like all the rock stars, at 27: Hendrix, Joplin, Morrison, that blonde bloke with the fit wife … Kurt Kobain, Amy Winehouse, who's next eh? Talking of Amy, you know that model that got snuffed down west, Lamorna Rain? Her name was Amy, her real name, and she was the fucking image of my Dan, well weird or what?'

'Really?' Fitzroy said letting Daniel roll.

'Yeah, except for the hair. Dan had real short hair when she died, to her shoulders before, and Lamorna Rain had that really long look, long and blonde, down her back, could have been wigs I suppose, well known for it, well, that and her great arse. Well tasty. I'd have given her one.'

Sam felt Treloar bristle, rested her hand on his arm, leaned over and kissed his cheek whispering "Steady" in his ear.

'You don't look very much like your sister then,' Fitzroy said, 'well, not if she looked so much like Lamorna Rain, if you don't mind my saying, just an observation, no offence intended.'

'None taken mate. We weren't related, why would we? Dan was adopted before I was born. My Mum had a thing about the name Daniel, that's how we both ended up with the same fucking name. Total crap or what?'

The conversation carried on for a further fifteen minutes with Fitzroy asking relevant bureaucratic questions about Dutch procedures and Anglo-Dutch liaison.

'Well, I think we've covered everything I need Mr Beaumont. Thank you again for taking the time out of your schedule. How long have you been a bike courier, do you enjoy it?'

'Well I'm freelance really, just work when I want to. Don't need the money, but it's great exercise and it gets me out of the house, meeting people and the like. I started with this mob at the beginning of the year. They're a good bunch; we had a great picnic party in Regent's Park May Bank Holiday weekend. Fucking brilliant.' He smiled looking into the near distance as if remembering. 'Well, if we're done here I'll be on my way.'

'Goodbye Mr Beaumont,' Fitzroy said standing and

extending his hand.

As Beaumont wheeled his bike away Treloar stood, walked across the courtyard area as if to enter the bar, and watched the slight figure cross the piazza, steering his bike by the saddle alone, weaving expertly and quickly through the crowds.

May this year

He'd been buzzing after talking to Fitzroy, decided to go back home, take the afternoon off, think. He had headed north through the piazza then away on the bike towards Covent Garden underground station then west and north; glided, practically floated through the lunch time people cars and buses. Charing Cross Road, Tottenham Court Road then east along Euston Road. Busy busy.

The newspaper billboards jumped out at him from the wide pavement outside Euston station as he went past, and he smiled when he saw that the lovely Amy's funeral was still going big and that pictures of her with anyone that counts were still a good draw.

The traffic was quieter as he reached Islington and turned into Upper Street from Pentonville Road, not much, but he had more time to think. Not so much to dodge and miss, watch out for.

'What the fuck was that all about?' he wondered. 'Haven't got a fucking clue.' He had been going to get there early to see if there were any watchers but couldn't because a rush job had come in and he didn't want to upset the boss, yet at least. 'Didn't matter anyway, that fucker Sam Scott was obvious straight away, from all the stuff on the TV when those girls in Cornwall went missing - she'd been there with a face like a smacked arse, couldn't miss it. What the fuck was she doing here? And the fucking ex, what the fuck was HE doing here?!'

He had deliberately told Fitzroy, loudly so Scott would hear, that he'd like to screw Amy, to wind them up, see what happened, but he hadn't been expecting the jump from Scott's mate. As soon as he'd seen it he recognised him from pictures online and the papers, even from the back. 'Christ! Who do they think they are, and what the fuck are they doing here? And what the fuck's it got to do with the Cloggy police?'

'Didn't give anything away though,' he thought as he cycled slowly past The Chapel, 'didn't want to piss them off, get them even more interested, but they haven't got anything. No way. Can't have. But what the fuck is Fitzroy really doing and what the fuck are Scott and fucking Treloar doing and why were they trying to fucking well hide?'

He got off, wheeled the bike across the pavement outside the newsagent, leaned it against the window, went in and bought the dailies to search through and clip, with a pizza and beer.

Thirty Seven

Fitzroy's 'little place' south of the river was in fact the entire top floor of a converted warehouse in Bermondsey. Reached by a large grilled service lift, it was all exposed brickwork and massive beams; very open plan; very desirable.

'Great place,' said Treloar admiringly, taking in the large and extensive views over the Thames.

'Phil's just finished a double barn conversion,' said Sam, 'so he knows what he's talking about.'

'Ah well, I can take no credit whatsoever for this place,' said Fitzroy, 'it came like this. I just threw in the furniture and paintings.'

'Something smells good,' Sam said.

'No credit there either I'm afraid,' Fitzroy said with a lopsided grin, 'roasted vegetable lasagne courtesy of the local deli. But, I can guarantee the quality, everything they do is wonderful.'

After they'd eaten and were seated on leather sofas with coffee and tiny nut biscuits, Treloar turned the conversation to Daniel Beaumont.

'What did you make of Beaumont?' he asked the other two.

'Well, I can't think why, but he seemed familiar somehow,' said Sam with a frown.

'Just another anonymous bike courier I expect,' said Fitzroy, 'they all look alike apart from the colour of their lycra; similar build, similar age, helmets.'

'No it wasn't that. Let me think.'

'I noticed something strange about him,' said Treloar. 'When he approached the table at the pub he was limping quite badly. But when he wheeled his bike away he was walking normally. I thought it odd so I watched him walk until he was out of sight; no limp.'

'Talking of his bike, did you notice the make?' Fitzroy asked.

'Oh yes,' Treloar replied, 'Bianchi. Coincidence?'

'Surely not'.

'That's it!' Sam exclaimed. The two men looked at her. 'That limp, that gait, I saw exactly the same thing on the CCTV coverage from the kindergarten. I'd swear to it; Daniel Beaumont was in Amy's street.'

'When? Which day?' asked Treloar.

Sam sighed. 'I don't know. But recently, certainly over the last few days, and definitely since Amy's funeral.'

'What if it was him delivering the hair? Was he carrying anything?' asked Fitzroy.

'No. I would have registered that. He was just walking away from Amy's on the other side of the road, towards the heath. And he didn't have his bike.'

'We need to have another look at that footage,' said Fitzroy.

'Yeah,' said Treloar. 'Too many things now to be just coincidence: the sister lookalike, the Dutch connection, the Bianchi bike, the limping figure in Amy's street.'

'Let's find out where he was when Amy died,' said Fitzroy.

'It was a Sunday,' Sam said, 'so he probably wasn't working.'

'So,' said Treloar, 'let's find out what he was doing.'

'If he's our man he's a smart one. I'll bet you'll find he was at a party in Regent's Park. Big place Regent's Park,' said Fitzroy.

Thirty Eight

Fitzroy and Sam reviewed the video from the kindergarten while Treloar waited impatiently at Amy's. They agreed that it was him and it was the day that the hair arrived through Amy's letterbox. Fitzroy put in a general enquiry to the Cavendish bike courier service about deliveries in that area on that day. Sam watched as he smiled and shook his head at the reply.

'Well he's a clever bastard,' Fitzroy said as he put the phone down. 'There was a delivery to a hotel at the end of Amy's street that day and our boy was the courier. They have the signed paperwork, but let's check with the hotel.'

'So where was his bike?'

'Good question. Let's ask.'

Over at Amy's Sam and Fitzroy sat in the rear garden. Treloar joined them with coffee. Sam had spoken to the hotel and they had confirmed the date and time of the delivery. When she had asked what was in the package they had told her some sample linen napkins sent on spec by someone looking for new business. They had kept the napkins but ditched the paperwork and packaging. They could not remember the name of the company. They remembered the courier because he had asked permission to leave his bike in their car park whilst he visited the heath to go swimming; he felt it would be safer there as they had CCTV cameras.

'So, he had an excuse to be walking down Amy's street without his bike if anybody checked. Smart,' said Fitzroy.

'Right Sam,' Treloar said, 'ring them back. He must have acquired the napkins to get that hotel onto his delivery route. Ask them to put them aside and we'll pick them up. It's a long-shot but he may have left some trace on them and we may be able to link him to them through the original supplier. That will prove the delivery was bogus.'

Sam sipped her coffee reflectively and turned to Fitzroy. 'Did you notice that when you mentioned his sister he immediately volunteered that Amy looked like her? You hadn't mentioned Amy and he had no expectation that you would, given what he'd been told about the nature of your meeting.'

'Well it is a major news story at the moment and the

resemblance is striking,' Fitzroy replied.

'Yes,' Sam continued, 'but then he mentioned the hair, "except for the hair". Why would he draw attention to the hair?'

'Because he's playing with us,' said Treloar 'OK. Did we check what he said about where he was that Sunday?'

'Yes,' said Sam with a sigh, 'I checked with his workmates and several confirmed that he was at the picnic in Regent's Park he mentioned yesterday, and two say there are loads of video clips and photos to prove it. Maybe it wasn't him? Maybe it was a random encounter?'

'It was him,' said Treloar. 'Come on Sam, a random encounter? In London maybe but not that part of Cornwall. No it's him; he's the stalker and he's the killer.'

'I agree with Phil,' said Fitzroy. 'There's too much connecting him: the link to The Netherlands, the lookalike sister, his presence in Amy's street, and he's fucking weird, he was so … hyper; I'd swear he's on something. Could be him and a partner, one here, one in Cornwall? In my experience psychopaths are drawn to each other, they recognise each other, much like Masons. Shame we don't have cause to check his phone records. Back in the day I could have swung that, but not in the current political climate.'

'Leave that with me,' said Treloar quietly.

'Really?' said Fitzroy with a smile and a raised eyebrow.

'Oh no,' said Sam.

'You don't have to know anything about it Sam. I'm making the call,' Treloar said pointedly then turned to Fitzroy. 'Contact from an old case with … useful skills.' And with that he picked up his coffee mug and walked back into the kitchen, pulling his mobile from his pocket.

'Useful skills? Fitzroy asked.

'Don't ask,' said Sam firmly, picking up her own phone to check messages.

Treloar and Sam had come across Jamie Deverell when they were investigating some violent sexual murders in Porthaven on the south Cornish coast. At first he had been considered a suspect but he was ruled out and had proved very useful to Treloar in uncovering the true killer. Jamie was an expert hacker.

Jamie Deverell lived at Linton Crucis in the New Forest, in a

285

former 13th century abbey. He and his childhood friend, Alasdair Frobisher, ran a highly successful security software company from offices in the grounds. Treloar reached him on his private line at the first attempt. Jamie was always in the office. After a few pleasantries Treloar explained what he wanted and Jamie promised to get back to him later that day.

Fitzroy had returned to his office to check on any information coming in on similar murders or stalking incidents, leaving Sam in the garden at Amy's waiting for Treloar. She had a message to call Superintendent Winters but Frosty could wait. It was a pleasant sheltered garden scented by the lilacs that bloomed along its walls. The lawn was in need of mowing.

Treloar had asked Jamie to check Daniel Beaumont's phone for the period since the date of the first strange phone call on the notes he took at his meeting with Amy on the day of her death. He had given him numbers to run the calls against: Amy's home, mobiles and office, her parents' home, her agent's mobile and home amongst them. But he had asked Jamie to focus on, and call him back urgently, on activity in the week prior to Amy's murder. Jamie rang at noon.

'There was nothing matching your numbers in the week prior to Lamorna Rain's death but the strangest thing is that there was nothing at all from late on May 1st to late evening of May 4th.'

'Nothing?'

'No. I'd say the phone was switched off over that period. Alisdair is checking for its physical location as we speak. I'd say your man left it at home when he went Cornwall.'

'If he went to Cornwall.'

'Well, that's my point. I recognised the dialling code for a number he called twice on May 1st, as the same as Lamorna's parents' home number. I reverse directoried the number and it's for a 'Lower Farm Holidays'. Hang on a sec … that was an email from Alisdair. Beaumont left his mobile switched on and it didn't move from his home address cell tower over that weekend. Are you OK Inspector?'

'Fine thank you Jamie,' Treloar replied woodenly.

'Right I'll carry on checking back from May for you and call you,' and with that he hung up.

'This is not like you. You don't doubt yourself, never,' Sam said fiercely.

'He rang Dylan. Why would he ring Dylan? Fitzroy must be right: they're a team.'

'Rubbish. He did not ring Dylan he rang the holiday business. Think about it. He tracked her to Cornwall. He found out she was going to her parents; the agency receptionist told him that. Lower Farm is one of the nearest places for him to stay to their house and it's the very closest to yours. He would have known about your relationship.'

Treloar sat silently shaking his head but Sam ignored him and continued.

'If he was smart enough to leave his mobile in London when he went to Cornwall, wouldn't he have been smart enough to use a payphone or a friend's phone or a client's phone to contact Lower Farm if he were involved with Dylan? Wouldn't he have called Dylan's mobile or their home? It's not Dylan, you've convinced me of that. It's Daniel Beaumont. He's the stalker; he's the killer. Let's check flights to Newquay, trains, car hire. Does he have access to a car? He didn't ride that bloody bike to Cornwall.'

'OK. Check. Do it. I'll check with Lower Farm; I'll talk to Hope, off the record. She knows I believe Dylan is innocent, she'll help.'

Fitzroy was back and he was excited. It turned out that it wasn't just the courier company at the picnic in Regent's Park, but several neighbouring businesses plus all their families: several hundred people. When Fitzroy had questioned the people to whom Sam had spoken more closely it transpired that nobody could actually recall speaking to Daniel. But when they had all been discussing it later in the week he had known all about it; he recounted specific incidents, even conversations, so they all assumed he had been there.

'Anyway, I looked at the Internet and there's loads of footage on Facebook, even on the courier company's website. He could easily have fabricated his presence at the picnic from those images. He spoke about it as if he were there, they had expected him to be there, they assumed he was there; very clever. Much better than saying he was home alone.'

'OK,' said Treloar nodding, 'he's back in the frame.'

'I agree,' said Sam, 'but not proving he was there does not

prove that he wasn't.'

'I like him for it,' said Fitzroy, 'he was very ... intense, manic almost.'

'What did your Dutch pals say about him again?' Sam asked.

'They said he was distraught. At first he was hysterical then inconsolable. There's no chance he pushed her, all the witnesses said it was an accident, she just stepped into the road without hesitation, not looking, straight under the tram. Marieke said he was more like a man who had lost a lover, the love of his life, rather than a sister.

But there's more, and this is the really interesting part. My search came back. Since the death of his sister, there have been two suspicious deaths of young women in the Greater London area, who bear a strong resemblance to Daniele Beaumont: Melissa Stanley-Beale and Christiana Trent.'

'What?' exclaimed Sam.

'Oh yes indeedy,' said Fitzroy with a huge grin.

'Christ,' said Treloar. 'Well we've heard back from my ... associate, and there was a call placed from Beaumont's mobile to Lower Farm Holidays on May 1st.'

'Lower Farm Holidays?' Fitzroy asked.

'That's the business of Dylan Maddox. It's adjacent to the mine where Amy was found; the mine is on Maddox land. It's a camp and caravan site with a few holiday farm cottages.'

'Could our man be working with Maddox?' Fitzroy asked.

'No we don't think so,' Sam replied, 'Lower Farm is an obvious place to stay if you are following Amy. It's close to her parents' home and the next land to Phil's where the party was on May 1st. Plus it's casual, easygoing. That campsite is not like a hotel, you don't register, nobody shows you to your room carrying your luggage.'

'Sam's right,' said Treloar, 'I've spoken to Hope Maddox, Dylan's wife. She has no record of anyone named Beaumont making a booking that day, but again, it's all rather slapdash especially if Dylan took the booking which she says he must have because she was in the farm shop all day. People with tent pitches go wherever they want in that field; it's a free for all. They can pay in advance over the phone with a card or pay cash on site.'

'He's been very clever. Why would he use his own mobile to ring?' asked Fitzroy.

'I've thought about that,' said Treloar. 'We know that someone spoke to the receptionist at Amy's agency and extracted the fact that Amy had gone to relatives. Amy's only relatives are in Cornwall. He would have known that if he was stalking her, it's common knowledge. I think he was excited, carried away by the chase. He was in a hurry. He found Lower Farm Holidays online and rang. He didn't know he could have paid by cash, Dylan would not have volunteered that information, so he paid by card. Dylan would have wanted to secure the money in case the guy changed his mind and didn't turn up. It was perfect: an anonymous, convenient place to stay.'

'Do we have enough for a search warrant on his home?' Sam asked.

Fitzroy grinned. 'I think I can swing that. Anyway, this bugger's so cocky, if we asked he'd probably offer us a guided tour.'

Sam's phone buzzed as a text came in. 'Shit, it's Frosty again. I've ignored her twice, I'd better call.' She stood up from the table and walked across the lawn.

'Where does he live?' asked Treloar.

'Islington. Gibson Square. I know it; it's near the Almeida theatre ….' He trailed off looking at Sam who was rushing towards them ashen faced.

'What the hell?' Treloar asked as she reached the table.

'I have to get back. I have to go now. Tamsin Thomas is dead.'

Thirty Nine

Tamsin Thomas was dead but Henry York hadn't killed her; well not directly. In fact, it could be said that Sebastian Thomas had killed her, but again, not directly. That week there was a small fun fair on Lemon Quay in Truro. Nobody paid any attention to another father and daughter strolling, laughing, hand in hand. Nobody saw the man stop to talk to a second man who took the girl's hand. Nobody was looking as the first man turned and walked quickly away through the crowds. Nobody heard the second man drop the girl's hand to answer his phone, saying, "be quiet for God's sake Tammy this is business and it's important."

But plenty of people saw a small figure running, shouting the name "Hal," the crowds parting before and then staring in horror as she hurtled straight out into Lemon Street and the path of a small delivery van. Later, several would say that the van had been speeding, but that those auto-part delivery vans always are, but others, the majority, said that the distraught young woman driving didn't stand a chance; nobody could have stopped.

Everybody said they would never forget the sight of the rag-doll body flying through the air and the sickening sound of her head thudding into the cobbled street, blood mixing with the rain water in the gunnels by the kerb and flowing slowly away.

In Superintendent Winters' office Sam was trying to hide her frustration with little success.

'With Treloar on leave, I need you back here Sergeant. I really cannot understand why you were still up in London. With Dylan Maddox in custody, this so-called stalker is irrelevant to our enquiry.'

'Yes, but surely,' Sam said, 'we must be absolutely certain that it was Maddox. It seems extraordinary that both Dylan Maddox and another person were targeting Amy Angove.'

'That is for the Met,' Winters snapped. 'I have met DCI Fitzroy and I am aware of his ... rakish charm. I see the appeal ...'

'Really Ma'am!' Sam interrupted, furious at the aspersion.

'Oh Sam, I have asked you not to call me Ma'am. Anyway I want you to finalise this business with the Thomases. The CPS is considering what if anything we can charge them with. The wife's complicity is obviously a complicating factor, and York is probably back in the US. I want you on it. Really, I cannot understand your reluctance to finish this.'

Well, Frosty was obviously still unaware of her contretemps with Sebastian Thomas, Sam thought. She would have to tread carefully.

'Christ, what a fucking disaster,' said Tom Grigg. 'No sign of Henry York. The boat was found moored off the French coast near Roscoff; no money, no passport, no kit. You know what I think of Frosty, but I have to agree; I bet York's home free and I doubt we'll pursue him.'

'Well when he finds out what has happened I bet he'll be devastated,' Sam said, 'from what Lily told us he was genuinely fond of the girl and she adored him. Strictly speaking he's blameless for her death. By the time it happened she was back in the care of her father and the van was travelling too fast. No, it's bloody Kate Thomas who's to blame. '

'Well, everyone should take some share of the blame here: the parents, York, the driver.'

'Huh,' Sam said with a snort, 'I bet the others are suffering more than Kate Thomas; she's probably glad to be rid of the girl.'

'Sam,' said Grigg sadly, 'the death of a child is not something you ever recover from.'

'Well I think it's like a Greek tragedy. Euripides' Medea; Jason's wife kills their children to punish him for his infidelity and rides off into the sunset in a chariot.'

'Oh I think there will be a price for Kate Thomas,' said Grigg. 'What will she have left? Sebastian and York will turn against her and when word of the extent of her involvement gets out she'll be a pariah.'

'Well the CPS must be able to proceed against her for something.'

'Don't be too sure. Broken woman, devastated mother punished beyond the power of the law, suffering a life sentence. I can hear her barrister now.'

Forty

Whilst Tom Grigg and Sam Scott bemoaned the inadequacies of the justice system, Treloar and Fitzroy were literally taking the law into their own hands: breaking into Daniel Beaumont's house in Islington, albeit armed with Fitzroy's freshly acquired search warrant.

The house was in Gibson Square, a classic London square of terraced houses surrounding a railed central garden. Beaumont's house was rather shabbier than most on the outside, but inside it was a shambles and filthy There was an overwhelming smell of burnt toast and spoiled milk.

'I'll take up here,' said Fitzroy, threading his way through the piles of newspapers which lined the stairs. Treloar worked his way down the hallway through more piles of newspapers and stacked empty pizza boxes, pulling on a pair of latex gloves. He opened the first door to his left.

The front sitting room was obviously not used. It was relatively tidy, but dusty and strung with cobwebs, and it smelled of damp soot. Above a dirty fireplace hung a portrait, presumably of a woman from the clothes, but the face was not visible as it was obscured by red paint, clearly hurled from a distance to leave dried rivulets running down to the mantelpiece, pooled in the hearth and streaked across the carpet. He closed the door.

The second door opened onto a very different scene.

'Ben! Down here!' he called and walked slowly into the room. This had once been a second sitting room, but its chairs and sofa were barely discernible beneath the piles of newspapers, magazines and hundreds, maybe thousands, of photographs. In one corner, leaning against the wall, was a dead tree branch. As Treloar approached he could make out tatty photos mounted in laminated plastic and framed with silver tinsel. At the top, shaped like a star, was a photo of Amy.

He heard Fitzroy on the stairs, 'Jesus Christ, it's like camera city up there; a room stuffed with cameras, printers, laptops, telephoto lenses and Christ knows what. He entered the room and joined Treloar by the tree. 'What the hell?'

'Look,' said Treloar pointing to the star, 'it's Amy.'

'Yeah, and here's Christiana Trent,' said Fitzroy pointing at another framed photo. Treloar was studying a row of boxes next to the tree. There were three; labelled: 'Melissa', 'Christiana' and 'Amy'.

He opened the 'Amy' box. It was full of newspaper cuttings and pictures cut from magazines and printed from the Internet. There was also a folder of photographs on glossy computer paper.

'Look at these,' he said thumbing through the prints. 'Fucking bastard.'

Fitzroy looked over Treloar's shoulder at the images which had obviously been captured in Amy's house without her knowledge. One showed her holding an open jiffy bag as red tulip petals fell to the floor, a look of shock and fear on her face. He walked back to the tree and looked more closely at the 'decorations'. 'Here's one of Christiana Trent with an envelope outside an office. She's looking frightened too. Our guy's a watcher. He's a coward. He gets off on their fear.'

Treloar was still gazing at the image of Amy in his hand. 'If he's got into Amy's and set up a camera to get these ...' he turned to face Fitzroy, 'what are the chances that he's watching us now?'

'Good point my friend,' Fitzroy replied scanning the room.

And they were right. As Daniel sat in the cycle café his phone beeped. He wasn't expecting anything and frowned as he opened the image. Fuck!! The bastard cops were in his house, in his tree room, touching his work! How the fuck?

Suzie, the waitress watched in surprise as her new regular threw down the menu he'd been studying and dashed out of the door and over to his bike. Fifteen minutes later he stormed through the front door in Gibson Square.

'Get out! Get out! GET THE FUCK OUT!'

He threw back the door to his tree room where Treloar and Fitzroy were patiently sorting through the contents of the girl boxes. Ignoring them, he turned and shouted towards the wall next to the tree, 'DAN? .... How did they get in? ....
Bollocks! How could you let them? It's our place. No-one comes here. It's ours .... For us. You and me. You knew! Why did you let the bastards in? .... How could you? .... Stupid! Bastards!' and with that he burst into tears, turned on his heel and fled back down the hallway and out through the open front door.

'Jesus, he's a complete nut-job,' said Fitzroy.

'Yeah, but he's getting away,' said Treloar stumbling through the pizza boxes in the hallway, 'Come on!!'
The two men rushed out after Daniel Beaumont, leapt into the Morris Minor and sped off after the fleeing bike.

Daniel sped out of Gibson Square and onto Richmond Avenue. He hurtled across Liverpool Street and on towards the Caledonian Road with the Morris Minor in hot pursuit. When he reached 'The Cally', as it is known locally, he turned left, pedalling furiously away.

'He's heading for the Regent's Canal I'll bet!' Fitzroy shouted. 'He'll be able to get onto the towpath where we can't follow and then he's got the whole length of the Grand Union Canal!'

As they drew close Treloar was watching the manic figure who was cycling madly but frantically tugging at something on his left wrist. As they drew closer still he could see that Beaumont was trying to pull off a wristband. 'What is he doing?'

At that moment the bike was forced to swerve out into the road as a bus pulled away from the kerb. Fitzroy was hot on his heels. Suddenly, the combined efforts of steering, changing up the gears, and trying to rid himself of the wristband defeated him and as he passed the accelerating bus he lost control, skidded and slid towards the pavement.

Fitzroy slammed on the brakes, 'Christ we've got to get him up! He's going to go under the bus!' he shouted reaching for the door handle, 'It'll kill him!'

'Exactly,' said Treloar icily, grabbing the other man's arm and pulling him back from the door. And with that there was a sickening crunching sound as a double decker London bus rolled over Daniel Beaumont's prone body.

Over the coming years, the two men in the car would work together on several occasions and become fast friends, but they never spoke of that moment again.

Epilogue

When suspicions of Daniel Beaumont's involvement in Amy's death had become public knowledge, a Dr Ivan Speer, who was a therapist at a private drug and alcohol rehabilitation centre near Fowey had come forward to the police with a video taken at a similar centre in Surrey the previous year. It was of the Beaumont siblings and he thought it might shed some light on Daniel's personality and his relationship with his sister. Back in Cornwall, Treloar and Sam watched it in silence.

'Well I can certainly see the amazing likeness to Amy. Daniele doesn't sound remotely like her but the physical resemblance is uncanny. It could be Amy at the time we got married.'

Oh Christ,' Sam said softly.

'What?' Treloar asked.

'Oh Christ, Oh Christ, I need to talk to Colin.' She picked up her phone and punched a speed-dial number. 'Col it's Sam. That photograph you found of Amy at the mine, was it just of Amy?'

Sam lifted her hand to her cheek as she listened. 'No that's it. Thanks. Bye.'

'What is Sam?' asked Treloar urgently, sensing her disquiet.

'The photograph they found at the mine was of your wedding day. It showed Amy standing next to Beatriz. It's not Amy he built the cell for it's Beatriz; it's not Amy he's obsessed with, not anymore, it's Beatriz. Oh my God!'

'What?!'

'The photographs in your hallway; Lucia saw it; she showed me.'

'WHAT?'

'They were a series taken over the course of the barn conversion. But in every one that featured both Beatriz and Dylan there was ... there was a noose around Bee's neck.'

'That's ridiculous.'

'No. No it's not, ask Lucia. Somebody had taken the original image and manipulated it; photo-shopped it or whatever. Fuck. I didn't make the connection. I didn't see the photo from the mine. I've been too distracted, too fucking distracted.'

'OK. OK. Let's think. What are you saying?' said Treloar calmly.

295

'I'm saying that whilst Dylan did not kill Amy he certainly has plans for your sister and we convinced Frosty to cut him loose.'

'Shit. I'll call Bee. No. I'll call Lucia. You call Tom.'

'Phil I'm so sorry, I should have seen it sooner. Don't give Lucia a hard time.'

'That's not why I'm calling. Believe me, if there's going to be a confrontation we want Lucia. She's very ... effective in a fight.'

Treloar phoned Lucia and told her to find Beatriz and to stay with her until he called.

'My mother put the originals up not me,' he told Sam. 'You don't notice things you live with. I knew what was in the photographs so I doubt I gave them a second glance.'

'Exactly, But Lucia was seeing them on the wall for the first time so she looked. Someone, with access to your home, took the originals and replaced them. That person must have had both access to your house and the skills to do the manipulation. You told me last year that Dylan and Hope had keys for any deliveries and tradesmen needing to get in to do work when you weren't there.'

'Well the Maddoxes certainly have the kit; Hope does all the marketing for the businesses. I should have seen it. Dylan has always been obsessed with the Pitt-Townsend hangings at the mine, even as a kid. He used to try to scare the girls with tales of the doomed sister and her mad mother.

I knew that it wasn't about Amy, Christ I shouted about it to everyone who'd listen, but I never thought about Bee, she's Hope's best friend for Christ's sake.

At Lower Farm Treloar and Sam sat at the kitchen table with Hope Maddox. Dylan was not there.

'It wasn't Dylan,' she said quietly.

'What are you saying Hope?' asked Treloar.

'It wasn't Dylan,' she repeated.

'Of course it was Dylan! I've seen the photographs that he manipulated, Lucia showed me. I've seen the photograph of Bee we found in that ... cell he built. You can't protect him Hope,'

'It wasn't Dylan. It wasN'T DYLAN! IT WAS ME! IT WAS ME, OK?'

'What?' asked Sam.

'I did the photographs. I put them in your hallway. Dylan couldn't have done that. He doesn't know how. He wouldn't wish Bee harm. It's Amy all over again.'

'But why would you do it?' Treloar asked, 'You love Bee.'

'I was sick of it. Sick of hearing about her; how beautiful, clever, fit, funny, accomplished she is. I was just sick of it. I do love her but I was so angry. I needed to do something so I doctored the photos. It was harmless. Nobody even noticed and nobody got hurt and I felt much better.

'But what about the cell?' Sam asked.

'Oh you just don't see it do you? It's for him, it's for Dylan. It's just his place to be, like a shed or something. He used to go there and play old CDs; music from the World Wars and sad songs like that Art Garfunkel I played at Amy's funeral. He asked me to do that. I saw no harm in it. I know he didn't kill her. If it hadn't been for poor Amy nobody would have given it a second thought. But you all jumped to conclusions. Poor Dylan, you all misjudged him, even you Phil who've known him for years. You said he would never have hurt Amy, how could you think he'd hurt Bee?'

Treloar shook his head. 'You're right Hope, I'm sorry. I did rush to judgement. Coming after Amy and with it being Bee, I didn't think it through.'

'OK Phil. I'm sorry too, about the photos I mean. It was petty and childish; spiteful. I kept the originals. I'll give them back of course.'

'But what about Dylan's fixation on Bee?' Sam asked.

'Oh that will pass, just like it did with Amy. I'm not a fool and please don't pity me. I know Dylan loves me and he adores Bethan. It's just that he has this muted passion for other women if that makes sense. I can live with that. It's harmless, he'd never, ever act upon it and he's mortified that you all know about it, especially Bee. It's rather sad really.'

'Can't he get help, counselling of some sort?' asked Sam.

'Yes. He's had that. When he was at school he went on a residential placement, all rubber bands and mantras. It's actually getting better. It's not as bad with Bee as it was with Amy apparently. Edmund has told me that, he knows about it.'

'Why didn't you say something sooner?' asked Sam.

Both Hope and Treloar looked at her. 'What?' she asked.

'Betrayal,' said Treloar quietly.

'Exactly,' said Hope, 'he'd be mortified if anyone knew, especially you Phil. I could never hurt him like that.'

'Where is he Hope?' asked Treloar.

'Radgell.

'Of course, Ochre. She offers sanctuary to waifs and strays; anyone in need. Call him Hope. Call him and tell him to come home. He has nothing to fear now. It's over.'

As they walked towards the car he put his arm around Sam's shoulder and pulled her towards him.

'Come on Sam, I could murder a pint.'

LONDON STALKER
BURIED

The funeral took place today at a London crematorium of Daniel Stephen Beaumont who was widely suspected of the stalking and murder of supermodel Lamorna Rain and HR manager Christiana Trent.

Beaumont was killed in a road traffic accident on The Caledonian Road when his bicycle went under a London bus during a police pursuit in Islington.

Police have discovered overwhelming documented evidence of his stalking activities at his home in Islington, and further evidence which links him to a campsite in Cornwall near the scene of Ms Rain's death as well her home in Hampstead Heath, and the apartment building in The Barbican where Ms Trent was found dead by her father.

A source close to the police investigation confirmed that Beaumont had also been suspected of involvement in the death of Melissa Stanley-Beale, who fell to her death from a car park near Oxford Street last year.

Speaking exclusively to this newspaper a former therapist of Beaumont, Dr Ivan Speer, said, 'he was a very troubled individual with deep rooted issues around his parents and his adopted sister.............' But Ms Suzie Simmonds a waitress at the cycle café in Shoreditch where Beaumont was a customer said, 'I can't believe it, he was always so sweet; very quiet and polite.'

As a matter of course where the police are involved in a death, the incident on The Caledonian Road has been referred to the IPPC, but sources have told the London Evening Standard that they expect no further action.

SILENT GULL

By

L. A. Kent

If you enjoyed Broken Dove, read the first two chapters of Silent Gull, #3 in the Treloar series; available mid 2016; starting over the page.

One

It was cold on the water. It was late November in Cornwall. It was late evening. A figure clad in a wetsuit, in a navy blue kayak, was pulling against the inflowing waters of the tide across the River Fowey from the Fowey side. A bright intermittent moon was shining off the water then disappearing behind sweeping clouds. The kayaker moved silently and expertly between the boats moored in the channel, then hugged the far side of the river which was uninhabited and safe from prying eyes. It steered into a tributary, where the going was easier, and glided up to a small jetty where a second figure clad in jeans and a dark hoodie was waiting, breath misting in the cold air.

A large tanned hand reached down to grab the prow and secured the kayak to a ring before moving to repeat the action at the stern. The paddle was handed up and then the paddler raised its arms and was lifted onto the jetty and into a passionate embrace. The paddler pulled a beanie off its head and a mass of red curls fell down its shoulders.

'Hey Babe,' said the lifter, smiling to reveal perfect white teeth in a tanned handsome face with piercing sapphire eyes. He was a good-looking boy.

'Hey Hitch,' said the girl returning his smile.

Her name was Georgiana Spargo and her father, Christian, was one of the most feared and despised men in Cornwall. If he had known the purpose of her crossing and who she was visiting, he would have killed her with his bare hands.

At the end of the jetty were a series of old terraced buildings and a thatched roundhouse, all entirely in darkness. The lovers should have been alone. But someone was watching and listening. A man was standing inside the roundhouse in the darkness having just emerged from the flotation tank. He should not have been there at night. What psychologist Dr Ivan Speer, ever on the lookout for an opportunity for blackmail and betrayal, with all his experience of troubled minds, should have remembered, was that secrets are dangerous, and even other people's can get you killed.

Christian Spargo resented Jackson Power. How could anyone leave California for Cornwall; abandon the weather, the space, the money, the opportunities? Christian's greatest regret in life was that he hadn't left for the US years ago. Opportunity lost. His dreams had been limited to the narrow grey horizons of the UK.

The US would have understood him; appreciated him; valued him; Christ, honoured him! Here he was treated with civil contempt. Oh, they respected his money and feared his assumed violence, but they didn't like him. They bridled at his uncouth presence in their riverside idyll. Just like his hero, Napoleon Bonaparte, he was misunderstood and despised. They had a stereotypical image of a gangster and they had pinned it on him.

But the real reason for his hatred of Jackson Power was a bitter, festering commercial defeat. Christian had been about to exchange contracts on the purchase of Seal Hall when he was outbid by a ridiculously higher offer by Power, the Hollywood superstar, much to the delight of the local community. Everyday, Christian could stare from the upstairs windows of his substantial home, Corsica House, set among the evergreen trees above the narrow streets of Fowey, across the Fowey River to the domain of his enemy on the top of the opposite wooded slope. He tried not to, but sometimes it was irresistible.

Power, a Minnesota farm boy whose real name was Rolf Lindström, had shot to fame in the nineties when he had been cast as an unknown Hollywood newcomer to play the hero in the first of a phenomenally successful series of movies about a fictional medieval kingdom. Twenty years later he was a multi-millionaire with a beautiful wife Erin, a family home on Mulholland Drive in Los Angeles and millions of devoted fans. He had gained great fame and fortune, but he had lost his eldest son.

Jackson and Erin had named their four children for their Hollywood favourites. The eldest, a boy, Ford after director John Ford; then daughter, Davis, after actress Bette Davis; son Hitchcock, known as Hitch, after director Alfred Hitchcock; and finally daughter Gardner, known as Posy, after actress Ava Gardner. All had been wonderful in their Camelot life until Ford fell in with the wrong crowd, took to drugs, escalating to heroin, and despite his parents' frantic efforts and copious cash, died of a massive overdose in a seedy motel on Hollywood Boulevard the previous year.

Erin had turned to her therapist, but bereft and inconsolable, Jackson Power had left for Europe. He had toured the continent fleeing his pain and eventually found himself in London. Sitting in the bar of the Savoy hotel, he had been leafing aimlessly through a back copy of Country Life magazine when he had come across an estate agent's details of a property for sale in Cornwall: Seal Hall. He knew it was perfect for a project that had been ripening in his mind. He phoned the agent and secured the property sight unseen. Over the course of the following eighteen months he had created 'The Valley of the Tides: a therapeutic centre for traumatized young addictive personalities and their families'.

Seal Hall, originally a Tudor manor, had served over the years as a boys' boarding school, a TB sanatorium and a hotel. Consequently there were a number of existing buildings beyond the main hall which were turned into facilities from therapy and treatment rooms to swimming pool, gym and flotation tanks. The interior of the hall had been gutted and transformed into the equivalent of a luxury hotel and spa to accommodate both patients and their parents. Steps led from Seal Hall's gardens down to the water's edge on a tributary of the Fowey River. Here were the chapel and graveyard of the original Tudor estate, the swimming pool, boat storage and a small jetty and a flotation tank in a thatched roundhouse.

The following morning Christian Spargo's thoughts were for once not turned toward his nemesis across the water, but to his youngest daughter, Georgie. She had come home very late the previous night, in fact, it must have been the early hours of the morning. Since the summer she had been unusually quiet. Normally the girl was full of life and laughter but for the past few months she had been distracted and distant. Of course what he didn't and couldn't know, was that Georgie was constantly thinking about Hitch Lindström, and obviously unable to share her thoughts with her father.

Georgie Spargo had met Hitch Lindström on 20 June at 21:37. He was attending the 21st birthday celebration of his best friend, Kit Penrose, at Sam's in Fowey and she was waiting on tables. The attraction between them had been instant and electric. Even Kit, who by that time had visited several pubs and bars and consumed a substantial number of beers, noticed. Kit worked at The Valley of the Tides as a gardener/handyman and lived in a small terraced house in Fowey which he had inherited from his grandmother. When Hitch needed to stay overnight in Fowey, this

4

is where he stayed.

Christian stood on the patio outside his drawing room in the pale early morning light gazing at the river where a mist was creeping along the water towards the sea like a predatory ghost. The air was still and silent. Threads of smoke drifted from an occasional chimney. He was pondering what to do about Georgie; whether he should speak to her mother or to his wife, Lana, who was nearer in age to his children. His elder daughter, Josephine, was of no use. She was living in London and wasn't close to Georgie anyway, and his son, Leon, he was a boy and therefore useless when it came to emotional issues.

One of the many myths surrounding Christian was that he had dumped his first wife, Lizzie, for a newer, younger model: Lana. In reality Lizzie had left him. She had gone off 'to find herself' and he had little contact with her. He smiled to himself as he recalled one of Napoleon's sayings which he thought entirely appropriate to his relationship with his first wife and her quest: 'Never interrupt your enemy when he's making a mistake.' As he chuckled softly the silence was broken by a piercing scream coming from low across the water. Hopefully that's Power dead, he thought. He was half right; it wasn't Power.

Two

If Christian Spargo was one of the most feared men in Cornwall, his younger brother, Gideon, was one of the most feared in Europe. Were a seagull to fly westwards some 40 miles from The Valley of the Tides it would reach Newlyn, where it could fly over the fish market to land on the roof of a terrace of stone cottages, home to Abraham Spargo, Christian's father, and son, Gideon.

Here, at his bedroom window, for hours on end, sat Abraham Spargo watching the world go by like a beady-eyed, silent gull. Long gone were the days when he had ruled his boys with an iron rod. Now he was marooned in this cold room, at the mercies of his deranged son Gideon. It was Gideon who now ran the family fishing fleet, supposedly his main occupation. But Abraham knew that the boy had inherited his father's taste for smuggling and had expanded it into darker realms. Gideon had no boundaries. If there was money in it, Gideon would smuggle it: alcohol, cigarettes, drugs, weapons, people … Abraham was scared of his son Gideon, although he would never admit it. So, he remained silent.

Christian on the other hand was a 'legitimate businessman', with his holiday camps and hotels, his bars and clubs across the county. Sneering at his brother he would often say; 'If I'd wanted to profit from human misery, I'd have become a dentist.' But Abraham remembered that in his youth, his elder son's hands had not been so squeaky clean. And Christian was the only person Abraham knew who was not frightened of Gideon. Well, apart from his granddaughter Georgiana, but then she was frightened of nobody and nothing. He adored her. And he didn't see enough of her since Christian had moved them all to Fowey. All his grandchildren … gone away.

Gideon had never married; never given him grandchildren. Abraham knew why, but didn't dare speak of it. So, in his silence he brooded, and the thing he dwelled on the most, was not the knowledge of his son's many terrible deeds, but the fact that he had cost Abraham his dearest, oldest friend: Jago Treloar.

Further back along the coast towards Fowey is the port of Falmouth, one of the world's deepest natural harbours set in one of Cornwall's larger extended wooded valleys. Home to dockyards, boatyards, and a healthy tourist trade, Falmouth is a larger version of Fowey. Here on a bluff overlooking the estuary, a former hotel had been converted into a hospice for police officers. It was into this building on that cold late November morning that D I Félipe Treloar, son of Jago, walked with a heavy heart. Treloar hated these places. For a man who saw more than his fair share of death and suffering, he had a morbid dread of serious illness and the natural end of life.

Treloar was the son of a Spanish mother and a Cornish father, with blonde blue-eyed good looks which made him a favourite of the media and hence the Chief Constable. He was the head of a small team in Devon & Cornwall Police which handled serious crime and he had a reputation for getting results.

He had come to visit his former boss and mentor, a retired Detective Chief Superintendent, Joe Thwaite. Every visit he was reminded of the man he had worked with, a big booming Yorkshireman who instilled terror into the ranks. As Treloar crossed the polished wood floor towards the reception desk he glanced around at the soothing primrose walls and the bold seascapes. He recognised some new additions as the work of his near neighbour and friend Ochre Pengelly.

Having signed in, he slowly climbed the stairs to the first floor like a reluctant schoolboy on his way to the headmaster's office. He walked along the plush carpeted hallway to the end and knocked on a door before opening it. He entered the room to be met by the customary stuffiness: a mixture of too much heat and too much cleaning product.

Joe Thwaite, now a frail wraithlike figure, was sitting in a reclining armchair in the bay window facing out over the dockyard. Treloar felt his spirits lift; the last time he had visited Joe had been confined to bed but as he approached he could see the man looked much improved.

'Morning Boss,' Treloar said, laying a hand on the older man's shoulder.

'Hello there lad,' Thwaite replied. 'Good of thee to come so quick.'

Treloar smiled as he reflected on how his former boss's accent seemed to get more pronounced with every visit. Probably too much time alone with his past.

'I got your message.' The younger man said, sitting in the second chair in the window.

'Aye, well. I wanted to tell thee something whilst there's time. It's been weighing on me of late.'

'What is it Boss? Something from one of our cases?'

'Nay lad, not exactly. More like one that got away. A right bastard I never nailed. More like a right bastard and his spawn …' he broke off, coughing and reached for a box of tissues. Treloar poured and handed him a glass of water.

'Ta lad,' he said recovering, 'where was I?'

'A bastard and his spawn?'

'Aye a right bastard if ever there were one. And we never got the bugger, not for 'owt major.'

'OK … how can I help?'

'I want you to nail him. And I'll give you cause. His youngest's an evil shite who likes to hurt people and loves nowt but money. He has no soul, none lad.'

'Who are we talking about?'

'Gideon Spargo. He's the worst of 'em, but they're all rotten them Spargos.'

Treloar looked surprised. Of course he knew of the Spargo family and the many lurid stories that surrounded them, but nobody had ever been able to convict them of anything that sent them away for any serious time.

Thwaite noticed the look on his protégé's face.

'Aye, I know, many 'ave tried. But none of had thy reason.'

'My reason?'

Thwaite fell silent for a while, gazing out to sea and then sighed deeply.

'Spargos, one or all of the bastards, are responsible for what happened to thy father.'

Treloar started in his chair. His father had gone missing, presumed drowned, whilst swimming in a cove near the family farm on the north Cornish coast some years previously. Despite himself he raised his voice. 'What? You're saying the Spargo family made my father kill himself, drown himself?'

'Nay lad … They made him disappear but thy father's not drowned. He's alive and well.'

About the authors

The Treloar series is written by husband and wife team Louise Harrington and Andy Sinden, under the pen name L A Kent.

They have lived in Cornwall for many years and love the wild beauty, endlessly varying landscape, and changing weather of the place. Here they bring to life Detective Inspector Félipe Treloar with his Spanish family heritage and the often violent disturbed criminals he and his team encounter.

They have travelled extensively across the world and also draw on time spent in other amazing locations for their stories.

More can be read about L A Kent and Treloar's team at the web site, www.lakent.co.uk, where many photographs of the books' settings can also be found.

Also by LA Kent

ROGUE FLAMINGO

By

L. A. Kent

Rogue Flamingo launched the DI Treloar series:

A lawyer's body is found on the beach in the small Cornish village of Porthaven, staked out with a tarred bag over its head, just as the peak summer season gets underway. When a second body is found bizarrely fixed to the floor of a building not long afterwards, the laconic police surgeon remarks 'Well, psychopaths need holidays too'; and DI Treloar, a maverick to some bosses but a driven, committed investigator to his fellow officers, takes charge. When more bodies turn up, Treloar and his team are at first unsure - accident or murder?

There seems to be no connection between the victims whose murders are violent, with escalating viciousness and sexuality. What is going on? Could they have brought their fates with them, festering secrets from the past? Could either of the two mysterious men staying at the camp site be involved?

Is it one or more doing the killing? What about the rabble of students in the big house or the local recluse and his enigmatic brother? What about embittered locals resentful of incomers buying up their village?

And who is the extraordinary female, obsessed with birds, institutionalised in the south of France as a child, who reflects on her past as the story unfolds?

Then a brutal attack on one of their own shocks Treloar's team and their focus switches in an unexpected direction when a heartfelt injustice surfaces.

Available from all good book shops and as an ebook.

For more information about the Treloar series, the characters and the authors, and beautiful photographs of Cornwall have a look at:

www.lakent.co.uk.

CPSIA information can be obtained
at www.ICGtesting.com
Printed in the USA
BVHW072351130920
588716BV00006B/565